MW00719011

The Life and Times of Jamie Lee Coleman

a novel

The Life and Times of Jamie Lee Coleman

a novel

MICHAEL E. GLASSCOCK III

GREENLEAF
BOOK GROUP PRESS

This book is a work of fiction. Names, characters, businesses, organizations, places, events, and incidents are either a product of the author's imagination or are used fictitiously. Any resemblance to actual persons, living or dead, events, or locales is entirely coincidental.

Published by Greenleaf Book Group Press
Austin, Texas
www.gbgpress.com

Copyright ©2014 Michael E. Glasscock III

All rights reserved.

No part of this book may be reproduced, stored in a retrieval system, or transmitted by any means, electronic, mechanical, photocopying, recording, or otherwise, without written permission from the copyright holder.

Distributed by Greenleaf Book Group

For ordering information or special discounts for bulk purchases, please contact Greenleaf Book Group at PO Box 91869, Austin, TX 78709, 512.891.6100.

Design and composition by Greenleaf Book Group
Cover design by Greenleaf Book Group

Cover images:
©iStockphoto.com/EduardoLuzzatti-Eduardo Luzzatti Buyé
©iStockphoto.com/shulz
©iStockphoto.com/Coldimages
Back cover images:
©iStockphoto.com/Frider

Publisher's Cataloging-In-Publication Data
Glasscock, Michael E., 1933-

   The life and times of Jamie Lee Coleman : a novel / Michael E. Glasscock III.—First edition.

   pages ; cm—([Round Rock series] ; [Book three])

   Issued also as an ebook.

   ISBN: 978-1-62634-044-2

   1. Abused children—Tennessee—Fiction. 2. Widows—Tennessee—Fiction. 3. Musicians—Alcohol use—Tennessee—Fiction. 4. Tennessee—History—20th century—Fiction. 5. Historical fiction. I. Title.

PS3607.L27 L54 2014

813/.6   2014936278

Part of the Tree Neutral® program, which offsets the number of trees consumed in the production and printing of this book by taking proactive steps, such as planting trees in direct proportion to the number of trees used: www.treeneutral.com

Printed in the United States of America on acid-free paper

14 15 16 17 18 19   10 9 8 7 6 5 4 3 2 1

First Edition

This novel is dedicated to the memory of my friend
Sarah Cannon, a.k.a. Minnie Pearl.

"Country music is three chords and the truth."

—Harlan Howard

"It's a marvelous feeling when someone says 'I want to do this song of yours' because they've connected to it. That's what I'm after."

—Mary Chapin Carpenter

"I think my fans will follow me into our combined old age. Real musicians and real fans stay together for a long, long time."

—Bonnie Raitt

Prologue

You are about to read my autobiography. I've taken some literary license in writing it. I obviously can't remember every word that was spoken, but the dialogue is as close as I can recall. All the characters are real and their names are accurate. The events occurred as I describe them. The dates are approximate, as I can't pinpoint exactly when each episode occurred.

No one assisted me with the writing of this book. I take full responsibility for any deficiencies. Several people did help me survive a turbulent childhood and eventually saw to it that I reached manhood. I thank them from the bottom of my heart. If these friends and mentors hadn't been there for me, I wouldn't have survived to tell this story.

First and foremost on that list would be Frances Washington. Jake Watson, Yolanda, Casey Jones, Axelrod Mahoney, Sam Ledford and his daughter, Joy, all did their part to help me mature into the man I am. My special thanks go to my wife, soul mate, and best friend, Melody. You'll learn who all these people are in due time, and you'll know why I think they're such remarkable individuals.

Jamie Lee Coleman
Round Rock, Tennessee
August 3, 2003

Part One

Chapter 1

"The love of my life
Is another man's wife
And our stolen kisses
Are now just wishes."

Chorus of "Stolen Kisses"
My First Platinum Single

Round Rock, Tennessee
January 1962

It wasn't much of a window: small, cracked in two places, and fogged with age. But it was my window to the world. On that overcast, drizzle-laden January day, I was a skinny ten-year-old looking out at the trucks slowing for the curve at the bottom of the small hill where I lived. I saw license plates not only from Tennessee, but also from faraway places like Kentucky, Illinois, and Indiana.

The rough plank floor on which I stood was cool and slippery from the constant drip of rainwater sliding down the tarpaper wall. My cold bare feet were calloused and my toenails long and dirty. Outside, a big semi braked hard and threatened to jackknife before the driver could get it under control.

"Jamie boy, fetch me a bucket of water."

My mom whispered when she spoke, for thick yellow and odorous pus ran freely from her ears in the fall and winter months. She said her voice seemed loud to her at those times. I could only get her to hear me by shouting. Pop, whose low and raspy voice was the work of cigarettes and moonshine, could barely make her understand his rambling utterances. I remember her with balls of cotton stuffed tight in both ears. If they hurt, she didn't mention it. She seldom complained.

I slipped on my worn high-topped tennis shoes and took the bucket down the wet hill to the pump. Our family shared the hand pump with our neighbors, who were mostly kin. The cast-iron monolith stood on a concrete slab not five feet from the curve in the blacktop.

With the bucket hung on the spout, I raised the handle and pushed until rusty, sulfur-laced water flowed in spurts like blood from a severed artery. I quit when the thing was three-fourths full, for walking up that slippery, mud-soaked hill would slosh a good third out.

The drizzle had picked up a bit, the drops licking my face like a friendly cat. I figured Pop would be sopping wet when he got home from the shirt factory. About halfway up the hill, I slipped a little and for a moment thought I might slide back down. When I got to the door, my shoes were black with thick, sticky mud. Mom kept a burlap sack for wiping our feet. I picked it up, scraped my feet as clean as I could, and carried the bucket to the kitchen where I set it on the floor beside the small table Mom used to prepare our meals.

Our shack sat about halfway up the hill and the folks above were not kin, which irritated Pop. The Coleman clan and a handful of Smiths and Crocketts inhabited Beulah Land. In all, there were no more than ten or twelve families.

The big room of the shack measured twelve by fifteen feet with one corner set aside for the kitchen. Mom had a small icebox that Pop had pulled from the county dump. We only got ice when Lester, my uncle, who had an old pickup, could afford gasoline to take Pop to the icehouse. Three kerosene lamps supplied light. In the cold months, heat came from the big black cast-iron stove on which Mom cooked our meals.

Attached to this room, like knots on a log, were the two small rooms where my parents and I slept. Theirs had a worn mattress slapped on the floor, covered with a ragged quilt. A small rope strung at one end of the room served as a place to hang their clothes. My room, the only one with a window, was half the size of theirs. I slept on a pile of burlap sacks, and I hung my meager clutch of pants and shirts on a rope, like my parents did.

"Light a lamp, son. It's hard to see in this corner," Mom said.

She kept the lamps on the table in the middle of the room, the one on which we ate our meals. Three ladder-back chairs with hard wooden seats were pushed under the table. A small couch, its springs dangerously near the worn cloth covering, sat next to the table. The room otherwise was empty.

I lit the lamp with a wooden kitchen match and the wick burst into a yellow flame, its soft glow giving the corner of the room a different character. Mom's busy hands, rough and calloused, deftly peeled the potatoes.

I placed a second lamp on the table for our supper. Long shadows flickered against the tarpaper walls. The two-mile walk from town would take Pop a good hour, so I didn't expect to be eating for a while. No clock or watch among us, the Coleman clan depended upon the height of the sun to determine the time of day. Past sundown, we judged the hour by the rumble of our stomachs or the heaviness of our eyes.

In my dark room I sat listening to the weak signal from the clear-channel WSM tower in Nashville on my crystal radio. It was an odd contraption of Uncle Lester's making. A hand-me-down he no longer needed or cared to own.

There had been army maneuvers in Parsons County back in 1943, and sticky fingers lifted some materials. Lester managed to confiscate a set of earphones belonging to a field radio. He kept them squirreled away under a loose board in his room for years. While working in Nashville at the stockyards in the mid-fifties, he found a small paperback book on prisoner-of-war crystal radios in an army and navy surplus store.

Lester collected a rusty double-edged razor blade, a cardboard tube from a roll of toilet paper, a safety pin, and a string of copper wire he picked up at the city dump. He attached these to a small board about eight inches square. He found two old extension cords at the dump and stripped off the insulation. He used one for an antenna, and the other he attached to a pipe driven into the bare earth for a ground.

That crystal radio and my window were my connection to the outside world. By moving the point of the safety pin across the surface of the razor blade, I could hit one spot that sent the signal to the earphones. Then I'd lose myself in the music and let my mind drift to a safe and wondrous place.

* * *

An hour later, Pop came in the door and stomped his brogans until the shack shook and my safety pin lost its signal. When I went into the big room, I saw that Pop was wet as a skunk and dripping rainwater on the hard, rough floor. Pop's hair, wet and tangled, hung in his eyes. We ate supper in silence, for Pop didn't believe in idle chatter. Mom placed a rare glass of sweet milk in front of me. I washed down the dry, week-old bread from the Salvation Army thrift store and stuffed boiled potatoes into my mouth.

"You get out of school tomorrow, come to the shirt factory. We got loading to do," Pop said.

"They pay me?"

"One, maybe two dollars you do a good job."

After supper, with the dishes washed and stacked, and Pop smoking on the couch, Mom whispered into my ear, "Tomorrow's payday Friday."

Back in my room, I put on the earphones and lay on my burlap bed with country music filling my head. My cousin Billy, Uncle Lester's boy, had showed me how to use a comb and tissue paper to make a Jew's harp. I used it to keep good time with the music despite the fact I knew little about what I was doing. That night WSM played songs by Patsy Cline, Cowboy Copas, Little Jimmy Dickens, and Hank Snow, and at some point, I fell asleep, letting my *instrument* drop to the floor. I awoke the next morning with a crick in my neck. With the sweet milk still cold, I had the treat of Cheerios in one of Mom's cracked mixing bowls before I did my one chore, taking Pop's slop jar to the privy.

It was a rusty fruit juice can, the jagged cut at the top formed by an ancient opener. Pop referred to it as his slop jar nonetheless as if it assured him some station in life. I had to be careful not to cut myself on the top. When I picked it up, the smell of piss was strong and stung my nose. I carried it down the slippery, mud-laden hill to the privy where I dumped its contents into one of two holes. Then I relieved myself, listening to my stream hit the stagnant shit and pee of my kin and watched idly as a black widow spider spun her web over my head.

* * *

At the final school bell on Friday afternoon, I grabbed my books and wandered down the long hill to town. Crossing the square where the whittlers sat on the courthouse steps and chewed tobacco, I passed Bradshaw's Drugstore and crossed the alley to the loading dock of the shirt factory where Pop and his coworkers carried boxes of folded shirts into the open door of a big semi-trailer rig. Supervisor John Wilson, a cigarette dangling from his lips, marked off each box stacked on the floor of the trailer.

"I'm here to work, Mr. Wilson," I said, walking up the steps.

He glanced at me and asked, "How much can you lift, boy?"

"Enough, I reckon."

"Them boxes weigh out at thirty pounds. Reckon you can lift that much?"

"I reckon I can."

"Well, you're big for your age. See what you can do."

Three men besides Pop worked on the dock, and despite the overcast sky and chilly temperature, their shirts stuck to their chests and perspiration trickled down their cheeks. Each man carried two boxes. I followed one of them back into the factory, picked up one box, and carried it out to the trailer. It didn't seem heavy to me. The semi was already half full by the time I started, which meant we'd be finished before sundown. That suited me fine, for the narrow blacktop to Beulah Land would be dark on our way home.

Mr. Wilson kept looking at his watch and finally said, "Speed it up, boys. We ain't got all day. Time's a wasting."

Near dusk, the supervisor closed and locked the big roller door. After he clicked the padlock together, Mr. Wilson reached into his shirt pocket and took out a wad of bills. He asked the men to form a line, and as he passed each one, he peeled off three fives. To me, he handed a one-dollar bill, which I shoved into my overalls. Pop slipped the bills into his shirt pocket, the one in which he kept his smokes, and motioned for me to follow him.

Pop walked with a long stride, so I had to stretch my legs to keep up. When I saw where we were headed, my stomach tightened. I hated the damned place and the man who lived there. I thought he was lower than a snake's belly. The house sat on a side street just off Main not two blocks from the factory. A white frame, it had a roofline with two gables facing the street. The neat yard held short clipped grass, and stepping-stones of Tennessee flat limestone led to the front door.

The bell didn't work, so Pop curled his fist and beat on the door. A few minutes later, Deacon Dallas Clark opened it and said, "Howdy, Gilbert. I've been expecting you."

The deacon was a pious acting man with a thin mustache atop a short upper lip. His black hair was cut in a military style and his beady eyes were the color of dirty dishwater. His teeth appeared so perfect I suspected they might be false like Miss Smotherman's, my teacher.

Pop followed the deacon to the kitchen at the back of the house. It was a bright room with yellow walls and windows covered with sheer white curtains. A row of glass gallon jugs filled with a clear liquid sat on the countertop.

The deacon asked, "One do you, Gilbert?"

"I reckon."

Pop pulled the bills out of his shirt pocket and handed one of the fives to the Deacon, who took out his own wad and selected two ones. Then Pop picked up one of the jugs and headed for the door.

"Oh, Gilbert," the Deacon said, "remember, a Christian man is prudent."

We weren't out the door or across the yard before Pop unscrewed the top of the jug and brought it to his lips. He threw his head back and took in the shine like a sword swallower in the circus.

Night fell like a curtain and by the time we reached the two lane highway that would lead us home it was black as a coal bin. The stars were so bright and plentiful they covered the sky like a big blanket. While I watched, a shooting star raced across the sky then disappeared. An owl hooted in the distance and sent a chill up my spine. Mom considered them to be terrible bad luck and I took it as an omen of things to come.

As most do in the country, Pop and I walked down the middle of the road ready to jump to the shoulder the second we saw a beam of light. We hadn't gone a mile when a big truck came barreling around a curve in front of us, and we had to scramble to one side. Pop let the jug hang loosely in his right hand as we walked, and from time to time he'd swing it up to his lips.

The singing started out soft and quiet, almost as if he was talking to himself. The closer we got to Beulah Land, the louder his voice got. Despite its raspy quality, Pop's voice was rich and mellow, and he could carry a tune. His songs were different from the ones I heard on my crystal radio. Pop's were more like ones an old-time folk singer such as Woody Guthrie or Pete Seeger would sing. Some dated to the Civil War and most likely the American Revolution. The Appalachian Mountains are full of such songs, passed on from father or mother to daughter or son.

I held Pop's arm and helped him climb the muddy slope to our shack. He stepped on my foot three or four times before we made it to the door, and a ragged pain shot through my toes and settled in the heel.

Mom had heard us coming and stood in the doorway. She had supper waiting but not on the table. Pop staggered to his chair and slammed the jug on the table in front of him. His face was beet red, the whites of his eyes watery and crisscrossed with crimson arteries, the pupils narrow and unfocused. He picked up the spoon beside his plate and then mine and held them in his right hand just so, the curved surfaces facing each other. He began to tap them on first his left hand and then his right knee in a snappy rhythm, all the while keeping time with the song he sang, an old Irish folk ditty. My right foot kept time with the spoons, and soon Pop's whole body swayed.

Mom shook her head and placed supper in front of me. She filled her plate but left Pop's empty, for she knew he'd soon fall asleep in his chair.

By the time Mom and I finished eating, then washed and stacked the dishes, Pop's head rested on his crossed arms atop the table, soft gurgling sounds emanating from his half-open mouth. I got on one side and Mom the other, and between the two of us, we managed to lift Pop and half-walk, half-drag him to the bedroom where we let him slide onto their mattress. He would lie there fully clothed and drunk as a skunk until morning. Mom went back to the kitchen, and when she was out of sight, I reached into Pop's shirt pocket, removed his pack of Camels, and the remaining twelve dollars. I took two fives and then turned the cigarettes upside down and shook three out. Sliding them into my pocket, I took the ten dollars plus my one to Mom.

"You're a good boy, Jamie. I reckon we'll eat this week."

I took one of the lamps to my room, placed it on the floor beside the burlap bed, and pulled out the cigarettes. Placing one in my mouth, I struck a kitchen match on the rough floor and held the yellow flame to the tip. I inhaled deeply and gave a sigh.

When the cigarette held no more than a small ash, I ground it into the wooden floor and pushed the butt through a crack between the boards. I was listening to Marty Robbins sing "El Paso." Mom came into the room, picked up the lamp, raised the chimney, and blew out the flame.

"Time you was asleep, Jamie boy."

* * *

The morning sun crept across my face, creating a crimson flare behind my eyelids. I awoke to Pop yelling, "Where's my goddamned slop jar?"

My heart pounded and my ears rang as if I had a bell stuck in my head. I'd forgotten to bring the damn thing back from the privy the day before.

I pulled on my pants, jacket, and shoes and ran out the front door and down the hill to the privy. The air was damp and cold and I wrapped my arm around my chest for warmth. In the distance a crow cawed. When I reached the privy, the latched door wouldn't budge.

"Who's in there?"

"Can't a man take a crap in peace around here?" Uncle Lester yelled back.

"I need the slop jar, Lester. Hand it out."

The door swung open, and Lester, pulling up his pants, poked the fruit juice can at me. "Go on now. Best shake a leg."

When I opened the door, Pop stood in the clothes he'd slept in, his pants wet at the crotch, his hair tangled with sweat and hanging in his eyes. He smelled of shine, piss, and sweat.

"Come here, you little asshole, and give me my goddamned slop jar!" he yelled.

As Pop yanked the can from my hand, the ragged edge took a slice out of my thumb. Then the old man slammed his open fist upside my head. Staggering away from Pop, I tried to gain my balance but fell to the floor. Pop dropped the can, grabbed my jacket collar, and lifted me to my feet. Then he curled his right hand into a tight fist and hit me square in the eye.

I slumped to the floor, tears filling my eyes, and curled into a ball, waiting for Pop to kick me. Instead, he pulled his dick out and filled the fruit juice can to the top.

"Take this to the privy, you little shit, and don't you ever forget to bring it back."

Blood dripped from my cut finger, and Mom, her face ashen, brought a rag from the corner kitchen and wrapped it around the cut. She glared at Pop with narrowed eyelids, deep lines forming at the bridge of her nose.

"Don't you be staring at me, woman. I'll beat the shit out of you, too."

Her eyes dropped to the floor, and she moved away from me. I picked up the can, my thumb in Pop's piss.

Nausea gripped my stomach as I went down the hill once more, holding the can as steady as I could. As I opened the door to the privy, Uncle Lester's wife was pulling up her drawers. Aunt Lulu sometimes forgot to latch the door and got herself exposed to neighbors and kin alike.

She was a big woman, tall and wide. "Jamie, don't you be looking at your old aunt like that. It ain't Christian."

Then spying the swelling of my eye and the redness of my cheek, she said, "Come here, son, let me look at you. Gilbert done that?"

"Yeah."

She touched my face. For a large woman, she had gentle but calloused hands. She ran her finger over the swelling so lightly I barely felt her touch.

"Your mom got any ice left, son?"

"No, she ain't."

"Come over to my house and I'll fix you an ice poultice. Take some of that swelling out."

"Thanks, Aunt Lulu, but Pop's already madder than a wet hen, and he might need to use the slop jar again."

"Well, if the old bastard falls asleep, come on over."

I opened the door to the privy and dumped Pop's piss into one of the holes. Then I latched the door and pulled down my pants. I kept an eye on that black widow spider while I freed myself of some damn loose bowels.

Pop was asleep when I got back up the hill. Mom worked in the corner kitchen, and she wouldn't meet my eyes.

I put the slop jar beside the mattress and left. In my room, I stood and looked out my broken window at the blacktop below. I watched a big semi, the air brakes squealing, enter the curve, and I could hear the driver doing a double clutch shifting into a lower gear.

If I ran, could I catch him?

Chapter 2

Between the Coleman clan, the Smiths, and the Crocketts, we almost filled the school bus that stopped at the bottom of the hill right at 7:00 A.M. That next Monday after receiving Pop's whipping, I stood with my cousin, Billy Coleman, Lester's boy, waiting for the bus. The day before, I'd slipped over to Lester's house and let Aunt Lulu put the ice poultice on my eye.

Billy said, "Look here what I got, Jamie."

He pulled a Red Man tobacco pouch out of his overalls. I could see half of a night crawler wiggling, trying to get itself deeper in the pile of dirt.

"What you doing with that?"

"I got some line and a couple of hooks in my pocket, too. You and me can go fishing. Play hooky."

"Last time we played hooky Mr. Youngblood paddled us hard."

"The principal ain't gonna know. Don't be a damn sissy. Hell, ain't nobody gonna know."

"How you figure that? Miss Smotherman won't see us in our seats? She ain't blind, you know."

"She ain't gonna be there. She went to see her sister in Atlanta. We got us damn substitute the whole damn week."

* * *

A big-busted girl named Sally Watson lived two miles from a back shoot off Dale Hollow Lake. While Mr. Arnold, the bus driver leered at her climbing the steps, Billy and I pulled ourselves through the rear window and dropped to the ground. Just as we touched solid earth, Mr. Arnold put the bus in gear.

We walked down a limestone county road to the lake. A blue jay swooped low over our heads and landed on a fence post. The bird eyed us for a moment and then took wing and disappeared into the woods. In the distance, a crow cawed. The sun was playing peek-a-boo with some low-hanging clouds and I wondered if it was going to rain. The air was still, no sign of a breeze at all.

I reached into my overalls and pulled out two cigarettes. "Want a smoke?"

"Sure."

I struck a match against the denim fabric of my overalls and lit the cigarette. Billy did the same. We walked along the gravel road in silence, blue smoke swirling around our heads like small tornados.

Dale Hollow Lake's coastline stretched six hundred miles or more, and the spring-fed water was so clear you could see fish ten feet below the surface. It remained cold and pure enough to drink all year long.

We stopped at a small park next to a boat ramp, where concrete picnic tables sat like sentries. Billy pulled the line out of his overalls and then the Red Man pouch with the night crawlers along with a small piece of cardboard with two fish hooks. He handed one hook to me. "Ain't you got no sinkers and corks?" I asked.

"We can make sinkers out of a rock. We don't need no floats. Hell, you'll know it, you get a strike."

Billy searched around the bank until he found two small rocks and handed one to me, and I tied it about eighteen inches above the hook. Then Billy and I threaded the squirming night crawlers over the sharp hooks. I hated the damn things because, small as they were, they reminded me of tiny snakes.

We walked out to a small point and dropped our lines into the cold water. The lake stretched wide and dead calm that morning, and in the distance a smallmouth bass jumped and flipped his tail, sending rings of small waves in all directions.

My cut finger throbbed. A red streak peeked out from under the piece of dirty tape and marched across the back of my hand.

"What we gonna do with these fish we catch?" I asked.

"I reckon we'll take them home and eat 'em."

"Then Mom'll know we played hooky."

"Free fish ain't nothing to sneeze at, Jamie. Hell, she'll be damn glad to get 'em."

At that moment, Billy's line made a big circle in the water, ripples following as it picked up speed. Billy yanked the line and started wrapping it around his palm and elbow as fast as he could. Then what looked like a two-pound smallmouth bass broke the surface, his tail beating furiously. Billy pulled the fish out of the lake and removed the hook. He threaded a line through the mouth and gills, tied a small twig to it, and threw the fish back into the water.

"You ain't got no bucket, best way to keep the fish fresh," Billy said.

I nodded and said, "That's for sure."

In the space of an hour, Billy caught two more fish, and so did I. Around noon, we pulled the catch out of the water and headed back up the limestone road toward home and Billy's fridge.

We'd walked along the blacktop for about fifteen minutes when I heard a car creeping up behind us going slow, its engine straining. My mouth went dry when I turned to look at it. Through the windshield, Sheriff Strawberry Wilson stared at us. Everyone in Beulah Land including me, was scared shitless of old Strawberry.

During the war, he'd been a truck driver, carrying produce back and forth between East Tennessee and the Texas Rio Grande Valley. In his youth, his hair had been the color of a morning sunrise. But his nickname was said to be due to the strawberry birthmark on the right cheek of his ass and not the hue of his hair.

He'd defeated Jasper Kingman in the 1956 election and had been sheriff ever since. A family man with Christian values, he was a favorite among the citizens of Round Rock. Known as a tough but fair sheriff, only the rowdy Coleman clan ever crossed his path.

"Billy, we're in bad trouble," I whispered.

He looked around and said, "Oh, shit."

We stopped dead in our tracks, for we knew old Strawberry would chase us to the ends of the earth to catch us. He pulled the patrol car to the shoulder and said, "Nice catch you got there, boys. Where'd you find them?"

Billy looked the sheriff in the eye and said, "That off-shoot down Watson Road."

"I reckon I'll have to take my fly rod down there this evening. Now hop in the car, boys. You're going to school. I know Mr. Youngblood will be delighted to see you."

The sheriff swung open the passenger door, and Billy, holding the fish to his chest, climbed into the patrol car. I climbed in next to him.

"You best take those beauties to Mrs. Nolner in the cafeteria and ask her to ice them down. Be a damn shame to waste the likes of them," Strawberry said.

When the sheriff pulled into the school parking lot, Billy looked old Strawberry in the eye and said, "I ain't lookin' to get me another lickin', Sheriff. Reckon you could jest let us out?"

Strawberry Wilson threw his head back and laughed so hard that tears came to his eyes. "Hell, son, you know damned well I can't do that. You got to learn from your mistakes. A good solid licking is about the best way I know. Come on now. Let's go see Mr. Youngblood."

The three of us got out of the patrol car, and the sheriff followed us into the grade school. The recess bell had just sounded as we walked into the long hall, and students were running toward us like a stampede of wild horses. I could feel my face flush and I bit my lower lip so hard I tasted blood. Several students from town stood to one side and gawked at the sheriff. Then they started laughing.

When we walked into the principal's office, Miss Campbell, his secretary, looked up with a worried expression and asked, "Is there something wrong, Strawberry?"

"No. I've just got a couple of rambunctious boys here who need a little discipline. Mr. Youngblood in?"

At that moment the principal walked into the room. Mr. Youngblood, just a bit over six feet three, had been a star basketball center on the 1952 UT varsity team. He remained strong as an ox despite his biscuit poisoning. That's how we describe pudgy folks in Round Rock. Though he continued to use one, he had no need of a paddle, for his rawboned hands could still reach around a basketball and were sufficient to raise whelps on any student's scrawny ass.

"Howdy, Strawberry, I see you found my missing students. What have they been up to?"

Billy, who still held the fish, held them up.

"Well, boys, they are a fine catch, but you need to do your fishing on the weekends—not during school hours. I'll take care of things from here, Strawberry. Thanks."

The sheriff smiled, tipped his Stetson, and left.

Mr. Youngblood said, "Come into my office, boys. I think you know what comes next."

Billy grimaced on the tenth lick, but his eyes never showed one sign of fear. I, on the other hand, couldn't help myself, and tears flowed down my cheeks like the rapids on Widow's Creek.

"You boys know not to play hooky. Next time, it'll be fifteen licks instead of ten. Now take those fish to Mrs. Nolner," Mr. Young-blood said as he placed the paddle in the corner.

Mrs. Nolner ran the cafeteria and taught the girls' home economics classes. A tall woman with gray hair done in a bun at the nape of her neck, she had a ready smile that could disarm the rowdiest boys at lunchtime. When Billy handed her the fish, she laughed. "Where did you catch these beauties?"

"Down Watson Road where the boat ramp is."

"I'll put them on ice for you. Come by at last bell. I'm not here, ask for Molly Johnson."

* * *

I had to keep shifting the cheeks of my skinny ass on the hard seat of my desk. The substitute teacher couldn't keep any of our names straight. She called me Billy Coleman all afternoon and gave us a pop math quiz just before the afternoon recess bell.

I still limped a little as Billy and I strode to the cafeteria to pick up our fish. Mrs. Nolner had wrapped them in a day-old copy of the *Nashville Tennessean* newspaper along with a few cubes of ice.

We rode the school bus home and divided the fish evenly when we stepped off at Beulah Land.

Mom's eyes widened when I showed her the two smallmouth bass, but she didn't ask where they came from. Lester had brought her some ice that afternoon so she placed the fish in the icebox. "Go over to Aunt Lulu's and ask her for some lard. I ain't got none left after frying them potatoes last night."

Noticing the red streak that had advanced up my arm, she said, "Come here, Jamie boy, and let me look at that redness."

I held my arm up in front of her. "It ain't sore or nothing."

She placed her hand over the area and said, "It's right hot to the touch, son. We best be going to see Dr. Kate. Come on now."

Mom grabbed her ragged coat, and we started down the hill to the blacktop. It took us an hour to reach town and another ten minutes to reach the Round Rock Medical Clinic. Jazz, the receptionist, pulled back the glass window when we walked in and asked, "What's wrong, Mrs. Coleman?"

Mom and I followed Jazz down a long hallway to a small room. Minutes later, Dr. Katherine Marlow, the town's only physician, walked in. Dr. Kate, as everyone called her, was a tall, slender woman with cropped blonde hair and royal blue eyes. "What seems to be the problem?" she asked.

"My boy cut his finger yesterday, and he's got a red streak running up his arm. I'm right worried about it."

"Let me look, Jamie," Dr. Kate said. "Does it hurt?"

"I reckon not."

She took my arm in her hand and ran her long, slender fingers over the reddened area. "It's hot to the touch." Then turning to Mom, she said, "It's infected. He'll need a tetanus shot and some penicillin."

I grimaced. "I don't want no damn shot, Dr. Kate."

"Sorry, son, you just don't have a choice," Mom said. "And please don't use that awful language. You sound like your father."

My skinny ass was already so sore I could barely walk, and the trip from Beulah Land to town had made me miserable. The thought of having a needle stuck in such a tender spot made me cringe.

Mom turned away when Dr. Kate pulled my pants down. I yelled bloody murder as the needle sank its full length into the muscle. Not caring what Mom thought, I screamed, "Damn, damn, damn that hurt!" as I pulled up my pants.

"I ain't got no money to pay you, Dr. Kate. I'll try to scrape some together in the next month and bring it to you," Mom said.

"Don't worry about it, Mrs. Coleman. Jamie needed the shot. That's what's important. Let me look at the arm in about a week."

Mom and I left the clinic as dusk was descending on Round Rock and started the long trek home, as usual walking down the middle of the blacktop. Two big trucks forced us to the shoulder about half a mile from Beulah Land. We didn't arrive at the shack until after dark, and our teeth were chattering as we climbed the hill. When we walked in, Pop was sitting at the table with a scowl on his leathery face. "Where the hell you been?" he asked. "I'm hungry, woman. Where's my damn supper?"

"Me and the boy had to go see Dr. Kate. Jamie's got a bad infection in his arm because of your slop jar. He needed a penicillin shot."

"Leave my damn slop jar out of this, woman. I want my supper. Get your ass over there and fix it right now. And I don't want no damn sassy back-talk neither."

Without a word, I walked to my room where I donned my headphones and listened to my radio. I could hear Mom throwing pots on the stove over the sound of the music.

Thirty minutes later, as we ate supper, I pierced my tongue with a sharp fish bone. I pulled it out and slipped it under my plate. Pop crunched his bones and swallowed the bits.

"This is right good eating, ain't it, Gilbert?" Mom said.

"I reckon so."

"Still, Jamie, it ain't right to play hooky. School is more important. You need to get your learning."

Pop crunched another big bone and held his fork in midair for a second. "I quit school when I was Jamie's age, and it never hurt me none."

Mom just looked at Pop but didn't say anything. I knew she'd quit after the fifth grade. She glanced at me and said, "Edwina Taylor told me about a job at the shirt factory. I reckon I might try to get on there. I could buy you some real brogans for this cold weather. Ain't good to wear them tennis shoes in the snow."

Pop laid his fork on the table, looked at Mom, and wrinkled his forehead. "I'll have to study on that, woman. I ain't sure I want you working at the shirt factory." Then getting up from the table, he said, "I'm going over to Lester's."

Mom clinched her jaw and her eyes bore a hole in the back of his head as he walked out the door. She shook her head and picked up the plates and threw them on the back table.

When Pop went to Lester's, Billy came to our place. At the door of the shack, Billy said, "Come out, Jamie." Then, so Mom wouldn't hear him, he whispered, "I got us some smokes." We sat with our backs against the shack and lit two Camels that Billy had lifted out of Lester's shirt pocket. It was cold and the night cloudy for I couldn't see a single star or even the moon.

"Damn if them weren't good small-mouths. I damn near got a bone caught in my throat, though. They're right full of them," Billy said, taking a draw on his cigarette.

With the January chill in the air, I pulled my jacket collar up and shook a little as I inhaled. I coughed a bit and took another drag. The Crouch family, who lived in the shack above ours, had a battery radio tuned to WSM, and we could hear Patsy Cline's voice floating toward us through the cold air.

"I wish I had a radio like that," I said as I took another drag on my smoke. "You ought to lift your smokes off your mom. I like them filters.

"Hell, them things are for sissies, Jamie," Billy said.

We finished smoking, then I stood and stomped my feet. "My damn feet is cold, Billy. I got to go in,"

"Me, too," Billy said as he headed down the hill.

I went to my room and donned the headphones of the crystal radio. I had a hard time finding a signal, and it took me ten minutes to get the tip of the safety pin in exactly the right spot. Because of the storm coming in from the west, the static made it almost impossible to hear a single song. I did catch a favorite, Patsy Cline's "I Fall to Pieces."

As I did many nights, I fell asleep with the headphones on my ears. Pop woke me when he came back up the hill from Lester's, singing at the top of his lungs. He kept singing as he undressed, and I heard each shoe drop.

The thin wall separating my parents' room from mine was only one layer of thin boards nailed on their side of the two-by-four studs. I heard some muffled grunts and groans and Pop's foot hitting the wall and knew they were at it, doing what Mom called *her duty*. I could always tell when they'd been at it because their room had a peculiar odor the next day.

The previous month Mom had come to my room one Saturday afternoon and said, "Jamie, borrow your cousin Billy's bike and ride to town for me. You know where the Esso station is across from the courthouse?"

"Yeah."

"Here's a quarter. There's a machine on the wall in the men's room has some things in there I want. Put the quarter in and pull the handle. A piece of foil will drop out, and that's what I need. I usually ask your uncle Lester to do it for me, but he ain't around."

"What's in the foil?"

"It keeps me from being with child when I do my duty. That's all you need to know."

* * *

A week hence, payday Friday, Pop came home with one of Deacon Clark's gallon jugs and was singing a song about a whore in Galveston who took on a sailing ship full of pirates. I'd never heard it before.

Pop skipped supper and went directly to his room where he sat on their mattress, drank and continued to sing at the top of his lungs. I drowned out his raging with the headphones. Not three minutes after he passed out, Mom pried the jug from his death grip and took it outside and smashed the glass into a hundred pieces. The shine seeped onto the cold, bare ground like blood from a freshly cut wound.

I awoke to Pop's bellowing the next morning.

"Where's my jug, woman?"

Mom stood in the corner kitchen frying an egg and didn't answer him. He staggered into the room, his hair tangled, his clothes rumpled, and his eyes as red as a baboon's ass.

"I said where's my goddamned jug, woman?"

She just glared at him. He leaned on the table, burped, and hung his head. Whispering now, he said, "Where's my jug, woman? Tell me now or I'll beat the shit out of you."

Her eyes narrowed, and her lips pressed into a fine, thin line. Then she said, "I broke the damn thing last night. All the shine is seeped into the ground by now where it belongs."

Pop gave her a slap with the back of his hand that shook her whole head. She backed away, but he hit her again and I heard her cheekbone crack.

I tried to pull Pop away, and as I grabbed his arm, he hit me full in the face, smashing my nose. The blow brought a mixture of blood and tears dripping to the floor. Pop hit me again in the same swollen eye.

"I hate you!" I screamed as I grabbed my jacket and ran from the room. A heavy frost on the ground caused me to slide down the hill to the blacktop. Once on the asphalt, I ran as fast as my feet would carry me. My thin jacket rippled in the wind, and though chilled to the bone, I didn't stop.

A good mile away, I could hear Pop yelling, "Come back, you little shit!"

There was a cold wind blowing out of the north. Big black clouds lay like puffs of cotton on the horizon, and I thought for sure I'd get caught in a downpour if I didn't find shelter soon. My heart was racing and I felt a little dizzy.

I stumbled along for a quarter mile, gasping for breath, my side aching. Finally, I stopped and sat on the top of a rail fence along the side of the road. My stomach growled, and I shivered as I wrapped my arms around my chest. I didn't know what I was going to do, but I knew one thing for certain: I'd never go back to that damned shack as long as I lived.

* * *

By mid-morning, the sun hung in the eastern sky, and the temperature had worked its way up a bit and that cold wind had died down a little. I walked along the road facing traffic. Several cars and a few trucks passed, and I had to scramble to the shoulder when I heard them coming. Mr. Culpepper, a neighbor farmer, stopped his pickup on the shoulder across from me. Rolling down his window, the old man said, "Where you headed, son? Need a lift? I reckon I can turn around."

"I reckon not. Thank you, though," I said as I continued walking.

My chills were gone by the time I spied a gravel road leading up a long hill.

At the top of the hill, I could see a white frame house in need of paint with a whitewashed picket fence surrounding it. A big barn sat behind the house, and I thought the loft would be a good place to hide. I might be able to steal some food when the folks were gone.

I approached the house and looked for signs of the owner. Seeing no one, I walked over to the barn and tried the big doors. They were unlocked, and I went inside. I saw a loft and a ladder, so I climbed up and lay on some loose hay. The loft was dry, warmer than the outside, and it protected me from what was left of that wind. I drifted off to sleep in a matter of minutes.

Chapter 3

A beam of sunlight crossed my face, awakening me. I sat up, stared into the light, and saw the outline of someone peering into the barn.

"Come out here, young man, and let me get a look at you."

My muscles tightened and sore spots popped up all over my body as I climbed down the ladder. I walked through the big doors and put my back to the sun. There in front of me stood an old lady. She didn't come up to my shoulder, and she had jet-black hair pulled tight in a bun at the nape of her neck. High cheekbones anchored translucent skin that fell in folds down her face like heavy drapes. She had the blackest eyes I'd ever seen, framed by small oval-shaped spectacles. There were some raised black spots on her face, with a few sparse hairs sticking out of them.

"What, pray tell, are you doing in my barn?"

"Sorry, lady. I ain't gonna give you no trouble. I'll run along now."

"What's your name, son?"

"Jamie."

"And your last name?"

"Coleman."

"Come closer so I can get a look at that eye."

The old lady had wrinkled, spotted hands with long fingers. Billy had told me a witch lived somewhere in the county. She closed the gap between us, and I shut my eyes and held my breath. Her touch, as soft as Aunt Lulu's, didn't hurt a bit. In fact it felt soothing as she stroked my swollen eye.

"Who did this?" she asked.

"I run into a damn door."

"Tell me the truth, son."

I bit my lip, looked away, and scraped the loose dirt with my tennis shoe. Pop had told me if I ever told anyone that he'd hit me or Mom, he'd beat the shit out of me.

The old lady tapped her foot on the bare ground.

"Pop done it."

"Which Coleman is your father?"

"Gilbert."

"Who is he in relation to Junior and Lester?"

"They're my uncles."

"So you live in Beulah Land?"

"Yeah."

"So, Jamie Coleman, do you have a middle name?" she asked.

"Lee. I reckon that was Mom's name before she hooked up with Pop."

"That would be her maiden name."

"Most folks just call me Jamie Coleman."

"I think you should use your middle name as well. It's a famous southern name and you should be proud of it. You should call your-self Jamie Lee Coleman. It has a nice ring to it. Come to the house and I'll put some ice on that eye. From the looks of you, it's been a while since you've had a square meal."

I followed her to the house. She walked fast for an old lady, and I hurried to keep up with her. A little black-and-white mutt sat on the steps of the back porch. Glancing at the dog, she said, "Come in, Bandit, and I'll feed you, too. He's kind of like you, Jamie; just showed up here unannounced about two days ago. He immediately stole my heart. That's why I call him Bandit."

The back hallway held a refrigerator outside the door to the kitchen. A Coca-Cola wall clock, with the big hand missing, hung over the fridge. The old lady went to the refrigerator and took out some ice cubes. She wrapped them in a dishtowel and handed it to me. "Hold this on that eye, Jamie. It'll take some of the swelling out." Then handing me the wet cloth, she said, "Wipe some of that dried blood off your nose."

She fed the dog first, some dry food out of a paper bag with Purina written across the top. I watched as the little dog gobbled the food down so fast it disappeared in seconds. I said, "He's a hungry little fucker, ain't he?"

She gasped, and her face changed color like one of those blinking neon signs. She gasped, "Jamie, child, where did you learn such language?" Then glancing skyward, she said, "Lord, give me strength. He's just a child."

 She motioned for me to sit at her kitchen table while she fixed me a sandwich. While she worked at the stove, she asked, "How old are you, son?"

"Ten."

"You in the fourth grade?"

"Third."

"You put back a year?"

"Yeah."

She placed two grilled cheese sandwiches and a glass of milk in front of me. Then she sat across from me and watched me eat while she sipped coffee. I ate the two sandwiches and downed three glasses of milk.

"When was the last time you had a bath, Jamie?" she asked.

"I ain't too fond of baths, lady. Don't take one unless something special's happening."

"I think your first square meal in several days could qualify as something special. March into the bathroom and take a bath. Wash your hair, too. There's a new toothbrush in the medicine cabinet. Looks like those teeth could use scrubbing. Throw your overalls and that tattered shirt out when you take them off, and I'll burn them later. I still have a few things of my grandson's stashed away. You don't have to refer to me as Lady. My name is Frances Washington. Most people call me Miss Frances. You may as well."

I liked the old woman, and I was thankful for the sandwiches, but I didn't want to take a damn bath or have my clothes burned. I studied on this for several seconds, trying to decide if I should make a dash for the door. But Miss Frances had been nice to me, and I felt I owed her something for fixing my lunch so I decided I'd do it.

"Where in Beulah Land do you live?" she asked.

"Just up the hill from the well."

"You take baths in cold water?"

"Mom heats a kettle of water for me and pours it in the five-gallon tub we use for bathing, but it's still cold as a witch's tit."

She groaned and then said, "We have hot water, so be careful. I don't want you scalding yourself."

I sat in the steaming water for the better part of an hour. When it cooled down, I'd add a bit more hot water. It was my first real bath and I had to admit, I liked it. The fact that I could add hot water, on demand, fascinated me. After I'd scrubbed myself so hard my skin turned pink, I washed my tangled hair.

Miss Frances opened the door and placed her grandson's shirt and pants on the sink. When I saw it swing open, I covered my privates, but in all honesty, the water was so black I couldn't even see my dick. When I stepped out of the tub, my fingers and toes were as wrinkled as a bull's sack.

I picked up a comb and ran it through my hair, slicking it back on my head. The grandson's pants and shirt were a little small for me, but I managed to pull them on. Then I opened the door and looked out in the hall. I didn't see the old lady anywhere. "Where are you, Miss Frances? I'm done bathing."

"In the living room."

She sat by the fireplace smoking a cigarette and reading a book. Her index finger flew across the page, and her lips moved, making her cigarette flop up and down, spewing ashes into her lap like sparks from a raging fire. Years later I realized she was a speed reader. Able to consume a novel in an hour or so. Bandit lay at her feet, snoring in his sleep. When she saw me, she said, "My goodness, Jamie, I hardly recognize you. Come over here and tell me about yourself."

I sank into the soft cushions like an angel sitting on a cloud. I took the crushed Camel cigarette I'd lifted off Pop out of her grandson's shirt pocket and slipped it into my mouth, then lit it. While I'd never smoked in front of Mom or even Pop, for that matter, I had no such restriction when it came to strangers.

"My God, Jamie, don't tell me you smoke cigarettes."

"Reckon I do."

"When did you start?"

"About three year ago. Why?"

"Children shouldn't smoke. It'll stunt your growth."

"I ain't small, Miss Frances. Hell, you can see I'm a right good size for my age."

"At any rate, smoking can't be good for a child."

"You smoke."

"I admit I don't set a good example."

"I ain't quitting, Miss Frances."

"Do you inhale?"

"You mean, suck the smoke up?"

"Yes."

"There any other way?"

"If you must smoke, just puff like I do."

"I'll try, Miss Frances."

"Where did you get the cigarette in the first place?"

"My old man's pocket. Sometimes at Thompson's Grocery."

"Where do you get the money?"

I didn't answer and she shook her head.

We sat there staring at each other for a few seconds, and then she asked, "Your daddy hit you in the face like that very often?"

I looked away.

"You have any brothers or sisters?"

"I had a little brother for a while. Pop picked him up one night and shook him real hard to make him stop crying. The baby went to sleep and didn't never wake up again. He's buried in the cemetery behind the high school."

She sat there puffing on her cigarette, the blue smoke whirling around her head. and I did the same. Looking around the room, I saw more books than they had in the high school library. An upright piano sat behind the sofa and caught my eye. I kept giving it sideways glances, and she asked, "Do you like music, Jamie?"

"Yeah, I like Patsy Cline and Marty Robbins a lot."

"Are they singers?"

"Grand Ole Opry on Saturday night. I listen to them on my half-ass radio."

She took a deep breath and shook her head. "So they're what we call *Country Singers*. Are they popular?"

"I reckon."

"Do you play any musical instrument?"

"I got me a juice harp."

"I don't know what that is, Jamie.'

This time I shook my head. Hell, I thought everyone knew what a damned juice harp was. I was beginning to think the old lady didn't even know nothing about the Opry. "Billy showed me. You take a comb and some tissue paper and hum through it."

"So you do like music. That's wonderful! I notice that you keep looking at my piano. Do you play?"

"I ain't never tried."

"My daughter used to play that one when she was about your age. Took lessons for five years and then gave it up. Shame, because she could play by ear. Know what that means?"

"Nope."

"She could read music, but what she really liked to do was play things she'd heard on the radio. It seemed to come naturally to her. Some people have a gift."

"What's it mean to read music? That don't make no sense."

"Go over to the piano and bring me that sheet music and I'll show you."

I saw a piece of paper that had a picture of a woman on it dressed in a funny-looking outfit. I'd never seen one like that on any of the women in Round Rock. Picking it up, I took the paper back to the old lady.

She took it from me, and pointing to the top of the page, she said, "This is called sheet music. This one is titled 'April Showers,' a popular song."

Opening it up, she said, "These lines have little dots with flags on them. They're called notes. Each one corresponds to a key on the piano. When you read music, you look at each note and then push down the key that corresponds to that note. This notation over here shows you how fast to play the notes. This is in four-four time. That

MICHAEL E. GLASSCOCK III

means you play all the notes in this segment called a bar to a beat of four. When you see musicians tapping their feet, they're keeping time."

"Damnation, that's right hard, ain't it? Don't reckon I'll be doing much music reading."

I'd always wanted to play a musical instrument because melodies sort of floated around in my head. Most were those ready-made songs I heard on the Grand Ole Opry. But some melodies were mine. I'd never heard them anywhere except in my head.

"You reckon I could do that? Play by ear."

"Want to try?"

"I reckon I would."

Pulling the piano bench out, I sat down. The first thing I did was start striking the white keys one at a time. As soon as I caught a melody, like magic, all the fingers of my right hand started to work together.

I played all the melodies that were spinning through my head with my right hand, and in a few minutes, my left hand started to insert the base notes. It was as if I had no control over my own hands. They just did what they needed to do. It felt spooky.

In all my life, I'd never had as much fun as I did that day playing the old lady's piano. I have no recollection of how long I sat there, but it must have been the better part of an hour. I glanced over at her once and saw tears sliding down her furrowed cheeks and thought she must be the saddest old lady who ever lived.

My forearms were aching by the time I finished, and my heart pounded. The old lady sat there shaking her head. "You seem to have a natural talent, Jamie. That's so wonderful. There're people like you all through the Appalachian Mountains. I think of them as prodigies."

"I don't reckon I know what that is."

"Someone who is born with a specific talent. It just comes naturally to them."

"Hell, I didn't even know I could play the damned piano. I'm right glad I can. I just wish I'd tried the one Miss Smotherman plays in our auditorium as school."

"What's going to become of you, Jamie Lee Coleman?" she asked.

"I don't reckon I know what you mean."

"I want you to live with me so I can look after you."

"I don't reckon I could do that, Miss Frances."

"You have other plans?"

I felt my unplanned, hasty retreat from Beulah Land made me something like a ghost looking for a body to inhabit.

"Reckon what Mom and Pop would say?"

"These matters are settled in court, but I doubt the judge would rule in their favor."

"I might just hitch a ride down to Nashville. Get me a job."

"I think you're a little young to be hitching rides, and you're much too young to get a job. No one would hire you. This is a good offer, Jamie. You need to take it."

"Well, I'll think on it."

"I hope you'll consider staying. I'll call Jake Watson, my attorney, and get things rolling in case you decide to accept my offer.

"There're a few habits you'll have to work on if you do decide to live with me. To start, please refer to me by my name or ma'am, as in 'yes, ma'am' or 'no, ma'am.' Whenever you address an individual who's older than you, it's important to show respect. When you're talking to a man, it would be 'yes, sir' or 'no, sir.' The cursing must stop as well as the use of that awful word *ain't*. We'll work on the smoking later. Now, there're a few things I'd like to know about you. Are you a good reader?"

"I can read."

"Go to the last shelf of the bookcase next to the door and bring me a book."

I pulled a little book off the shelf without looking at the title and took it back to her. She smiled and said, "That one's in German. I don't think that would be a fair test. Try again."

The second book was *The Adventures of Huckleberry Finn*. She said, "This is more like it. This might even ring a bell for you. Open to the first chapter and start reading."

None of the Coleman clan owned a book. Miss Smotherman read to me and my classmates, and tried to get us to take books out of the high school library, to no avail.

I opened the book and stared at the page. I didn't know half the words, and those I did recognize looked funny. I stumbled through one paragraph, and she said, "That's enough. You have some work to do in this area. You must learn to read, Jamie. It's very important.

"What's twelve times twelve?" she asked.

I stared at her.

"Ten times twelve?"

I shook my head.

"Where's the country of Egypt?"

"It ain't in America, that's for damn sure."

"Who's the president of the United States?"

I shrugged.

She brought her hand to her mouth. "My God, child, you're practically illiterate. Do you even go to school? "

"Sometimes."

"Well, in the future you will have to go to school every day. When I was younger, I was a school-teacher. So, I will tutor you and help you get your grades up. Then we'll get you into the proper grade. No playing hooky. Come, let me show you where you will sleep if you do decide to stay with me."

Miss Frances led the way back down the hallway toward the

bathroom. The room was at the end of the hall next to the bathroom and contained a spindle bed so tall I'd have to stand on a stool to climb onto it. A brass lamp sat on a bedside table with a marble top, and a chest of drawers stood in the corner. On the bedside table, beside the lamp, was an honest-to-God radio. I could feel my heart race. Never in my wildest dreams did I think I would ever own or be able to listen to a real radio.

* * *

Back in the living room, Miss Frances asked, "What's your decision, Jamie?"

I bit my lower lip and looked at the floor. I'd never known such a conflict of feelings. I liked the old lady and she'd been nice to me, but I didn't care much for her rules. But given my choices, going back to Beulah Land or staying with her, the decision was easy. What swayed me more than anything were the radio and the piano.

Looking up at my new mentor, I said, "I reckon I could try it for a few days. But I ain't promising nothing."

Miss Frances smiled and said, "I'll call my attorney."

About four o'clock that afternoon a car pulled up to the front gate and a man got out of the backseat and started up the walk. He was a handsome older man with gray hair and wore a suit and tie, which was unusual for Parsons County.

Miss Frances met the man at the door while I stood by the fireplace with my back to the gas logs.

"Jake Watson, meet Jamie Lee Coleman," she said.

Taking my hand, the man said, "Pleased to meet you, young man." Then turning back to Miss Frances, he said, "Could we talk alone for a minute, Miss Frances?"

"Anything you want to say can be said in front of Jamie. I don't want to keep secrets from the boy."

"Have a seat and let's talk about this. You're what, Miss Frances, eighty-five?"

"Something like that."

"You have no domestic help, high blood pressure, and arthritis. Do you think you can raise a young boy by yourself?"

"I raised Little Joe. Granted with help from Persifor, but I know what I'm doing. Don't patronize me, Jake. Just arrange for a court date."

"You're sure about this?" Jake Watson asked.

"I am."

* * *

Two days later, I sat at a table with Mr. Watson and Miss Frances in the Parsons County courthouse. Mom was sitting across the room at another table, crying. Pop glared at me with meanness radiating from his eyes. I figured if he wasn't in the courthouse with all the people sitting around, he'd just smack me a good one across my face. Just the thought of that made my stomach burn.

Judge Grant looked down on us like God in heaven. Perspiration trickled down my rib cage despite the cool dampness of the court-room.

Mr. Watson stood and addressed the judge: "Your Honor, I've filed a petition with this court to have one ten-year-old boy by the name of Jamie Lee Coleman removed from his parents' custody and rendered to the care of Miss Frances Washington. She'll become responsible for his housing, clothing, and nutrition, and will supervise his attendance at school.

"This change is in the interest of the boy's general health and well-being. It's made necessary by the fact that he currently resides in an abusive home caused by his father's drinking. The boy has survived numerous assaults."

The judge looked at Pop and said, "Do you have anything to say, Mr. Coleman?"

Pop stood, looked Judge Grant in the eye, and said, "Good riddance, Judge. He ain't a good boy. No, sir, he ain't nothing but trouble." Then he sat down and looked out the window.

I could feel my stomach tighten and I took a deep breath. Why did Pop hate me so?

Judge Grant glanced at Mom and asked, "Mrs. Coleman?"

Mom stood and looked at me, her eyes red as fire. "I'll miss the boy, but I reckon it's for his own good. I ain't got no objections."

The judge brought his gavel down hard and said, "So be it. This court is adjourned."

Watching Mom and Pop walk away from the courthouse brought bile to my mouth, and I spit it on the bare ground. I felt an ache in my stomach and a sense of emptiness. Suddenly, I realized I'd miss Mom something awful.

The taxi that had brought Miss Frances and me to town took us home. It wasn't a taxi like you'd see in a city with a sign on top, just a four-door Ford sedan that Jerry Whittle used to take folks around the county.

Bandit was sitting on the front porch waiting for us when we pulled up to the picket fence.

After supper, while we sat in front of the fireplace, Miss Frances laid out the rules for my behavior. She took a puff on her cigarette and said, "You'll take a bath every day and wash your hair every other. You will feed Bandit and the chickens I keep in a pen behind the house. There will be no playing hooky. The bed is to be made daily and no clothes can litter the floor of your room. You'll learn proper English, forget the words *shit, damn, hell, and ain't*. Fingernails must be short and clean. Do these things in good spirit and you can listen to the radio at night before going to sleep."

I stood there with my mouth open like an idiot at the state loony farm and thought, *Fuck this shit! I ain't taking no damn bath every day and I sure as hell ain't gonna give up cussing.*

Chapter 4

There's a certain advantage to buying used shoes at a thrift store, be it the Salvation Army or Goodwill, for they are broken in, well worn, soft, and easy on the heels and toes of big, calloused feet. Until that following Saturday morning when Miss Frances and I went to Dawson's Dry Goods Store, I'd never donned a new pair of brogans.

Jerry Whittle picked us up around ten in the morning. A middle-aged man with graying red hair, Jerry had a pleasant smile, though his teeth were sparse and stained yellow from tobacco.

It was the first week in February, and the tree branches looked like skeletons. A gentle mist and drizzle covered the landscape, and the day had a forlorn feel to it. The grandson's jacket I wore was at least one size too small, and my feet were jammed into my old tennis shoes, the laces long gone.

Mr. Dawson walked with a stoop so bad he looked up at people from under bushy eyebrows. His shirt, though buttoned and fixed with a broad yellow tie, was big and loose at the collar, and his coat hung loosely off his thin frame, the sleeves covering his thumbs.

"Morning, Miss Frances. How may I help you?" he asked.

"I need to outfit this young man: shirts, pants, cap, shoes, underwear, socks, handkerchiefs, and a good warm jacket."

Turning to me, he asked, "What's your shoe size, son?"

I stared at him.

Miss Frances said, "You best measure Jamie, for I doubt he knows these things."

I did okay until Mr. Dawson measured the inseam of my pants leg. When the man held the tape in my crotch, squashing my testicles, I jumped as if the old man had hit me with a cattle prod. Mr. Dawson wrote the number of inches on a notepad. For the shoes, I stood on a metal slab with a slide on it and numbers printed in white letters. I needed a size nine in a D width, which Mr. Dawson said was large for a boy my age.

"We'd like to leave the clothes Jamie has on so you can discard them, Mr. Dawson. I want Jamie to go home in a new outfit," Miss Frances said.

I went into a dressing room, removed her grandson's tight clothes, and left them on the bench. I would have saved them for Billy, but I knew they'd be too small for him. Then I pulled on a new pair of Jockey briefs, pants, shirt, and socks and slipped my feet into the new brogans. While Miss Frances wrote her check, I donned the new windbreaker and cap with flaps that I could pull over my ears.

It took three trips out to Jerry's car with Mr. Dawson, Miss Frances, and me carrying the sacks of clothes. When he saw us struggling out to the car, Jerry jumped out and opened the trunk.

As he crammed sack after sack into the trunk, he looked at me and said, "Jamie, son, you're going to have all the girls chasing you around the school yard."

I could feel my face flush. "I don't care too much about girls, Mr. Whittle. They kind of make me nervous if you know what I mean."

Jerry laughed. "I know exactly what you mean, son. Please call me Jerry. Mr. Whittle makes me feel old as Methuselah."

The taxi driver opened the back door and Miss Frances got in, followed by me. As Jerry drove, I looked out the window at the passing landscape and thought how nice it was to be riding in a car instead of walking along the blacktop. When we passed Beulah Land, I tried not to look up the hill but couldn't help myself. It had only been a few days, but it seemed like a lifetime to me. Thin trails of black coal smoke cut through the gray sky like worms from the tops of the tin roofs of the tar-paper shacks and I thought how cold it would be inside my old home. I gave a slight shiver, and Miss Frances glanced at me with a look of compassion.

Jerry Whittle turned onto the long drive and at the top of the hill parked in front of the picket fence. Then he helped us carry the sacks of new clothes to my room where we stacked them on my bed. Miss Frances gave Jerry a dollar more than usual for helping.

By suppertime, I had two Band-Aids taped to my heels, and I limped like an old man.

Bandit sat at my feet during meals because I'd slip the little dog a small morsel from time to time. I did this clandestinely, for Miss Frances thought it crude.

Glancing at me, she said, "Let me see those fingernails, young man."

I pushed them in front of her and held my breath. When feeding the chickens their evening rations, I'd dug a small hole in the dirt with my fingers to hide a plug of Red Man. On top of that, I'd failed to trim them when I took my bath that morning.

"There's enough dirt under there to start a garden, Jamie. As soon as you finish eating, march to the bathroom."

After supper, we sat in the living room in front of the gas logs and smoked. When she looked away from time to time, I'd inhale deeply and let it out slowly with my head turned to one side.

"Why don't you get that book and I'll read you a chapter," Miss Frances said as she dabbed her cigarette into the ashtray. "I want you to learn to read. It'll enhance your life and round out your character. We'll start with fiction."

"I don't reckon I know what fiction is, Miss Frances."

"When someone tells you a story he made up, when the story isn't based in fact, then it's fiction."

"You mean a lie?"

"It's just a story someone made up from his imagination. Let's read the book and I'll explain as we go."

I handed the book to her, and she motioned for me to sit on the couch. Bandit crawled up beside me, and she began to read.

When Miss Smotherman read to our class, her voice was a monotone, and the majority of the time I fell asleep. With Miss Frances it was different. She took on the character of each individual. She used a different voice for Huck than for Jim. Through the whole book, which took us two weeks to read, she explained what the author attempted to convey to his reader. Not that I understood all she told me, but I did remember she said Huck was a captive of his environment, much as I was.

After the first chapter, she closed the book and said, "Time for bed, Jamie. Don't forget to brush your teeth and turn off the radio promptly at ten."

I took off my new clothes, placed them on the rocker beside the bed, and donned the pajamas Mr. Dawson had insisted Miss Frances buy. I picked up Bandit and stepped on the stool and climbed into the big bed, sinking into the softness of the feather mattress.

The little dog crawled to the foot of the bed and was sound asleep in seconds. The radio, tuned to Ernie's Record Shop in Gallatin, Tennessee, featured Ernest Tubb that night.

Miss Frances came in later, turned off the radio, and said, "It's ten, Jamie. What did I say?"

"Yes, ma'am, I'm sorry."

When she left, I picked up the radio, placed it on the pillow next to my ear, and turned it back on. *I ain't in prison, Miss Frances.* I reckon there were just too many changes going on in my life. Some I liked okay: others I hated. I'd decided to stay with Miss Frances because as bad as the rules were, the thought of going back to Beulah Land was a whole lot worse.

* * *

Miss Smotherman took a double look when I walked into the classroom Monday morning. Billy wrinkled his nose when he saw me in my new clothes and grimaced as if he'd smelled a polecat. A couple of the girls actually smiled at me.

At the first recess, Roger Williams, the town boy who always made fun of my ratty clothes, walked up to Billy and me and said, "I sure ain't never seen a clean Coleman before. Even when they ain't covered with grime, they still remind me of niggers."

"Listen, prissy pants, you better go before I beat the shit out of you," I said, though in truth I wasn't sure I wanted to ruin my new clothes.

Roger stuck out his tongue, and that stupid act of defiance shot through me like a bolt of lightning. My muscles quivered and my heart raced. I rushed Roger and hit him squarely in the chest with my head.

Billy roared, "Fight!"

Encircled by students, we rolled around on the ground, each one of us trying to get an advantage, a chokehold or a half nelson. I felt my right knee rip through my pants leg and a sharp pain shot up to my groin. In one great straining effort, I was able to get the upper hand and rolled on top of Roger, pinning his shoulders with my knees.

"Hit him, Jamie!" Billy yelled.

"Give up, prissy pants, and I'll let you up," I said, looking down into Roger's mean black eyes.

"Bullshit," Roger said and rolled onto his right side, throwing me off.

This resulted in more thrashing and rolling around as each of us tried to better the other. I was furious. I'd ripped my new pants, and my knee was bleeding. Finally, with great effort, I was able to twist Roger's arm behind him.

I kept pressing Roger's arm until he started crying. At that, I figured I'd won the fight and let go. Standing, I turned my back to Roger. The next thing I felt was a rock hitting the back of my head. Everything went black for a moment and I fell against Billy, knocking him to the ground.

Out of the corner of my eye, I saw Roger running toward the schoolhouse with Billy in hot pursuit. They tangled on the steps just as Roger attempted to open the door.

Five minutes later, the three of us sat outside Mr. Youngblood's office, Roger with his right hand cupped under his nose trying to stop the bleeding and Billy with a rapidly swelling right eye.

Billy and I got fifteen licks, but Roger got off with ten. That pissed me off because Roger was the one who started the whole ruckus.

"How come Roger only got ten licks?" I asked Billy.

"Hell, Jamie, Mr. Youngblood give us ten last week and promised us fifteen if we got in trouble again. Can't you remember nothing?"

On the bus home Billy said, "Let's go to the pool hall in Round Rock tomorrow."

"I can't play hooky no more. Miss Frances told me not to."

"You letting that old lady tell you what to do?"

"She's a nice old lady. I ain't gonna play hooky."

"You turning into a damn sissy on me, Jamie?"

"I ain't no sissy. Let's go after school. I'll ask Miss Frances if I can walk home."

"Hell, that's a goddamned five miles, Jamie."

"Don't matter. We stay at the pool hall for an hour, I still got time to get home by dark."

"Think you can do that in them new brogans?" Billy asked with a grin.

* * *

The school bus arrived at 6:30 every morning and took a route that bypassed Beulah Land. At 4:00 each afternoon, Bandit met me at the mailbox, and the two of us walked up the long drive together. On this particular afternoon, when I walked into the living room, Miss Frances was reading and smoking in her chair. When she saw my torn pants, she asked, "What happened, son?"

"A town boy named Roger Williams picked a fight."

"The banker's son?"

"I don't rightly know. I whipped him good, though."

"How did he pick the fight?"

"He said even clean I reminded him of a nigger."

Miss Frances put her hand to her mouth. "Oh, dear me. I'm so sorry, Jamie. That's a terrible word used for colored people. Pay no attention to it. You've got to stand up for yourself but, if possible, it's best to do so without resorting to violence. Better go change clothes."

That night, while Miss Frances fixed our supper, I sat at the kitchen table and did my arithmetic. I said, "Reckon it'd be all right if I walked home tomorrow instead of taking the bus?"

She stared at me. "Why would you do that?"

"Billy, my cousin, and me want to go to the pool hall. He wanted to play hooky, but I told him I couldn't."

"It should be 'Billy and I' want to go. Try to use proper English, Jamie. I don't think pool halls are a good place for young boys. However, I'm so pleased you've been honest with me, I'm going to give my permission. That is, if you get Jerry to drive you home. I don't want you walking that distance by yourself. It's another three miles to here from Beulah Land."

Never in my wildest dreams did I think Miss Frances would let me go to the pool hall. I simply couldn't believe it.

"Thank you, ma'am, but I ain't got no money to pay Jerry."

She shook her head. "Jamie, son, please don't use that awful word. I'll give you the money."

We had country ham, creamed corn, and green beans for dinner that night. I sure enjoyed Miss Frances's cooking and I usually ate till I thought I'd pop. But it made me feel bad that I was eating so well and Billy wasn't. So I swallowed a bit of ham and asked, "If we have any food left over tonight, you reckon I could take some to Billy?"

"Billy is Lester's boy?"

"Yes, ma'am."

"I'll put what we have left over in a plastic container and wrap it in aluminum foil. You'll need to ask the woman in the cafeteria to keep it in the refrigerator for him. Then he can take it home. Do you think that will upset his mother and father?"

"Aunt Lulu won't mind but I don't know about Lester."

"Well, we'll try this one time and if everything goes well, we can send food on a regular basis."

*　*　*

The next day, when I told Billy about the country ham Miss Frances had sent him, he said, "Hell, Jamie, that was right nice of the old lady. Thank her for me. We ain't been eating too good since my old man got his hours cut at the shirt factory."

Then, when I told him what Miss Frances had said about playing pool, he didn't believe me until I showed him the two dollars.

"Hell, Jamie, you walk home you can keep the two dollars."

"That old lady's too nice to me. I ain't... I'm not going to do that."

We walked down the hill to town after the last bell. I carried my books held together with an old belt I'd found in the chest of drawers. It was one of those cold, damp days that Tennessee is famous for in February. I pulled the collar of my new windbreaker around my neck and yanked the flaps of my cap over my ears. A buttermilk sky hid the sun.

The pool hall was in the corner of an old brick building at the bottom of the hill from the shirt factory. The rest of the structure housed the Parsons County Feed Store, so there were salt blocks stacked in front of the building along with sacks of feed.

Two men were playing eight ball when we walked into the pool hall. The one who was lining up a shot had a cigarette dangling from his mouth and squinted to keep the smoke out of his eyes. He had a hooknose, a two-day stubble, and long black hair down to his collar. A scar ran down his right cheek ending at the corner of his mouth, giving him a permanent sneer.

The other fellow I knew, for the man lived in Beulah Land, one of the Crockett clan by the name of Sylvester. He was a rotund little fellow with pink skin and sparse hair who reminded me of a suckling pig. He had beady, close-set eyes and one that wandered so you never knew whether or not he was looking at you or somebody else.

The main light in the pool hall came from fixtures that hung low over the two tables. Flickering Coca-Cola and 7-Up neon signs cast long shadows against the cracked plaster walls. The floor was unpainted concrete. Hank Musk, the owner, kept a vigil on everything that went on. He was an old man with heavy jowls and sacks of skin under his eyes that gave him a hound dog look. His gray hair was unkempt and tangled. An avid Red Man chewer, he kept a tin can not unlike Pop's slop jar at his feet.

Billy and I had never played pool. Until that day, all we'd ever done was to stand around and watch. We never had the seventy-five cents it took to get a table. In his practical way, Billy had come up with a scheme for us to get our game.

Crushed cigarette packs, old candy wrappers, and discarded butts of cigarettes and cigars littered the concrete floor. Billy thought the two of us could sweep the rubble, and Mr. Musk would give us a free game.

Though it was Billy's idea, I was to make the arrangement, so I said, "Mr. Musk, sir, Billy and me would like to strike a deal with you."

He looked at me with watery eyes and a deadpan expression. In a cigarette voice, he said, "Deal?"

"Yes, sir."

"What kind of deal?"

"I reckon we could sweep the floor for a game."

"It don't need sweeping."

"Reckon there's anything else we could do? We ain't got the money."

Old Musk glared at me while he was thinking. Then he looked back at the pool table and watched the two men argue about a shot Sylvester had just made.

Finally, he said, "The Coke and cigarette machines need filling. You do that you get one game. Don't even think about lifting a pack of smokes. I'll know it right off. Got it?"

"Yes, sir, Mr. Musk. Show us what to do."

The Coke machine was empty, and it took us fifteen minutes to fill it from the wooden cases in the storeroom. The cigarette machine was easier.

"Hell," Billy said, "how's he going to miss one pack out of all these?"

"You want to play a game you best put that in with the rest."

Billy turned the pack over in his hand and stuck it in the slot with the others.

When we'd finished filling the vending machines, Hank motioned for me.

"Grab the broom out of the storeroom and sweep the damn floor. It ain't a bad idea."

There being only one broom, Billy and I took turns. The room seemed to grow as we worked. I looked at the Coca-Cola wall clock. By the time we finished, we'd put in an hour's worth of effort.

Billy and I'd watched eight ball so we had a fair idea of what to do when we racked the balls. What we didn't know was the skill it took to sink a ball in a pocket without scratching. We were so bad, Sylvester and the hook-nosed man stopped their game and stood watching us make fools of ourselves.

"You got to put some backspin on that cue ball, Jamie," Sylvester said. "You don't it'll follow the six ball into the pocket, and you'll scratch. You'll have to spot the six ball and lose a shot."

"I don't reckon I know how to do that, Sylvester."

"Put some chalk on the tip of the cue, and then line up on the lower half of the cue ball. That way when you hit the damn thing, it'll go forward but with some backspin. When it hits the six ball, the cue ball will come back at you instead of going into the pocket."

I hit the cue ball, but the stick dug into the felt of the table top, ripping it. I grimaced.

Hank yelled, "I hear a rip?"

"Yes, sir."

"It ain't too bad, Hank. Little duct tape will fix it," Sylvester said.

"Hell you say. Let me look."

He lifted his big frame out of the chair and waddled over to the table. Bending over the rip, he said, "I ought to have my damn head examined, me letting you boys at my pool table. Look what you done, boy. You got the money to pay for this?"

"No, sir, I ain't got no money."

My hands shook like a man with palsy, and my mouth was so dry, I couldn't swallow. Billy stared at Hank with sheer terror etched into his round face.

"Get the fuck out of here and don't be coming back."

I dropped the cue on the floor and followed Billy out the door, slipping once on the slick concrete floor.

It was dusk when we ran up the hill to the square where Jerry Whittle kept his Galaxy parked at a reserved spot the sheriff had marked for him. Strawberry Wilson said a town the size of Round Rock needed a taxi service, and he aimed to keep Jerry Whittle happy.

Jerry sat in the car with the windows rolled up, his head cocked back on the seat, sound asleep. When I rapped on the window, Jerry jumped and hit the horn ring.

Jerry rolled down the window and said, "Jamie, son, don't ever do that again. You scared the shit out of me. Shake the damn car or something next time. What you want?"

"Me and Billy want a ride home."

"You got two dollars?"

"Miss Frances gave it to me."

"Hop in. Billy gonna get off at Beulah Land?"

"Yes, sir."

We climbed into the back, and Billy asked, "You got a smoke, Jerry?"

"Yeah, but I ain't giving you none. Damn things cost too much, and besides you're a youngun. Damn things'll stunt your growth, and you're a little shit as it is."

About halfway to Beulah Land, Jerry rolled down his window and spit a mouthful of tobacco juice into the wind, splattering the window next to where I sat.

I had an uneasy feeling grip my stomach when Jerry stopped in Beulah Land. I looked up the hill, wondering if I could see Mom. It seemed like a hundred years since I'd left.

Bandit was waiting in front of the picket fence when Jerry pulled up to Miss Frances's house. I gave Jerry the two dollars and climbed out. Bandit came over and licked my hand. I picked up a stick and threw it into the field next to the house. Bandit took after it like a scalded rabbit.

Forgetting it had rained the previous evening, I ran into the field and sloshed through one mud puddle after the other before falling headfirst into a three-inch stand of water.

Covered from head to toe with mud, I walked onto the back porch and fed Bandit. Miss Frances opened the door and, seeing me, said, "Dear me, perhaps Jake is right. Jamie, honey, I know you're just a child, but can you at least try to stay clean?"

I looked at the floor and said in a whisper, "I'm right sorry, Miss Frances. I wasn't thinking. Please don't be mad at me."

A smile crossed Miss Frances's face and she reached out and tousled my hair. "I'm not mad at you, son. I just want you to be more careful. Now tell me about your game of pool."

Chapter 5

Around the first of March, Miss Frances handed me a package wrapped in slick red paper and tied with a white bow. She said, "You can't carry a piano on your shoulder. This way you can take your music wherever you go."

I ripped open the package and found a used Gibson guitar. I took to the instrument like a dung beetle to a pile of shit. Though well used and possibly abused by its previous owners, it nonetheless had a mellow tone.

The next morning the ground was covered with a layer of bright snow six inches deep. Drifts had piled up against the barn, and they looked three feet high. The bare limbs of the maple trees, covered with snow, dripped under the weight and looked like white weeping willows against the cloud-filled sky.

I was strumming the catgut strings, trying to get the right sound with clumsy, untrained fingers, when the front door opened and a tall, thin man with sandy hair and deep-set blue eyes stepped into the living room, followed by a big black Labrador.

The man extended his hand. "I'm Joe Stout, Miss Frances's grandson. You must be Jamie."

"Yes, sir, we've been expecting you. We thought you might get here yesterday."

"I had a little trouble with my pickup in Little Rock. Nothing serious. Where's Mother Washington?"

I tilted my head. "Kitchen."

"This old boy's name is Poncho. Who's the pooch?"

Bandit and the Labrador were doing their own introductions.

"We call him Bandit."

Miss Frances had told me Joe was a veterinarian and lived in a place called Utopia, Texas. He was trying to get a new practice started.

"It must be a right smart drive from Texas to Parsons County. How far you reckon it is?" I asked the doctor.

"Right at a thousand miles, give or take a few."

"What's the weather down there?"

"When I left it was in the low eighties."

"Wow! And us with all this snow. Ain't—isn't that something."

The doctor laughed and shook his head. "I see Mother Washington has got you on the Proper English Program. I had that one myself a few years ago."

I gave a deep sigh. "It's right hard, isn't it?"

"Yes, it is. Go back to practicing your guitar. I'm going back to see Mother Washington," Dr. Stout said as he headed for the kitchen. A few minutes later, there was a faint knock on the front door. Miss Frances seldom had visitors, so I thought it unusual.

I placed the guitar on the table and, followed by Bandit, walked the few feet to the door. When I opened it, Mom stood smiling at me. She'd walked the three miles from Beulah Land through six inches of snow.

"Howdy, son. I done missed you so much, it burns my stomach."

I hadn't seen Mom in three months. My lips were so dry they stuck together, but I managed to say, "Hi, Mom. Come in. You need to get warm."

She looked into the room and, hesitating, shook her head. "I don't reckon it'd be proper, me barging in like that."

At that moment, Miss Frances and the doctor walked into the room. When Miss Frances saw Mom, she said, "Mrs. Coleman, please come in out of the cold. Surely you didn't walk all the way from Beulah Land?"

"It weren't nothing."

"Come in and warm up. I just made a pot of tea. Here, let me take your coat."

After Miss Frances brought the tea pot and cups from the kitchen, the four of us sat and drank hot tea mixed with sweet milk. The doctor told us how hard it'd been to heat the old house when they had nothing but coal grates. That was when Miss Frances had taken him in, at age nine, some twenty years before.

Mom's cup and saucer rattled a little as she lifted it to her lips. I'd forgotten how dry and calloused Mom's hands were and how wrinkled her thirty-year-old face was.

Judge Grant had given Mom visitation rights, excluding Pop. Until this morning she'd chosen not to seek me out. I knew it'd be a lie if I said the situation didn't trouble or mystify me. As I sat watching Mom strain to be sociable, I wondered what was going on in Beulah Land. Billy had shunned me of late, and I knew little of the gossip I used to get from my cousin.

The tea gone and Mom warmed, Miss Frances said, "My grandson will take you home, Mrs. Coleman. I'll not have you walking in this weather."

Then Miss Frances went into the kitchen and gathered some Irish potatoes, green beans, and a big slice of country ham. She wrapped them in aluminum foil and came back into the living room. Handing the food to Mom, she said, "Please take this home with you Mrs. Coleman. We have more than we need and I don't want it to go to waste."

Mom took the food and said, "That's right nice of you Miss Frances. Thank you."

I saw a worried look on Mom's face and I knew what she was thinking. Pop would be mad if he knew where it came from. I just hoped he didn't hit her.

I rode with them, the red Ford F100 with Texas plates sliding back and forth across the road for lack of chains. When we got to Beulah Land, each shack, including Pop's, had a thin trail of black smoke arising from the galvanized pipes sticking through the tin roofs.

I sat in the middle of the bench seat, and when Mom got out, she leaned over and kissed me on the cheek. Her lips felt like sandpaper.

"Good-bye, Jamie boy. You be good and mind Mrs. Washington."

I watched her climb the snow-covered hill to our shack, slipping every now and again until she reached it. She turned, waved, and went inside.

I was scared Pop would stick his head out the door and holler at me, but he didn't. I wondered what it was like for her there without me to help her. Then I felt a little guilty for running out on her. At that moment, I realized how much I missed my mom. Would I ever get over losing her?

*　*　*

The doctor stayed for three days. He said he needed to get back to his practice because he'd left some sick animals in the care of a colleague. The morning he was to take off, I got up late, for it was a Saturday. As I walked toward the kitchen, I heard him talking to Miss Frances. I stood by the refrigerator and tried to decide if I should go in. I listened for a moment and realized they were talking about me.

"Please keep it down, Joe. I don't want to alarm Jamie."

"He seems like a nice kid, but for God's sake he's a Coleman. Just think of all the problems we've had with those people."

"He's a good child and he's trying hard. He misses his mother, and he's having to cope with a whole new way of life."

"I hate to say this, Mother Washington, but you're too old to do this. And you're not in the best of health."

"I'll decide when I'm too old, young man. Now you take care of your business and I'll take care of mine. Jamie stays."

I could feel my face heat up. *What if something happens to Miss Frances? Is she sick? Could she die?*

Running back to my room, I threw myself on the bed and buried my face in the feather pillow, thinking, *I won't go back to Beulah Land.*

When I didn't come to breakfast, Miss Frances came to check on me. Seeing me fully clothed with my face buried in the feather pillow, she tapped me on the shoulder.

"Jamie, are you okay?"

The pillow was wet when I raised my head. "I'm fine."

"Why have you been crying?"

"Stomachache."

"What's our arrangement, Jamie?"

"Truth."

"Tell me."

"Dr. Joe don't like me."

"Were you eavesdropping?"

"Yes, ma'am."

"Joe likes you, Jamie. He simply thinks I'm too old to raise a young boy by myself. He's mistaken, but he means well. Now I don't want you worrying yourself over nothing."

"Yes, ma'am."

I reckon her reassurance should have put my mind at ease, but it didn't. I was afraid Dr. Joe would keep at her until she threw me out. What would I do? Where would I go? Why did he hate me?

Miss Frances, Bandit, and I stood on the porch and watched Dr. Stout drive away. The snow, gone two days, had left a muddy mess of the yard and a few shallow ruts in the limestone driveway. She waved one last time as the pickup turned onto the county road, and I noticed dampness in her eyes. *Does she like him more than me?* That thought made my stomach hurt.

* * *

The school year ended around the middle of June. My grades had moved from F to straight B during the months I'd been living with Miss Frances. By late June, we'd settled into a comfortable existence, for the three of us were now a family: Miss Frances, Bandit, and me. I hadn't seen Mom since that day in March. Miss Frances and I went to the First Baptist Church every Sunday morning in the back of Jerry Whittle's Ford. I was learning about Christ in Sunday school, so each night I said a prayer asking for Mom's safety.

I reckon the routine of my day gave me a sense of security. I arose promptly at 5:30 each morning, bathed, fed Bandit and the chickens, and then ate a big breakfast of scrambled eggs, toast, bacon or sausage, and some of Miss Frances's homemade jam. I spent my days with Bandit exploring the farm. I'd have a sandwich for lunch and then practice either the piano or the guitar for a couple of hours in the afternoon. Then Bandit and I would go out looking for adventure. In the late afternoon, after feeding Bandit and the chickens, I practiced the piano, guitar, or both for an hour and then did the homework Miss Frances insisted I do till supper, which we had promptly at six thirty. Since school was out, the homework consisted of assignments

Miss Frances gave me. Sometimes the home work was a series of math problems or a chapter to read in the encyclopedia. After supper, I studied until eight o'clock. Miss Frances read one chapter from some book we'd jointly agreed upon, then I went to bed.

Saturdays we went grocery shopping. One July afternoon we were in Thompson's Grocery laying in supplies when I turned a corner, pushing a cart in front of me, and almost knocked Mom off her feet. She had a sack of Irish potatoes in her hand.

"Jamie, you give me a fright, son. You doing okay?"

"Yes, ma'am. You?"

"Why I'm just fine, son. You here alone?"

"Miss Frances is on the other side in the meat market."

"Well, you tell her I said hello. I got to be going now."

She turned and hurried away without looking back, and I felt my stomach drop to my knees. I stood there staring into space until Miss Frances walked up and asked, "Jamie, what's wrong?"

"It ain't nothing."

"It isn't anything. What happened?"

I looked away. "I just saw Mom."

"That should make you happy. How is she?"

"I don't know. She didn't say much, just hello, then good-bye."

"I know you miss her, Jamie. It's only natural."

"Why won't she come see me? You know, at our house."

"I have my suspicions, son, but I don't know for sure. I do know she loves you very much. I believe this arrangement is as hard on her as it is for you."

A week later, again in Thompson's, I looked up one aisle, then another for Mom, but to no avail. It was my job to push the cart around the store while Miss Frances loaded it. I kept asking her for white bread, and she refused, always with the same answer: "White bread has all the nutrients taken out at the bakery. Wheat bread is good for you."

I did develop a taste for raisin bran, and she was delighted that I'd get iron and roughage. I wondered, *How can raisins contain iron? What's roughage?*

That Saturday, as usual, Jerry Whittle sat patiently at the curb waiting for us. He always helped load the paper sacks into the trunk of his car. Jerry and I were placing the last of the sacks in when I saw Pop walking down the street toward us with one of the deacon's glass jugs swinging freely from his hand.

Miss Frances sat in the backseat checking the sales slip as she did each Saturday, so she didn't notice him. I bit my lip and looked away as if that would make Pop disappear. Jerry, aware of my situation, narrowed his eyes and motioned for me to get in the car.

It being a warm day, the windows were down. Jerry had just slipped behind the wheel when Pop got even with the car. He leaned through the back window, his flushed face and watery blood-laced eyes inches from my face, and belched. The stench of his shine-soaked breath made me gag.

"Well, if it ain't Jamie Lee Coleman. The little smart-ass thinks he's so special. You ain't been missed at all, just you remember that."

In a calm voice, Miss Frances looked past me and said, "Mr. Coleman, you are inebriated and making a fool of yourself. Kindly take your head from the window so Mr. Whittle can proceed."

It looked to me as if Pop didn't understand a word she'd said. I wasn't exactly sure what *inebriated* meant, but seeing Pop's condition, I figured it had something to do with being drunk as a skunk. Pop pulled out of the window and hit his head on the top of the frame. He stepped back a step or two, and Jerry gunned the car, leaving Pop staggering to keep from falling.

"I'm sorry, Jamie," was all Miss Frances said.

I felt my face flush and my stomach tightened into a knot. I don't think I'd ever hated the old bastard as much as I did that day. I was so embarrassed I could barely breathe.

Jerry helped us unload the groceries, and Miss Frances gave him a one-dollar tip. I helped her take the groceries out of the paper sacks and then we stacked them in the pantry. I couldn't believe all the food we had to eat. It would have lasted us a month in Beulah Land.

While she placed a can of pork and beans on the bottom shelf, she said without looking at me, "I know it upset you to see your father like that. It seems to be a Coleman affliction—alcoholism."

"I don't reckon I know what that means, Miss Frances."

"It means someone who needs to drink alcohol like the moonshine your father prefers. He is addicted, which means he has little or no control over his need. Some scientists believe it may even be hereditary."

"Hereditary?"

"Passed on from one generation to another."

I swallowed hard and said, "Uncle Junior and Lester both like their shine."

"I know that very well, but I don't want you worrying about yourself. It's not something that always happens. Now why don't you and Bandit go outside for a while, enjoy this glorious day."

It was a clear, cloudless day in the mid-eighties and Bandit and I went to our favorite spot in the small woods just behind the barn. The creek that ran through the maple, oak, and birch trees was shallow with rocks in the middle that created a rippling sound I found soothing. The shady spot I liked most was in the middle of the woods and had a large boulder on which Bandit and I could sit and watch the minnows and crawfish scamper about in the clear water.

A solitary beam of sunlight filtered through the leaves and created a spot of brightness where we sat. Bandit lay curled at my feet sound asleep, soft gurgling sounds emanating from his open mouth. Occasionally, he moved his paws, as if he was dreaming of running.

I lay back on the rock, my face illuminated by the sunshine, and thought about Miss Frances. I wondered if she realized how much I appreciated all the nice things she did for me. For the first time in my life, I actually felt lucky. But for the grace of God and Miss Frances I would still be in Beulah Land fighting with Pop. *Why haven't I told her how I feel?* I wondered.

After supper, we started a new book, *The Swiss Family Robinson*. By the end of the first chapter, I had an idea.

"I want to build a tree house, Miss Frances, in that big oak beside the barn. You know the one with the low hanging branches."

She folded the book and set it on the table next to her chair.

"I'd be afraid you'd fall, Jamie, break an arm or something. I don't think that's a good idea. Besides, who would help you?"

"You could."

She laughed and said, "You've got to be kidding."

After each chapter for a week, I brought up the subject of a tree house, and she always said no, and each "no" became more emphatic than the preceding one. In desperation, for I thought she had mixed feelings about my persistence, she said, "I give up. I can't help you build it for obvious reasons, but I will help you design it. There're still a few of my husband's tools in his garage. Joe took most of them to Texas."

My eyes widened and I said, "Oh, Miss Frances, thank you so much. I know it'll be a wonderful tree house. You reckon there's enough tools left to do the job?"

* * *

The following Saturday afternoon, after the groceries were in the pantry, Miss Frances and I walked out to the big oak tree and studied its limb arrangement. Two low branches ran at right angles to each other, and we decided these could support the floor

Back at the kitchen table, on one of my blue-lined notepapers we drew up the plans for the tree house. Then we went into Mr.

Washington's garage, and Miss Frances located a hammer, a coffee can full of six-penny nails, and a hand saw. I climbed the ladder to the loft and found enough two-by-fours and one-by-sixes to build three tree houses.

I carried the lumber out to the tree and stacked it in neat piles. Miss Frances stood and watched with a broad grin. My pulse raced each time I ran back to the garage for another load. The tools were last.

It being summer and the days long, I worked on the floor until six o'clock. Big blisters poked out of the insides of both thumbs and I had a bleeding finger where I'd jabbed myself with the saw, but I'd never been happier.

The third Saturday, as Jerry was unloading the car, he said, "You building that tree house, Jamie?"

"Yes, sir."

"Need some help?"

"I would be much obliged, Mr. Whittle, if you'd tell me how to build the roof."

So for the next four Saturdays, Mr. Whittle spent an hour helping me after unloading the groceries. It was a fine tree house. We painted it barn red with some paint I found in Mr. Washington's garage. It had a tin roof that Jerry Whittle brought from his farm tied to the top of the taxi, and a real window, bigger than the one in my room in Beulah Land. I could even raise and lower it to let in air. We made a rope ladder that I could pull up like the drawbridge of a castle.

The afternoon we finished, Mr. Whittle, Miss Frances, Bandit, and I stood under the oak tree and admired our work.

Miss Frances said, "The two of you have done a wonderful job."

I said, "Thank you, Mr. Whittle. I don't reckon I could have done it without your help."

"You're welcome, son. You done a good job."

That evening while I played a new song I'd heard on the radio,

"Crazy," written by Willie Nelson and sung by Patsy Cline, Miss Frances started coughing. She was red faced and having trouble catching her breath. Her eyes bulged a little, and I feared for a moment she was dying.

I rushed to her side and slapped her on the back, which did seem to help a little. She looked up at me, her eyes wet, and said, "It's the cigarettes."

I said, "I'll quit smoking, Miss Frances, if you will. I promise."

Spittle seeped from the corners of her mouth, but it didn't lessen the smile that formed in her reddened cheeks. "We'll quit together."

Chapter 6

Miss Frances had tutored me all summer, so when school started in late August, she convinced the principal to move me up to the fifth grade where I should have been. I was amazed by how much I'd learned under her strict guidance. It was a new experience not being one of the dumbest students in class. I'd become a ferocious reader over the summer and fell asleep every night with a book in my hand.

My grades steadily climbed, and Miss Smotherman smiled like a Cheshire cat when she handed me my first report card.

"I knew you were a smart boy, Jamie, even if you are a Coleman," she said.

My cousin Billy stopped speaking to me. "You ain't nothing but a damn teacher's pet," he'd yelled across the school yard. My new station in life pissed him off. He couldn't abide the changes he'd seen in me. The last time I'd brought him a plate of food from our house he'd thrown it on the ground and stomped on it.

Around the middle of September I stepped off the school bus to find Bandit waiting for me as usual. I collected the mail, and we strolled up the long limestone driveway to the house. As we approached, I noticed an unfamiliar car parked at the picket fence. It had Putnam County license plates. *What's someone from Cookeville doing here?* I wondered.

As I stepped onto the porch, the door opened, and a tall woman said, "You must be Jamie. I'm Amy's mother."

Who's Amy?

Miss Frances said, "Come back in an hour, Mrs. Blackman, and Amy will be ready."

The woman got in her car and drove away, leaving me in a state of confusion. In the living room, sitting on *my* couch, was a skinny girl. She had hair the color of cinnamon and the palest skin I'd ever seen. I thought she looked like a ghost. Her eyes were a brilliant green and held a hint of mischief. They were hidden behind a pair of horn-rimmed glasses. When she stood, she was damn near as tall as me.

"This is Amy Blackman, Jamie. I'm going to tutor her three days a week. She's having a little trouble with math. She's a very bright girl, but numbers seem to be a problem for her. Like I told you when you first came to live with me, in my younger days I was a teacher. I sometimes tutor young people who are having trouble in school. Sort of like how I've helped you."

Amy closed the gap between us and extended her hand. "I'm pleased to meet you, Jamie. Miss Frances has been telling me about your musical talent. I hope you'll play for me sometime."

I must have looked like an idiot standing there with my mouth open. When I took her hand, she gave it a squeeze and smiled. It was then that I noticed the splash of freckles across her nose and cheeks.

I felt my face flush. I wasn't accustomed to shaking hands with girls. Hell, I stayed as far away from them as possible.

"I reckon I'll go do my chores while y'all study," I said, rushing from the room.

While feeding the chickens, I contemplated the situation. I'd be lying if I said it didn't irritate me to have a girl taking Miss Frances's attention away from me. *At least it's only three days a week. What if she ends up liking Amy better than me?* I didn't even want to consider that possibility.

After feeding Bandit, I swung my guitar over my shoulder and went to the tree house. I'd been spending a lot of time there since Jerry Whittle and I'd finished it. I could practice without bothering Miss Frances. It wasn't that she didn't like listening to me. I just didn't want to disturb her reading.

Mrs. Blackman must have been running late, for Amy wandered into the backyard and looked up at me. "Can I come up?" she yelled.

No one except Jerry Whittle and I had climbed the rope ladder. It was my territory, my tree house. I didn't want to share it with anyone, let alone a girl.

She stood there, arms crossed over her flat chest, and stared at me. I stared back, feeling hot all over.

When I didn't answer, she wandered over to an elm tree about ten yards away and sat with her back against the trunk. Looking up, she said, "Play for me."

The only person who'd ever heard me play the piano or guitar was Miss Frances. Who did Amy think she was, ordering me around? I pulled up the rope ladder and went into the far room of the tree house, where I sat looking out the window at Cooper Mountain.

Moments later, I heard Mrs. Blackman yell, "Come on, Amy, time to go home."

I waited for a few minutes and then went back out onto my little porch. Thankfully, the yard was empty.

* * *

At the dinner table that evening Miss Frances said, "Amy said you were rude to her this afternoon. That doesn't sound like you. What happened?"

"I don't like her. She's nosey and bossy."

"You're not jealous, are you? Does it bother you that I'm tutoring her?"

I shrugged and didn't say a word. I kept my eyes on my plate, avoiding her gaze. Then I took a bite of country ham and washed down the saltiness with a gulp of milk.

Miss Frances laughed. "You're the apple of my eye. No one could take your place. Amy is a temporary student. As a favor to me, please be nice to her."

"How much longer you reckon she'll be coming here?"

"She's a smart girl but has poor study habits. She's doing very well. My suspicion is, she'll only need help for about another six weeks. Surely, you can be a gentleman for that length of time."

"I reckon I can. I'll try for you."

"That's my Jamie."

* * *

The following Wednesday when Mrs. Blackman dropped Amy off, I opened the door for her and said, "Hi."

"Hi yourself, Jamie Lee Coleman. I play the piano. Maybe we could try a song together after Miss Frances finishes with me."

"I think that's a capital idea," Miss Frances said, entering the room. "In fact, we'll stop a few minutes early so you'll have time."

I was mortified. What if she played the piano better than I did? What if I couldn't keep up with her? What if she didn't like my kind of music? But I'd made a promise, and I knew Miss Frances would want me to honor it. Still, I said, "I'm not sure I'll have time to do my chores if I do that." I looked at Miss Frances with pleading eyes.

"If you begin now, you'll have plenty of time. Come, Amy, let's get started."

I knew I was doomed. I shook my head and headed for the chicken yard with Bandit close behind. As I watched the hens peck the grain from the bare ground, I wondered what kind of music Amy liked. All I knew was what I'd heard on WSM. I didn't listen to rock and roll. It was too loud, and I couldn't understand what they were singing. In fact, I considered most of the songs to be idiotic.

Bandit gobbled down his dinner in record time. "Slow down, Bandit. You wanting to hear me make a fool of myself?" I asked out loud.

At that moment, Amy opened the back door and said, "Come on. I'm ready."

I followed her down the long hallway like a man being led to the gallows. When we got to the living room, Miss Frances sat in her chair with a look of anticipation on her face. "I'm ready for my concert," she said.

In my anxious state, I'd forgotten to bring my guitar. "I'll have to find my guitar. I think it's in my room."

I went to my room and stood looking at my guitar on its metal stand, the one Miss Frances had bought me at the beginning of summer. I sat down on my straight-back chair and hung my head. I did not want to do this. I didn't like girls, and I particularly didn't like this girl. Why did Miss Frances care for Amy so much? A good five minutes passed, and I finally realized I couldn't put off the inevitable any longer. I had to put up or shut up.

When I got back to the living room, Amy pulled out the stool and sat at the piano. Looking up at me, she asked, "What do you like?"

"Crazy."

She laughed. "You're a Patsy Cline fan. So am I."

With that, she started playing the melody, and I jumped right in. Before I realized it, I was singing the chorus at full volume. Then she joined in. I'll admit we sounded good together, and before long we had that old living room shaking with our music. I glanced over at Miss Frances and saw that she had her eyes closed. She had a big smile on her face and kept perfect four-four time with her foot.

We played a variety of songs for thirty minutes or so, and by the time Mrs. Blackman knocked on the door, we were exhausted but exhilarated. I'd never had so much fun in my life and could have gone on for another hour. I actually hated to see Amy and her mother leave. Miss Frances and I followed them out to their car, and I held the door open for Amy. As she slid onto the front seat, I said, "That was great, Amy. Let's do it again on Friday."

She smiled and said, "You're really good, Jamie. I love your voice. It sent chills up my spine."

I felt as if I'd walked into a furnace room, I was so hot all over. I might have only been ten years old, but at that moment, I decided I might actually like girls.

* * *

It was the middle of October when my life fell apart. Bandit and I'd been to the creek, and when we walked into the living room, I thought Miss Frances might be asleep in her chair. As always, she held a book in hand, but her index finger wasn't flying across the page. I started to go to my room so I wouldn't wake her, but just as I turned to leave, I noticed she didn't seem to be breathing. That realization startled me and my heart raced. I crossed the room quickly and stood looking at her intently. Her eyes were closed and she did not take a breath. There was little question in my mind that something bad had happened. I ran down the back hall to where the telephone rested on a small shelf and picked up the receiver, my hands shaking. I couldn't remember Dr. Kate's number so I told the operator, "Please get Dr. Kate for me and hurry."

"Round Rock Medical Clinic," Jazz said. "Can you hold a minute?"

"No!" I shouted into the phone. "No! I've got to talk to Dr. Kate, now! Please, Jazz, now!"

"That you, Jamie?" Jazz asked.

"I've got to talk to Dr. Kate. Now!"

"Okay. Hold on."

Two seconds later, Dr. Kate asked, "What's wrong, Jamie?"

"I think something bad has happened to Miss Frances. She ain't breathing much."

"Go sit with her, Jamie. I'll be there in a few minutes."

I walked back to the living room with Bandit trailing behind me. I was hyperventilating and my head felt as if it was going to split right down the middle. I couldn't swallow and my hands trembled. When I got back to Miss Frances, she had not moved. She still looked asleep, but I was sure now that she was not breathing. I'd never seen a dead person but I knew that Miss Frances had passed. And I knew that I loved her with all my heart. How could I possibly live without her? She had literally saved my life.

I sat on the floor and pulled Bandit to my chest. Then I wondered out loud, "What's going to happen to me? I can't go back to Beulah Land. I won't."

A little sob escaped my lips, and then my whole body shook and tears streamed down my cheeks. I buried my face in Bandit's fur and cried harder than I had ever cried in my life. I had never felt so frightened. Not even when Pop beat me.

I had lost all sense of time when I heard a car race up the long driveway and skid to an abrupt stop at the picket fence. Moments later, Dr. Kate rushed through the front door and went directly to

Miss Frances. She placed her right index finger on the old woman's neck, felt for a carotid pulse, and shook her head. Then she reached down and lifted me to my feet. She engulfed me in a bear hug and said, "Jamie, honey, Miss Frances is dead. I'm so sorry. I know you loved her very much and she loved you, too. You were the apple of her eye. We'll all miss her."

I held on to the doctor with all my might. I was afraid if I let go, I might die, too. Dr. Kate kept her arms around me until my sobs began to subside. I looked up at her with wet cheeks and asked, "What's going to happen to me?"

Looking out the window, Dr. Kate said, "We'll know very soon now. Jerry Whittle just delivered Jake Watson."

The attorney entered the room minutes later and walked over to where Dr. Kate and I stood hugging each other. He glanced at Miss Frances and then looked directly at me. Then he said, "Miss Frances has made arrangements for your care. She thought of everything. Please don't be frightened. You're going to be looked after. I know this is a terrible loss for you. I will do the best I can."

I shook my head. I had no idea what the attorney was talking about. I did latch on to the thought that I would be looked after. Finally, confused, I asked, "What's going to happen to me?"

"Miss Frances asked me to take care of you if anything happened to her, and I agreed. I would like for you to come live with me. I will be responsible for all your material needs. I'm an old bachelor, don't know the first thing about young people, but I'll do the best I can. Are you game?"

I nodded my head and whispered, "Yes, sir."

You could have knocked me over with a feather. Anything was better than going back to Beulah Land and Pop. I still missed my mother something awful, but I'd gotten used to a new life and had no intention of going back to my old one. I knew I'd never forget Miss Frances and all the nice things she'd done for me. I'd miss her something awful, just like I did my mother.

"Thank you, Mr. Watson. I'd appreciate that. What about Bandit?"

"I think we can make room for your dog. Gather your things, and as soon as the sheriff gets here, we'll go to my house."

* * *

I placed all my clothes in a cardboard box and zipped my guitar into its canvas cover. I started out of the room and suddenly turned back. Walking over to the bedside table, I unplugged the radio and placed it in the box on top of my clothes. I was sure Miss Frances would want me to have it.

Then I walked onto the back porch and collected Bandit's bowl and bag of dog food. I lifted Bandit's leash off its hook and attached it to the dog's collar. The two of us walked down the long hallway to the living room and out of Miss Frances's house for the last time. I found Jerry Whittle waiting for us with Jake in the backseat. Jerry had left the trunk open so I would have a place to put my belongings. I opened the back door and let Bandit in first, then climbed in beside Jake. "I'm real sorry about Miss Frances. We'll all miss her a lot," Jerry said as I slammed the door.

We rode in silence. I couldn't believe I'd never see her again. I'd never hear her read me another story. I bit my lip, trying to hold back the tears. No matter how much pain I created, the tears came anyway. They just slid freely down my cheeks. Jake noticed but didn't say a word. He had a look of anguish on his face.

When we passed Beulah Land, I turned my head and looked away. I had no desire to see my old shack. I did wonder how Mom was doing. Was Pop still beating her? It seemed to me that is was taking much too long to reach Round Rock. It was like the place had actually moved. I knew that couldn't be. Then I whispered to myself, "I reckon I'm just not thinking straight."

I just stared into space with random thoughts drifting aimlessly through my mind. When the car suddenly stopped, I looked through the windshield at a large house. Miss Frances's house was a modest, sturdy structure and comfortable, a mansion compared to Pop's shack in Beulah Land. But Jake's house was a real mansion. It stood three stories high with a porch on three sides. It was a blue Victorian with white shutters and white gingerbread trim, and a gazebo in the yard. The house was on a cul-de-sac that contained no other structures.

While Jake paid Jerry, I removed my box of clothes from the car's trunk. Somehow I'd managed to get Bandit's bowl, his food, and the radio in the box as well. I wandered up the steps to the long porch and looked out at the dense forest surrounding the house. The trees were ablaze with red and gold. A gentle breeze ruffled the leaves and a cascade of them fell to the ground. Bandit pushed his shoulder against my leg like a cat and whimpered.

"It's okay, fellow. This is our new home."

"Come in and I'll show you around," Jake said, opening the door.

I clung to the box and Bandit's leash as we walked into a large hall that had a high ceiling. A magnificent crystal chandelier hung from an open rafter. A spiral staircase led to the upper floors. I stood there, mouth agape, and wondered how I would manage among such splendor. I glanced from side to side as I followed Jake down the long hallway. I saw a large living room with overstuffed sofas and chairs, and then we passed the dining room that contained a long table with at least twelve chairs. At the end of the hallway, Jake turned into an incredible room. The walls contained walnut bookcases filled with more books than I'd ever seen in one place. At the far end was a huge brick fireplace. Over the mantel hung a portrait of a man who looked a little like Jake. Two red leather chairs with ottomans were in front of the fireplace, and beside it were two large stereo speakers.

In one corner was a grand piano, its top open. I'd never seen one except in a magazine. I wondered if Jake would let me play it but decided to wait a while before asking.

"I thought Miss Frances had a lot of books," I said. "You've got more than the library."

Jake said, "Some I inherited from my father. That's a portrait of him when he was on the Tennessee Supreme Court. You're welcome to read any of my books. Just put it back exactly where you found it. Yolanda has them arranged by author. Come, I'll introduce you to Yolanda. She's my housekeeper."

With my guitar slung over my shoulder and the box of clothes still clutched to my chest, I followed Jake to the kitchen. Yolanda turned out to be a small woman with fine features, skin the color of milk chocolate, and short, curly white hair. She smiled as we entered the room.

"Yolanda, I'd like to introduce Jamie Lee Coleman. He'll be living with us now."

She extended her hand, and when I took it, she gave me a gentle squeeze. "I'm pleased to meet you, young man. I'm so sorry about Miss Frances. She was a wonderful woman and I know you'll miss her. Welcome to Mr. Jake's house. What's your dog's name?"

"Bandit. He's well behaved."

"I'm sure he is. Let me show you to your room."

She opened a door that led to a set of back stairs. I followed her up to the second floor with Bandit at my heels. We stepped into a hallway and passed several doors before she stopped in front of my new room. What I saw flabbergasted me. A beautiful walnut sleigh bed was nestled in one corner. Two leather chairs sat at the foot of the bed with an antique table between them. A Tiffany lamp was on the bedside table, and a huge cherry armoire took up a good part of one wall. There was a dressing room attached to a large bathroom containing a deep claw-footed tub. The fixtures were gold plated.

I let my breath out slowly. I'd never seen anything like Jake's house. I wasn't going to look a gift horse in the mouth. I just wished Miss Frances could live there with us.

"My room's off the kitchen," Yolanda said. "If you need anything, all you have to do is pull this cord."

"Thank you, Yolanda. I think I can manage. If you need any help around the house, I'm used to doing chores."

"You just get settled in. Supper will be ready in about thirty minutes."

She left, and I placed the box with my clothes on the floor. Then I stooped and removed Bandit's leash. "We're going to like it here, Bandit. I can already tell." I hung my one Sunday suit on a hanger and placed my underwear, socks, and shirts in the drawers. I placed my guitar on one of the chairs and plugged the radio into a wall socket before putting it on the bedside table. Next, I went into the bathroom. Turning on the water as hot as I could stand it, I stripped and slid into its depths. I lay back, the water to my neck, and soaked.

With my eyes closed, I thought of Miss Frances, my first real bath, and my new clothes. How stupid I'd been to even think of not staying with her. I'd learned so much since that cold day in January. She'd shown me a whole new world. But I suspected Jake was going to show me even more. Suddenly I realized that amidst all the splendor of my new quarters, I'd still miss my tree house, Miss Frances, and Mom.

Chapter 7

Yolanda was a marvelous cook. She used vegetable oil, not lard like Miss Frances. She did season our green beans with a piece of pork, but they weren't greasy. Her cornbread was light and melted in my mouth. I can't even describe the desserts. I'd never heard of a lemon tart, but I came to love them, along with black bottom pie and ladyfingers.

That first meal with Jake and Yolanda was memorable in many ways. For one thing, the three of us ate together. In the 1960s housekeepers, particularly black ones, didn't do such things. But I was soon to learn that Yolanda and Jake had an unusual relationship. There appeared to be a closeness between them that even a ten-year-old could grasp.

The table was set with solid silverware, china plates, and crystal glasses. Everything was so heavy I couldn't believe it. I tried to remember everything Miss Frances had taught me about table manners. I even kept my left hand in my lap. Jake had a bemused smile on his face as he watched me struggle.

After eating, Jake and I adjourned to the library. Jake pushed a book in one of the cases, and to my amazement, a section swung open to expose a rack filled with bottles. He took one off the shelf and poured a dark liquid into a small crystal glass. Closing the section, he said, "I prefer a little Spanish port following supper. I have some Coke in this small refrigerator. Would you like some?"

I nodded. "Yes sir I would."

He removed a green bottle of Coke, used an opener to remove the top and handed it to me. "

Shall we listen to some music? I understand you're a fine musician."

"I can play guitar and piano. That's a nice one in the corner."

"It belonged to my mother. I've had it in storage for years but decided to take it out recently. You're welcome to play it anytime you like."

"Thank you, Mr. Watson. I really appreciate that."

"When we're alone, call me Jake. When adults are around, best call me Mr. Watson. What kind of music do you like?"

"Mostly country and a few popular songs. I hate rock and roll. Why would anyone listen to music if they couldn't understand the words? They jumble together and are drowned out because the bands are way too loud."

"That makes two of us. Ever heard an opera?"

"I don't rightly know what that is."

"It's a story set to music and sung by professional singers. They date back to the seventh century. I have a marvelous stereo system. If you like, we can listen to one for a few minutes."

What was I going to say? I couldn't refuse the man who'd stepped in to save my life.

"Okay by me."

"We'll start with a comic opera by Mozart called *The Marriage of Figaro*. I've got a libretto. That's an outline of the story the opera tells. The singing will be in Italian."

Jake went to a cabinet and removed a small booklet. Handing it to me, he said, "Just read along as the opera progresses. It may be a little hard for you because you've never done it. You'll catch on quickly."

The music was unlike anything I'd ever heard. The singers had powerful voices and the women had really high-pitched ones. I tried to keep up, but it was fruitless. By the time the Countess and Susanna were dressing Cherubino as a girl, I was totally confused. I finally just gave up and listened.

To his credit, Jake made me listen for only thirty minutes. Seeing my discomfort, he said, "It takes a while to appreciate opera. I won't force it down your throat. Grab a book and go to bed."

I picked a book at random. It was John Updike's *Rabbit, Run* published two years earlier. In my new bedroom, I brushed my teeth, put on my pajamas, and crawled into my big bed. I climbed right back out because I'd forgotten to pick up Bandit. There was no way the little dog could jump that high. Settling into the soft feather mattress made me think of my old bed at Miss Frances's house. A pang of sadness swept over me. I already missed her so much it hurt me to breathe. It seemed to me that I was always missing someone, first Mom and now Miss Frances. As I lay there staring into the black void of my room, I wondered how my life was going to change in the weeks and months to come. How would living with Mr. Watson compare to my time with Miss Frances?

* * *

The funeral took place the following Tuesday. Jake and I walked down the hill to Main Street and found our way to the First Baptist

Church where Miss Frances and I'd attended services. The street was filled with cars and pickups, and the church parking lot was full. By the time we got there all the seats were taken, and I had to stand in the back. Jake had a reserved seat because he was a pallbearer.

The first thing I noticed was the colored people sitting where our choir should have been. They wore purple robes with gold sashes around their waists. Brother Abernathy's wife sat at the piano.

Dr. Stout and April Simpson, Jake's partner, walked in a side door and took a seat in the first pew. They both looked like they'd been crying.

Brother Abernathy said a few words about Miss Frances that I thought summarized her as well as anyone could. Then Dr. Stout got up and said he'd asked the choir from the colored Baptist church to sing some spirituals Miss Frances was partial to. When they stood and sang, I could feel my spine tingle. Their voices blended together with a richness that I'd never heard. They reminded me of the opera singers. I wasn't familiar with the songs they sang.

The first was "Swing Low, Sweet Chariot." A young colored woman sang the opening stanza with a crystal clear voice that rang to the rafters. I thought she could have sung in that opera Jake had me listen to. By the time the choir finished the song, my heart was pounding. Next an old man, his face wrinkled as a prune, with a deep, gravelly voice, sang "Nobody Knows the Trouble I've Seen." By the time they finished with "Steal Away," there wasn't a dry eye in the church.

Then Dr. Stout read two poems he said Miss Frances liked. After that, Mrs. Abernathy played a medley of Miss Frances's favorite hymns.

When it was all over, Jake and the pallbearers lifted the casket and walked down the aisle to the front door. Dr. Stout and Miss Simpson followed. While the pallbearers slid the casket into the hearse, Dr. Stout and Miss Simpson talked to a colored man and woman I'd never seen before.

I started to walk over and tell the doctor how sorry I was about his grandmother, but in the end I didn't. He seemed like a nice enough fellow, but I couldn't help remembering he'd wanted Miss Frances to send me away.

Jake rode to the cemetery with the other men, but I couldn't bring myself to see her lowered into the ground. I said my good-bye silently as the hearse drove away. Then I walked up the long hill to my new home, feeling a mixture of sadness and uncertainty about the future.

* * *

Life in Jake Watson's house was different. The only chore I had was feeding Bandit. I missed the chickens. I loved to watch them waddle down the plank from their house so I could feed them grain on the bare ground. And I missed the woods, the creek, my tree house, and Amy. But most of all, I missed Miss Frances. I could read well, but I missed the way she interpreted a story. I even missed the school bus, for now I could walk to school. It was just a few streets over from Jake's house.

In the afternoons I'd play Jake's piano. It had a rich sound that made Miss Frances's old upright seem tinny. And I'd practice my guitar in my room with the door closed so I wouldn't disturb Yolanda.

One evening after dinner, when Jake and I retired to the library, as we did every night, he said, "I bought a new album today I think you might find interesting. It's by a classical guitarist named Andres Segovia. He's a Spaniard and, like you, self-taught. He gave his first concert at age sixteen, and now at sixty-nine he goes all over the world. I'll be interested to hear your thoughts."

I don't know what I expected when Jake lowered the stylus onto the record. What I did hear thrilled me. I'd never heard the guitar played like that. Segovia used the fingers on his right hand to pluck the melody while strumming the chords. Soon an orchestra joined in, and the room filled with incredible music. My head was swimming. *If only I could play like that*, I thought.

Jake watched my amazement with a bemused smile. "I thought you might be impressed," he said.

"Would it be okay if I listened to the record after school? I'd like to see if I can copy some of what he does. I'll be real careful"

"I only have one request. When you're ready, I'd like to hear you play."

* * *

Christmas came and I got to decorate my first Christmas tree. I'd never had one in Beulah Land. On the Friday before Christmas, I went to the Ben Franklin Store on Main Street and bought presents for Yolanda and Jake with money from my allowance. Jake now gave me five dollars a month to spend any way I wanted. I bought a handkerchief for Jake and a bottle of hand lotion for Yolanda. I wanted to buy a present for Mom but had no way to give it to her. Even if I did, Pop might throw it away when he found out it came from me.

On Christmas morning the three of us sat in the living room next to the tree. Jake and Yolanda sipped on their coffee mugs while I opened my gift. When I ripped off the red paper, my eyes widened. Yolanda and Jake had given me a small stereo set of my own for my room. After opening the box and carefully removing it, I said, "Thank you so much. Now I can listen to Mr. Segovia in my room."

In the weeks following Christmas, I listened to the Segovia record every day. In fact, by January I'd almost worn that record out. To my own amazement, I'd learned a lot from Segovia. I got terribly discouraged at times because I had to learn everything by trial and error: a lot of error. Being a natural musician has its advantages and disadvantages. While it was easy for me to pick up a tune, the mechanics of the difficult finger movements required to copy the Spanish guitarist were challenging.

On the second Saturday in January, after one of Yolanda's wonderful suppers with all the trimmings, I said, "I reckon I'm ready to give y'all that concert I promised." So, the three of us adjourned to the library. Jake and Yolanda each had a glass of port, and I positioned myself on a ladder-back chair. I'd gone to the school library and looked up Segovia in the encyclopedia. There was a picture of him sitting on a plain chair, his foot on a stool, his leg supporting the guitar.

I used two large books because we didn't have a stool. Even though it wasn't a "real" concert, I felt nervous. I didn't want to disappoint Jake and Yolanda. My mouth was a little dry and my hands felt cold. I'd read that Segovia soaked his hands in warm water before a concert because of his nervousness. That thought reassured me.

I'd picked the opening of Beethoven's Fifth Symphony in C minor. In truth, I didn't know exactly what that meant, but that was how it was described on the album jacket. I plucked the famous repetitive first four notes and was soon lost in the beauty of the piece. I didn't open my eyes until the last chord. When I did, I was surprised to see Jake and Yolanda staring at me open mouthed.

Jake was the first to speak. "My God, son, you learned all that from listening to a record?"

"Yes, sir."

"This calls for another drink," he said, heading back to his bottle of port.

When he returned, he said, "I'll try to find you a teacher, but there's no one around here who could help you. There has to be a classical guitarist in Nashville. I'll contact one of the recording studios. Maybe I can get someone to work with you two Saturdays a month. Jerry Whittle can drive you down. What do you think?"

What did I think? It scared me a little. What if I wasn't good enough? What if they made fun of me? But in the end, I said, "I think I'd like to try."

* * *

The third Saturday in January of 1963, Jerry Whittle and I headed for Nashville. Jake gave me five dollars for gasoline and said he'd look after Bandit. Yolanda packed us a lunch of sandwiches and potato chips. I placed my old guitar on the seat beside me for the trip south.

As we drove through Cookeville, I wondered how Amy was. I hadn't seen her since Miss Frances passed. Jerry had his radio tuned to WHUB, the Cookeville radio station. A live program was in progress. A country artist sang an old Appalachian folk song I'd never heard. What really caught my ear was her yodeling. I couldn't imagine how she made that sound.

In my first ten years of life, I'd never been out of Parsons County. All I knew about the outside world I'd learned from reading books. I'd set aside *Rabbit, Run* because I couldn't understand what it was about. I realized I did better with adventure stories and westerns.

As we left the plateau and descended on Highway 70 toward Carthage and Lebanon, I watched the landscape change from mountains to rolling hills. We crossed the Caney Fork River two or three times and drove along the Cumberland River in Carthage.

I had been quiet the whole time. Everything was so new and exciting, I couldn't believe how lucky I was. I turned to Jerry and said, "I really appreciate you doing this for me. And I couldn't have made my tree house without your help. Thank you so much."

Jerry glanced at me and said, "I lost my son when he was about your age. Drowned in Dale Hollow Lake. We were fishing for smallmouth bass in a john boat. I didn't insist on a life jacket because the boy could swim."

Jerry bit his lip and his eyes started to tear. "He fell over the side when I made a quick turn as we were heading back to the dock. He must have had a cramp or something because by the time I got back to where I'd seen him go down, he wasn't there. I jumped in and dove after him, but I was too late. I ain't never got over it, Jamie. Don't reckon I ever will. You might say I like dealing with you because you remind me of my boy."

I shook my head. "I'm so sorry, Mr. Whittle. That's just plumb awful. I just can't imagine anything worse."

We rode in silence the rest of the way and arrived in Nashville around eleven and drove up Lower Broad to West End Avenue, where we found the music school on a side street. Jerry parked the car at the curb and, turning around to face me, asked, "You want me to come in with you?"

"I can do it by myself."

I walked up the sidewalk, wondering what lay ahead. I had the name of the guitar teacher written on a piece of blue-lined note-book paper. I'd be lying if I said I wasn't nervous. My palms were already wet and I kept swallowing hard. In reality I'd only played for four people. I knew and trusted them. How would I do with a total stranger? Stepping onto the wide porch, I knocked on the door.

Mr. Arbuckle answered. He was a tall, slim man with silver hair that came to his shoulders. He was dressed in jeans, a turtleneck sweater, and a tweed jacket with leather patches at the elbows. I immediately focused on his fingers. Like mine, the nails of his right thumb, index, and middle fingers were longer than the others. Firm calluses had formed on the tips of his left-hand fingers.

"Jamie?"

"Yes, sir."

"Come in and we'll go to the practice area."

I followed him down a long hallway to a big room with a fire-place. There was a piano in one corner and several chairs and a sofa. Music stands were scattered about.

"Have a seat and tell me about yourself."

"What do you want to know?"

He smiled. "How old are you? How long have you been playing the guitar? Who was your first teacher? Those kinds of things."

He seemed like a nice fellow, and I felt comfortable with him. Clearing my throat, I said, "I'll be eleven in three days. I've been playing for almost ten months, but I've never had a teacher." Then I thought about the Spaniard. "I did listen to a record by a man named Segovia."

Mr. Arbuckle leaned against his desk and set his cup down. He had a confused expression on his face.

"You're self-taught?"

"I reckon."

"What other instruments do you play?"

"Just the piano."

"Can you read music?"

"I do everything by ear. I do know the notes."

"Hand me your guitar."

I unzipped the canvas cover and handed the instrument to my new teacher.

Me. Arbuckle took it and plucked a few notes. "Did you tune this yourself?"

I nodded.

He said, "Turn away from me and face the wall." Then he struck a chord. "What was that?"

"G 7."

After running through a series of chords, he started plucking single notes, asking me each time what it was. Finally, he said, "You've got perfect pitch. Can you play something from memory?"

"I do all the time."

Handing me my guitar, he said, "Let me hear something from that Segovia album."

I closed my eyes and started. After two pieces, he said, "Stop."

Opening my eyes, I saw that he held a guitar. It looked older and more used than mine. Mr. Arbuckle strummed a few chords. The sound was mellow and rich. Then he did a quick riff and nodded at me. I followed his exact notes.

We kept doing that back and forth for several minutes. Finally, he placed his guitar in a stand and asked, "You're from Round Rock?"

"Yes, sir."

"I've heard about natural musicians from the mountains of East Tennessee all my life. Frankly, I doubted they existed until today. You're a prodigy, son. Do you even know what that means?"

"Miss Frances told me it was someone who had a natural talent of some kind. That's all I know."

"It means you have a talent few people understand. At your young age, it makes you something of an oddity. Mozart was a prodigy. Ever heard of him?"

I nodded, remembering the opera that Jake had shared with me.

"I'm not quite sure how to handle you, Jamie. You'll be a challenge to say the least. I'm not even sure I should teach you to read music. That might stifle you. I'll give it some thought. That'll be it for today. I'll see you in two weeks."

* * *

Jerry and I ate our lunch by the lake in Centennial Park. Yolanda had made us Swiss cheese sandwiches and placed a bag of potato chips in each brown paper sack as well as two homemade chocolate chip cookies.

Jerry took a bite of his sandwich and asked me, "How did it go with the music teacher?"

"Okay, I reckon. He's a right nice fellow, and he plays the guitar real good."

"You gonna keep coming back?"

"Sure."

Pulling out his pocket watch, Jerry said, "We got some time, Jamie. Want to go by the Ryman Auditorium? You know, where they broadcast the Opry. I reckon we could take a tour."

My eyes widened like pie plates, and I swallowed the last bit of my sandwich.

"Are you kidding? Yes."

Jerry wadded his paper sack up and threw it in a trash can. I did the same with mine and tossed the last of my potato chips to the swans.

Back in the Galaxy, we drove to Broadway and stopped just past Fifth Avenue. Jerry parked at a meter in front of the Ernest Tubb Record Shop, and we wandered up to the entrance of the Ryman Auditorium.

Jerry bought tickets with his own money, and the two of us followed the tour guide into the auditorium. I stayed real close so I could hear everything the woman said. I hadn't expected the church pews, but the tour guide said the place had once been a tabernacle. The stage looked smaller than it had on Jake's television. The big canvas backdrop touted the benefits of Martha White Flour. Looking up at the balcony, I figured that would be the best seat in the house.

For a few minutes I tuned the tour guide out and just let my imagination run wild. I tried to envision myself standing up there on the stage with the pews full of people. What would I play for them? Would I be alone or with other musicians? Would the audience like me? While these questions frightened me a little, they nonetheless made my heart pound with excitement.

Until that moment, I'd never thought of playing my guitar professionally. All I'd ever considered was the pure joy the music brought me. Then I wondered, *Reckon I could make a living playing the guitar?*

Part Two

Chapter 8

In January of 1968, the day I turned sixteen, Jake and Yolanda threw me a birthday party. Two friends from my sophomore class came as well as Miss Smotherman, my third grade teacher. Mr. Arbuckle drove up from Nashville with his wife. My high school English teacher, Mrs. Woods, came but a few minutes late. Amy, who was a week older than me, drove herself from Cookeville. After Miss Frances's death, Amy and I didn't get to see each other, but we did talk on the phone occasionally. Because Jake refused to have anything to do with phones, I had always gone to a friend's house to make the calls. Since there was a long distance charge, I would ask the operator for the amount so I could give that to my friend's mother.

The year before, Amy and I had seen each other at a state debating contest. Amy had filled out nicely, and I was looking forward to dating now that she could drive. Jake refused to have anything to do with automobiles, preferring to have Jerry Whittle chauffeur him around.

I hadn't dated much because I spent so much time practicing my guitar and the piano and I didn't have access to a car. But on occasion, I would ask one of the girls in the class behind me to go on a date. She would borrow her father's car and we would park on some country road and do a little heavy petting.

Mr. Arbuckle and I'd become good friends. He'd decided against teaching me to read music, letting me expand my repertoire at my own speed. I'd learned a great deal in the five years we'd worked together. I was much more relaxed playing in front of strangers.

We'd asked everyone not to bring gifts, but they did anyway. Mr. Arbuckle brought a Segovia album. I'd personally invited Mom, but she hadn't responded to the note I sent by Jerry Whittle. I continued to be mystified by the fact she continued to shun me. I'd occasionally see Pop staggering around Round Rock, but I stayed clear of him.

The party finished with ice cream and cake. I'd made a wish before blowing out the candles. Amy had asked me what it was, but I refused to say. It was a simple, straightforward wish that my new family, Jake and Yolanda, stay safe. I couldn't bear the thought of losing another mentor. I still missed Miss Frances something awful.

Dr. Stout had settled on her farm a few months after his grandmother's funeral in 1962. He ran his veterinary practice out of Miss Frances's converted barn. Every stray cat and dog ended up there, and his field was full of rescued horses, goats, sheep, and any other type of hoofed animal one could imagine.

That evening when Bandit and I crawled into the big sleigh bed, I lay awake listening to WSM as I did every night. Thinking back to my crystal radio, I marveled at how my life had changed in the past six short years. I felt aglow with my new existence.

* * *

Then, a couple of weeks later, it quickly began to unravel. It started one morning when I fed Bandit. The little dog didn't eat his dry dog food; he just looked at it. That was not the Bandit I knew. Bandit generally gobbled down his breakfast. Next, I noticed that the dog was having trouble breathing.

Jake now gave me an allowance of five dollars a week and I'd mowed lawns the previous summer, so I had some cash on hand. Since Jake hated telephones, we didn't have one in the house. I walked down the hill to Jerry Whittle's stand and found him asleep behind the wheel, his head laid back on the headrest. From past experience, I knew not to startle him, so I pushed gently on Jerry's new Ford Galaxy and the man roused, shaking his head.

"I need to go out to Dr. Stout's," I said. "We need to pick up Bandit first."

By the time we arrived at Jake's house, Bandit was wheezing, gasping for breaths. I picked up the little guy and went looking for Yolanda. I found her in the kitchen, cleaning up the breakfast dishes. When she saw Bandit in my arms, she asked, "What's wrong with Bandit?"

"I don't rightly know, Yolanda. I'm scared to death."

"You taking him to Dr. Stout?"

"Yes, ma'am. Jerry Whittle is waiting outside for us."

"Well, I'm sure the doctor can take care of Bandit. He's a good vet. Let me know what he said when you come back."

Full of dread, I carried Bandit to the car. We sat on the backseat while Jerry headed for the Stout farm. Bandit's heart pounded in his chest and his eyes were glazed.

I found Dr. Stout in the barn delivering a colt. The mare lay on her side as he guided the newborn out of the birth canal. Spying me, he said, "Hi, Jamie. I'll only be a minute."

He wiped the fluids from the colt and cut the umbilical cord.

Then the little fellow tried to stand. After three or four attempts, he managed a wobbly stance, all four legs outstretched.

Dr. Stout closed the stall door and, seeing my dog, asked, "What's going on with Bandit?"

"He didn't eat this morning and he's short of breath."

The doctor took a stethoscope out of his pocket and placed it to Bandit's chest. He listened for a few moments and then said, "Take him to my exam room over there and put him on the table, Jamie."

I walked across the bare concrete floor to a small exam room and placed my dog on the table.

Dr. Stout followed me into the room and, placing his stethoscope on Bandit's chest, listened some more. Then he asked, "How old is Bandit?"

"I don't know for sure. I think he was a pup when he wandered up to Miss Frances's house. That would have been in 1962."

Dr. Stout shook his head. "I'm afraid this isn't good news. Bandit has congestive heart failure."

"What's that mean?"

"He doesn't have long to live. I can treat him, but he'll only last a month at best. I recommend putting him down."

If he'd hit me over the head with a shovel, it wouldn't have hurt nearly as much. I stared at him in disbelief. Dr. Stout wanted to kill Bandit? I couldn't believe I'd heard those words. A sense of panic gripped me. Bandit was an integral part of my life. He'd been with me since my first day at Miss Frances's house. How could this be happening?

"There's no hope?" I asked.

"I'm sorry. He's drowning in his own fluids. What do you want to do?"

"I need a few minutes alone with him."

"Take your time. When you're ready, come find me."

I picked up my friend, held him tightly to my chest. Bandit licked my face. Then I walked across the field to the woods where we used to play. After climbing the fence together, we sat on the big rock and watched the minnows scamper about in the clear water. I stroked his head and rubbed his ears, and he whimpered softly, snuggling his nose into my armpit. Tears slid down my numb cheeks. We sat there, shivering in the cold January morning, for the better part of an hour. The sky was overcast and a brisk north wind picked up, rustling the leaves that covered the ground beneath the bare tree trunks. It was the second saddest day of my life.

As I held the little dog close to my chest, my thoughts drifted back to the first day Miss Frances had adopted Bandit and me. I remembered how Bandit would meet me at the mail box when I stepped off the school bus. And how Bandit had kept me warm at night by snuggling up close to my back in our big bed. In truth, Bandit had been the one constant in my new life.

Dr. Stout was mucking the birthing stall when I walked into the barn. "Have you made a decision?" the doctor asked.

I nodded as I walked into the exam room and placed Bandit on the examination table. Dr. Stout followed me and went to a cabinet where he removed a syringe and a vial of amber liquid.

"Is this going to hurt Bandit?" I asked.

"No. I'll just slip a small needle into one of his veins. I know this is hard, Jamie. I had a dog named Napoleon when I was your age. I loved him so much it made my heart ache when he died."

I held Bandit close, shielding his eyes from the veterinarian as he slipped a needle into Bandit's leg vein. I watched Dr. Stout draw some blood and then push the plunger on the syringe until it was empty. Bandit took a deep breath and went limp. I shook all over, tears streaming from my eyes. I held Bandit for a few minutes longer, burying my face in his fur. I didn't want to let go. I thought the doctor might have to pry my fingers loose. Finally, my head reeling, I let go and looked at the doctor through blurry eyes.

"I know it's hard, son. Just remember you've saved him a lot of suffering."

"What happens now?"

"I have a small cemetery out back. I'll take care of everything. You can visit anytime you like."

Wiping my wet cheeks, I asked, "How much do I owe you, Dr. Stout?"

Shaking his head, he said, "You're family, Jamie. You don't owe me anything."

* * *

I didn't go to school that day. When Jerry dropped me off at the house, I tried to pay him, but Jerry refused to take the money and said, "I know you're hurting real bad, son, and I'm sorry. It ain't easy losing something you love."

I went to my room and closed the door. Then I picked up my guitar and I played for hours, skipping lunch.

Late that afternoon, Yolanda stuck her head in and asked, "What did Dr. Stout say, Jamie?"

"Dr. Stout put Bandit down."

"Oh, child, I'm so sorry. Can I bring you some supper?"

I simply shook my head.

Jake knocked on my door when he got home from the office.

"Come in," I said;

Jake walked to where I sat strumming my guitar and placed a hand on my shoulder. "If Joe Stout put your dog down, it was for the dog's own good. You do understand that don't you?"

"Yes, sir. It's just that Bandit was my best friend. He'd been with me since I first went to Miss Frances's house. I don't know what I'll do without him."

"Do you want another dog? I suspect we can find one for you."

"No, sir. I don't think I could do that. At least, not now. Maybe later."

Jake shook his head and left the room. As he closed the door, he looked back at me and said, "Time heals all. You'll get over this. Try to be brave."

I fell asleep reading and awoke once in the night, feeling for Bandit with my foot. When I realized he wasn't there, I wept. He had become a part of me. We'd been together so long, done so much. I wondered how I'd manage without him.

We had an algebra test that day, but I hadn't studied for it. I went to the kitchen as usual for breakfast, but found that I had no appetite. I excused myself and went to my room where I quickly scanned the workbook. I didn't care if I passed or not. I didn't care much about anything that morning. Before leaving for school, I took Bandit's food and water dishes to the big trash can in the backyard. I simply couldn't look at them any longer.

* * *

The first Friday in February, the teachers had a conference in Cookeville, and we got a free day. Since the loss of Bandit, I'd been feeling terribly sad. One question that kept eating at me had to do with Mom. Why had she abandoned me? She'd come to Miss Frances's once when I lived there, and I ran into her that time at Thompson's Grocery. Other than those two times, I'd had no contact with her. Didn't she love me anymore? Had Pop poisoned her against me?

At the end of summer, I'd taken some of my money and purchased a ten-speed bicycle. I didn't ride it much because I could walk most places in Round Rock. On that day, I decided to ride out to Beulah Land. I hadn't been there but once since I'd run away. That was the day Dr. Stout drove Mom home after she'd walked through the snow to Miss Frances's house. Then I'd sat in his truck and watched her climb the hill to our shack.

I kept the bike on the back porch, and when I went to get it, the tires were flat. It'd come with a small pump that attached to the frame. It took several minutes, but I finally got them inflated.

As I coasted down the long hill to town, I wondered if I should take Mom something. I felt a little guilty living in a fine house while she was stuck in a tarpaper shack. It was a feeling that swept over me from time to time. I kept thinking once I got out of school and started making money, I'd buy her a real house.

I stopped at the Ben Franklin Store on Main Street. Walking up one aisle and down another, I searched for something I thought she might like. Then I saw it. Blue in color and holding about an ounce, the bottle had a label that said Genuine Lavender Perfume. It seemed the perfect gift.

I gave the salesclerk a five-dollar bill, and she handed me seventy-five cents in change. Slipping it and the bottle into my trouser pocket, I got on my bike and headed for Beulah Land. It was only a two-mile trip. Pop and I used to walk it when we'd both been working at the shirt factory.

It was a cold, overcast day. I'd worn a heavy sweater, windbreaker, leather gloves, and a wool watch cap. By the time I was halfway there, I was sweating. A harsh north wind stung my cheeks and chapped my lips. It was about three o'clock when I reached the water pump at the bottom of the hill below our shack. I figured Pop would still be at the shirt factory. It being Friday, he'd stop to see the deacon on the way home. Most likely I'd have at least a couple of hours with Mom.

There were three malnourished-looking children playing hide-and-seek when I chained the bike to a small oak and climbed the hill. The children ran after me, their eyes watering in the cold, their cheeks as red as mine.

It appeared that nothing had changed as I approached the door of our shack. I knocked once and waited. The children gathered around me and one, his nose running, asked, "Who are you, mister?"

I shook my head and said, "Nobody."

When there was no answer, I knocked again, harder this time. A few moments passed and Mom swung the door open. When I saw the cotton in her ears, I remembered her hearing loss. She gave me a toothy grin, her teeth black with decay.

"Jamie boy, how are you?"

"May I come in?"

She hesitated. Glancing down the hill and biting her lower lip, she motioned me in. The interior of the shack looked like it had the day I left. She did have a kerosene lamp lit because of the dark day. The iron stove on which she cooked barely heated the room, the cold wind seeping through the numerous slits in the tarpaper.

"I ain't got nothing to give you, son."

Pulling the small bottle from my trouser pocket, I said, "I don't need anything. I brought you a present. I hope you like it."

I don't think she knew what it was. She turned it over in her hand and said, "It's real nice, son."

"It's perfume," I said. "Open it and put some on."

She smiled and twisted the top off. Then she dabbed some on her index finger and rubbed it behind her ear.

I think we both felt a little awkward. We hadn't seen or talked to each other in five years.

"That were real nice of you, son. I'll keep good care of it."

It hurt me to see her like that, to hear her talk. Her hands were calloused and red, the skin rough to the touch. I wanted to do something for her, to ease her pain.

Then I heard something that made my blood run cold. It was Pop's gravelly voice. The shirt factory must have let out early. He was singing at the top of his lungs, like he always did after he'd had some of the deacon's shine.

I froze. God only knew what he'd do when he found me with Mom. There was no way out except by the front door. The only window faced the front. I was stuck. I'd have to do something to pacify him. Keep him away from Mom.

My dry mouth made it impossible to swallow. My hands shook, and despite my heavy clothing, I felt a terrible chill.

The door swung open, and Pop staggered in. His hair was disheveled, his eyes bloodshot. In the darkened room, he had trouble focusing, and it took him a moment to realize I was there.

"Jamie Lee Coleman!" he bellowed. "The boy whose shit don't stink." Then he lunged at me. I stepped aside and he rammed the door frame.

He shook his head and glared at Mom. "You let him in?"

She nodded.

"Damn you, woman. Ain't I told you not to have nothing to do with that boy? Ain't I?"

"He's our son. I love him even if you don't. Leave us alone."

He backhanded her so hard, spit flew from her mouth. She stumbled back, grabbing air, and fell, striking her head on the table. There was a soft moan and her body went limp. I looked on in horror. Kneeling beside her, I tried to find a pulse in her neck, then her wrist. There was none. Mom was dead.

I spun around, picked up a ladder-back chair, and swung it with all my might at Pop. He ducked the first blow, but I kept at it until he was on his knees, covering his head. "Stop it!" he yelled. "Stop it!"

"Go to hell! I'm going to kill you!" I screamed.

I kept pounding until Pop slumped to the floor and didn't move. I didn't bother to check for a pulse. I hoped the bastard was dead. Still shaking with rage I kicked him hard in the chest and gasped for air. Finally, I stopped and looked down on my poor mother. I sat next to her and pulled her up so I could cradle her in my arms. I stroked her face softly with the fingers of my left hand. I rocked back and forth as tears streamed down my cheeks. In a soft, hoarse voice I said, "I'm so sorry. I'm so sorry. I should have protected you. I should have stood up to the bastard. I love you, Mom. I love you so much. I'm so sorry. Can you ever forgive me? Why didn't I do a better job? I'm so sorry!"

I shook all over. I gently lay her back on the floor and stood. My brain simply wouldn't work. I didn't know what to do. Would the sheriff think I'd killed them both? I knew Jake was a lawyer, but I doubted he could save me. In my panic, I thought I had only one choice. I had to run away. Put as much distance between me and Round Rock as possible.

The children were still outside the door when I opened it. I didn't know if they'd heard the fighting or not. All I knew was that I had to get away. I pushed past them, then ran and slid down the steep hill to my bicycle. Hands trembling, I unlocked the chain, jumped on my bike, and pedaled back to town. I mumbled to myself the whole time. I couldn't believe my mother was dead. I had this terrible burning sensation in my gut and my hands shook so hard I had to grip the handle bars so tightly that my knuckles were white. *My Mom's dead—my Mon's dead. Oh Jesus my poor mother is dead.*

It was starting to get dark when I reached Jake's house. Yolanda would be in the kitchen cooking supper, and Jake was supposed to work late that night. I ran to my room. I kept my money in a Mason jar at the back of the armoire. When I counted it out, I had one hundred fifty dollars. I placed it in my wallet and pulled some clothes off their hangers. Jake had given me a small suitcase one Christmas, and I filled it. Then I grabbed my guitar and quietly left the house.

The cold wind did little to remove the perspiration from my brow. I could feel it run down my cheeks mixed in with the tears I shed for Mom. I couldn't believe she was dead. As I walked down the long hill to town, I kept thinking, *Why didn't I stop him? I just stood there and let him kill her. I'll never be able to look in a mirror again.*

The suitcase slapped against my leg as I hiked out to the highway. My mind felt numb. I stumbled along, oblivious to my surroundings. My head pounded and ached. I stopped on the gravel shoulder just outside of town and sat on the suitcase. Cars and pickups whizzed past. Several minutes went by and I heard the squealing of air brakes. Looking up, I saw an eighteen-wheeler skid to a stop about ten yards from where I sat. It took me a few seconds to realize the driver was offering me a ride. I picked up the suitcase, grabbed my guitar, and ran to the cab.

Swinging open the door, I climbed up the steps. The driver was a skinny fellow with black hair tied in a ponytail. A cigarette dangled from his mouth, the blue smoke swirling around his head.

"Where you headed?" he asked.

I had no idea. In my state of agitation, I didn't even know what direction we were facing.

"Where're you going?" I asked.

"Memphis," he said.

"That'll do just fine."

The cab was hot. The driver had the heater going full blast, so I took off my jacket and sweater. I placed them in my lap and set my guitar on the floorboard at my feet.

The radio was tuned to WSM's Friday night Opry. We listened in silence. At Cookeville, the driver pulled onto the new section of Interstate 40 West. I closed my eyes and tried to wash my memory clear of the afternoon's events. It didn't work. Hard as I might, all I could see in my mind's eye was Mom lying dead in that cold shack.

"You ate?" the driver asked.

I opened my eyes. "No, sir."

"We'll pull in at Lebanon. There's a new restaurant there called the Cracker Barrel. It's got good country cooking."

I wasn't hungry, and I doubted I could eat.

The driver had to park on the shoulder of the highway because the truck wouldn't fit in the lot. The place was crowded even at eight o'clock. I went directly to the restroom and washed my hands. I washed them six times, as if I could wash my sin away. I'd killed a man, my own father. Granted, I hated him and he needed killing, but nonetheless, I felt ashamed and horrified.

I ordered a hamburger with fries and a Coke. Dwayne, the driver, asked for country ham, green beans, creamed corn, and sweet iced tea. I managed to get the burger down, though I choked a couple of times.

By eight forty-five we were back on the interstate headed toward Nashville.

"What time you reckon we'll make Memphis?" I asked.

Dwayne looked at his watch. "I'd say one o'clock. You got a place to stay?"

I shook my head.

"You can bunk at my place. I've got room."

I'd figured on staying at a motel, but with my limited funds, a free room sounded pretty good. Besides, I had no idea where I was headed.

"Thanks," I said.

* * *

We pulled up to a trailer on the outskirts of Memphis in a suburb called Bartlett around one thirty. Dwayne pulled out a flashlight and led the way to the trailer. When we stepped into the trailer, I realized Dwayne was a bachelor. Dirty dishes filled the sink and empty beer cans littered the floor.

"I ain't had time to clean up, left in a hurry last week. Don't mind the mess."

I set my suitcase on the cluttered floor and glanced around. There was a bedroom in the back, but only one. Where was I to sleep?

"The dinette makes a bed. I'll get some bed clothes. Bathroom's there," he said, pointing to a door just past the refrigerator. "Want a beer?"

"No, sir."

"Cut the 'sir' crap," he said as he grabbed a Budweiser. "You can take the crapper first."

He took a sheet, pillow, and blanket from a closet and threw them at me. Then he walked into the bedroom and shut the door. I was dead tired but doubted I'd sleep.

I stripped to my skivvies and took my travel kit, another gift from Jake, to the bathroom. After brushing my teeth, I peed. Staggering to the dinette, I dropped the table and pulled the cushions over it to make the bed. Then I placed the sheet and blanket over them. I flipped off the overhead light, dropped onto the cushions, and fell asleep.

Sometime in the night I felt a hand on my leg. It was creeping up to my crotch. I didn't know what was going on. "What're you doing?" I asked, assuming it was Dwayne's hand.

"You're a good-looking kid, Jamie. Why don't you come back and sleep with me?"

Sitting up, I swung my legs off the bed and turned on the light. Dwayne was naked, a big grin on his face.

"What's going on?" I asked.

"You ever had your cock sucked?"

"What did you say?"

"Some guys like pussy. I like cock," he said.

I pulled on my pants and shirt, then socks and shoes. "Look, fellow. I've heard about you guys. I like girls, not boys. Why don't you go back to bed and I'll just leave."

Dwayne actually got a hurt look on his face. Then he smiled. "It's okay. You don't have to leave. You don't know what you're missing, though. I give great head."

"I'll take your word for it."

I picked up my suitcase and guitar and left.

Chapter 9

The temperature was in the mid-twenties, the sky cloudy. I couldn't see shit, and I shook like a damn epileptic. I was lost on a side road in the middle of nowhere, with nothing to do but start walking. I had no idea what quadrant of the compass rose I was in. I wondered to myself, *how did I get in this mess?* Then it hit me. *I'd killed my worthless father.*

An hour later, I heard the unmistakable sound of eighteen-wheelers. Thinking the interstate must be ahead, I picked up my pace. In the distance, I could see lights. My teeth chattered as I broke into a run, my guitar flapping against my back, the suitcase bumping my leg. My heart was pounding. I thought it might burst.

The lights belonged to an Exxon station beside a Waffle House. Rushing through the front door, I collapsed into a booth. In the one next to me there were a couple of men who looked like truck drivers. A black short-order cook pressed a spatula on sizzling bacon, and an overweight woman with a cigarette dangling from her thin lips waddled over to take my order.

I didn't bother looking at the menu. I asked for scrambled eggs, bacon, coffee, and orange juice. I still shook, the chill so deep I wondered if I'd ever be warm again. I kept my eyes down and tried to compose myself. I had no idea what lay ahead or where I'd eventually end up. I couldn't believe how drastically my life had changed in less than twenty-four hours.

"What're you doing out here in the middle of nowhere, honey?" the waitress asked as she placed my food on the table. "I ain't seen you drive up."

"I hitched a ride."

"Where're you headed?"

I didn't want the conversation, preferring to be left alone. When I didn't answer, she wandered off and filled the truck drivers' cups.

The warmth that finally settled over me was welcome. I pulled off my watch cap and opened the windbreaker. I devoured the breakfast and glanced at the wall clock. It read six o'clock. I must have left Dwayne's trailer around five, which meant I hadn't had much sleep. I certainly wasn't tired; my nerves were too on edge.

The men in the next booth walked to the cash register. After paying their bill, one came back to where I sat. He was a heavyset fellow with a pot belly hanging over his belt. He had a stubble of black beard and curly black hair that fell in ringlets over his collar. He wore jeans, cowboy boots, and a navy pea coat.

"You hitching a ride?" he asked.

I nodded.

"Where're you headed?"

"Nowhere particular."

"I'm on my way to New Orleans."

I took the last bite of eggs, gulped the cool coffee, and paid my bill.

As we walked to the truck, the man stuck out his hand. "Name's Harry Wilson. What's yours?"

My heart leaped into my throat. What if the police had an all points bulletin out for me? It just rolled off my tongue. "Luke," I said.

The cab was still warm as we climbed in. As I settled on the passenger seat, I asked, "You're not a cocksucker, are you?"

Harry grabbed me by the shirt collar and asked, "What the fuck are you talking about? You take me for a fucking queer?"

"Sorry. The last guy who picked me up wanted to suck my cock."

"I ain't got no desire to suck your damn cock."

He'd left the big diesel running. Buckling his seat belt, Harry threw the gear box into first. We rode in silence through Memphis. In Batesville, Mississippi, we stopped to fill the big tanks with diesel. Back in the cab, we continued south. Harry said, "Sorry I yelled at you, Luke. Can't understand why a man would want sex with another man. It don't seem natural."

I nodded, relieved.

* * *

We stopped in Jackson, Mississippi for lunch, again at a Waffle House. The temperature had risen to the high forties and the sun beat down on us from a cloudless sky. I was thinking I might like living a little south of the Mason-Dixon Line.

I ordered a hamburger and hash browns since they didn't offer fries. I'd been lucky with my cash. I hadn't had to spend any except on food. I had no idea what I'd do in New Orleans or where I'd stay. I assumed I'd find a job somewhere. Doing what, I didn't know.

Back on the road, Harry asked, "Where're you from, Luke?"

"Tennessee."

"What part?"

"East."

He let it drop. Most likely he'd figured out I was running away from something.

"What about you?" I asked.

"Cairo, Illinois."

"You come to New Orleans often?"

"Once a week."

"I need a job. Any thoughts?"

"How good are you on that guitar?"

I shrugged. "Pretty good."

"I'd go to the French Quarter. Might have to start by sweeping floors, but it could lead to a gig."

* * *

Harry let me off at a truck stop on the outskirts of New Orleans. We shook hands, and he said, "You can catch a city bus over there. It'll take you to Canal Street. From there you can walk to the French Quarter."

"Thanks, Harry."

I'd read a lot about New Orleans, particularly Andrew Jackson's exploits during the War of 1812. The British troops weren't prepared for the way Jackson managed the battle. His Tennessee sharpshooters decimated their ranks, the Treaty of Ghent unknown to both sides. I was looking forward to seeing Jackson Square and the French Quarter, and learning more about New Orleans.

I had to transfer to another bus about halfway to the center of the city. That was a little confusing. And I had a terrible time understanding the driver. I assumed he was a Cajun. I'd read about them, too, thanks to Miss Frances.

The bus stopped in front of the Federal Building on Canal Street, and I stepped off. The temperature hovered in the low seventies. It was another clear day. Shading my eyes from the bright sun, I stopped at a Walgreens and asked directions to the Quarter. The cashier said, "It starts behind this store. Just walk out the back door."

Carrying my worldly possessions, I wandered down Bourbon Street and was amazed by what I saw. It didn't look anything like I'd expected. I knew the buildings would be old and have lots of wrought iron. What I hadn't counted on were the numerous bars. It seemed every twenty yards or so there was a strip joint or bar. Even at eleven in the morning, most were in full swing. I hadn't antici-pated seeing so many hotels and restaurants either.

As I walked down Bourbon Street a patrol car eased past me at a crawl. I glanced over my shoulder and saw a policeman eying me from the driver's seat. My mouth went dry and I got a sharp pain in my stomach. Were the cops looking for me? Was there a warrant out for me? I swallowed hard and looked straight ahead and watched the patrol car turn off on to a side street.

I stopped and glanced in every bar, trying to muster the courage to ask for a job. When I reached the last one on Bourbon Street, I set my jaw and walked in. My mouth was so dry I doubted I'd be able to speak, let alone ask for a job. But I had no choice. It was now or never.

The bar was called the Triple J Lounge. A few men sitting at the bar were nursing beers. No one looked up. The bartender was a young black guy who looked to be in his twenties. The only other person there was the waitress.

Slipping my suitcase under a table, I placed my guitar in a chair and took a seat. The waitress wandered over to take my order. She didn't look much older than me, had blonde hair I figured came out of a bottle, brown eyes, and a sweet smile.

"What you want, honey?" she asked, pencil in hand.

"Hamburger, fries, and a Coke. The manager around?"

"Triple J owns the place, but he sleeps till two most days."

I was intrigued. "What kind of name is Triple J?"

She laughed. "Jimmy Joe Johnson is his name, but everyone calls him Triple J. You looking for a job?"

"Yeah, any thoughts?"

"I'd try to hire on as a janitor. Triple J fired Amos last week. That's why the place is such a mess."

"Where's a cheap place to find a room?" I asked.

"There's a vacant room in my boarding house. It's not fancy, but affordable."

"Can you give me the address? I'd like to get my stuff settled."

After I finished eating, she jotted the address on the back of a blank restaurant check. I gathered my belongings and headed for the door. The waitress stepped in front of me and asked, "What's your name, honey?"

"Luke. What's yours?"

"Casey Jones. And before you ask, I'll tell you. My father named me after the famous railroad engineer from Jackson, Tennessee. My old man worked for the Union Pacific Railroad."

* * *

The boarding house was on Prytania Street. It was a three-story Victorian that reminded me a little of Jake's house. It wasn't in great repair, but I figured the rooms would be cheap. The manager was an old guy who looked like a holdover from the nineteenth century. His handlebar mustache and mutton-chop sideburns reminded me of a character in a bad western movie. He looked me in the eye and asked, "How old are you, son?"

"Eighteen."

"You wouldn't lie to a fellow, would you?"

I swallowed hard. What if he won't rent me a room? Where will I stay? I swallowed hard again and said, "I wouldn't lie to you, mister. Honest, I'm eighteen."

"The owner finds I rented a room to a kid, he'd be pissed. You got a driver's license?"

No. Of course not. I'd always used Jerry Whittle just like Jake and Miss Frances. Why would I need a driver's license? I shook my head and said, "No, sir. My folks couldn't afford a car so I never needed a license."

"You got money?"

I took a roll of bills out of my pocket and asked, "How much is a room? For a week?"

"Fifteen dollars a week in advance."

I peeled three fives off and handed them to him.

"You better not be shitting me, son. We'll both be in trouble."

Even though the house wasn't in great repair, the rooms were okay. Mine was on the third floor, and I could see the Mississippi River from my window. There was a bathroom down the hall that served four rooms. I hung my clothes in the closet and placed my guitar under the bed.

After freshening up, I walked around the city for a few hours and arrived back at Bourbon Street around five in the afternoon. When I reached the Triple J, Casey was scurrying from table to table trying to keep up with the onslaught of patrons. Every barstool was occupied, and people stood guzzling drinks. The bartender ran from one end of the bar to the next.

When Casey saw me, she hurried over. "You get a room?" she asked.

"Yes. Is Triple J here?"

"Fat guy in the corner."

Glancing at Triple J, I decided he needed three names. His neck looked bigger than my waist, and folds of fat circled it like a necklace. His pudgy hands resembled porterhouse steaks ringed with link sausages, and his belly was so huge I doubted he'd seen his dick in years. Long, greasy black hair, uncombed, reached his collar. He wore a jumpsuit and house slippers. Dark, beady eyes peered at me beneath bushy eyebrows as I approached.

"Sir, I'm looking for a job," I said. "I heard you needed a janitor."

As he leaned the chair back, I wondered if the legs would break. Crossing his beefy arms over his massive chest, he said, "You heard that, did you? Who from?"

"Casey told me."

"How old are you?"

"Eighteen."

"Your name?"

"Luke."

"That it? You ain't got a last name?"

"I go by Luke."

"You got a Social Security card?"

"Never needed one."

"Good. Dollar sixty an hour's minimum. I'll give it to you in cash, no questions asked. Payday's Friday. I need a busboy, too. You can work six to twelve busing, then spend a couple hours cleaning up after closing. That's midnight weekdays. Friday and Saturday it's two in the morning."

I didn't reckon I had much choice. The hours didn't seem too inviting, but I decided I'd make it work. "Where's the janitor's closet?"

"Next to the men's room," Triple J said, waving toward a hallway.

It was already five-fifteen, and Casey had her hands full, so I jumped right in. I'd never bused a table in my life, but it didn't look too hard. I found one of Casey's trays and headed for an empty table littered with dirty plates and beer bottles. Scooping them up, I carried them to the kitchen.

The odor of melting fat filled the small space as a heavyset black woman fried hamburgers, the staple of the bar's menu. A short, skinny black man rinsed dishes under a running faucet. No fancy dishwashing machines in the Triple J Lounge.

An hour later, things slowed for a few minutes, and Casey flagged me down. "Thanks, Luke. Want a burger?"

"It free?"

"Sure. The only benefit offered by the Triple J Lounge."

"Then, yeah. I'm really hungry."

I went to the back of the bar and sat at a small table with two chairs. I looked around the room but didn't see Triple J. That suited me just fine. I really didn't like the fat man very much.

Casey brought the hamburger to the table a little later. She sat with me for a couple of minutes until the place started filling up with the late crowd.

I said, "Thanks, Casey. The hamburgers in this place are actually pretty good."

"It's good that the bar has some saving grace. It's about the only thing," Casey said.

I laughed and took a bite of my hamburger.

Later, when Casey got ready to leave, the night waitress came in and introduced herself. Her name was Maggie, and she looked as if she might be in her mid-thirties. She had the wrinkles of a heavy smoker and yellow stained teeth.

Before she left, Casey pulled me to one side and said, "Here's your share of my tips."

I shook my head. "You don't need to do that. I was glad to help. I reckon that's part of my job."

"It's customary for a waitress to share her tips with a busboy."

"Well, maybe tomorrow. That is, if I still have a job."

* * *

Around nine o'clock, three black guys walked in and wandered over to an elevated platform I hadn't noticed before. An old upright piano like Miss Frances's was shoved against the wall.

One man was older than the other two. He was bald with a fringe of kinky white hair. When he smiled, his gold-capped incisors glittered in the subdued light. Even though the sport coat and slacks were threadbare, I thought he looked distinguished. The young guys, wearing turtle-neck sweaters and jeans, looked to be in their thirties. Each had a bushy Afro. One carried a bass wrapped in a canvas cover, and the other held a black tenor saxophone case.

While they prepared their instruments, the older man sat at the piano and began to play. Soon the other fellows joined in. I stood transfixed. I'd listened to some New Orleans jazz on Jake's stereo, but that was nothing like hearing it live. I'd always loved the mellow sound of a sax, and that fellow was a master. The piano player had fingers I envied. He was doing incredible runs.

"Tables need busing!" Triple J yelled across the room. He was still sitting in the same chair and had a scowl on his beefy face.

I nodded and got back to work.

The crowd now was mostly drinkers who appreciated the trio. After each set there was thunderous applause. I joined in. Every forty-five minutes, the guys took a short break. During a lull, I walked over to the leader.

"Great music," I said. "Your runs remind me of Art Tatum."

The man held a tumbler in his hand, and I got a whiff of bourbon. He smiled, his gold caps sparkling in the dim light. "Hey, man, can't get a better compliment than that. What's your name, kid?"

"Luke."

"Sit down. I'll buy you a drink."

"Thanks, but I'm working and I don't drink. What's your name?"

"Axelrod Mahoney."

"What do you call your trio?" I asked.

He laughed. "The Mahoney Trio."

I felt a little sheepish. I should have assumed that would be the name. But, I was a little naive to say the least. I suspected that would soon change.

The trio played off and on till closing. As they gathered their instruments, Axelrod said, "Hey, Luke. We jam at an after-hours place if you want to come."

"Thanks. I've got to clean up now. Where is it?"

He jotted down an address, and I slipped it in my pocket. I thought I might wander over after I'd finished.

The place was a mess. Cigarette butts littered the floor. Dirty drink glasses and empty beer bottles cluttered the bar and tables. It took two hours to tidy everything up. Before she left, Maggie came over and said, "Thanks for all the help, Luke. Here's your cut of my tips."

I shook my head. "You don't have to do that. You worked hard tonight."

"But it's customary."

I gave a sigh and asked, "You're sure?"

Handing me several wrinkled bills, she said, "Yes. See you tomorrow."

Around two o'clock, I called Triple J's apartment upstairs and told him I was leaving.

He said, "Don't leave until I get down there. I want to make sure you did a good job."

I heard him clomping down the back stairs and held my breath. What if he didn't like what I'd done? Would he fire me like he had Amos?

When he entered the bar, he had a big cigar dangling from his mouth and was dressed in a terry-cloth robe and those ratty slippers.

He glanced over the room and said, "I like having a white guy working for me. This ain't a bad job you've done, Luke. Do this every night and we'll get along just fine."

I nodded and walked out the door. I didn't trust Triple J, maybe it was the beady eyes that made me think that, but at least it was a job. I was feeling good; I had found a job and a place to live in one day. Even after the stress of the past two days, I wasn't tired, so I decided to go to the afterhours club where Axelrod was playing.

The place wasn't far from the Quarter. When I walked in, it was dimly lit, and you couldn't cut the cigarette smoke with a knife. The club only had about fifteen tables, each one occupied by black couples. The men looked rough, but the women were dolled up in fancy dresses and high-heeled shoes. Mine was the only white face in the crowd, but no one paid any attention to me as I stood against the back wall.

Axelrod and his guys were playing on a small stage. There was no amplification because the place was so small. Axelrod had a tumbler of bourbon sitting on top of the piano, and he'd pick it up every few minutes and take a swig. As soon as it was empty, someone would place another one there. The bass player had his eyes shut, swaying with the music.

Around three in the morning, I began to fade. In Round Rock, I went to bed at ten. I figured it would take me a while to adjust to my new life. As I thought of home, I was overcome with sadness. My mom was dead and I'd killed my worthless father. I missed Jake and Yolanda and felt terrible that I'd left without saying good-bye.

With a heavy heart, I walked to the boarding house.

Chapter 10

I awoke at nine the next morning and was still groggy when I stepped into the shower. I wanted to locate the library before going to work. I'd left Round Rock so quickly I'd failed to bring a book. For me to be without a book was unheard of. I carried one everywhere I went.

There was a small café a block from the boarding house. I stopped in for a croissant and coffee. I liked the half milk mixture with chicory. I learned from the cashier that the Main Library was on Loyola Avenue. I found it without difficulty and soon walked out with *Topaz* by Leon Uris and *When She Was Good* by Philip Roth.

Casey Jones was entering the lounge as I walked up. Her eyes were puffy and bloodshot.

"Hey, Luke," she said. "You got any aspirin?"

I shook my head. "Headache?"

"I must've gotten a bad bottle of beer last night."

I laughed. She smiled and went directly to the restroom. The chairs were still on top of the tables just as I'd left them the night before. The bartender hadn't arrived yet, and the place was as quiet as a tomb.

Wandering over to the piano, I pulled the stool out. I hadn't played since my hasty departure from Parsons County. Flexing my fingers, I did a few quick runs and tried to copy what I'd heard Axelrod do the evening before. It didn't work. I'd tried to imitate Art Tatum before and hadn't been successful. It was frustrating because I could play almost anything I heard. I simply didn't understand the whole concept of jazz.

After thirty minutes I was getting closer, but was still off.

I felt a hand on my shoulder and looked up to see Axelrod standing behind me.

"Luke," he said, "how'd you do that?"

"I know it's terrible. I just can't get it right."

He sat down beside me. "That's my composition. Was last night the first time you heard it?"

I nodded.

"You're close. What I can't understand is how you can play something after hearing it once."

"I can play most anything I hear, except jazz."

"Then you're a natural. You just need to loosen up. The secret is improvisation. What most people don't understand is that jazz is based on a form that is similar to the classical sonata allegro. The solo is where you improvise on the chord progressions and melody. A good jazz pianist like Art Tatum can play an out-of-tune piano and make it sound right."

Then he proceeded to demonstrate what he'd just said. He'd play for a few minutes, and then I'd try to imitate what he'd done. After thirty minutes of his tutoring, I had the basics. That's not to say I was pleased. But at least I had a start.

After we'd finished, I asked, "What are you doing here so early?"

"Triple J was supposed to leave my money with Jim, the bartender. I guess he hasn't come in yet."

Glancing at my watch, I said, "It's almost eleven. He should be here any minute."

"Let's see if Casey has the coffee ready," Axelrod said.

We wandered over to the urn and filled two cups, then sat at a back table. Axelrod took a sip and said, "You ever think about going professional?"

My life had been turned upside down. I'd planned on college and then a master's and PhD in English literature. That had been Miss Frances's wish for my future. Now that seemed highly unlikely. I shrugged and said, "I've got to make a living somehow."

"It's a hard life. Very few people reach the top, but those who do get rich. Most of us simply survive. It's a combination of talent and luck. Drugs and alcohol take their toll."

"I'm not worried about that," I said. "I've seen firsthand what alcohol does to a person."

Triple J surprised us when he entered the room. He strolled over to our table and sat down. His hair was uncombed and his eyes bloodshot. Bags of redundant skin under each eye looked deep enough to hold a jigger of gin.

"I thought you slept till two," Axelrod said.

"Couldn't sleep. Hey, Axelrod, I've got a pussy joke for you."
Axelrod rolled his eyes.

Triple J placed his massive elbows on the table, leaned forward, and said, "Two colored girls meet on Canal Street. One says, 'I heard you got married. Is it so?' Then the other girl says, 'It sure is. I can't hardly touch it with a powder puff.'"

He laughed so hard his whole body shook, the folds of fat jiggling like a bowl of gelatin. Spittle formed at the corners of his massive mouth, and he coughed, gasping for breath. I thought the joke was funny, but I felt sorry for Axelrod. He looked dismayed.

"Here's another one," Triple J said. "Two colored girls are having their picture taken. The photographer is using a portrait camera. He sticks his head under the black drape to adjust the focus. One girl asked the other, 'What's he doing?' She says, 'He's got to focus.' The first girl says, 'Both us?'"

This time he laughed so hard the salt and pepper shakers fell to the floor. I grinned but didn't laugh. Axelrod just raised his eyebrows.

Casey walked over and said, "There's a call for you, Triple J."

Still laughing, the fat man pushed himself up from the table and waddled to the pay phone next to the restrooms.

I glanced at Axelrod and asked, "How do you deal with that racist shit?"

He shook his head. "Believe it or not it's better here than most places in the South. Worst place I've ever been is Mississippi."

"You think the civil rights movement will change things?"

"I hope so. But I know human nature. It'll never go away completely. I've just learned to work around it."

"How?"

"Back in the fifties the boys and I were playing black nightclubs in Mississippi. We had a new Chevy van so we could haul Willie's bass. I'd had our name printed on the doors, 'The Mahoney Trio.'

"I was behind the wheel when a redneck sheriff pulled us over. He didn't even bother to get out of the car. He just rolled down the window, and yelled, 'What're you doing with that van, boy?' I said, 'I'm taking it to my boss, Mr. Mahoney.' Then the idiot nodded and said, 'That's all right then. Just be out of Calhoun County by sundown.'"

I shook my head. "I've never understood racism. We don't have many blacks where I grew up, but the whites don't treat them very well."

"Where you from, Luke?"

"East Tennessee."

"Ever been to Memphis?"

"Drove through is all."

"You ought to visit Beale Street. Listen to some blues. You play anything besides piano?"

"Guitar. It's what I like best."

"Try some jazz on your guitar. See how you like it."

"You think I could make some money playing guitar?"

"What kind of music you like best?"

"Classical and country. I know that's a little weird, but it's the truth."

"Can you sing?"

"A little."

"You can't make much money in classical. Hell, I'd go country if I was you."

"That would mean Nashville, and I need to stay out of Tennessee for a while."

"You in trouble with the law?"

I shook my head. "I just don't want to go back to Tennessee."

"There's always the Louisiana Hayride over in Shreveport."

"I used to listen to that on KWKH," I said. "I'd forgotten about them."

"It's always been a good place for a country musician to get started. Hell, even Elvis played the Hayride."

Triple J came back to the table and handed Axelrod an envelope I assumed held cash. Jim was behind the bar by now, and patrons were beginning to file in. I didn't start work till six that afternoon, so I decided to look around the city. I said good-bye to everyone and left.

I wandered over to Jackson Square and found the Central Grocery. I'd read they were famous for their muffuletta sandwich, and I was determined to try one. When I walked into the grocery I spied two policemen in the back of the store. They were buying coffee at a small bar. My pulse quickened as it did any time a spotted a policeman. I was sure that I was on someone's wanted list. How long could I keep up my charade? Would I spend the rest of my life in prison for killing a worthless bastard?

I went to the counter where they sold the sandwiches trying to keep my face turned away from the policemen. My pulse was still racing as I placed my order. After I paid for my sandwich, I sat on a bench in the pedestrian mall and ate hoping the policemen wouldn't notice me when the left the grocery. The iron fence was covered with paintings and sketches, the artists sitting next to their work.

I finished my sandwich and threw the sack in a trash can. Then I wandered over to look at the paintings. Most were pencil sketches of famous landmarks in the French Quarter. Some of the oils were of landscapes set in the Mississippi Delta and showed well-known plantation mansions dating back to the Civil War. I had been fascinated by the War between the States because I occasionally found minié balls buried in the dirt on Miss Frances's farm. And, I'd read several of her many books on the subject.

Later, I walked along the levee and watched a tug push three barges filled with sand, the tug's stack belching black diesel smoke. The temperature was warm, the sky clear. A tourist sternwheeler passed in the opposite direction, the patrons hanging over the rail and waving their hands.

On my way back to the boarding house, my mind was flooded with thoughts of Round Rock. Since the weather was so warm and wonderful in New Orleans, I wondered if it was snowing at home. Actually, I'd been thinking of Round Rock a lot in the past few days, and the friends I'd left behind. And I continued to regret the fact that I hadn't told anyone good-bye. But as I thought of it, how could I? I'd looked forward to spending some time with Amy. I'd hoped that we could play music together again as we'd done at Miss Frances's house when we'd first met. Now that would never happen. A sadness settled over me as I climbed the three flights of stairs to my room. Once there, I sat on a ladder-back chair and strummed my guitar. Maybe I would learn something about the Memphis blues after all.

*   *   *

I liked Maggie. She was all business. I figured she'd been a waitress for a long time. I kept waiting for nine o'clock to roll around so I could listen to Axelrod and his fellows. They showed up right on time and went to playing immediately.

While I bused the tables, I would from time to time just stand and listen to the trio. Then I'd look across the room and see Triple J glaring at me.

After the lounge closed, I was able to clean the place in a little over an hour. Triple J came down from his apartment when I called and said, "You're doing a good job, Luke. I like having a white guy working for me."

I said, "Thanks," and left. Axelrod had asked me to come to his jam session, but I wanted to get to bed. I wasn't sure I wanted to be a professional musician if I had to stay up all night.

At the boarding house, I climbed the three flights of stairs and went to my room. I'd just turned off the light and crawled into bed when I heard a faint knock on the door. I slept in my BVDs so when I opened the door, I stood behind it.

In the hallway, back-lit by the dim overhead light, stood Casey in a sheer, very short nightgown. She held two beer bottles and a small purse. Without being invited, she walked in and went directly to my bed where she sat down and glanced up at me.

"Close the door, Luke, and come here," she said, patting the sheet next to her.

Closing the door, I did as I was told. As I sat beside her on the bed, she twisted the tops off the two beers and handed me one. I promptly set it on the floor.

"I don't drink, Casey. Thanks anyway," I said.

"Really?" Smiling, she said, "Surely you have some vices."

"I guess not."

"I brought some weed."

"What's that?"

"Marijuana, silly."

"That's illegal."

She rolled her eyes, blew out an exasperated breath, and said, "That's what makes it fun. Come on, smoke a joint with me."

I shook my head.

"You're no fun, Luke. I swear, a good-looking guy like you ought to loosen up," she said as she placed her hand on my bare thigh, her fingers inches from my crotch.

In the soft light of my bedside lamp, I could see her erect nipples through her sheer top and the cleavage of her pale breasts. I'd be lying if I said the combination of her probing fingers and the sight of those knockers didn't arouse me.

She smiled at my involuntary response. "So, you don't have ice water running through your veins after all."

"I guess not."

She took a swig of her beer, picked up the purse, and removed a small cloth pouch. Removing a piece of cigarette paper, she sprinkled some marijuana over it. Then she rolled it lengthwise and licked it. She lit the joint with a Bic lighter and inhaled deeply. She held her breath for a few moments, then slowly let out the blue smoke, its sweet smell engulfing my face.

Lying back on my pillow, she handed the joint to me and said, "It won't hurt you, Luke. It'll just relax you. Believe me, honey, you need relaxing."

To say I was tense would be an understatement. In truth, at

sixteen, I still hadn't been with a woman. I'd done the usual heavy petting with some of my girlfriends, but I'd never gone all the way. God knows, I'd wanted to, but the girls had always stopped at the last minute. Frankly, I'd never understood how they managed that.

I was racked with indecision. I knew what alcohol did to people, but I had no experience with marijuana, no idea what it did to a person's brain. Holding the joint in my hand reminded me of smoking with Miss Frances. I inhaled and immediately started coughing.

She laughed. "Take it in slow and hold your breath for a few seconds. Then let it out."

When I exhaled, the room tilted and I felt light-headed. But I also felt fabulously relaxed. I took another draw and handed it back to Casey. We passed it back and forth until the butt was so short we couldn't hold it.

"Put this out," she said, handing it to me.

When I stood, a wave of dizziness gripped me, and I staggered to the other side of the room where I'd left my shoes. I placed the butt on the floor and extinguished it by grinding it into the hardwood floor.

As I approached the bed, I saw that Casey was wearing nothing but a smile. It reminded me of Marilyn Monroe's famous quote about her calendar picture. I slipped out of my BVDs, turned off the light, and lay down beside her.

Casey wrapped her arms around me and kissed me on the lips, letting her tongue find mine. I didn't know if it was the marijuana or just my excitement, but I'd never had such an erection. We caressed and explored each other's bodies for a long time, increasing my need for release. Casey was in no hurry. I, on the other hand, exploded sending a wad of semen onto Casey's belly.

I could feel my face redden and a said, "I'm so sorry. I just couldn't hold it anymore."

She laughed and pulled me to her. "Don't be silly. A young guy like you can get it back up in a minute or two. Just relax, Luke. We've got all night."

Luckily, she was right. I did get it up again and she rolled on top of me and slipped me inside her. I still came before she did but she did make it a few seconds later.

Afterward, we lay in each other's arms and fell asleep. I awoke once in the night to Casey's snoring. It was a new experience for me to share my bed with anyone except Bandit. I had to say, I thoroughly enjoyed it.

The next morning, Casey rolled on top of me, and we did it again. By the time we'd finished, both of us were sweating. She smiled and said, "I could get used to this, Luke. I hope that doesn't scare you."

No, it didn't scare me. I liked it too much. But would it lead to a romance? I doubted it. I liked Casey, but I knew I didn't love her. Besides, my life had been turned upside-down, and I had no idea where I was headed or how I'd get there.

I rubbed my nose against hers and said, "It doesn't scare me a bit. I'm not so sure about your weed, though. I've got a throbbing headache this morning."

We got out of bed around nine o'clock, and I lent her my robe so she could go back to her room without arousing suspicion. I let the hot water run over my head for a long time in the shower and thought about the marijuana I'd smoked the evening before. It had definitely increased my sex drive and my pleasure. That in itself made me wonder if I should continue to use it. Plus the headache was killing me.

Before she left for work, Casey stopped by to return my robe. Her hair was in a ponytail and her cheeks were rosy. Her eyes sparkled as she stepped into the room. Handing me the robe, she said, "Here you go, handsome." She gave me a peck on the cheek and left.

If nothing else, my new life had taken some interesting turns. New Orleans was a far cry from Round Rock.

Chapter 11

On the way to work that afternoon, as I passed the corner of Bourbon and Royal, I spied a young black guy playing a tenor sax. He wore dark sunglasses and had his instrument case open on the sidewalk. It was filled with one- and five-dollar bills. Tourists wandered by, and a few stopped to listen before throwing a bill into the case.

Casey looked a little haggard when I arrived at the Triple J. A few strands of hair had pulled out of her ponytail, and her eyes had a dull cast. When she saw me, her demeanor brightened.

She wandered over, and I asked, "Rough shift?"

"Triple J's on a rampage. Don't go near the fat bastard."

Then she turned and grabbed a tray of food from the kitchen pass-through window.

I bused tables at a ferocious rate once Maggie arrived. Luckily, Triple J didn't materialize until it was time for the Mahoney Trio.

As soon as Axelrod pulled out the piano stool, the boss was arguing with him. I had no idea what it was about and decided to mind my own business.

At the trio's first break, I pulled Axelrod aside and said, "I saw a guy on the street today playing a sax. People were throwing money in his instrument case. I thought I might try that with my guitar. What do you think?"

The black man took a swig of bourbon and said, "You might pick up a little change. It'd give you some experience playing a crowd. Someone might see you and arrange a gig. Hell, I'd do it."

"Where should I stand?"

"Anywhere on Bourbon Street."

* * *

On the way to work the following day I left the boarding house earlier than usual. I didn't have a guitar case, just a canvas cover. There was a small hat shop on Royal so I went in and bought a black cowboy hat with a silver headband. I figured I could turn it upside down on the sidewalk in front of me.

I'd decided to stand on the corner of Bourbon and St. Louis Streets. It was a Friday, and a lot of tourists milled around both streets. I got there at four o'clock so I'd have two hours to play before going to work.

Peeling the cover off my guitar, I placed it on the sidewalk and took off my hat. My mouth felt like it was full of cotton, and I kept swallowing and licking my lips. Other than Miss Frances, Jake, Yolanda, Mr. Arbuckle, and Amy, I'd never played in front of anyone. At that last moment before starting, I couldn't decide what to play.

Finally, I just started strumming a few chords. Several people stopped for a second and then moved on. After a few moments, I began to loosen up. It being New Orleans, I thought I might play a song I'd learned from listening to a Count Basie record on Jake's stereo. It was a classic 1940s boogie-woogie piece.

I was picking the melody and throwing in chords at a furious rate. People began to stop and listen, their feet tapping to the fast beat. Seeing the smiles on their faces brought joy to my heart. It was a natural high, far greater than the one I'd received from Casey's marijuana.

Within minutes, a crowd of thirty or so people stood in front of me. Anyone wanting to walk down the street had to cross to the other side. When I finished, there was generous applause, and some of the people in front filled my hat with five- and ten-dollar bills.

Next I played my own rendition of "Granada." The crowd continued to grow, and finally, a policeman wandered over and said, "Move along, folks. You're blocking the street."

No one moved. I held my breath. *What if he arrested me? They'd know who I really am.* My heart pounded and I stopped playing. I scooped up my hat, threw my guitar over my shoulder, and started down Bourbon toward Triple J's.

The crowd dispersed and I picked up my pace. As I passed a bar, someone grabbed my arm. I thought it was a cop and tried to pull away.

"Slow down, kid. I want to talk to you," a man said. "Come in here for a minute."

I looked past him into the bar. It was dark inside and crowded. I figured the man must be the manager. He certainly didn't look like a cop.

"What do you want?" I asked.

"To give you a job."

"I've got a job."

"Doing what?"

"I'm a janitor at the Triple J Lounge."

He laughed. "You shitting me?"

I shook my head.

"Don't waste your time with that nonsense. Hell, you're the best damn guitar player I've ever heard. I'll give you a hundred bucks a night plus tips."

"What's your name, mister?" I asked.

"Sam Ledford. I own this joint."

"Let me think about it and I'll get back to you tomorrow."

I wasn't about to take a job playing in a bar without talking to Axelrod and Casey. I didn't care much for Triple J, but at least the fat bastard had given me a job when I really needed one.

* * *

That night when Axelrod took his first break, I went to his table and told him what had happened. He was sipping on a tumbler of bourbon. "Hell, Luke, that one's easy. Take the gig."

"I'll need to give Triple J a week's notice."

"Just leave. The bastard doesn't deserve notice."

"That wouldn't be right."

"You're too good, Luke. You need to look out for yourself. If you take the gig, you'll need to join the AFM."

"What's that?"

"American Federation of Musicians. We have a local chapter."

"Would I need a Social Security card?"

"Sure."

"What if I don't join? Can I still play?"

"Yeah, but you'd miss out on some benefits, might not get paid scale."

Triple J sat in his chair near the bar, guzzling a draft beer. During a lull, I wandered over and said, "Sir, I need to give a week's notice. I'm quitting."

He looked up at me with those beefy eyes and said, "Just take the fuck off. Go on. Beat it."

I just stared at him. He owed me eighty dollars for five days' work. I needed that money.

"I've got a week's pay coming," I said.

"Like hell you do."

I took off my apron, walked behind the bar, pushed Jim aside, and opened the cash register, and I took out the money owed me.

Triple J roared like a wounded lion. He tried to get out of the chair, but gravity proved to be a more powerful force than his flabby muscles could overcome.

"Somebody get me out of this fucking chair," he bellowed.

No one moved.

I waved to Maggie as I walked out the door. Triple J was still screaming obscenities as I stepped onto Bourbon Street. It was only ten o'clock, so I wandered over to Preservation Hall. A skinny old black man was doing a tap dance on the sidewalk as I walked up, his steel-tipped shoes keeping perfect time to the fast rhythm seeping through the open windows.

Inside, the place was packed. I had to stand in back. A group of ancient black men played genuine New Orleans Dixieland jazz on the small stage. The audience clapped their hands and stomped their feet after each set.

Around midnight I wandered home. I climbed the three flights to my floor, stopped, and descended to the second. At Casey's door I knocked gently. There was no answer. I knew she must be there so I did it again, louder. The door swung open, and Casey, silhouetted by her bedside lamp, stood staring at me, her slim body outlined in her sheer nightgown. Her hair was disheveled, her eyes sleepy.

She smiled and grabbed me by the wrist, pulling me into the room. "Hi, handsome," she said, drawing me to her. Wrapping her arms around my neck, she planted a wet kiss on my lips. "Come to bed, sugar," she said in a sleepy, guttural voice.

We made gentle love for a long time, caressing and exploring each other's bodies. It was less intense than our first time, and I figured that was because we hadn't used marijuana. That fact alone told me I shouldn't get hooked on the stuff. Afterward, we fell into a deep and restful sleep.

Sometime in the middle of the night, Casey awoke and slowly walked her fingers up my thigh to my crotch. My response made her laugh. When I opened my eyes, she said, "It's that time again."

I rolled on top of her and said, "You're wearing me down, girl, and I love it."

When it was over, we held each other in a firm embrace, and I stroked her cheek gently with the back of my hand. We fell asleep again, and I didn't stir until morning.

I awoke to the aroma of brewing coffee. Opening my eyes, I glanced across the room to see Casey filling a cup from an electric percolator. She smiled and said, "I've got to have my coffee in the morning. Want some?"

"Sure."

She brought me a mug, and I pushed my pillow behind me and sat up. She settled beside me. The coffee was strong and filled with chicory.

"That was a pleasant surprise, you showing up at my door. What were you doing off so early?"

"I quit last night."

"How did the fat ass-hole deal with that?"

"He refused to pay me so I took what he owed me out of the cash register."

She laughed. "I guess the SOB finally met his match. Good for you, honey. Everyone else is scared shitless of Triple J." Then she frowned and asked, "What are you going to do for a job?"

"I've got a gig at Sam Ledford's bar playing the guitar."

"You're a musician? I didn't know that."

I guessed she hadn't noticed my guitar when I'd walked into her room the evening before. I'd placed it on the floor behind the door. I threw the covers back and walked naked across the room. Picking up the guitar, I peeled the canvas cover off and returned to the bed. Casey stared at me with wide eyes, a wicked smile on her face.

"What kind of music do you like?" I asked her.

"Anything, honey, just play whatever you want."

I strummed a few chords and then picked out the melody of Elvis's old song, "Love Me Tender." Then I looked into Casey's eyes and in a soft voice started to sing. Her mouth opened slowly, and she gripped my thigh, her fingernails biting into my skin. When I finished, she said in a hoarse voice, "Luke, sweetie, that made chills run up my spine."

Amy had told me that the first time I'd sung for her. Thinking of my old life, I was overcome with sadness. It must have shown on my face because Casey said, "Luke, honey, you look like you've seen a ghost."

I gave her a wary smile and said, "I have."

She pulled me to her, wrapped her arms around me, and held on tight as if the slightest breeze would blow me away.

"Someday I'll level with you," I said.

"What does that mean?" she asked with a puzzled expression.

"Things aren't always what they seem. Life gets complicated sometimes if you know what I mean." Then smiling, I dressed, slipped my guitar into its case, and left.

* * *

I had less than two hundred dollars to my name. The thought of making a hundred bucks a night seemed an impossible dream. I showered, shaved, and dressed in my best trousers and button-down shirt. I wanted to talk to Sam Ledford.

His bar was called Play It Again Sam. I walked in around eleven o'clock. The joint was packed with tourists. I didn't see him anywhere, so I wandered over to the bar and asked, "Where's the boss?"

The bartender was a gorgeous blonde with the bluest eyes I'd ever seen. Tall and slim, she wore jeans and a tank top sans bra. She raised her pale eyebrows and asked, "Who wants to know?"

"Obviously, me."

"I'm supposed to be impressed. Who the hell are you?"

"My name's Luke."

"Luke what?"

"Just Luke."

"What, like Cher?"

"I guess."

"He doesn't come in till two. What do you want?"

"He offered me a job."

"Doing what?"

"Playing the guitar."

She rolled her eyes. "Guitar players are a dime a dozen. What's so special about you?"

"I guess the way I play. What's your problem?"

"I don't have a problem. What're you talking about?"

"You seem awfully tense. Are you having a bad day?"

She laughed so hard, tears come to her eyes. "I'm sorry. I *am* having a bad day. Why don't you come back at two? I'm sure Sam wants to talk to you."

Turning to leave, I asked, "What's your name?"

"Joy Ledford. I'm the boss's daughter."

* * *

I'd become addicted to muffuletta sandwiches since arriving in the Big Easy. It was close to noon, so I walked over to Chartres Street. I'd been told the Napoleon House had the best muffs in town. When

I walked into the dining area, I heard Beethoven's Fifth Symphony playing softly in the background. The room had a fourteen-foot ceiling with fans hanging from it, and the tables were covered with white tablecloths.

The sandwich was good. Finishing with a cup of espresso, I watched tourists wander down the sidewalk outside. I wondered how Jake and Yolanda were. I missed them more than I could have imagined. I often thought of Amy, too. I found it hard to comprehend how drastically my life had changed.

As I sat thinking of my friends, I wondered what the reaction had been to the discovery of my dead parents. Should I call the City Café and ask Dorothy to get Jake on the phone? I felt so conflicted it made my stomach burn. I just didn't know what to do. Were the police looking for me? I wished I had access to the *Round Rock Courier* or at least the *Nashville Tennessean*. I made a mental note to stop by the library to see if they had any Tennessee newspapers. Besides, I needed some new books. I wanted a biography of Jean Lafitte.

Feeling stuffed, I decide to stroll over to Jackson Square and pick up a copy of the *Times-Picayune*. Since I didn't have a television or radio, I'd become dependent on the newspaper to stay current. The big news that day was the Tet Offensive in Vietnam. I shuddered, knowing I'd have to register for the draft in two years.

Walking along the iron fence, I once again glanced at the oil paintings and charcoal sketches of familiar New Orleans tourist attractions. I nodded to the artists as I strolled by. It was a balmy day with a slight breeze off the water. The river was a beehive of activity. Boats of all kinds steamed up and down the Mississippi in front of the levee. *I'll have to take a ride on one of those tourist boats one of these days*, I thought.

A few minutes before two, I went back to Bourbon Street. When I walked into Sam's place, it was still packed. Joy was scurrying from one end of the long mahogany bar to the other, filling mugs with draft beers. It didn't appear that her temperament had improved.

I spied Sam at a corner table, eating lunch. "May I sit down?" I asked.

He wiped some mustard from his chin and said, "You decide to take the job?"

"Yes, sir."

He nodded. "Want to start tonight?"

"That would be great. How long do I play? What time?"

"Start around nine. Take the usual breaks. I expect you to perform for at least two hours."

"Not a problem."

"See my bookkeeper in the office. She'll get you signed up."

I didn't want to talk to the bookkeeper, I didn't have a Social Security card and couldn't get one because I didn't have a birth certificate. Besides, I'd have to give my real name. I didn't know what to do, and my stomach burned at the thought of losing this job.

Clearing my throat, I said, "Couldn't you just pay me as an independent contractor? I'd rather not be an employee."

He frowned and placed his hamburger on his plate. "Why don't you want to be an employee?"

"I'd just rather be independent. I'd also like to be paid in cash every evening after I finish performing."

I knew I was pushing the envelope, but I didn't think I had a choice.

Sam frowned and asked, "How old are you?"

"Eighteen."

"I don't even know your name."

"Luke."

"That's it?"

"Yes, sir."

"Why do I get the impression you're hiding something? Are you in trouble with the law?"

"No, sir."

"Everyone has a last name for Christ's sake. Don't give me this bull-shit."

My mind raced. What was a good name to go with Luke? Watson? Johnson? Crutcher? I finally decided on Montgomery. "It's Luke Montgomery."

"That's better. If you weren't such an incredible musician, I'd throw your skinny ass out of here. Come back at nine."

Chapter 12

I arrived at Sam's around 8:30 with my guitar over my shoulder. Joy was still behind the bar. When she noticed me, she gave me a halfhearted wave. I tipped my head in response and looked around for Sam. He wasn't there. *Surely*, I thought, *he'll show up to hear me play.*

I'd been practicing all afternoon and had a lineup of songs I planned to perform. The list contained some classical, boogie-woogie, and jazz. I didn't think the crowd would like country. I intended to do some Johnny Mercer songs as well as some of Elvis's material. I'd just figure it out as I went.

Alcohol flowed like a raging river, and the crowd was loud and talkative. Would anyone even be able to hear me? I didn't like amplification and didn't want to use it. But I might not have a choice. I glanced at the small elevated stage next to the bar. A microphone on a stand stood in front of a lone chair.

At the bar, I asked Joy for a glass of water.

"Little nervous, are you? You don't want a beer?"

Nodding, I said, "Yes, I'm nervous. No, I don't want a beer. I don't drink."

She handed me a tumbler of ice water and said, "I'm looking forward to hearing you. Sam's a hard guy to please. He must see something in you."

"Where is Sam?" I asked. "Isn't he going to introduce me?"

Joy smiled. "There he is," she said.

Sam pushed through the tables and stepped onto the stage. Taking the microphone off the stand, he said, "Ladies and gentlemen, I'd like to introduce your entertainment for this evening. Please welcome Luke Montgomery, a young man with extraordinary talent."

The talking and laughing continued unabated. I stepped onto the stage and sat in the chair. I glanced at Joy, who smiled and mouthed a silent "good luck."

Sam had taken a seat at the back of the room with his arms crossed over his chest, waiting for me to start. I could barely swallow. How in the hell was I going to sing? I'd just have to put that off until I got warmed up or thrown out of the joint. I'd never been so scared in my life.

It was so noisy, I could barely think. No one even looked at the stage. It was if I didn't exist. I wondered if I was simply invisible. Not knowing what else to do, I started strumming a few chords. I remembered the people on the street had liked the Count Basie boogie-woogie number. So I tore into it with all I had. I doubted anyone in the back of the room could even hear it. *Maybe I should move the microphone down even with the guitar*, I wondered. I didn't want to do that, though, preferring the natural sound.

A few people next to the stage stopped talking and fixed their eyes on me. I switched to a classical Segovia piece. Slowly, like a wave sweeping over the compact sand of a far-away beach, the crowd began to go quiet. Tables farther and farther from the stage went silent. I glanced at Sam and saw a smile on his face. That gave me confidence, and I moved next to a jazz tune.

After twenty minutes of instrumentals, I decided to try a song. Racking my brain, I wondered what this crowd might like. I was pleased with the attention they'd given me so far. Then I did something that would later become a trademark for me. I looked at the crowd and asked, "Anyone have a request for a song?"

A man at a table about ten feet from the stage stood. He was stoop-shouldered, with white hair and a face as furrowed as a cotton patch. Next to him was a woman who appeared to be as old, smiling sweetly. The man said in a shaky voice, "Emily and me are celebrating our sixtieth anniversary. Could you sing 'I Love You Truly'?"

There was applause as the old man took his seat. I watched him place his arm around his wife's shoulder and pull her to him. Luckily, I knew the song. I'd found a copy of the sheet music in the piano bench at Miss Frances's house the week I'd moved in. It's very sentimental and had been written around the turn of the century.

I picked out the melody and stepped down from the stage. Strolling to their table, I looked directly into the woman's eyes and began to sing. Tears slid down her plump cheeks, and she took a handkerchief out of her purse and blew her nose. The old man beamed. When I finished, she stood and threw her arms around my neck. The audience didn't respond at once. In fact, as that old cliché states, you could have heard a pin drop. Then like a wave crashing on a sandy beach, the sound of people standing and applauding reached me.

Back on the stage, I played for another fifteen minutes and took a break. Sam was smiling from ear to ear when I approached his table. All he said was, "You didn't disappoint me, Luke."

I walked over to the bar and asked Joy, "May I have another glass of water?"

She bore her blue eyes into mine and bit her lower lip. I thought it made her look sexy. I could almost see the gears turning in her head. *What is she thinking?*

After filling a tumbler with ice water, she set it on the bar in front of me. Then she placed her hand on my arm and said, "I barely know what to say. I've never heard a performance like that. It was awesome. I apologize for being so flippant earlier today."

I could tell she was truly moved, and I could feel my face flush. "Thanks. Does the boss ever give you a day off?"

She smiled, and I noticed what she had the whitest teeth I'd ever laid my eyes on. And her lips were full and sensual. I had an almost uncontrollable desire to place mine on them.

"I get Sundays off."

"Would you like to do something with me tomorrow?" I asked, dreading the answer.

"Sam doesn't want me dating the help. But if you'll keep your mouth shut, I'll do it anyway. Deal?"

"Deal. May I have your number?"

She jotted it on a cocktail napkin just as the waitress stepped up to the bar with a drink order. Joy said, "I get off now. See you tomorrow."

I started playing again around ten-fifteen and went on for another hour. I kept getting encores, but my voice was giving out so I begged off.

I'd had the foresight to place my cowboy hat on the stage, and after each set, people filled it with five- and ten-dollar bills. When I finished, Sam gave me my hundred bucks. I sat at the bar and counted it all. The tips amounted to fifty dollars. I'd made more money that evening than I'd ever earned at a single job.

Back at the boarding house I stopped at Casey's room but didn't get an answer when I knocked. I guessed she was on a date. That thought bothered me for some reason. Then I remembered Joy and brightened up.

* * *

The next morning I slept late, showered, shaved, and went down the street for my usual croissant and coffee. I'd moved up to espresso. I bought a Sunday *Times-Picayune* and took it back to my room. Around noon I went downstairs to the hall pay phone and called Joy.

She answered on the third ring. "Hello," she said.

"Hi, it's Luke."

"Hi, yourself. What's the plan?"

"I thought I'd leave it up to you."

"Let's meet at Jackson Square, and then decide how to spend the afternoon. Let's say around one o'clock."

"Sounds great. See you then."

It was the first week in February, and the weather was great. It was another cloudless day with a soft southerly breeze. I had to admit, I loved the warm temperatures. I'd been told to dread the muggy summers, but I hadn't experienced one yet.

Joy took my breath when she walked up. She wore a tight miniskirt and a tank top, again sans bra. Her hair was in ringlets that fell to her shoulders. Her full lips were the color of raspberries, and she wore high-heeled sandals, exposing perfectly manicured toes.

I, on the other hand, felt like a bum. I only had one pair of nice trousers and they needed a trip to the cleaners, so I'd worn jeans and a sweatshirt. I made up my mind at that moment to buy an outfit with my new money.

"Hi, Luke," she said. "I'm starving."

"Where do you want to eat?" I asked.

"Let's go to the Court of Two Sisters. They have a great jazz brunch."

I'd walked past the place several times, and it looked awfully expensive. I still had the money in my wallet from the previous evening, so I knew I wouldn't embarrass myself. But in truth, I didn't want to spend much of it.

She grabbed my arm and pulled me along. I couldn't back out. I just swallowed hard and hoped it wouldn't break me.

We had to stand in line for about thirty minutes. While we waited, Joy had something called a Mimosa and I sipped a Coke. A maitre d' seated us at a small table under a huge tree.

After going through the buffet, Joy looked me in the eye and said, "Tell me your story, Luke. I want to know more about you."

"What do you want to know?"

"Your real name, for starters. And where you're from. Your accent isn't familiar."

I didn't even know I had an accent. I couldn't level with her. I didn't know how to respond. Finally, I said, "Wouldn't you rather I remain a mystery?"

"No. Quit stalling."

"Okay, under one condition. Tell me about yourself first."

She shook her head and let out an exasperated breath. "You know I'm the boss's daughter. I live in my own apartment in the Quarter. I'm taking a break before going back to school. I start a master's in psychology next fall at LSU. I have no brothers or sisters, and yes, I'm a daddy's girl. My mother died in childbirth."

I stared at her. The poor kid had grown up without a mother. I felt so sad for her. I reached across the table and took her hand. "I'm sorry about your mother. Mine's dead, too," I said. "I'm from Tennessee, the eastern part of the state. Luke is a nickname. I never use my real name anymore. I'm sorry, but I can't tell you why."

"Well, that's better than nothing," she said. "But that still leaves a lot of unanswered questions. Why in the world can't you use your real name?"

"I just can't. Please don't push me on it."

"How old are you?"

"What difference does that make?"

"I'm not sure I want to go out with someone younger than me."

"I told your dad I'm eighteen."

"So you are younger than me. But you *are* eighteen?"

I nodded, feeling badly that I continued to lie about my age. But what choice did I have? No one would hire a sixteen-year-old.

We made idle conversation while we ate. At one point I asked, "Since you're into psychology, are you a B. F. Skinner disciple?"

"How do you know about Dr. Skinner?" she asked.

"I read his biography. He did a lot of experiments with rats. The guy who really fascinates me is Freud. I've read two of his biographies. I love reading about interesting people. It's a hobby for me."

"I'm not a Skinner disciple. His work kind of scares me."

We went back through the line for dessert. Joy picked up a lemon tart, and I chose a flourless chocolate cake. Both of us had coffee.

The bill wasn't as expensive as I'd feared. Joy insisted on leaving the tip but I wouldn't let her. I paid, and we wandered down the street, looking into antique shops. When I took Joy's hand, she squeezed it and held on.

"What do you want to do?" I asked.

"Let's go to my apartment," she said.

She led me to a building on Royal Street. Her apartment was over an antique shop. It was a small one-bedroom affair with high ceilings and a wrought-iron porch. The furnishings were modest but in good condition.

"You want a beer?" she asked.

"I don't drink, remember?"

"What's that about?"

"Alcohol addiction runs in my family."

She shrugged and sat on the couch. She patted the cushion next to her and said, "Sit with me."

I did. Her miniskirt rode up on her thighs. Her legs were slim and shapely, the ankles small. She slipped off her sandals and pulled her feet beneath her. I thought she was the sexiest woman I'd ever laid eyes on.

She smiled and placed her head on my shoulder. I put my arm around her, and for the longest time she didn't move or say a word.

"You're an interesting guy, Luke. I've never met anyone quite like you."

I assumed that was a compliment, but I wasn't sure. I realized I was a neophyte when it came to women. I'd never made love until I met Casey. Looking at Joy, I knew I wanted to devour her with kisses.

She sat up and faced me. A smile crossed her lips, and she asked, "What are you thinking?"

"That you're the most beautiful woman I've ever been with."

"Are you trying to get into my pants?"

"The thought crossed my mind."

"Ever made love in the afternoon?"

I shook my head.

"It's very French," she said.

She stood and pulled me to my feet. Then she led me to her small bedroom. The big four-poster bed reminded me of mine at Jake's house. She threw back the covers, fluffed the pillows, and pulled her tank top over her head. Her breasts were full and well-rounded, the nipples pink and erect. Next she slipped out of the miniskirt and her bikini panties. Naked, she put her arms around my neck and kissed me full on the lips, a wet, lingering kiss.

I stripped in a clumsy charade of falling clothes and crawled into bed next to her. Pulling her to me, I kissed her gently and caressed her breasts. I'd been able to manage my premature ejections a little better than that first time with Casey, but as soon as Joy returned my kiss I couldn't help myself. Joy made a face when she realized what had happened.

"I'm sorry, Joy, I couldn't help myself."

"Don't worry. This'll give me a chance to introduce you to cunnilingus."

I had no idea what she was talking about. She spread her legs and pushed my head between them. Then she told me what to do.

She made it very quickly and, by then I was ready to go. I pulled myself up and kissed her again and slipped inside her. I tried really hard to hold back but I couldn't and exploded.

"I'm sorry, Joy. I'm actually a little new at this."

She laughed. "That's okay, you got me off. I'm well satisfied. When you recover I'll introduce you to a little act known as fellecio.

She did, and afterward Joy cuddled up to me and whispered into my ear, "I love the sexual revolution."

My head felt light. Joy had opened up a whole new world for me. I didn't say anything, just held her tightly against me.

"Why don't you move in with me?" she asked in a hoarse whisper. "I know it's sudden and crazy, but two can live cheaper than one. Just don't tell Sam."

I sat up and gazed into her beautiful face. "You're serious?"

She nodded.

We showered together, and later Joy fixed dinner for us. We ate by candlelight. She had a glass of red wine, and I stuck with Coke.

"I practice my guitar every day. Do you think the neighbors will mind?"

"I doubt it."

"I really like working at night. That way I can spend the day reading and practicing."

"You must read a lot," she said.

"Three or four books a week. One of my mentors was a speed reader who managed two or more a day."

"Someday I hope you'll tell me the truth about yourself," she said.

I stared into her enchanting blue eyes and said, "I will. I promise."

* * *

Climbing the stairs to my room, I met Casey coming down. She was dressed in jeans and a sweatshirt. She smiled when she saw me.

Grabbing my arm, she asked, "Luke, honey, how's the new job?"

"Great. I love playing in front of an audience. It sure beats being a janitor."

"Triple J still hasn't found anyone to replace you. I think he's sorry he didn't let you give that week's notice."

I wanted to tell her I was moving out, but for some reason I felt badly about it. I liked Casey and we'd been intimate. Why did I feel disloyal? Would I continue to see Casey? It didn't make sense if I was living with Joy. What if Casey wanted to make love? My head was swimming.

"Where're you headed this time of night?" I asked.

"I'm out of coffee. Can I come up after I get back?"

"Sure."

I was packing my suitcase when she knocked on the door. I opened it and ushered her in. When she saw what I was doing, she asked, "You moving out?"

I nodded but didn't know what to say.

A smile crossed her face, dimples forming in her smooth cheeks. "You find a new girlfriend?"

"I'm moving in with her."

"Lucky girl. Who is she?"

Should I tell her? It might get back to Sam.

"Her name is Joy. She tends bar."

"So I've lost my squeeze," she said.

I laughed. "I'll miss you, Casey. You've been great to me."

She moved into my arms and kissed me on the lips. Pulling back, she looked into my eyes and asked, "Want to roll in the hay one last time?"

Feeling her lithe body next to mine, her firm breast pushed into my chest, overrode any hope I had of resisting. "Why not?" I said.

We made love off and on most of the night. Sleeping, waking up, doing it, and going back to sleep. The next morning I was exhausted. Pussy-whipped would be the more accurate term.

Casey rose on one elbow and gazed into my eyes. I noticed the black roots of her blonde hair and thought of Joy, a pang of regret sweeping over me. Casey smiled and said, "Your girlfriend's taught you a few new tricks."

Chapter 13

After my first week, Sam upped my pay to two hundred dollars a night because his business had doubled. When I performed, there was a line to get in. People stood in the back, and the cocktail waitress took them drinks. I was becoming more and more confident on stage.

In my mind, the performer with the most stage presence was Elvis. I loved the way he'd walk out before an audience and just stare at them for a few moments. Then he'd raise his lips into a snarl that ended in a big smile. I'd seen his NBC TV December 3, 1968 special on Jake's television and it had blown me away. His career had been in a downward spiral and that show had revived it. Thinking about it, I had no intention of rotating my pelvis, but I did want to come up with an original opening.

Mardi Gras came and went. I was glad when it was over. I'd never seen so many people wandering up and down Bourbon

Street. Alcohol flowed faster than the Mississippi. Joy and I did watch some of the parades from our balcony, and I caught several trinkets thrown from the floats. The thing I enjoyed most was the gorgeous women who were mooning people on the street. When Joy caught me gawking at them, she poked me playfully on the shoulder.

Joy and I'd settled into a stable relationship. When I was performing, I'd glance her way and see her smiling at me. I'd get a lump in my throat and smile back. We did everything together when we weren't working. And when we made love, I felt as if we were one. If Sam knew, he never let on.

* * *

One Sunday morning in May, I'd just finished reading the paper when I made a snap decision. Joy had gone to the grocery store, and I was alone so it was a perfect time to call Amy. I'd been planning on contacting her to see what was going on in Round Rock. I knew I could trust her not to give me away. I hadn't seen her since my birthday party in January.

I got her mother's number from information and placed a straight station-to-station call. Amy picked up the receiver after two rings. "Hello," she said.

"Amy, it's me," I said.

"Jamie Lee Coleman! Where are you? I've been worried sick about you."

"What's going on in Round Rock?"

"You mean about your mother and father?"

"Yes."

"Your mother's dead, but I guess you knew that. One of your uncles found your father unconscious beside your mother. I assumed you did that. Dr. Kate revived him and called the sheriff. Your dad admitted hitting your mom. He's in jail awaiting trial. Where *are* you?"

I couldn't believe my ears. I wasn't a murderer. The cops weren't looking for me. I was a free man.

"Jamie, answer me."

"I'm in New Orleans."

"What in the world are you doing there? When are you coming back?"

"I'm not. I have a new life."

"I don't understand what that means."

"I'm working as a musician, making good money. I've got new goals."

"You're not going to finish high school?"

"No."

"I can't believe this. I think you're off your rocker. Jake and Yolanda have been sick with worry. Please contact them."

The next thing I heard was a dial tone. I'd obviously pissed her off. And I felt like a coward. More than a coward. I felt ashamed and mortified that I'd been such a dolt.

Joy had walked into the room unnoticed and had been listening to the one-sided conversation for a few minutes. When I replaced the receiver, she asked, "Who's Amy?" she asked.

"A girl from home. We've been friends since grade school. She lives in Cookeville, Tennessee."

"Is that where you're from?"

"No. I'm from a little town about twenty miles north-east of there—Round Rock."

Joy flopped on the couch and stared at me. "Is there something you need to tell me?"

I had dreaded that day. Having to tell Joy who I was and where I'd come from. I sat next to her, took her hand in mine, cleared my throat, and said, "I ran away from home. My father killed my mother. Hit her hard and she fell and struck her head on a table leg. I attacked him—wanted to kill him. I pounded him over the head with a chair. I left him a bloody mess on the floor of our tarpaper shack. I hoped I'd killed him, but according to Amy, the sorry bastard lived. He's awaiting trial now. I thought the police were after me. That's why I took an alias. My real name is Jamie Lee Coleman."

As I related the tale, it seemed bizarre even to me. But Miss Frances had always said fact could be stranger than fiction.

Joy was speechless. After a period of awkward silence, she said, "Your name is Jamie, not Luke."

I nodded.

"What did you mean about a tarpaper shack? I don't understand."

"We were dirt poor. We lived in a place called Beulah Land. It's about two miles out of Round Rock. Just a bunch of illiterate, drunken fools huddled together in tarpaper shacks. One privy for ten families. One well. No electricity. No running water. Not exactly heaven—more hell than anything."

"Your father beat your mother regularly?"

"Yeah. When I tried to help her, he'd beat me, too. That's why I ran away the first time."

"First time?"

"I was ten. He'd beat me for trying to help her. So, I grabbed a jacket and ran out the door. I ended up on a farm owned by an old lady named Miss Frances Washington. She took me in and basically saved my life. Took legal custody of me."

"What do you mean, saved your life?"

"She taught me to read. Cleaned me up, bought me clothes, helped me improve my grades. That sort of thing. And she gave me my guitar and encouraged my music. I loved her with all my heart. I thought I'd never get over her dying."

"I still don't understand. Did you go back to your mother when Miss Frances died?"

"No. Her attorney, a man named Jake Watson, took me in. When I thought I'd killed my father, I'd gone to see my mother to give her a present. My father came home in a drunken rage and hit her."

Joy had a stricken expression on her face. She shook he head and asked, "How am I going to deal with this? You're not the person I thought you were."

"Sure I am. Nothing's changed but my name. I told you Luke wasn't my real name when we met."

I thought Joy was acting silly. I was beginning to wonder if I should've told her everything, but she'd said she wanted to know.

She sank back into the cushions of the couch and closed her eyes. She didn't say a word. For a moment, I thought she'd gone to sleep. I was getting hungry and wanted to go to the Court of Two Sisters. Since our first date, we'd had brunch there almost every Sunday.

I just sat and stared at her. Finally, she opened her eyes and said, "Kiss me. I want to be sure it's really you."

I pulled her to me, and kissed her hard. She moaned, and in a matter of seconds, we were engaged in wild lovemaking on the couch. Pillows flew across the room, and at one point we rolled onto the floor. That didn't slow the action.

Minutes later, exhausted and spent, we lay in each other's arms, breathing in short gasps. Joy rolled on top of me and laughed. "Well, Jamie, alias Luke, I guess you're the same guy."

When we returned to the apartment after brunch, I placed a call to the City Café and asked for Dorothy, the owner. "This is Jamie Lee Coleman. When Jake comes in tomorrow, ask him to call me." I gave her our phone number and replaced the receiver.

It made me feel free—unencumbered to think that I could finally stop living a lie. I could use my own name without worrying the police were going to arrest me, and above all, I wasn't a murderer.

And my worthless father would rot in jail for killing my mother. Maybe there was justice after all.

* * *

Monday morning at eight o'clock the phone rang and I answered. Jake asked, "What are you doing in New Orleans?"

"I'm working as a musician. I'm making good money."

"Why did you run away, and when are you coming home? Yolanda and I have been worried sick about you. When we heard about your mother and father, we thought your disappearance had something to do with that. Did it?"

"I thought that I'd killed the bastard and that the police would be looking for me. I was scared, Jake. No, terrified."

"That's understandable, but you knew I'd be there for you. I would've taken care of everything. Surely you trust me. When are you coming home?"

From the way Amy had responded to the same question I wasn't sure I should level with Jake. But he'd been a wonderful friend and mentor. I had to be honest with him. Swallowing hard, I said, "I'm not coming back."

There was a short silence, and then he asked, "Are you going to finish high school there?"

"No, sir. I'm going to become a professional musician."

"You're only sixteen, Jamie. That's no life for someone your age. Besides you've got to get an education. High school dropouts don't do well in the modern world."

"Miss Frances always told me I could become an educated individual by reading. I'll continue to read, learn new things."

"She wouldn't approve of this, and you know it. Don't be a fool, Jamie. Come home."

My stomach burned and I shook my head, thinking, *There's no way I'll ever convince Jake that this is the right decision.* I didn't know what to do. I couldn't just hang up like Amy had done. I owed Jake better than that. Finally, I cleared my throat and said, "I've got to do this, Jake. If I don't make a go of it, I promise I'll come back to Round Rock and finish high school."

"That's a promise?"

"Yes, sir."

"You'll come home?"

I said, "Yes, sir," then replaced the receiver.

I sat in the overstuffed chair in our apartment and stared at the wall. I didn't know when I'd return to Round Rock. First, I had to see if I had what it took to be a star. I wanted to accumulate a bigger bankroll before starting out on a new venture. Over the past few weeks, I'd decided I was going country. I felt my guitar work and voice would get me there. Axelrod was correct. New Orleans bars were a trip to nowhere. I had big plans.

* * *

That night when I went to the bar, Sam waved me over. Motioning to a chair at his table, Sam said, "Have a seat, Luke, or should I call you, Jamie? Joy's been telling me a strange story about you. Is it true?"

I nodded. "Yeah. It's true. I'm sorry I deceived you. I thought I'd killed my father and the cops were after me. That's why I lied about my name. I'm really sorry, Sam. You've been really great to me. I wouldn't have done that if I hadn't thought I had to."

"Is that all you lied about?"

I just couldn't tell Sam the truth about my age. Number one, I was too young to be working in a bar and number two, I'd told Joy I was eighteen as well. She already didn't like the fact that she thought she was two years older than me. I was gripped with indecision.

Finally, I let out a deep breath, and said, "That's all. I just lied about my name. Nothing else."

Sam raised his eyebrows. "You're sure?"

"Yes, sir. I'm sure."

* * *

Things just kept getting better. Sometimes it made me nervous. I was taking home more than five hundred bucks a night, six nights a week. I couldn't believe I was raking in twelve grand a month. I paid half the rent and contributed to the grocery bill, but that left a lot over. I had a lot of money to put away. But, first I had to decide where to place it.

When I realized I wasn't wanted by the police, I'd called Nashville and ordered a birth certificate. I took a copy to the Social Security office on Poydras Street and applied for a card. Once I received it, I joined the AFM because Axelrod had said I should if I was going to be a professional musician.

With my new Social Security card, I'd started a savings account at the Chase Bank on Royal. By July, it contained a little over forty thousand dollars. I'd just deposited some cash and was headed out the door when the branch manager stopped me.

"Have you got a minute?" he asked.

Wondering if I'd done something wrong, I said, "Sure."

He motioned for me to sit across from his desk. I pulled out a chair.

"I've noticed that your savings account has grown considerably in the past few weeks. Are you aware that you're barely getting three percent interest?"

Actually, I'd not even considered it. The bank was just a safe place to hold my cash. It seemed better than the Mason jar I'd used before.

"Are there other alternatives?" I asked.

"Do you know anything about the stock market?"

I shook my head. "No, sir."

"You're obviously making a lot of money right now. The mistake most young people make is that they spend cash as quickly as they make it. You seem different. That tells me you need some guidance. We have a trust department that can help you get into the market. That's where the real money is made. Pick the right stocks, and you can double and triple your funds."

"Sounds good to me. Who do I talk to?"

He took a business card out of his desk drawer and handed it to me. "Mr. Flanagan is on vacation this week. When he gets back, I'll have him call you. Give me your phone number, please."

I scribbled our home phone number on the back of a deposit slip and left the bank. I felt excited. Now there was a real possibility that I could reach my goal of financial independence and someday start out on my own.

* * *

Since I'd been playing regularly at Sam's bar, I'd looked out over the crowd several times to see Axelrod in the audience. For some reason he always left just before I took a break. In the past week I'd gotten the idea there were other musicians showing up to hear me. I didn't quite know what to think of that.

One evening, during my last set, Axelrod walked in and stood in the back of the room. I finished my song and, looking over the audience's heads, said, "Axelrod, please don't leave. I want to talk to you."

The old man glanced at his watch and nodded.

We sat at the bar. Axelrod had bourbon and I sipped a Coke. "You're doing well, Luke. You're a fine musician. I still want you to join the AFM."

I realized that I'd not had a chance to tell Axelrod my real name. I felt I had to set the record straight.

"I've already joined the AFM. And, Axelrod, there's something I need to tell you. My name's not Luke. It's Jamie Lee Coleman. I know that seems strange, but I had to use an alias because I thought I was wanted by the police. That's all settled now, and I can tell people who I really am. I hope you'll forgive me."

Axelrod had a strange expression on his face, but a moment later he smiled. "Hell, son, don't nothing surprise this old man in this day and age. I'm really happy for you."

"How are your guys?"

"We've got a new gig. I couldn't deal with Triple J any longer. Fat bastard is losing it."

"I worry about Casey and Maggie," I said.

"They've both quit. I don't know where they are."

Axelrod grew silent and stared across the room. I could tell something was bothering him. I touched his arm and asked, "What's up?"

"I'm going to do something I know I shouldn't. I'm going to give you some advice."

"You know me. I'm always open to new ideas. I can take advice."

"Don't stay in this gig too long. It's okay for a while. Save some money, get a little more experience, but move on. You've got the makings of a star. Don't waste it in a lousy French Quarter bar. This whole damned city is corrupt as hell. The Mafia runs a lot of the bars on Bourbon Street and those they don't own outright they shake down the owners of the other bars for protection. And the police look the other way because a lot of them are on the take."

To say I was shocked and felt totally naïve would be an understatement. I shook my head and asked, "You think Sam pays protection?"

"I don't' know but I wouldn't be surprised. All I'm saying is get out while you can."

* * *

The following week I received a call from Mr. Flanagan at the bank. He asked me to come in for a consultation.

In his office, Mr. Flanagan said, "Mr. Coleman, I have a suggestion for you."

I shrugged. "Sure. What do you have in mind?"

"I'm a trust officer, not a broker. I'm more comfortable dealing with mutual funds and fixed-income annuities. According to Mr. Burch, you're interested in growing your funds rapidly. I think you should move your money to a full-service brokerage house."

I'd been half-expecting the conversation. Mr. Flanagan had never warmed up to me. For one thing, I think it bugged him that I was so young and pulling in so much cash. If he'd known how young I actually was, he'd probably have had a stroke.

"I assume you have a suggestion," I said.

"Paine Webber is a stable, old-line house. I can give you the name of an excellent broker."

"That sounds good to me. I really appreciate all you've done for me, Mr. Flanagan."

I'd learned that a little flattery goes a long way, particularly with bureaucrats. And I considered all accountants and bank officers to be bureaucrats. He cut me a cashier's check for fifty-five thousand dollars. Even at three percent interest, my continued deposits had added up quickly.

Mr. Flanagan gave me the name and telephone number for the Paine Webber broker. I called the gentleman the moment I got back to the apartment and set up an appointment for the following morning.

* * *

Mr. Abernathy met me at the door. He was a tall, cadaverous man with premature silky gray hair. He wore a Brooks Brothers suit, a white shirt, and a striped tie. The broker smiled as we shook hands.

"We're delighted to have you as a client," Mr. Abernathy said. "Jerome Flanagan hadn't mentioned how young you are. You've accumulated quite a nice nest egg. Let's make it grow together."

"That sounds good to me. I'll level with you, Mr. Abernathy. I'm in a hurry. I want to be in growth stocks. I like companies like Texas Instruments and IBM."

He laughed. "So does everyone."

"I'd like to learn all I can about investing in the market. Can you point me to some good books on the subject?"

"Of course. Once you get a feel for how things work, I think you'll find investing quite fascinating. Successful investors study companies carefully. You already have a good start if you've been studying annual reports. I assume that's how you learned about IBM and Texas Instruments."

"Yes, sir."

"Try to know something about the CEO and other officers as well as the makeup of the company's board of directors. I'll guide you, and as you gain more knowledge, you can help me pick your stocks."

"That sounds good to me. Thanks for your help," I said, taking the man's hand.

* * *

In October I'd been at Play It Again Sam for nine months. Sam was raking it in, and so was I. We'd changed my name from Luke Montgomery to Jamie Lee Coleman on the marquee outside the bar with no explanation. I thought it odd that people didn't seem to care what my name was. I'd set a goal of a hundred grand before I struck out on my own. I was getting close. Joy and I were tighter than ever.

I wasn't sure I could leave her, but I figured we could keep up by phone and we'd visit each other periodically.

She'd started working on her master's in September and only tended bar on Saturdays. She was at school all day, and I was gone until late at night. We still had fantastic lovemaking sessions. In fact, I was beginning to think I was in love. That thought both excited and scared the hell out of me.

I'd been working on my show but still hadn't come up with what I considered a good opening. I loved the way Mr. Cash walked out on stage and said, "Hello, I'm Johnny Cash."

I finally hit on it. That evening when I walked out on the stage, I strummed a few chords and did a quick boogie-woogie run. Then I smiled so broadly the audience could see my tonsils and said, "Well, I guess you know who I am or you wouldn't be here."

Then I'd play nonstop for an hour. I'd learned I could really stir up the crowd by stepping off the stage and walking to some old lady's chair and singing her a love song. They'd blush and finally cry, but they all ate it up.

During my break, young women would approach me and want their pictures taken with me. I'd place my arm around their shoulders and one of their friends would make a snapshot, the flash almost blinding me.

I had hotel keys slipped into my pocket by young and middle-aged women who'd wink and say things like, "You're so adorable. My panties are wet just looking at you."

I'd usually blush, and they'd double up with laughter. I often wondered what most of them would do if I'd indicated I was ready to accept their offer.

Since Joy only worked on Saturdays, she watched me like a hawk, but she knew me well enough not to be jealous. I think it turned her on that women found me attractive, and she wasn't above a little friendly ribbing.

I knew this because one night, she'd said, "Listen, big guy, just because those silly girls fawn all over you doesn't mean you're all that hot. Those broads get starry eyed at anything wearing pants."

Sam had figured out our situation simply by observing his daughter's demeanor when we were together. There was an obvious tenderness between us. We didn't try to hide our feelings. Sam never said a word to either of us. I suspected he wasn't too happy that Joy was involved with a musician, though he knew I was a straight arrow. He was impressed that I didn't drink or do drugs and that I managed to hold onto my money.

* * *

One night in late December, I finished my first set and took a break. A young fellow walked up and said, "Jamie, I'd like to talk to you for a minute."

He was about my height and looked to be in his early thirties. He wore jeans, a cowboy shirt, and boots. His hair was dark brown, wavy, and combed straight back from his forehead. His eyes looked like small dark pools of motor oil dripped onto a garage floor.

We sat at the bar, him with a beer and me with my Coke. He introduced himself by saying, "My name's Colt Walker. I'm putting together a country band and wondered if you'd like to be the lead singer."

I'd been thinking I was ready to move on. I hadn't quite decided how to do it. I didn't know a damn thing about Colt Walker, but figured I could find out one way or another.

"What's your background?" I asked.

"I'm a banjo picker. I've worked as a studio musician in Nashville for the past four years. Before that I toured with a couple of bands you wouldn't have heard of. I'm ready to take the next step."

"How did you hear about me?" I asked.

"One of my friends here in New Orleans told me you were the best guitar player he'd ever heard. After catching your show, I have to agree."

I had no contacts and didn't know the first thing about acquiring bookings. On the spur of the moment, I decided I'd join up with Colt Walker and try to learn the business.

"What're you paying?"

"The going rate, you know, scale. If we do well, I'll give everyone a bonus."

"I'm making three grand a week here," I said. "Scale doesn't sound too exciting."

Colt's eyes widened. I don't think he had a clue about how well I was doing. Seeing his shock, I said, "I've saved a bundle. I'm interested in learning the business, so I can afford to take a cut. I'll have to give Sam a month's notice."

We shook hands, and he said, "There's one more thing. I know and you know you're going to be a superstar. You'll eventually outgrow us. While you're with our band, just remember who's boss."

Chapter 14

When we got back to the apartment that night I closed the front door and locked it. Then turning to Joy, I said, "We need to talk for a few minutes."

"What about?"

She had a suspicious expression. I cleared my throat and said, "I signed on with a band tonight. I'll be traveling with them for the next few months."

Joy's face drained of color and then slapped me with all her might. Reeling from the blow, and in a state of shock, I asked, "Why'd you do that?"

"You signed on with a band without talking it over with me, you thoughtless shit. I can't believe this."

"Come on, Joy. You knew I'd eventually have to leave the bar. It's not like I'm going to abandoned you. I love you."

"You don't treat people you love like that. You've made a selfish and thoughtless decision without even considering my feelings. I can't believe this."

Then she spun around and stormed to the bedroom. The door slammed and I heard the lock latch. I stood there feeling like a jerk of the first degree. I'd never considered talking to Joy until after I'd made the deal with Colt. I felt really sorry for what I'd done and desperately wanted to make it up to her. I knocked on the bedroom door and said, "I'm sorry Joy. I don't know what I was thinking. may we talk about this?"

"Go away, asshole. Leave me alone."

"Please, Joy. Don't do this."

Silence.

I knew I'd made a mess of the situation and walked over to the couch. I took my shoes off and lay down. The overhead light was still on so I got up again and turned it off. I felt a sense of dread as I lay back down. Staring at the dark ceiling, I wondered how I might right things with Joy. Nothing came to mind.

One of the numerous neon lights on the street flickered off and on through the window and that irritated me. I lay awake most off the night. I finally fell asleep, I think, sometime around three in the morning.

I awakened when I heard Joy banging dishes around in the kitchen. Sitting up, I rubbed my eyes trying to clear my head. Slipping on my shoes, I stood and walked to the kitchen with a sense of dread.

"Joy, honey, I'm so sorry. Please forgive me. Let's try to patch this up. I love you so much it's killing me."

Silence.

"Come on, honey. We can work something out. *Please.*"

When she turned to face me I could see that her mascara had streaked down her cheeks. Her eyes were blood shot and swollen. My heart went out to her. Cautiously, I walked to where she stood and placed my arms around her. She buried her head in my shoulder and I could feel her body tremble.

I stroked her hair gently and whispered into her ear. "I realize now that I've made a terrible mistake. What I did was thoughtless and selfish. I was only thinking of myself and I know that wasn't right. When you love someone you have to take their feeling into account when you make decisions. When you're in a relationship you have to discuss major decisions. I've learned a lot from this experience. It'll never happen again."

Joy pulled back from my embrace and stared into my eyes. "I'll miss you so much. It scares the hell out of me that I won't see you again—ever."

"Don't believe that for a second. I'll always be there for you. I'll always love and protect you. I know we can work out something."

What we worked out was a compromise. I'd call from the road two or three times a week and try to visit as often as I could. It sounded reasonable at the time, but both of us were naïve. There was no way either of us could have understood the rigorous schedule the Walker Band would follow.

Sam was disappointed when I gave notice but wished me well. I agreed to stay through January. Joy and I had been able to keep the flame ignited in our relationship and I felt that things between us would become a stronger bond in the future. The day I left, Joy rode in the taxi with me to the Greyhound bus station. We held each other for a long time, then I kissed her and climbed the stairs. Looking out the window as the bus pulled away, I threw her a kiss and she returned it. I felt a deep burning sensation in my stomach and I wished I'd bought some Tums before I got on the bus.

I met Colt and the others in Houston the first week in February. He'd arranged a gig at a large dance hall in the Clear Lake area near NASA. He'd booked us into a Holiday Inn. Colt and his wife had a one-room suite, and each band member had a room to himself.

There were to be five of us in the band: Colt on banjo, his wife, Kelly, on fiddle, me as lead guitar, Butch Lee on rhythm guitar, and a guy named Mouse O'Brien on bass.

The morning after we'd all checked into the motel, Colt assembled the band in his suite for our first practice session. Playing with other musicians took a little getting used to because I'd always been a solo performer. The first practice session was a little tense. After two hours we were beginning to sound pretty good, though. Colt would start a run on the banjo, then I'd introduce the melody and the others would join in.

Kelly was an exceptional fiddler. She could make the fiddle sing with her powerful bow strokes. I figured she was in her mid-twenties. She reminded me a little of Amy because of her cinnamon hair and cream-colored skin. In high-heeled cowboy boots, she barely came to my shoulder. The thing I found most attractive was her infectious smile.

Butch was the oldest at forty-four. He looked like a guy who'd led a rough life. A heavy smoker, his face was deeply furrowed. He was great on rhythm guitar and kept us all in sync.

Mouse was a natural-born comic. He told one joke after another until our sides ached. A big man, he reminded me of Hoss Cartwright on the TV show *Bonanza*. He was incredible on the bass.

On the second day, Colt placed a tape recorder on the coffee table, and said, "Okay, y'all, let's get it right this time. We're going to listen to how we sound in one hour. Then we'll have some idea on the things we need to do to improve the situation." After the first hour of practice, Colt was pleased by how the band sounded. "That's pretty good, y'all, but I want it to be perfect. Let's keep at it till lunch and then we'll take a break."

Colt was molding us into a team. We ate together and traveled together. Colt paid all our expenses with his own Visa card. He'd bought a used Ford van the week before to haul the band from one gig to another.

The five of us rolled up to the dance hall in the van right at seven o'clock. It was a cavernous building that looked like a converted warehouse. The stage was elevated about four feet off the floor. Two long bars, one on either side of the room, served tap and bottled beer. No hard liquor. There were six bartenders, all gorgeous young women, at each bar. Tables were scattered haphazardly around the vast room, and the dance floor could hold thirty couples. We wore western-cut jeans, fancy shirts, cowboy boots, and black cowboy hats with feathered hatbands. Kelly kept her long hair in a ponytail.

Around nine o'clock on Friday evening, we walked out on stage for the first time as a band. The applause was tepid, to say the least. After all, we were an unknown quantity. Colt had been around enough to be relaxed, but my palms were wet and my mouth dry.

Colt had a good stage presence. He stepped up to the microphone and addressed the audience with confidence. He said, "Howdy, folks, I'm Colt Walker. Y'all ready for a little two-stepping?"

The response was a roaring, "Yes!"

Colt picked a Hank Williams piece on his banjo, and Kelly joined in on her fiddle. I kept rhythm with Butch by playing chord progressions. About halfway through the song, I stepped up and picked out the melody.

We played for forty-five minutes before taking our first break. The crowd was rowdy but rewarded us with loud applause after each song. Colt beamed from ear to ear as we left the stage and went to our dressing room.

"Good job. Y'all did great out there," he said.

Kelly went for beers while we discussed our next set. She and one of the bartenders brought us all one. I shocked them when I said, "Thanks, but I don't drink."

Butch said, "I reckon you do smoke a little weed."

I shook my head.

Kelly laughed. "You hired a damn teetotaler, Colt. I guess we can make him our sober designated driver."

While the rest of the band members sat in the dressing room and guzzled beer, I stepped out and went to one of the bars. Grinning, I said, "You got a Coke?"

The young bartender looked at me with a frown and said, "Well, yeah, I reckon so. Want diet or regular?"

"Diet would be fine."

"You're right good on that guitar, fellow. You ain't bad looking either. You got plans after your last set?"

I laughed. "Yeah. I've got plans. Mostly a girlfriend back home. But if I didn't, I'd sure like to take you out on a date."

She shooed me on and went back to work.

Back onstage, we dove right into a series of well-known country songs. After the first five, I stepped up front and started singing. What happened next shocked me as much as anyone in the band. All the couples stopped dancing and stared at the stage. They didn't move until I finished, and then they erupted with clapping and boot stomping. I stood there with my mouth open like the village idiot.

We did all instrumentals for the rest of the set, and I kept my mouth shut. I didn't want the other band members to be jealous. The crowd kept bringing us back for encores, and when we finally walked off the stage for the last time, the manager came over and congratulated us. He told Colt, "You and your band are welcome to come back anytime you want. Y'all were great tonight."

Colt was grinning as we piled into the van for the ride back to the Holiday Inn. "I'm so happy, I could bust a gut. Y'all were great out there. Hell, we've got us one fine damn band. Let's celebrate. I'm buying."

Later we congregated in Colt and Kelly's room to rehash the evening's performance. They were guzzling beer and smoking weed. The air was heavy with the sweet marijuana aroma, and it made me a little dizzy. It reminded me of my first sexual experience with

Casey. I turned away from my colleagues because that thought produced a bulge in the crotch of my jeans.

Kelly had pulled off her boots and was sitting propped up on their king-size bed facing the rest of us. Her eyes were a little glazed, and her infectious smile had turned into more of a leer. The top button of her cowboy shirt was undone, and her breasts strained against her black bra. I tried not to notice, but she caught me staring. Slowly and deliberately, she unlatched the second button and shifted her weight so her tits almost fell out. Colt was oblivious to all this. I looked away. I had no intention of messing with the boss's wife.

Butch had pulled me to one side that first day and told me in a low voice, "Watch out for Colt. He's got a mean streak, and he doesn't want anyone messing with Kelly. And he carries a small snub-nosed .38 in his hip pocket."

They were still partying around one o'clock in the morning when I went to my room. I was dead tired and couldn't wait to fall into bed. I didn't even read myself to sleep. I just passed out.

I didn't awaken until ten the next morning. I had a mild headache from inhaling their weed but otherwise felt great. After a breakfast of bacon and scrambled eggs, I went back to my room and practiced my guitar for about an hour.

There was a knock on my door, and when I opened it, Kelly stood smiling at me. Her shirt was properly buttoned, and her hair was in her usual ponytail. She said, "Colt wants to know if you can be ready to leave in thirty minutes."

"Sure. I travel light."

She just stood there smiling at me. Neither of us said a word. Finally, I asked, "Is there something I can do for you, Kelly?"

She winked at me and said, "Maybe." Then she turned and left. As she walked away in her tight jeans, I thought, *that's one round ass*.

* * *

We piled into the van and headed for I-45 North. Colt drove and Kelly sat in the passenger seat. Butch, Mouse, and I were squeezed together in the second row. Our luggage and instruments were assigned to the back.

It was a cool day and cloudless. I was delighted that Houston and New Orleans had similar weather conditions. I had to admit I liked the warmer weather of the Gulf over the mountains of East Tennessee. Round Rock was probably buried in three inches of snow.

Colt had lined up a gig in Fort Worth for that evening. Kelly was turned in her seat facing the three of us. She said, "Colt showed me the songs he wants to play tonight and I think he's nuts." Then she handed a hand-written list to Mouse.

Mouse glanced at it and then handed it back to Kelly. "We ain't getting between you two. Besides, Colt's the boss."

She flushed and turned back toward the windshield. Colt snickered, and she poked him in the ribs.

I'd picked up a paperback novel at a Walgreens and pulled it out. Turning to the page I'd marked, I started reading.

Butch asked, "How can you do that? I get sick as a dog if I try to read in a moving car."

I shrugged. "Doesn't bother me."

Kelly turned around again and said, "You're a odd duck, Jamie. You're not like any guitar player I've ever met."

Colt said, "Turn around, Kelly, and lay off Jamie. Mind your own damn business."

"You telling me what I can and can't do?"

"Yeah."

She crossed her arms and slumped in her seat. She didn't say a word for the next hundred miles.

Around noon, we took a Corsicana exit and stopped for lunch at a McDonald's. Kelly didn't speak to us as we ate. We all ordered a

Big Mac. Colt was doing a good job ignoring Kelly. The whole scene made me uncomfortable.

Back in the van, Colt said, "I think we should let Jamie do some more solos. That was a fantastic response he got last night. It'll help our image."

Butch and Mouse shrugged. Kelly nodded and said, "I want to do a duet with Jamie. Like Porter Wagoner and Dolly Parton."

Colt laughed. "You ain't no Dolly Parton, darlin'. But that's not a bad idea. What do you think, Jamie?"

"Suits me."

Soon it was quiet in the van. Kelly had placed her head against the door, obviously trying to sleep. Mouse and Butch stared ahead in a bored trance.

I racked my brain trying to think of a song that would lend itself to a duet featuring a man and a woman. I thought it should be funny and resemble some sort of banter between the two. Laying my head on the back of the seat, I closed my eyes and continued to think, but I couldn't come up with anything.

I realized that plenty of duets were out there. Loretta Lynn and Conway Twitty sang together, as did Tammy Wynette and George Jones. When I couldn't pinpoint a song that I thought would be good for Kelly and me, I decided to write my own. I worked it out in my head as we continued up the interstate.

By the time we arrived in Fort Worth, I had the lyrics pretty well figured out and the melody set. I called it "Mountain Love." In my room, I picked out the tune until I was satisfied. Then I called Colt's room and asked them to join me for a practice session.

The basic premise of the song was two young lovers arguing about which one loved the other the most. Kelly thought it was great, and I was pleased that she had a fine voice. There was no country twang.

Colt said, "You need to contact BMI in Nashville and license this song a soon as you can."

I shrugged and asked, "What's BMI?"

"They handle royalties for artists. It's very important to hook up with them. I've got their phone number and address. I'm amazed that you haven't heard of BMI."

"I'm still a little new to the business, Colt. I'll catch on to everything eventually, and when I do, all hell's going to break loose."

* * *

When Kelly and I did our duet that evening, it brought down the house. We always had two microphones on stage. I stood at one, and she was at the other. She'd place her hands on her hips and flip her ponytail around as we sang our lovers' quarrel. I had to admit, she looked damn cute. When we finished, the crowd went wild.

Perspiration glistened on Kelly's forehead as we took our bows. She was grinning, and her pale face was flushed. After the applause died down, she grabbed me, gave me a bear hug, and planted a kiss on my lips. Out of the corner of my eye I could see a scowl on Colt's face. When Kelly finally backed off, I glanced at Colt and shrugged.

Colt flew into a fast blue-grass piece, and we all joined in. Kelly stayed on her side of the stage, and I tried not to look in her direction.

We played well that evening, and I was becoming more accustomed to performing with others. I did three solo songs and received a standing ovation after each. I was becoming more relaxed on stage and knew I'd eventually venture out on my own, but I realized I still had a lot to learn about the business.

Back at the motel, I fell into bed around one o'clock as usual. I read for about thirty minutes before turning off the bedside lamp.

Sometime in the night, I felt the bed tilt. The next thing I knew I felt a body crawl on top of me. I could smell a familiar perfume and realized that it was Kelly in my bed smothering me with kisses. I rolled over and turned on the light. She was naked, her hair disheveled, her lipstick smeared. She looked up at me with a big grin on her face and said, "Well hello, handsome. I've got a little present for you—me."

I looked at her with disbelief. "How did you get in here?"

"I stole your other key."

"Where's Colt?"

"He's knee-walking drunk in our room. Don't worry about him. Let's do it."

I eased her off me and covered her with the bedclothes. "Kelly, I like you a lot, but you're Colt's wife. He might shoot us both. When you sober up, you'll agree."

Then she passed out. She lay there on her back, her eyes closed, her huge breasts hanging off each side of her chest.

I thought, *Now what?* My boss's wife lay beside me in her birthday suit, and her jealous husband carried a damn pistol in his hip pocket. I didn't know where her clothes were. She must have walked down the hall naked. How in the hell was I going to get her back to her room?

I grabbed her shoulder and shook her. "Kelly, wake up. For God's sake, wake up, girl. This isn't a good idea. Where are your clothes? Kelly, damn-it, wake up."

I realized there was no way to wake her. She was out cold. Colt would never believe me when I told him what'd happened. And I wouldn't blame him. I lay there trying to figure out what to do.

Finally, I went to the closet and removed an extra blanket I found there. Then I wrapped it around Kelly's nude body. I'll admit that I did make an approving study of her fine tits, flat stomach, and round ass. Under different circumstances, I'd have enjoyed making love to her.

I dressed, and she didn't stir as I lifted her into my arms. I carried her back to her room, placed her on the floor outside the door, and propped her against the wall. I hoped that she'd have no memory of coming to my room, and that she and Colt would figure she'd wandered out into the hall in a drunken stupor.

Needless to say, I didn't sleep well the rest of the night. I kept dreaming I was climbing a hill. I'd lose my footing and go careening back the way I'd come. Between dreams, I wondered what Dr. Freud would've thought.

When we assembled for breakfast at ten o'clock that morning, I was the only one without a massive hangover. Kelly's eyes were bloodshot, and she could barely hold her head up. She kept looking at me as if there was something she wanted to say and couldn't think of it. The three men had not bothered to shave, dark stubble covering their faces.

Colt was the first to speak. Glancing at me, he said, "You drive today, Jamie. I ain't up to it."

We had to be in Oklahoma City that evening, or we'd have stayed an extra night in Fort Worth so everyone could sober up.

I was in a quandary. Living with Miss Frances and then Jake, I'd never learned to drive. How could I explain that to Colt? He'd think I was nuts. The van had an automatic transmission so I wouldn't have to worry about shifting gears. I figured that was the hardest part of driving. And, of course, there was one more problem: I had no license.

It wasn't easy, but an hour later I was able to herd them into the van. Colt, Kelly, and Butch sat in back, and Mouse rode up front with me. I'd watched Colt, so I had a working knowledge of what to do.

It would have been better if I'd had a smaller vehicle to learn on. I almost sideswiped the car next to us as I backed out of the parking space. Then I ran over the curb while exiting the lot. My companions didn't stir. They were in some parallel universe.

We stopped in Ardmore, Oklahoma, so everyone could take a bathroom break and tank up on coffee. I sipped on my Styrofoam cup and thought of how much I missed the chicory brew of New Orleans. I'd tried to call Joy from Fort Worth a couple of times but couldn't catch her at the apartment.

The schedule Colt had laid out for us was rigorous, to say the least. It didn't look like we'd have a break for several months. I had no idea when I could get back to New Orleans to see Joy. My encounter with Kelly had made me horny as hell, and I desperately wanted to make love to Joy.

Kelly was the first to come alive. I watched her in the rearview mirror. When she saw my eyes fixed on hers, she smiled. Then she winked and blew me a kiss. Thank goodness, Colt was sound asleep. I was beginning to worry that I wouldn't be able to manage the situation. As much as I wanted to walk the straight and narrow, I had to admit Kelly turned me on. And I had the distinct impression she knew it. Did she remember coming to my room naked as a jaybird?

We checked into yet another Holiday Inn right after lunch. Colt suggested everyone take a nap so we'd be fresh for the evening show. I hadn't been hung over, but the stress of driving for the first time in my life had made me weary. After I'd checked into my room, I closed the blinds and pulled off my boots. Then I dropped onto the bed fully clothed and fell sound asleep. I woke up around four and took a quick shower.

Afterward, I went to the restaurant for a cup of coffee and passed the indoor swimming pool. Glancing in, I saw Kelly climb out of the water, a brief bikini clinging to her wet body. I stood and watched her dry off, biting my lower lip in an attempt to control my lust. I had to get laid soon, or I might make a terrible mistake.

She walked out of the pool area just as I wandered by. Her skin was covered with goose-bumps, and she shivered a little as she wrapped the towel around her shoulders. When she saw me, her eyes lit up and she slipped her arm in mine. "Hi, handsome," she said. "Walk me back to my room."

My heart was pounding and I could feel my groin tighten. She looked so damned sexy I thought I'd scream. She tightened her grip on my arm and said, "Colt's passed out cold. Want to make a quick stop at your room?"

"Well, yes, that would be swell, but not a good idea, Kelly. I admit you turn me on, and I'd love to have sex with you. But you know where that would lead. We'd both be in a cemetery somewhere."

"Don't be a chicken. Colt never has to know. You'd have the time of your life."

"I believe you. I just can't do it."

By this time we were at the door to her room. We stood there for a moment staring at each other, and finally, she slipped the card into the lock and opened the door. Before walking in, she pinched me on the butt and smiled.

That night we played to an appreciative crowd in another dance hall. Kelly and I brought the house down again with our duet. She teased me with her body all through the song. Colt had to be aware of the sexual tension between Kelly and me. Every time I glanced Colt's way, my boss was scowling. I caught Butch looking at me with raised eyebrows.

I've got to get this situation under control, I thought. *My damn career is going to get cut short before it starts if I don't.*

Chapter 15

The following day we left for Kansas City, Missouri. This time we weren't playing a dance hall. Colt had arranged a gig at a theater downtown. It had been an old movie house at one time and was now used mostly for touring Broadway shows. On this evening, Colt's agent had booked us with a band called the Mississippi Travelers. They were beginning to sell a respectable number of records and were an up-and-coming group. Our band was to open for them.

I was delighted that we'd have a full day of rest before performing. In the meantime I desperately needed to get to a bookstore. For once we didn't have to stay in a motel because the promoters had booked rooms at the Baker Hotel in the center of the city. It was an old establishment but had been completely renovated. The rooms were large and the bathtubs huge. The first thing I did was fill mine to the top and soak for thirty minutes.

We were to gather in the main dining room at seven o'clock for dinner. I dressed and went looking for a bookstore. I found a small, independent one a block from the hotel. I bought two novels and a biography of Booker T. Washington.

Back in the room, I finally made contact with Joy. She'd just walked into the apartment.

"I've been trying to call you for days," I said. "How are you, girl? Damn I've missed you."

"I've missed you, too, sweetie. It's so lonesome here it's killing me. If I didn't have school to keep me busy, I don't think I could stand it."

We talked for thirty minutes. I shuddered to think what the charges would be. I'd have to reimburse Colt because long-distance calls weren't part of our deal.

The hotel restaurant was elegant. Frankly, our crew seemed a little out of place except for Kelly. She looked ravishing. She'd done her hair in a French twist with a silver comb holding it in place. For the first time since I'd known her, she wore a dress. The neckline was low-cut, exposing the tops of her generous breasts. I tried not to stare, but I couldn't help myself. She caught me staring at her, and a sly smile formed on her face. Neither of us had mentioned the episode in my motel room. I was convinced she had no memory of anything that'd transpired that night. I hoped it stayed that way.

The men ordered steaks, but Kelly settled for fresh Alaskan salmon. They drank beer and I had my usual.

"What're you folks doing tomorrow?" I asked since we had the whole day free.

Kelly said, "I'm going to sleep late and have breakfast in bed. Then I'll figure out the rest of the day."

"I'll be with what's her name," Cole said with a grin, pointing at his wife.

Mouse and Butch didn't bother to respond.

"I'm going to read and practice my guitar," I said. "I bought three new books today, and I can't wait to get at them."

"Why do you read so much?" Kelly asked. "I've never known anyone who kept his nose in a book like you do."

"For one thing it passes the time, but I read mostly to learn new things."

"I've learned all I want to know," she said.

That was one of the things I loved about Joy. She was filled with intellectual curiosity. And she loved to read almost as much as I did. I thought I'd be bored as hell if I was hooked up with an air-head. I enjoyed the company of smart, strong women. I assumed that had to do with my association with Miss Frances. To say she was a strong woman would be an understatement.

* * *

We were scheduled for an eight o'clock start and were to play for about forty-five minutes to warm up the audience. Colt had told us it was a great opportunity. I wasn't so sure. We played it very straight that evening. Kelly and I didn't do our duet, which I thought was a mistake.

The Mississippi Travelers were fantastic. They had a tremendous stage presence and incredible energy. They harmonized beautifully, their voices blending as one. I stood in the wings and watched how they played the audience. The rest of our group remained in the dressing room where they could hear but not see what was going on.

After the show, I flagged down the leader of the group, Wally Simpson, as he left the stage. Extending my hand, I said, "Y'all were great out there. I can't believe how well you harmonize."

"Thanks. Like anything else, it takes a lot of practice. Y'all have a pretty good sound yourselves."

"We're just getting started. You got a minute?"

"Sure."

"Mind if I ask you a few questions?"

"Shoot."

"Someday I want to be out on my own. A solo act. Can you give me some pointers on how to get moving fast? Y'all have climbed the charts at rocket speed. How'd you manage that?"

Wally laughed. "It ain't rocket science to spin a pun. It's the deejays. Those guys are the secrete to everything. Get them on your side and it's all downhill after that."

"How do I manage that?"

"Payola is illegal. Don't ever forget that one. Hell, it's simple. Make the rounds, introduce yourself, and be nice to the guys."

"Go all over the country? Is that what you're saying?"

"No. Just start with the ones in Nashville. They have a big convention there once a year and you can schmooze the others then. Look, I've got to get moving. Good luck, Jamie. I think you're going to make it big. Just don't let it go to your head. There's always someone in the wings ready to make you a has-been."

I said, "Thanks, Wally, I won't forget that one."

Back at the hotel, we congregated in the Walkers' room and discussed our next gig. It was in Bakersfield, California, the following Saturday. The engagement after that was to be in Reno, Nevada. It wasn't Vegas, but it was close. Colt hoped to parlay that gig to one on the Strip. We were to stay in Reno for six weeks, the longest we had stayed in one place.

As we headed back to our own rooms, I pulled Colt aside and asked, "It'll take you guys at least three days to make the drive to Bakersfield. I need to make a quick trip to New Orleans. If I fly, I can meet y'all there. That okay with you?"

"Yeah. Just make sure you get there by the time we do. You need some cash?"

"I'm okay. I'll pick up my check when we get to Bakersfield."

I booked an American Airlines flight as soon as I'd ended my call to Joy. I was excited at the thought of seeing her. And I needed some lovemaking.

We said good-bye the following morning. Kelly grabbed me around the waist and pulled me to her. I was terrified she'd kiss me on the lips, but she simply gave me a peck on the cheek.

"I'm going to miss you, big guy. Don't do anything I wouldn't do," she said with a wicked smile.

I shook hands with the guys and said, "Y'all drive careful, now. Please get there in one piece. I don't want to go looking for a new job." Then I waved them off and took a taxi to the airport.

* * *

Joy met me at the gate. Her hair was in a ponytail, and she wore jeans and high-heeled pumps. She looked super. When she saw me, her face lit up like neon. She rushed into my arms and I hugged her. She felt light as I lifted her off her feet.

"I've missed you, sweetie," I said.

"I've missed you, too. Let's go home. I need you."

She'd borrowed her dad's Mustang convertible and had the top down. It was a balmy evening, a full moon hanging over scattered clouds. I placed my overnight bag and guitar on the backseat and climbed behind the wheel.

"I thought you didn't know how to drive," she said.

"It's one of many things I've learned in the last few weeks."

She slid into the passenger seat, and I drove us out of the parking lot. The wind whipped her ponytail as the car picked up speed. She placed her hand on my thigh and gave it a squeeze. The radio was tuned to a country station.

"I didn't think you liked country," I said.

"I put it there just for you."

"How's Sam?"

"Excited you're going to be here for three days. He thinks he can talk you into doing a few shows."

"He might if you let me out of bed long enough."

"I may keep you in bed the whole time," she said with a grin.

At the apartment, I followed her up the stairs and patted her beautiful derriere with my free hand. As soon as the door swung shut, clothes were dropped on the floor like a trail of crumbs leading to her king-sized bed. By the time she pulled back the covers, we were both naked.

There was no foreplay the first time. It was over in a matter of minutes. We lay in each other's arms afterward and just held on.

We awoke at some point in the night and spent a long and joyous time exploring each other's bodies. I remembered every fold and crease of hers and softly kissed every one.

The next morning we went to the Central Grocery for croissants and coffee. Then we held hands and walked along the levee.

"How do you like being on the road?" she asked.

"It's okay. I enjoy the music and the crowds. Staying in a strange hotel or motel every night isn't much fun."

She squeezed my hand and pulled me around to face her. "Have you behaved yourself?"

"Straight arrow, that's me."

"No groping the groupies?"

I shook my head. I didn't mention the fact that I lusted after my boss's wife.

* * *

We stopped in to see Sam around two o'clock and had a hamburger. The first thing he said was, "I hope you brought your guitar."

I nodded. There was nothing in my agreement with Colt that said I couldn't do a gig on my own if we didn't have an engagement. I thought it would be fun to perform solo again.

"I've got a jazz trio playing the bar, but you can do a show before or after them if that's okay."

"Not a problem. You are going to pay me?"

He raised his eyebrows. "You had to ask that question?"

Joy and I had dinner at the Court of Two Sisters for old time's sake. We'd fallen into our old, comfortable relationship. It was as if we'd never been apart.

"How's school going?" I asked as we finished our meal.

"Great. I like it so much I may go for a doctorate."

"Is Sam willing to foot the bill?"

She nodded.

"If not, I will."

Joy took my hand in hers and said, "You're so sweet. It's no wonder I love you so much."

That was the first time she'd ever said she loved me. I guessed it had been an unspoken acknowledgment between us. We'd just assumed we loved each other. As I thought of it, I knew I did love Joy.

But where would that love lead us? She was consumed by school, and I was an itinerant musician. I'd just barely turned seventeen, and she was six years older than me. How would that work?

I felt confused and irritable. Joy sensed my mood and asked, "What's wrong?"

I shook my head. "Nothing."

"Be honest with me."

I took a deep breath and held her hand. "I feel a little claustrophobic. I love you, but I don't know where it's going to lead us."

"It doesn't have to lead us anywhere right now. Let's just enjoy each other. I'm not pushing you to marry me for God's sake. All I said was I love you."

She'd made me feel a little more than foolish. I felt my face flush and wished I'd kept my mouth shut.

"Forget I said anything," I said.

"Yeah, right."

I paid the bill, and we started out for her father's bar. I looked Joy's way and saw that her lips were pressed into a thin line, her jaw tense.

"I'm sorry," I said. "You know I love you."

When she didn't answer, I grabbed her arm and spun her around to face me. Then I pulled her to me and kissed her hard on the lips.

She pulled away, turned, and started up the sidewalk at a furious pace. I had to run to catch her. "Damnit, Joy, stop this! We only have a few days together. We shouldn't be fighting."

Joy stopped dead in her tracks and turned to face me. She shrugged her shoulders and said, "You're right. I know you love me. We couldn't get married now even if we wanted to."

Then she slipped into my arms and kissed me on the lips. We held each other for several minutes, ignoring the stares of people walking past us.

"I've missed you so much it's killing me," I said. "I dread leaving you again."

"I don't want you to leave either, but you have a job. Somehow we'll get through this," Joy said. "Come on. We need to get to the bar."

When we arrived at Play It Again Sam's, we learned the jazz trio wouldn't start until nine o'clock. Glancing at my watch, I saw that it was eight. Should I do a show now or wait for their break? As if she could read my mind, Joy said, "Why don't you go on before the trio?"

The place was packed. I found Sam at the bar and said, "I'll go on now if you want me to."

"You got it," he said, getting off the stool.

He climbed onto the small stage and announced, "Ladies and gentlemen, we have a special surprise for you this evening. I've asked Jamie Lee Coleman to entertain you before our jazz trio begins their gig."

I'd unzipped the canvas cover and removed my guitar while Sam was talking. I eased the strap over my neck and stepped onto the stage. Everything seemed familiar and I shouldn't have been nervous, but I hadn't performed solo since I'd left and my mouth was a little dry. This was a crowd of tourists, and they didn't know me from Adam. They continued to talk as I strummed a few chords.

The boogie-woogie introduction I'd used before had always gotten a crowd's attention. I flew into it with all I had. Slowly, from the front of the room to the back, people began to grow quiet. As soon as I had their attention, I did a series of Patsy Cline songs I'd memorized when I was a kid listening to her on my crystal radio.

I played for about forty-five minutes, took three encores, and left the stage. Sam and Joy were waiting for me at the bar.

"You haven't lost your touch," Sam said. "If anything, I think your voice is stronger."

Joy grabbed my arm and started walking me toward the door. "Let's go, handsome. I don't want these women fawning over you," she said.

"May I get my guitar cover?"

We were in bed by nine thirty, and as Joy turned off the bedside lamp, she said, "Let's borrow Sam's car and drive over to Gulfport tomorrow. It's a nice trip along the water. We can have lunch and come home."

"Sounds good to me, " I said and then pulled Joy to me. I kissed her passionately as I cupped her breast in my hand. Then the covers were thrown off.

* * *

We left around ten o'clock the following morning. Joy drove. It was a clear day, and the radio announcer stated the temperature was eighty-eight degrees. Joy had a scarf tied under her chin, and I'd put on a Saints baseball cap. For once my guitar wasn't in the backseat.

Joy was a good driver and I felt safe with her. She didn't speed or cut in front of other cars. The road was a two-lane blacktop that ran right along the Gulf. I gazed out at the water to see several sailboats on the horizon. I wondered what it would be like to sail. The radio was tuned to a classical station, and Beethoven's Ninth Symphony blared from the car's stereo.

Completely relaxed, I closed my eyes and lay my head against the headrest. I felt happy to be alive and with Joy. As we sped along, I wondered how Colt and the gang were doing on their road trip. How far had they gotten? Were they in Arizona yet?

Suddenly, my ears were filled with the screeching of tires. It was so loud it drowned out everything else, the road noise and the symphony. I opened my eyes and sat up just in time to see an eighteen-wheeler slam head-on into our car.

When I opened my eyes again, I realized I was lying on the asphalt near the curb. All I could see was clear sky. I didn't hurt, but I did feel a little groggy. I tried to turn over so I could get up, but I couldn't move. It was if my back was glued to the road. Then out of curiosity, I tried to wiggle my toes. They simply didn't respond. I couldn't move my arms either. I tried again. Nothing.

It came down on me like an avalanche. I'd broken my neck and was paralyzed. I heard doors slamming and sirens in the distance. Several people walked over to look at me, and one man knelt beside me.

"You okay, fellow?" he asked.

"No. I think I have a broken neck. Please don't try to move me. Let the EMS do it. How is the woman who was driving our car?"

"I don't know."

Minutes later, I heard two sirens come to an abrupt halt and more doors slamming. I looked up to see a policeman and a medical tech. "How's the driver?" I asked.

The policeman shook his head. "She didn't make it. I'm sorry."

I hadn't thought it could get any worse until he uttered those words. The EMS splinted my neck and he and his partner placed me on a stretcher. I tried to look at the car as they carried me by it, but I couldn't move. Tears streamed down my cheeks.

The ride to Charity Hospital was a nightmare. All I could think of was lying paralyzed in a ward somewhere the rest of my life. I'd lost Joy. I'd lost my music. I'd lost everything. At that moment I realized that I'd rather be dead.

The emergency room resident took one look at me and placed a stat call to the neurosurgical resident. He was there in a matter of minutes. After examining me, he said, "I've got to get some X-rays of your neck. Then I'm taking you to the OR. We've got to move fast if we're going to get you decompressed and stabilized. Is there anyone with you?"

"No."

"You have family here?"

"No."

"How old are you?"

"Seventeen."

"We've got to operate. Do you understand?"

"Yes."

I couldn't sign a consent form because I was a quadriplegic, so the doctor asked a nurse to witness me agreeing to the surgery.

It didn't take long to do the X-rays, and I was in the OR suite within minutes. Nurses and doctors scurried around the room as the orderlies carefully transferred me from the wheeled gurney to the operating table. Everyone was masked so I couldn't tell which one was the doctor who'd examined me in the ER. A woman placed a tourniquet around my upper arm and I felt a needle stick in one of my veins. Then I lost consciousness.

I awoke in the recovery room, shaking like a leaf. I'd never been so cold in my life. Noticing that I'd awakened, a nurse came to my bed and covered me with two blankets.

"They dropped your temperature during the surgery. I'll get you warmed up in a few minutes. How do you feel?"

I felt groggy and disheartened. I still couldn't move my arms and legs. I stared into her brown eyes and said, "I still can't move anything."

Just then the doctor walked up and said, "Don't worry. Your cord wasn't severed, just contused. Once the swelling goes down, I think you're going to be fine. You'll be in a halo for several months, though. I'd guess about three all together."

I had no idea what a halo was. All I cared about was a full recovery. I heard Sam's voice in the background. "I want to see him now. I don't give a damn when visiting hours are!" he yelled.

Sam approached the bed and asked, "How are you, Jamie?"

"Tell me about Joy," I said.

Tears flooded his eyes. "She died instantly. You were thrown from the car."

"What happened? I can't remember anything."

"The eighteen-wheeler crossed the center lane. The police don't know why. The driver's dead."

Chapter 16

The doctors planned to keep me in the Neuro-intensive Care Unit for three of four days. On the day after my surgery, a woman came to my bed and said, "Good morning, Mr. Coleman. Are your parents coming in later today?"

I grimaced and squinted at the over-head light. "My mother's dead, and my sorry ass father is going to rot in prison for the rest of his life. What do you want?"

The woman looked to be in her mid-fifties and had gray hair pulled into a tight bun at the nape of her neck. She wore thick horn-rimmed glasses on a long narrow nose. She took a deep breath. "I'm Mrs. Labadie from the business office. I noticed that you don't have any health insurance. How do you plan to pay your bill?"

"I'm good for it."

"Do you have a job?"

"Yes, I have a job."

"Here in New Orleans?"

"No. I'm a musician. I travel with a band."

"This could be quite expensive, Mr. Coleman. Is there anyone who could help you with the bill?"

I sighed. "Look, lady. I'm good for it. I've got money. I'll write you a damned check when the doc lets me out of this place."

Mrs. Labadie shrugged. "Okay. I hope you make a quick recovery."

As she walked away, I wondered how much my bill would be. What I didn't realize at the time was that my hospital and rehab bill would nearly deplete my funds.

The doctors were giving me intravenous treatments with steroids. They said it helped reduce the swelling. It must have helped because feeling slowly returned to my arms and legs, then movement. That did make me feel better. At least I thought I might actually walk again. Being flat on my back was beginning to make me stir crazy and just a little claustrophobic.

I'd learned what a halo was: a device anchored into my skull and attached to my chest. It kept my neck from moving. I'd have to wear it for about three months if everything went well. The pins that held it to my skull went through the skin and had to be cleaned several times a day to prevent infection. I kept wondering who would do that for me once I was discharged from the hospital.

I still hadn't come to grips with the fact that Joy was dead. I simply couldn't believe it. I could not get her out of my mind. I kept going over the trip along the Gulf before we had the wreck. Each time I'd visualize Joy's face I would have a sharp pain in my chest. I was convinced I was suffering from a heart attack. I even wished I would have a heart attack and die. I had no desire to live. I wanted to die.

Sam, God love him, came to see me every day. I don't think I'd have made it without him. I could tell from his drawn features each time he came to visit that he was battling his own demons. I knew he missed his daughter as much as I did.

The accident had been written up in the newspaper. When I was finally moved to a room, Axelrod and Casey came to see me.

When Casey walked into the room and saw me, she started to cry. "Oh, Jamie, darlin', I'm so sorry about Joy. And I hate it that you have to wear that thing on your head. How long you got to do that?"

I glanced at Axelrod, who had a stricken look on his face but hadn't said a word.

"Doc says three months or so. I don't know what that means."

"I'll look after you, honey, after you get out of this place. Whatever you need, I'll get for you. Anything."

Axelrod nodded and said, "You name it, Jamie. We'll take care of it."

I started laughing. "I don't know what I'd do without you two. You've always been great friends. I'm not sure I deserve you."

Casey walked over to the bed and gave me a gentle hug. "I'm a little afraid to hug too tight, honey. We'll go now. Me and Axelrod just wanted you to know we're here for you."

"Please come back when I feel a little better. I'd like to know what's going on with both of you," I said with a grin.

* * *

After four days in the neuro-unit I was transferred to a semi-private room. It held two hospital beds side by side. There was a man who looked to be in his mid-fifties in the other bed. He stared at me when the orderlies wheeled me into the room but didn't say anything. The television was tuned to a soap opera and the sound was muted. Once the orderlies transferred me to my bed they elevated the head and left.

I lay there trying desperately to think through how I was going to deal with all the new challenges in my life. At lunch on that day I was hit with the first of many of them. The nurse came in and propped my head up with a pillow. She had brought a tray of food in with her and placed it on a table next to my bed. Then she began to feed me like a damned baby. The man in the other bed stared at me and then looked away. After about fifteen minutes the nurse took the tray away and left. A few minutes later another nurse walked in and went to the man in the next bed and pulled the covers back exposing a tube extending out of his abdomen. The tube was folded over at the end and wrapped with a rubber band. She took the rubber band off and placed large syringe into the opening of the tube. The syringe was filled yellow liquid. After emptying the syringe she removed it from the tube and replaced the rubber band. Then she left the room.

The man looked back at me and asked, "What happened?"

I was still sitting up so I could look into his eyes. "Wreck, broken neck. What's wrong with you?"

"Lou Gehrig's."

"I don't know much about that. Why are they feeding you that way?"

Then it hit me. He had been lying in the same position since I'd entered the room. He hadn't moved. He was paralyzed.

"There are two types," he said. "Bulbar and peripheral. I have the peripheral. That means the paralysis started in my legs and has moved slowly up my body. At some point I will be totally paralyzed. All I will be able to move are my eyes. At least now I can still talk but that will go too. So the future for me is the pits. Oh, the bulbar type is a little better. You're not paralyzed with that form; you just eventually run out of oxygen and die. You ever heard of the physicist, Stephen Hawking? He has the bulbar type." Then the man looked away again.

I felt like a total self-indulgent shit. I closed my eyes and tried to render myself unconscious.

* * *

The man in my room was named John Wilson. About three days after our talk he was discharged to home. His wife was a nurse and she had come to get him. She gave me their home phone number and said that John wanted to keep up with me and my career. I thought that was such a nice thing for him to do. Particularly with the terrible future he was facing.

* * *

I'd sent a wire to Colt as soon as I was conscious and orientated enough to dictate one. He and Kelly sent me a big bouquet of flowers. I had no idea if my career would ever get back on track. I still wasn't sure I'd ever walk again, let alone play the guitar.

Because of my injuries and the loss of Joy, I was overcome by a sense of despair. My stomach burned so badly I thought I'd never be able to eat again. I was consumed by hopelessness. The doctors placed me on some antidepressants, but they didn't work very well. The neurosurgical resident said part of my stomach pain was due to the steroids. He said they caused erosion of the lining of the stomach and could produce ulcers. So in addition to the antidepressants, he'd placed me on a prescription antacid. Most days I escaped by sleeping. It seemed I was sleeping my life away. I woke only when a nurse was poking me with a needle or trying to adjust my bedding, or feeding me. I knew I'd never forget the antiseptic smell of that hospital room as long as I lived. And every four hours someone was taking my pulse and blood pressure.

Over a period of weeks, I had a number of roommates. Most only stayed a day or two. I really didn't get to know any of them.

The damn halo was driving me crazy. My scalp itched, and I was feeling very sorry for myself. Movement was returning, but not fast enough to suit me.

I lay staring out the window one day when Casey walked in. She'd brought me a small bouquet of roses and three books.

"Hi, Jamie, how are you, honey?"

I didn't answer.

She came around and looked me in the eye. She evidently saw right through me, at least through to my sadness and depression. She pulled up a chair and said, "I know this is hard, Jamie. Losing Joy was awful, and having a broken neck isn't exactly fun. But you've got to get hold of yourself. You can't mope around like this. You've got to go on with your life."

"Why?"

"Listen to you. This doesn't sound like the Jamie Lee Coleman I know. You're made of tougher stuff. Buck up, honey. I know you can do it."

I could feel tears sliding down my cheeks. *How could I buck up? Why hadn't I been killed along with Joy? Or better yet, instead of Joy.* I wanted Casey to go away and leave me alone.

But she didn't. In fact, she came to see me every day. Each time she walked through the door she'd have something nice to say. She'd sit and talk to me for an hour, always encouraging me. Finally I began to come out of my funk. She told me one day she could see the progress each time she visited. I was doing better in rehab as well. While my mood wasn't light, it wasn't dark either. And the doctors were encouraging.

I was amazed that Sam, despite his own grief, continued to visit me almost every day. Close to the time of discharge, Sam came in early one morning and said, "Joy's apartment has eight months left on the lease, and I'm paying the rent. I want you to recuperate there."

"I'm not sure I can do that, Sam. How could I possibly sleep in our bed knowing that I'll never see Joy again and never feel her body next to mine?"

"It would be a waste to leave the apartment empty when you

obviously need a place to stay. I know it'll be hard at first, but you'll deal with it. You're strong. Look what you've endured already."

"I don't know, Sam. Let me think about it."

I relived my last fight with Joy over and over in my mind. She'd told me she loved me, and I'd been stupid enough to tell her it made me feel claustrophobic. How stupid. How completely and totally stupid I'd been. Every time I thought of our exchange I felt overwhelmed with a deep emptiness.

On the day of my discharge, Sam picked me up in a new four-door Ford sedan. I got the impression he never wanted a convertible again. We were quiet on the way to the apartment. Finally, I asked, "How are you dealing with it, Sam?"

He shook his head and said, "I lost Joy's mother to childbirth. Joy was all I had. My life is empty. I feel hollow inside. If it wasn't for work, I don't know what I'd do."

I knew somehow I had to get back to work. I had to hold my guitar and play. Could I do that in a halo brace? I didn't know, but I knew I had to try.

* * *

Sam parked the car on the street and placed a couple of quarters in the meter. I could feel a slight breeze off the river, and the sun beat down on us through a cloudless sky. I should have been happy to be out of the hospital and actually walking, but I wasn't. The thought passed through my addled brain that I might never be happy again. *Jesus, how will I ever be able to sleep in our bed?*

When we entered the apartment, it looked just as it had the day Joy and I left for Gulfport. An eerie feeling crept over me, and I said, "I don't think I can do this, Sam. There's too much of Joy here. I can still smell her perfume, for God's sake."

Sam shook his head. "I know it's hard. It bothers me to be here,

207

too. But you've got to be practical, Jamie. Joy would want you to be practical. You know that."

I couldn't move my head, so I had to turn my whole body to sweep the living room with my eyes. There were still some dishes on the rack in the kitchen. In the bedroom, the bed where we'd last made love remained unmade, the pillows scattered on the floor. I could smell the essence of Joy's being. Entering that room had been like having a knife jabbed into my heart. *Could I do this?*

Sam placed my clothes from the hospital on the dresser. He glanced at me and asked, "You going to be okay?"

"I don't know."

Sam made us coffee, and we sat in the living room and talked for a while. My mind was numb with grief. I hadn't realized how much I loved Joy until I'd lost her. Had I taken Joy for granted? Had I been that stupid?

When Sam left, I made the bed with clean sheets. Then I went to the kitchen to place the dishes in the cabinets. One of the glasses hadn't been washed completely, and when I picked it up, I saw Joy's lipstick on the rim. I held it to my lips.

I spent the afternoon watching television, something I'd never done in my life. I had no desire to read. I felt like a zombie. As hard as I tried to fight it off, I could feel myself slipping back into a deep depression.

I didn't eat dinner. I sat immobilized in front of the television until eleven o'clock and then went to bed. The doctor had given me some sleeping pills. I took two.

At some point in the night, I reached across the bed for Joy. Feeling the empty space sent a shudder through me. I got out of bed and went back into the living room and turned on the television. I sat there in a daze until sunrise. Had someone asked me what I'd seen on the screen, I couldn't have answered. I didn't bother to eat breakfast or lunch. I just sat in front of the television until darkness fell, the only light coming from the television screen.

* * *

I wasn't sure how I got there. Or what was going through my saddened mind. I just realized I was standing in the store staring at row after row of bottles. Some held clear liquids and others amber.

The salesclerk asked for identification. I had none. He must have seen the sorrow in my eyes because he said, "There're better ways to deal with your problems, son."

I just stared at him, then turned and left. It was ten o'clock in the morning. Sam's would be in the process of opening, so I wandered over to Bourbon Street. The janitor was taking the chairs off the tables when I walked in. Everyone else must have been in the kitchen. I went behind the bar and took down two bottles of vodka. I'd brought a large shopping bag with me and slipped them inside.

Back at the apartment, I filled a glass with ice cubes, orange juice, and vodka. I sat at the kitchen table and stared at the walls, slowly sipping on the potent mixture. The closest thing to a buzz I'd ever experienced had been from Casey's marijuana. The warm feeling that swept over me that morning worked its magic. I felt relaxed for the first time in weeks.

Casey showed up every afternoon on her way to work to clean the pins in my halo. She'd landed a job at a family restaurant on Canal Street. My eyes must have been a little glassy because she gave me a quizzical look. If she suspected anything, she didn't let on.

"How you doing, honey?" she asked.

"Fine. I'm doing fine."

"I bought us a new bottle of peroxide at Walgreens."

"Thanks."

She cleaned the skin where the spikes were inserted into my skull.

Her hands were gentle as she rubbed the Q-tips over the area. The feel of her soft fingers made me think of my aunt Lulu. Casey stood close to me as she worked, and I could smell her lavender perfume. It reminded me of the small bottle I'd bought for my mother the day she was killed.

"I'll come by after work to do this again," she said as she left.

"Thanks, Casey. I appreciate your help."

My alcoholic genes kicked in that day. I might as well have been drinking the deacon's shine. I managed to lift a couple of vodka bottles from Sam's bar each week. If the bartender realized what was happening, he never said anything to Sam.

Casey was an angel. She never failed to show up each day.

* * *

When it was time for my routine follow-up visit to Charity Hospital, I flagged down a taxi for the short ride to the huge medical facility that served the LSU and Tulane medical schools and residency programs.

I signed into the neurosurgery clinic and sat in the overcrowded waiting room surrounded by black people of all ages. Mine was the only white face in the group. When I was finally called to an exam room, I'd been waiting for two hours. The heat was oppressive, and the big fans just blew hot, stale air across the area.

The resident who had performed my surgery looked to be in his early thirties and had a good bedside manner. He seemed exhausted when he stepped into the room but, as always, had a smile on his face.

"How's it going, Jamie?"

"Okay. This damn halo is driving me nuts. My scalp itches like mad."

"Let me take a look," the resident said as he shined a pen-light on my halo pins. "Someone's doing a good job on these. Your girlfriend do this?"

"Just a friend. How much longer have I got to deal with this?"

"It's going to be awhile, Jamie. Let me see you in a month."

Back at the apartment, I realized I'd been living there for weeks and had yet to pick up my guitar or read a book. I watched television every waking hour as I sipped Screwdrivers. While I did feel relaxed, the depression only worsened. I'd taken to sleeping during the day when I wasn't watching the tube. I didn't even know what programs I watched or what day it was most of the time.

At the beginning of the fourth week, I was lying on the couch in a stupor when Casey walked in. When she finally shook me awake, she said, "Jamie, honey, this ain't going to cut it. You've got to quit this shit."

I looked into her eyes with my glazed ones. I couldn't keep them open and kept falling back to sleep.

The next thing I felt was a pitcher of ice water being poured over my head. That woke me up and got my attention. "What're you doing?" I yelled as I tried to sit up. My head was spinning, and I thought for a minute that I'd throw up on Casey.

She still held the pitcher in her hand. "I can't believe you're doing this to yourself. Do you think Joy would approve? You've got to stop wallowing in self-pity, Jamie. You've got too much to offer the world."

"Mind your own business, Casey. Leave me alone."

"I can't do that."

"Yes, you can. Leave. I don't want you here. Go pester someone else."

She stood there with determination in her eyes and looked down on me. My head hurt like hell and I felt like shit. She just stared at me. It made my skin crawl.

"I'm not leaving, Jamie. Not until I get you to face up to who you are—what you've become. You think Joy would have had anything to do with a bum? I don't think so. Get your sorry ass off that couch."

I couldn't hang my head in shame because of the halo. I did look around the room. The television blared as images flashed across the screen. Clothes lay draped over the furniture, and dirty dishes littered the kitchen table. I hadn't changed clothes since the previous day. An empty vodka bottle lay at my bare feet.

Fixing on my feet, I stared at them. Where were the calluses? Would I have new brogans before the first snow? Then I began to cry. First, just a few tears slid down my cheeks, and then I felt my whole body shake as I began to sob. Casey placed the empty pitcher on the coffee table, sat next to me, placed her arm around my shoulder, and pulled me to her.

I couldn't lay my head on her shoulder. I just let myself sink back into the soft cushions of the couch. When I finally stopped crying, I glanced at Casey and saw that her eyes were red and wet. I picked up her hand and held it to my lips.

In a hoarse voice, I said, "I don't deserve you. I'll try to get it together. I don't know how, but I'll try."

She squeezed my hand and kissed me on the forehead. "I'll help you. The first thing we're going to do is get you cleaned up and then we'll work on the apartment."

"Don't you have to be at work?" I asked.

"I can be a little late."

Since I'd been in the halo, I'd stopped taking showers and used the tub. Casey filled it with steaming water and helped me undress. After all, we'd once been lovers. She washed my back, my arms, my legs, and even my shrunken Peter. The water wasn't as black as when I'd taken my first bath at Miss Frances's house, but it was close.

When I was bathed, Casey dried me from head to toe with a clean bath towel and helped me dress. Then I went into the living room. The television was off; the dishes were washed. The vodka bottles, one full and one empty, had been thrown away. All the clothes had been picked up.

Casey held the framed eight-by-ten photograph of Joy and me that usually sat on the coffee table. She gave it to me and said, "Every time you look at this picture think how lucky you were to have loved Joy. To have known love at your age is remarkable in itself. And yes, I do know how old you are. You've got a wonderful talent and your whole life's in front of you. Don't you dare waste it."

I could feel the wetness of my eyes and felt embarrassed that I'd started crying again. I walked to where she stood and made an awkward attempt to hug her. My halo hit her in the forehead, and we both laughed.

* * *

That evening when she got off work, Casey brought me three novels and a biography of Dwight Eisenhower. I hadn't eaten all day, and when I told her this, she scrambled me two eggs and fried three strips of bacon. While I ate, she sat across the table from me, sipping on a mug of coffee. It reminded me of my first meal at Miss Frances's house. As I thought of her, I couldn't believe how long it'd been since the first time I'd run away from home. In a sense, I'd never quit running.

"Are you going to make it?" Casey asked.

"Thanks to you."

I'd forgotten what a sweet smile Casey had. How could I ever repay this woman? She'd shown me unconditional friendship—love. I guessed the best way to reward her was to get my life together. I made a solemn oath to myself that night—I would sober up and never, ever take another drink of alcohol as long as I lived.

* * *

I spent the next day reading. I still wasn't sure I could hold my guitar well enough to play. When Casey came to tend my scalp, she was delighted to see my transformation. I hadn't been boozing long enough to become addicted. I figured I'd be able to shake the family curse quickly.

"Well, look at you. This is more like it, Jamie. I'm so proud of you. I know you can do this," Casey said with a smile.

"Not without your prodding. Thanks for being such a great friend."

"You feel like venturing out?"

"I guess."

"Why don't you come by my new restaurant this evening for dinner? I'd love to introduce you to my boss."

"I reckon I could do that. Where exactly on Canal is it?"

"Three blocks to the right, off Bourbon Street. Place called Valerio's."

That evening I walked over to Canal Street and jumped on a streetcar for the short three-block ride. I'd only been out of the apartment to steal vodka from Sam and to buy a few groceries. And there was the trip to Charity Hospital. On all these excursions people did a double take when they saw my halo. At first it embarrassed me, but then I just let it roll off my shoulders. After all, there was nothing I could do about it.

The establishment where Casey worked was a small family-owned Italian café. I'd never eaten pasta until I'd come to New Orleans. It wasn't something on the menu at the City Café in Round Rock.

Casey's face lit up when I walked in the door.

"Oh, Jamie, honey, I'm so glad you came. Come on. I'll seat you at a table in the back."

"Suits me. I'm pretty hungry."

The restaurant was small, for it only had about twelve tables. They were covered with white table cloths and had a candle and holder in the middle. There was a big refrigerated case in the back near my table filled with Italian meats and cheeses. A big wine rack stood in one corner, and it was full of bottles lying on their side. The aroma and garlic and oregano filled the air and stimulated my appetite. During my funk I'd lost down to one hundred and sixty pounds from my usual one seventy-five.

The owner, a man who appeared to be in his mid-sixties with silver hair worn long, came over, and Casey said, "Mr. Valerio, I'd like to introduce my good friend, the famous singer, Jamie Lee Coleman."

I laughed. At the rate I was going, I thought I might have to go back to being a janitor. Well someday I might make it as a singer. Time would tell. "Nice to meet you, Mr. Valerio. Casey tells me the food here is wonderful," I said with a grin.

The man's face broke into a wide smile. His eyes literally sparkled as he said, "We pride ourselves in our family recipes. Enjoy, Mr. Coleman."

When he turned and left, Casey said, "I'm so excited that you came, honey. You need to be getting out of that apartment. I can't get over how handsome you look tonight."

I just smiled and thought back to my first experience with sex—with Casey. *My God that seems like a life time ago. In many ways it was.*

The angel-hair pasta with sautéed shrimp was delicious. Coffee and tiramisu ended a perfect meal. I left Casey a generous tip, which she promptly slipped into my shirt pocket.

"Don't you dare leave me a tip," she said.

"Okay. I'll think of something else."

I didn't bother with the streetcar on the way back to the apartment but walked the whole way. When I walked up the steps and entered the living room I was pleased to see that the place looked spotless. I read until I fell asleep with the book on my chest.

I finished the first novel, *The Godfather* by Mario Puzo, the following day. My guitar had been sitting in a wing-backed chair in the corner of the room since the morning Joy and I took our fateful ride. It was still in its canvas cover.

I gazed at it. *Have I forgotten how to play? Will my fingers work?* There was only one way to find the answer to those questions.

I unzipped the cover. The cool wood of the neck felt strange in my hand. The strings had lost some of their tightness, and I could tell without strumming them that they were out of tune. I didn't think I could sit on the couch and play. I'd sink too far into the cushions, so I went into the kitchen.

I'd never looked at the guitar when I played, like some artists did. Now that I couldn't bend my neck, it proved to be an advantage. Like most guitarists, I always tuned the G string first. My fingers felt stiff, and I had trouble bending them to press the strings on the frets. I'd kept my fingernails on my right hand too short, and I had difficulty striking the strings individually.

At first I simply strummed a few chords. Then I increased the rhythm. An hour later, things were slowly improving. I realized it would take weeks, but at some point in the future, I'd be back. *God won't that be wonderful.*

* * *

Three months after the accident, the doctors at Charity Hospital removed my halo. My neck was rigid, and I still had to turn my whole body if I wanted to look around at my surroundings. There were tears in my eyes when I took the hand of the young resident who had operated on me. "Thank you, Dr. Waldron. I'll never forget you."

He smiled. I'd never noticed what a really nice smile he had. Lately, I'd decided I didn't notice enough about people. I planned to change that. I wanted to know more about the individuals I came in contact with.

"You've been a good patient, Jamie. You'll do fine. One of the nurses told me she'd seen you perform at one of the bars on Bourbon

Street. She said you were spectacular. Are you planning on going back to performing there?"

I started to shake my head no when I realized that was impossible and started laughing. It felt so damned good to laugh. So good in fact that tears slid down my cheeks. "No, Doc," I said, "I've got other plans."

When I walked out onto the street, the sun beat down on me from a partly cloudy November sky. The temperature was mild, and I felt encouraged, happy to be alive. I hailed a taxi and went directly to the Paine Webber office to see Mr. Abernathy. We'd talked on the phone several times, but because of the accident, we hadn't met in person. My hospital bill had been a shocker. That and my living expenses for the past three months had badly depleted my portfolio.

"How bad is it?" I asked.

"You're not broke, but you've been hit pretty hard. When are you going back to work?"

"I'm still recovering, but I plan to start soon. When I do, you'll get steady checks."

Sam had offered me a stint at the bar, but I felt I should move on. Colt had replaced me out of necessity, so that option wasn't open. If you planned to be a country singer, the place to start was Nashville. So my next step was to head for Tennessee. But my first stop would be Round Rock. I wanted to see Jake and Yolanda. And if Amy was in Cookeville, I'd see her as well. The thought of visiting my old friends excited me. I still felt badly that I'd left without saying good-bye. I just hoped that they wouldn't hold that against me, that they'd greet me with open arms.

Chapter 17

I had avoided going to Joy's grave. I knew before I left New Orleans that I would have to say good-bye to her one last time. I called Sam the day before I was scheduled to leave to get directions to the cemetery.

New Orleans cemeteries are unique. Some date back to the 1700s, and most contain above-the-ground crypts because of the high water table. And there is always the threat of flooding.

I took a streetcar to the cemetery and found Joy's grave from a map supplied by the onsite business office. Sam had kept it simple. The inscription stated:

Joy Ledford

A true joy to all who knew her.

1946–1968

I sighed and placed the flat of my right hand on the marble. "I miss you so much," I said in a hoarse whisper. "How will I ever live without you?"

My eyes filled with tears and I dropped to one knee, still holding onto the marble. I stayed in that position for a full fifteen minutes, my shoulders shaking as sob after sob racked my body. Finally, I collapsed onto the grass, my head bowed as much as my neck would allow, and continued to sob.

An hour later, I stood and kissed her name in the inscription. "Good-bye, my love. I will carry you in my heart till the day I die."

* * *

I'd planned the trip carefully. I'd said good-bye to Sam, Axelrod, and Casey, my New Orleans family, on the evening before I left. And I bought a coach ticket on American Airlines from New Orleans to Nashville. The plane arrived in time for me to take a taxi from the airport to the Greyhound terminal on Murfreesboro Road. The bus trip to Cookeville took two hours. I'd called Amy, and she picked me up on the square. She was a senior in high school. I hadn't talked to her since that one phone call when I found out that my father was alive.

When I stepped down the bus stairs, I saw Amy sitting in a four-door 1965 Olds 88 parked at a meter. I walked to the driver's door, and Amy lowered the window. "Hi, stranger, long time no see," she said with a grin.

"It's been a while. You look great, girl. I like your hair short like that. Makes you look sophisticated."

She was wearing contacts. No more horn-rimmed glasses. She was dressed in jeans, penny loafers, and a Tennessee Tech tee shirt, which she filled out nicely. Her green eyes looked me over from head to toe. Then she smiled. "I've missed you, Jamie. God knows I was worried sick till you called me. I still can't believe you ran away. It's been over a year and a half since I've seen you."

"I've missed you, too. Nice car."

"It's a hand-me-down from my mother. You look different somehow. I can't put my finger on it," she said.

"A lot has happened to me in that time."

"Tell me about it," she said.

I told her about my trip to New Orleans, leaving out my problem with Dwayne the truck driver. How I'd worked as a janitor and then played guitar at Sam's bar. I explained how I'd signed up with Cole Walker and his band, never mentioning Kelly. I even told her about Joy and my broken neck.

When I finished, she glanced at me with a bewildered expression on her face.

"No wonder you look older," she said. "Are you home to stay?"

"Just a short visit."

"You're not going to finish school?"

I shook my head by moving my entire body.

She remained silent for a long time, the miles speeding by until we reached the outskirts of Livingston. "You want to stop for a Coke?" she asked.

"Sure."

I smiled when I saw the whittlers sitting on the courthouse steps. Every little town in Tennessee had its whittlers—old men with nothing to do but shave cedar blocks with sharp pocket-knives. It was a southern tradition.

There was an old-fashioned drugstore on the square that had a soda fountain. Amy parked on the street, and we went inside and sat at a long bar. We each had a Coke with a little cherry syrup. A small amount of perspiration had beaded across Amy's forehead. I took my napkin and blotted it dry. She smiled and said, "You not only seem older; you seem different. Maybe you're just more mature."

Of course, I was different. No one could go through what I had without it affecting him. I'd experienced too many losses: Miss Frances, Mom, Bandit, and then Joy. I'd been on my own all the time I'd been gone. I wasn't a high-school boy any longer. I had matured beyond my age and made decisions like an adult in his thirties. I was a man.

We arrived in Round Rock around seven o'clock. Jake and Yolanda were expecting us. Amy had been invited to stay. She parked the car in front of Jake's house and turned off the engine. We sat there a moment without saying a word. Finally, Amy asked, "Are you ready for this?"

I nodded. "As ready as I'll ever be. Let's go in."

We walked up the steps to the big porch, and I rang the door-bell. Yolanda opened the door and stood gazing at me.

"Lord, child, you are a sight for sore eyes. We've missed you so much. Come in this house this minute. You too, Amy."

Yolanda threw her arms around my neck and hugged me tightly. When she released me, she had a look of horror on her face." Lord, child, I forgot about your neck. I hope to Jesus I didn't hurt you."

I smiled and said, "No, ma'am, you didn't hurt me. It felt good having your arms around my neck. I've missed that act of kindness more than you'll ever know."

Jake shook my hand and wrapped his arm around my shoulder. There were tears welling up in the older man's eyes.

"I've been worried sick about you, Jamie. I'm so glad you're home," Jake said.

I'm so sorry I caused you and Yolanda so much trouble. I was scared to death and I thought the police were after me," I said, tears welling in my eyes.

"I told you on the phone that I could have taken care of that. You should have trusted me."

"It's not that I didn't trust you. I was terrified. I'm really sorry, Jake. Please forgive me."

"There's nothing to forgive. I'm just glad you're safe. We'll talk about things after we've eaten. Yolanda's made a special supper for you and Amy."

I'd forgotten what a good cook Yolanda was. We had a wonderful meal of country ham, candied yams, creamed corn, and fried green tomatoes. Where she'd gotten green tomatoes I couldn't imagine. I ate until I was stuffed.

After we finished eating, I walked Amy to her car. As she opened the door, I placed my arms around her waist and pulled her to me for a hug. She wrapped her arms around my neck gently and kissed me on the cheek.

"Thanks for picking me up. It's been great seeing you," I said.

"How long are you going to be here?" she asked.

"Two or three days. I've got to start making a living."

"Call me when you're ready to leave. I'll take you to Nashville."

I watched her drive away and thought how wonderful it was to have her as a friend, one I didn't have to be in love with to enjoy.

When I returned to the house, I had to recap everything I'd told Amy for Jake. I didn't leave out any details, as I had with Amy. Jake laughed at my encounter with Dwayne. After I'd finished my story, Yolanda said, "I've got to clean up the kitchen. Why don't you two go to the library and relax, I may join you later."

We sat in the library like we'd done when I'd lived there. Jake had a glass of port, and I pulled a Coke out of the small fridge.

Jake set his glass on the table next to his chair and turned to face me. Then he said, "I talked to Mr. Wallaby, the new high school principal, and he said he'd let you back in your old class."

I cleared my throat. "I'm not going back to school. I've got other plans. I want to be a professional musician."

Jake let out a loud, exasperated breath and said, "That's ridiculous, Jamie. You need an education to make it in today's world. Musicians lead a terrible life."

"I'm going to be a star."

Shaking his head, Jake said, "That's what every Tom, Dick, and Harry says, Jamie. Nine times out of ten they end up broke. I can't believe we're having this conversation. What would Miss Frances think?"

I knew he'd throw that one at me, and I was ready for it. I said, "I know what I want out of life, Jake. All I need to get there is in my fingertips and my voice. You know me. I'll never quit reading and learning new things. Miss Frances herself told me as long as I kept reading; I'd be an educated man."

I could see the hurt in Jake's face, and it made me feel terrible. But I knew I had to follow my gut. "I'm really sorry, Jake. I hate to disappoint you. You've been a wonderful friend. I couldn't have made it without you when Miss Frances died. You've always been there for me. I can never thank you enough."

Jake shook his head and said, "Give it a try, and get it out of your system. Then maybe you'll come to your senses."

"Thanks, Jake. I won't let you down."

We listened to Mozart's Symphony Number 40 in G minor until around ten o'clock, and then I excused myself and went to my old room. When I crawled into the big bed, I thought of Bandit. I hadn't realized how much I'd missed the little dog until that moment. I promised myself a dog once I got on my feet. I read until the book dropped on my chest and I slipped into a peaceful sleep.

* * *

I stayed for three days. I tried to visit all my Round Rock friends. I stopped by the clinic and spent some time with Dr. Kate and Jazz. Then I talked Jerry Whittle into taking me out to Dr. Stout's farm. I still thought of it as Miss Frances's, but made a concerted effort to refer to it as his.

The doctor had accumulated more acreage so he could accommodate the many hoofed animals he'd adopted. There must have been eight broken-down horses, three donkeys, six goats, and ten sheep wandering around. I didn't bother to count the dogs and cats.

One puppy caught my eye. His fur was white with black spots sprinkled across his back and belly. His eyes were barely open. I laughed as he stumbled around the yard. I figured he couldn't be over four weeks old. When I asked the doctor what he was, Joe smiled and said, "He's a sooner. Sooner be one thing as another."

"Please don't get rid of him. When I get my life in order, I want to come for him. What's his name?"

"I call him *Dog*. Why don't you name him?"

I rubbed the puppy's ears and picked him up. He licked my face and I started laughing. Then the little rascal peed on me. I knew I had the perfect name. I'd call him Fireman.

Amy picked me up the following morning. Part of I-40 was finished in places, and we didn't have to take that curvy stretch of US 70 from Cookeville through Chestnut Mound. I remembered Miss Frances telling me it was on a curve there where Joe Stout had lost his parents.

We made good time and stopped in Lebanon for lunch. I'd told her about the Cracker Barrel so we ate there. She'd been quiet on the trip, and I wondered if something was bothering her.

"You okay?" I asked.

"I'm worried about you, Jamie. You don't have a job and no place to stay."

"As long as I have my guitar, I'll never starve. If nothing else, I'll play on Lower Broadway for tips."

"That's a great plan. Now I'll rest easy," she said, rolling her eyes.

I placed my hand on her arm and said, "Please don't lose any sleep over me. I'm going to be fine."

"Well, at least you have confidence in yourself. I suppose that's half the battle."

* * *

In Nashville the next day I found a furnished one-bedroom apartment on Twenty-First Avenue close to Hillsboro Village and down the street from Vanderbilt University. It wasn't too far from Sixteenth

Avenue, better known as Music Row. I thought it would be an ideal location.

The Pancake Pantry was a small restaurant in the Village where people stood in line every morning for breakfast. I ate there the first day. There were only two waitresses, and they scurried about the place taking orders and filling coffee mugs. The coffee was as good as the pancakes, but I missed the chicory of New Orleans.

That afternoon I called my old music teacher, and when he answered, I said, "It's Jamie Lee Coleman, Mr. Arbuckle. I've just come to Nashville and wanted to say hello."

"Well, hello, yourself. I'm delighted you're here. What are your plans?"

"I've decided to be a country singer. Nashville is the place to be."

"That's for sure. How about coming to dinner tonight? I'd love to see you and catch up. You just sort of disappeared into the wood-work a year or so ago."

"Yes, I did. Sorry I didn't say good-bye. I'll fill you in when I see you. Dinner sounds great. I don't know where you live. We always worked together out of the music school."

"We live on Hampton Avenue, 226 to be exact. Do you have a car?"

"I'll take a taxi. What time?"

"Seven."

"Got it. See you then."

I still had a hard time associating dinner with the evening meal. In Round Rock everyone called it supper. I was excited to see my friend and teacher. I'd learned a great deal from Mr. Arbuckle.

Hampton Avenue was near the Green Hills Shopping Center, just off Hillsboro Pike, and it ran parallel to Golf Club Lane. The house was a traditional two-story brick with black shutters. The yard full of maple trees was carefully landscaped. The bare limbs of the maples were silhouetted by a full moon and they moved rhythmically from a soft northerly wind. I shook the chill from my shoulders and pulled my jacket close to my neck as I stepped out of the car.

I paid the taxi driver and walked up to the front door. When I rang the doorbell, I heard barking coming from the back of the house. Mrs. Arbuckle, accompanied by a black Lab, opened the door and said, "Come in, Jamie. I'm so glad you could come."

Her husband walked out of the kitchen with an apron around his neck, wiping his hands on its tail. "Did you bring your guitar?" he asked.

"No, sir."

"Not a problem. I have several."

Mr. Arbuckle had prepared a rack of lamb, green beans, new potatoes, and creamed corn. As he set serving dishes on the big table, he said, "Have a seat, Jamie. The girls will be here in a minute."

Taking my seat, I looked up to see the two daughters, Charlotte and Anna. I remembered them from music school where they'd also taken lessons. Both were excellent musicians in their own right. Charlotte, the blonde, was ten and played the piano, and Anna, an eight-year-old brunette, was a violinist.

I stood as they approached and pulled chairs out for them. "Great seeing you again. You've grown a little since I last saw you."

Both girls giggled and took their seats. Mrs. Arbuckle took a chair next to her husband. Mr. Arbuckle said, "Dig in. We're not formal in this house."

After a few bites, I said, "Wow! This is great. I didn't know you were such a good cook, Mr. Arbuckle."

"Flattery is always appreciated, young man. It's part of the performance gene we all have in this family."

We all laughed.

After dinner, we adjourned to their den. Mr. Arbuckle handed me a Martin guitar and said, "I think you'll find this instrument satisfactory."

It was in tune when I strummed a few chords. With its wonderful, deep resonance, it was a much finer instrument than my old Gibson. Charlotte sat at a grand piano, her sister picked up her violin, and Mrs. Arbuckle brought out a viola.

"You decide what you want to play, and we'll join in," Mr. Arbuckle said, picking up his guitar.

I fell back on my Segovia repertoire because I figured they would be familiar with the Spaniard's music. They didn't disappoint me. We played together for around thirty minutes, and then the girls had to do their homework. Mrs. Arbuckle followed them up the staircase to the second floor, leaving her husband and me alone so we could talk.

"So, tell me where you've been all this time, Jamie."

I told him about my adventures in New Orleans and finished by saying, "As I said on the phone, I've decided to be a country singer."

He shook his head. "That's a hard life. Are you sure it's what you want?"

"Yes, I love playing to a live audience."

"I wish you luck. How do you plan to start?"

That was a question I'd been bouncing around for the last few days. In truth, I hadn't a clue. "I'm open to suggestions," I said.

"I have a friend who manages studio musicians. I'll call him for you. They're always looking for a good guitarist. That'll put food on the table until you figure out the next step. Do you belong to the AFM?"

"Yes, sir. I joined when I was in New Orleans."

"That's essential. The AFM Local 257 here in Nashville was organized in 1902. You'll need to check in with them when you get time. Good luck."

"Thanks, Mr. Arbuckle. I really appreciate all you've done for me. And thanks for dinner. It was great. I usually exist on hamburgers and fries."

I stood and we shook hands.

"I'll call a taxi for you," Mr. Arbuckle said, reaching for a phone.

* * *

Several weeks later, I had the radio tuned to a country station while I shaved. I almost cut my throat when I heard Kelly and my replacement singing our duet, "Mountain Love." A pang of disappointment gripped me. I'd wanted to record that myself, and with Kelly. I just shook my head and went back to shaving. I had no idea when they'd recorded it or how the single was doing. I knew I needed to contact BMI and give them my new address. The royalties would mean additional income that I desperately needed.

As I thought about it, I realized I should concentrate on writing my own material. That's what the really successful country stars did. Johnny Cash was an excellent example. At seventeen, I'd had an unusual amount of experience with disappointment, loss, and heartbreak. Plus, I did have one heck of an imagination. Miss Frances had nurtured it from the very beginning.

I dressed, grabbed my guitar, and walked out of the apartment. There was an overcast sky and a slight drizzle formed a mist as I trudged along Twenty-First Avenue. A gentle breeze swayed the bare limbs of the maple trees. It only took me a few minutes to reach the studio where I'd lined up some work as a session musician with Mr. Arbuckle's help. There were numerous such studios in Nashville, some owned by big record labels and others that were small, private affairs in people's homes.

I liked working in the studio because the musicians were remarkable professionals. It also gave me an opportunity to meet some of the singers who were cutting records, as well as their managers. I was trying to learn all I could about the music business. As I thought about it, sometimes I felt like a sponge. There was just a lot to learn. And, I was in a hurry.

I'd just walked into the lobby of the studio, shaking the wetness off my cowboy hat, when a young woman came around a corner carrying two Styrofoam cups filled with hot coffee. We collided, and she fell flat on her ass, spilling coffee onto the tile floor.

She looked up at me with an expression of complete disdain. I bent at the waist and offered her my hand, saying, "I'm very sorry. I just didn't see you."

"Oscar will be furious I spilled his coffee," she said, taking my hand.

"I'd be happy to find some more," I said.

"Know where it is?"

"No."

"Come with me," she said, scooping up the two cups.

I followed her down a long hallway, wondering why she hadn't blessed me out for knocking her down. In the small kitchen, she threw away the dirty cups and picked up two new ones. Filling both, she handed me one.

As we walked back to the studio, she sipped on hers and asked, "You always that clumsy?"

"Not really. You're awfully understanding. Most folks would have cussed me out."

"Not my style. You didn't do it on purpose."

"You a musician?" I asked.

"Fiddle."

"Play in a band?"

"Just studio work."

We stopped at the spilled coffee, and I soaked it up with a paper towel. Then I threw it in a wastebasket. When we stepped into the recording area, she said, "That cup's for Oscar. He's the mixer."

I handed the cup to Oscar and turned back to the woman.

I smiled and extended my hand. "I'm Jamie Lee Coleman. Glad to meet you."

"Rhonda Utter," she said, taking my hand.

Redheaded fiddle players seemed to gravitate to me like flies to maple syrup, or maybe it was the other way around. So, after Kelly Walker, there was Rhonda. As we made small talk, she explained that she hailed from Newport, Tennessee, near the border with North Carolina. I thought her name was appropriate because she had the largest breasts I'd ever seen on a skinny woman. She had what I call snake hips, and in her cowboy boots she was only three inches shorter than my six-two. I later learned that she was a natural musician like me and could play the fiddle as if the devil himself was after her.

When the session began, we were doing backup for a young woman singer who'd just signed a contract. She looked to be in her twenties and appeared a little nervous. She had a lovely voice, but after the session, I decided she didn't have the spark it takes to make a star.

Rhonda was a better fiddler than Kelly, which is saying a lot. After we'd finished, I asked, "Would you like to have dinner with me tonight?"

She raised her eyebrows and let her eyes shift to one side as if she was thinking it over. Then she smiled and said, "Yes. That would be nice. What time?"

"How about seven?"

"That works for me. You'll pick me up?"

"Sure. Where do you live?"

"I have an apartment in Green Hills. It's on Richard Jones Road off Hillsboro Pike. I'm in building B, apartment five."

"Okay. I'll see you at seven," I said.

I didn't have a car or a license, so I called a taxi. When Rhonda opened the door, I realized I'd underdressed again. She wore a simple black but elegant dress with a gold chain around her long neck. Her hair was full and fell to her shoulders. She draped her coat over her shoulders and started out the door. When she saw the taxi, she asked, "Don't you have a car?"

"No."

"Pay him and we'll take mine."

She had a new green 1970 Chevrolet Monte Carlo. She slipped behind the wheel, and I sat in the passenger seat. I was accustomed to having people chauffeur me around, but as I closed the door, I felt a sudden sense of panic. The accident with Joy literally flashed before my eyes and I could feel my pulse quicken.

"Where're we going?" she asked.

Trying to remain calm or at least appear calm, I took a deep breath and said, "I've heard that Mario's is good. That okay?"

She nodded and drove down Twenty-First Avenue past my apartment house and cut across to West End Avenue. Mario's Italian restaurant was in an old house. As we walked in, I noticed the small bar to the left. It was dimly lit inside the dining room, and the waiters were all men dressed in tuxedoes. Chianti wine bottles with straw wrapped around them hung from the ceiling. The maître d', a tall good looking fellow, led us to a back table and opened Rhonda's napkin for her and placed it in her lap. As we took our seats I noticed a wrought iron rail and a set of steps leading down to a wine cellar.

"Would you care to see the wine list?" the maître d' asked.

I looked at Rhonda. "I don't drink. Would you like a glass of wine?"

"Sure."

I let her pick what she wanted because I knew nothing of wines. She chose a Merlot to go with a Caesar salad and veal, and I had angel-hair pasta and an Italian dinner salad.

While we waited for our food, I asked, "Could you tell me a little about yourself?"

"I'm from a farm family of five girls. All of us have musical talent to varying degrees. I took to the fiddle because of my father. I've been here for three years. The day I graduated from high school, I hopped on a Greyhound bus headed for Nashville. I knew at an early age that I wanted to be a professional musician."

"I know a man isn't supposed to ask a woman how old she is, but I'm a curious fellow."

She laughed. "I'm still young enough that it doesn't bother me. I'm twenty-one. You?"

Like all the women who had been in my life, Rhonda was older than me. In her case, by three years, and I wondered if I should lie about my age, but at the last moment I decided not to. I was tired of lying about my life. "I just turned eighteen. I hope that doesn't bother you."

"Why should that bother me? Now, tell me about yourself."

"Well, let's see. I'm from a place outside of Round Rock, Tennessee, called Beulah Land. It's a hillside of tarpaper shacks. I ran away from home the first time at age ten because of an abusive alcoholic father. A woman named Frances Washington took me in and saved my life. She died suddenly, and her attorney took me under his wing. Then my father killed my mother right in front of me, and I tried to kill him. In fact, I thought I had. So, I ran away a second time and ended up in New Orleans. I became a professional musician and here I am. Oh, yeah, my girlfriend was killed in a car wreck and I got a broken neck—a spinal injury and was paralyzed from the neck down for awhile. I was in a halo brace for three months. I guess that sums it up."

Rhonda had a stricken expression on her face. I thought for a moment that she was going to cry. She placed her hand on mine and said, "That's an incredible story. You poor thing, that must have been awful seeing your mother murdered like that."

Her hand felt warm against my skin, and as I looked into her hazel eyes, I saw true empathy. She smiled and I knew we'd be friends.

We finished our meal with spumoni and coffee. Mario himself came to our table to ask about our meal. He was a big, friendly man, and I liked him immediately. I later learned that he was somewhat of a mysterious fellow. There were rumors of possible Mafia connections but I don't believe they were true.

We drove back to my apartment, and when Rhonda parked in the alley behind the building to let me out, I asked, "Would you like to come up for a few minutes?"

She smiled and said, "Some other time. I've got an early session in the morning. Thanks for dinner."

I got out of her car and watched her drive away.

Something told me Rhonda would be a challenge.

Chapter 18

I didn't find out what a challenge it would be until the following week when we went to a restaurant called Rotier's on Elliston Place across from Centennial Park. It was a local hang-out for Vanderbilt students and musicians. We each had one of Rotier's famous hamburgers.

When she dropped me off at my apartment, I said, "Come up and listen to some music with me. I bought a new stereo."

She hesitated for a moment and then said, "I can only stay for a few minutes."

My apartment was on the third floor on the front of the building. We took the back entrance off the parking area. In the kitchen, I pulled a Budweiser out of the fridge and handed it to her.

"I thought you didn't drink," she said.

"I don't. I bought it for you."

I'd bought the stereo at Service Merchandise on Lower Broadway.

It wasn't expensive but sounded pretty good. I slipped in a cassette and went to sit next to Rhonda on the couch. It was a Frank Sinatra recording with some of his early hits.

"It's hard to beat Old Blue Eyes," Rhonda said, taking a sip of beer.

I hadn't been with a woman since Joy's death. I continued to think of her constantly and missed her so much it made my heart ache. But, I knew I had to move on. Joy would always be my first love, the love of my life. I didn't think anyone would ever take her place. And I was lonely. I missed having a female companion, someone to share my new life. I swallowed hard, moved close to Rhonda, placed my arm around her shoulder, and pulled her to me. She stiffened, removed it, and turned to face me, a smile on her face.

"Jamie, honey, I think you're a nice fellow, great looking, and a fabulous musician, but I'm not into guys."

My mouth dropped open, and I stared at her in a state of confusion. "What's that mean?"

"I like girls as much as you do. I'm a lesbian."

I'd just hit on a female Dwayne. "I don't understand this whole thing about same-sex attraction," I said.

"Of course not, you're straight. There's no way you could understand."

"I'm sorry I came on to you. I didn't know."

"Don't be silly. I'm flattered."

"Can we be friends?" I asked.

"Why would you even ask a question like that? I love having you as a friend."

I shook her hand. "Deal."

"I've got a great girl for you, Jamie. I've been trying to get in her pants for months, but she's straight. I think you two would make a great couple."

"She a fiddler?"

"Yes."

"Redhead?"

"A blonde with a figure to die for. I get wet just looking at her."

That was the strangest conservation I'd ever had with a woman. I actually felt a little uncomfortable.

"Will you introduce us?" I asked.

"She's on the road now with a band. She'll be back this weekend."

"When can I meet her?"

"I'll ask both of you to come to my apartment for drinks on Saturday afternoon. Well, Melody and I'll have a beer. You can sip on that damn Coke you like so much. I swear, Jamie, it just seems crazy for a musician to be a damn teetotaler."

* * *

I took a taxi on Saturday to Rhonda's apartment, and when I knocked on the door, it took several minutes for her to open it. When she did, there was a big smile on her face. "Come in, handsome. Melody isn't here yet. She called to say she'd be a few minutes late. Rest your bones on the couch while I finish washing my lunch dishes. I took a nap after lunch and left them in the sink."

I sat on the big leather sectional couch and stared at Rhonda's artwork. There were several prints of prominent buildings in and around Nashville. A Patsy Cline album played softly on a small stereo. I could hear Rhonda clanging dishes in the kitchen and I wondered what in the world she'd had for lunch.

There was a knock on the door and Rhonda yelled, "Get that, Jamie!"

I walked to the door, wondering what Melody would look like. Rhonda had said she had a body to die for. That would be nice, but

I was also fascinated by the fact that she was a fiddler. And I hoped she'd be smart and well read.

When I opened the door, my jaw slackened, and my mouth dropped open. I felt like a simpleton. Melody Chapman did, indeed, have a body to die for, as well as the most luxurious mop of blonde hair I'd ever seen. Her eyes were as blue as Joy's, and her face could only be described as angelic.

She smiled when she saw my expression and extended her hand. "You must be, Jamie. Rhonda says you're a great musician. I can't wait to hear you play."

I took her hand and found her shake to be firm and yet gentle. I motioned her in and said, "I understand you're a fabulous fiddler. We can probably make great music together."

Melody laughed and I blushed. I couldn't believe I'd said such a stupid thing. It was a cliché of the first magnitude. Rhonda came out of the kitchen at that moment, wiping her hands on a dish towel, and said, "I see you two have met. How about a beer, Melody? Jamie only drinks that fancy French water and Cokes. Have you ever known a musician who's a teetotaler?"

Melody laughed. "I didn't know there was such a creature. Yeah, I'll have a beer."

"Have a seat and I'll bring everything out. I've got some salsa and chips, too. Y'all get acquainted."

"So, where're you from?" I asked.

"You first," Melody said.

I told her the abbreviated version I'd told Rhonda, and she looked at me with disbelief in her eyes. Finally, she said, "Wow! That's quite a story. A lot of that material will come in handy when you start writing your own songs. My story can't hold a candle to yours."

"It's not a competition," I said. "I want to know more about you."

Just then Rhonda brought in a tray with our drinks and salsa. She placed it on the coffee table in front of us and sat down opposite me.

Melody picked up her Bud and tipped the bottle up for a long drag. She wiped her lips with the back of her hand and said, "I'm from a place called Yazoo City in Mississippi just north of Jackson. I came to Nashville right out of high school, just like Rhonda. My brother is a pharmacist in Memphis. My mother and father are teachers. I mostly do studio work, but on occasion, I travel with a band of no particular note. In fact, I don't know anyone who's ever heard of us. And let's see, I'm twenty-two. That's me in a nut-shell."

The three of us visited for another hour, and then I looked at my watch and said, "It's about dinner-time. Would the two of you like to join me?"

Melody looked at Rhonda. Rhonda said, "Two's company, three's a crowd. You two go on. I'll fix something here."

I stood and offered Melody my hand. Then turning to Rhonda, I said, "Thanks for inviting us. And for the snacks."

Melody nodded, and we walked out the door. She turned to me and asked, "Shall we take your car or mine?"

I laughed. "I don't have a car. I either walk or take a taxi. Where's your car?"

"That wreck of a Chevy station wagon over there."

I'd wanted to take her to Mario's because I thought that was the fanciest restaurant in town, but she said she wasn't that hungry and just wanted a hamburger. She suggested Tootsie's Orchard Lounge on Lower Broadway next to the Ryman Auditorium.

Tootsie's was a famous hang-out for country musicians partly due to its location across the alley from the stage-door. It was a small establishment that looked like a coffee shop you'd see in a low end hotel. There was "U" shaped counter and tables littered the floor. The waitresses wore jeans and men's button down shirts. All the tables were taken so we sat at the counter. It was so noisy we really couldn't talk, so we ate our hamburgers and whispered into each other's ears. That worked fine since we were sitting side by side. I actually thought it was a little sexy. I inhaled a lovely sent of lavender as I placed my mouth next to her ear.

The hamburgers were huge, greasy, and delicious. My fries were thick like they have in the country and greasy as well. I gobbled mine down but Melody ate like a perfect lady, taking small bites and wiping her mouth with her cloth napkin between bites.

After we finished eating, while I was paying the bill, she asked, "Ever been backstage at the Opry?"

I shook my head. "I took a tour of the Ryman when I was about ten, but I've never been to a show."

She grabbed my hand and pulled me up. "Come on," she said, "I'll take you."

We went out the back door of the restaurant and crossed the alley to the stage door. People were loitering around in hopes of seeing someone important. No one was impressed with Melody or me as she opened the door. There was a lone policeman sitting just inside. He appeared to be in his early to mid-sixties with a ring of white hair surrounding a bald head.

Melody said, "Harry, meet Jamie Lee Coleman. You got room for us tonight?"

"I've always got room for you, darlin'. Good to meet you, Jamie."

I was so excited I could barely contain myself. Melody pulled me along, and we squeezed between musicians waiting in the wings to go onstage.

I looked out at the auditorium and realized it looked just as it had when Jerry Whittle and I'd taken our tour the day I'd met Mr. Arbuckle. Except now the church pews were filled with several hundred people. The balcony was full with people hanging over the rail at the front and several people stood in the back. A huge ad for Martha White Flour hung on the back wall of the stage.

We stood right behind the curtains and watched the performers. I couldn't believe my eyes. The stage was full of people milling around aimlessly. Performers would hear their name called and then walk rapidly to the microphone, their band members trailing after them. An announcer would read commercials between acts.

I glanced at Melody and asked, "How can they let people wander around like that?"

"They use directional microphones that pick up only what's fed directly into them."

While we were standing there, Johnny Cash walked up and nodded to us. I had no idea he was such a big man. He towered over my six foot two height.

When Johnny Cash walked onstage, the crowd went wild. People came up with cameras and it looked like the place was in the midst of a lightning storm. He sang his own composition, "I Walk the Line." He'd had just done the soundtrack for the Gregory Peck movie of the same name. It had been made in East Tennessee not too far from Round Rock. It was a story about a small-town sheriff who put his career and marriage on the line when he fell for the young daughter of a local moonshiner.

Cash sang two more songs, and then signed off. I couldn't believe how much stage presence the famous singer had. *If I could just be half that good I'd be thrilled. I loved the way he said, "Hello, I'm Johnny Cash."*

I turned and glanced at the woman standing next to me. She looked very familiar. Then it dawned on me. It was Loretta Lynn. She smiled and moved onstage for her set as Cash was leaving the stage. The flashbulbs of the cameras were like lightning strikes. I wondered why the musicians didn't feel blinded.

Melody was enjoying my reaction to the celebrities. I'm sure I looked like a rube from the country. Then I laughed because basically that's exactly what I was. She grabbed my hand and said, "Come on, I'll introduce you to Mr. Acuff."

We wandered through the back hall to where the dressing rooms were lined up in a row. There were head shots of all the stars lining the walls. Most of them had been signed by the artist and most had which recording studio they represented on the bottom of the picture. I kept stopping to look at the pictures and Melody would pull me along. "Come on slow poke. I'll bring you back again sometime and you can dillydally all you want."

Roy Acuff's dressing room was in the back near the stage door and was larger than the others. He and his band were taking a break when we walked in. Melody told me later that he'd helped her get her first gig when she'd come to Nashville.

Roy Acuff was truly a legend in his own time. I'd listened to him on my crystal radio in Beulah Land when I was a child and couldn't believe I was actually standing in his dressing room. My pulse felt as if it was running a hundred miles an hour. He was a slight man with a full head of dark curly hair.

When the country star noticed Melody, he said, "Come here, sugar, and give me a hug."

Melody hugged him, and then, turning to me, she said, "Roy, I'd like you to meet my friend, Jamie Lee Coleman. He says he's a guitar picker, but I haven't heard him play yet. He may be for all I know."

Acuff said, "Glad to meet you, son. You seem awfully young to be in this business."

I swallowed hard and said, "It's an honor to meet you, Mr. Acuff. I've listened to you on the radio all my life."

"Hell, son that makes me feel old as hell. Want a swig of whisky? I've got some good Hamilton County shine over there in the corner."

"No, thank you. I appreciate the offer, though."

"You and Melody make yourselves at home. The boys and I've got to go on in a minute or two. By the way, this here is Howard, our Dobro player, and that's Charlie over in the corner. He plays a mean rhythm guitar."

I shook hands with both men and thought they seemed like really nice fellows. There was a tall man standing in the corner talking to a pretty brunette. He was dressed in a suit and tie, which made him look a bit out of place. He wandered over and said, "I'm Dr. Perry Harris." We shook hands, and I later learned he was an ear, nose, and throat specialist who was good friends with Mr. Acuff. He came to visit the famous musician every Friday and Saturday night. Dr. Harris was also Larry McNeely's father-in-law. Larry was the banjo virtuoso on the *Glen Campbell Goodtime Hour.*

A few minutes later, someone came to the door and said, "You're on, Mr. Acuff." Roy Acuff picked up his fiddle, and the three musicians left the room with Melody and me in hot pursuit. When Roy Acuff walked out onstage, he got the same response that Johnny Cash had. He and *his boys* played "The Great Speckled Bird," Roy's signature song, to thunderous applause. Then he balanced his bow on the tip of his nose and walked around the stage in a tight little circle. I thought the place would explode. I laughed so hard my side hurt.

They did one or two more songs and left the stage. I felt someone's presence and turned to see Minnie Pearl standing next to me. She had on that silly hat with the price tag dangling from it. I'd listened to her all my life as well, and when I realized who was standing next to me I felt like I was in the presence of royalty. When she noticed me staring at her, she smiled and said, "You're a handsome young fellow. What's your name, honey?"

I took her hand and said, "My name's Jamie Lee Coleman. I'm so excited to meet you, I can hardly stand it."

She laughed and stepped out on the stage. She told one corny joke after another and had the audience eating out of her hand. I got to know her as a friend later. She was a gracious and educated woman whose real name was Sarah Cannon. She'd grown up in the Colleyville section of Centerville, Tennessee, about fifty miles west of Nashville. She used Grinder's Switch as her fictional home-town when she was doing monologues on stage. It was just a railroad switch outside of Clarksville.

My head was reeling. I looked at Melody and said, "Honey, I can't begin to tell you how much I appreciate this. I'm not sure my old ticker can take much more of this excitement. Let's go."

We thanked the policeman at the stage door as we stepped through. The crowd of autograph seekers was still there shivering in the January cold. No one asked for our signature as we brushed by them.

We climbed into Melody's station wagon, and I asked, "Have you got your fiddle with you?"

"I don't go anywhere without my fiddle."

"Let's go to my place and make a little music."

She gave me a wry smile and said, "Just so you know up front, that's all I have in mind."

"What did you think I had in mind?" I asked.

"You're a man, sweetie. Need I say more?"

We drove back to my apartment house, and she parked behind the building. Her fiddle was in the backseat. She grabbed it, and we headed up the back stairs. In the kitchen, I asked, "Want a beer?"

"You having one?"

"I don't drink. Remember?"

She gave me a quizzical look and said, "A musician who doesn't drink? I thought Rhonda was kidding me."

I shook my head.

"No weed or coke?"

"Afraid not."

Then she did something that took me completely by surprise. She threw her arms around my neck and gave me a wet kiss on the lips. I held her around the waist and she leaned back, her beautiful blonde hair falling off her shoulders, and looked into my eyes.

"Where have you been all my life?" she asked.

"Waiting for you," I said.

"You're one smooth talker. Reckon I can trust you?"

"I'm a straight arrow, always have been. I hope you don't think that makes me dull."

She laughed. "There's nothing dull about you, darlin'. Just looking at you stirs my hormones. Oh, my God, I can't believe I said that."

"From where I stand, that's a good thing. Mine have been swirling through my veins and affecting my head since the moment I opened the door at Rhonda's."

"Let's sit on the couch for a moment and let things cool down," Melody said.

We sat next to each other in a stiff standoff. Finally, Melody asked, "How old are you, Jamie?"

I'd turned eighteen in January. I'd lied about my age for so long, I started to say twenty but didn't. I just couldn't bring myself to do it. I said, "I'm eighteen."

"Do you have a problem dating an older woman?" she asked.

"Not if you don't."

"I'm glad we got that settled. What do you like besides country?"

I picked up my guitar and strummed a few chords. Then I tore into a classical Segovia piece. To my astonishment, she took her fiddle out of its case and joined me note for note.

When we finished, she said, "I started studying the violin when I was five years old. I'm classically trained, and I play in the Nashville Symphony."

We jammed for two solid hours, and then Melody said, "I really like you, Jamie. I'm glad Rhonda introduced us. I've got to go now."

She placed her violin in its case and snapped it shut. I had the greatest desire to make love to her. Seeing the expression on my face, she said, "I can read you like a book, boy. Come on, walk me to my car."

I followed her down the steps, lusting after her round ass. At her station wagon, she placed the violin case in the backseat and turned to face me. She slid into my arms, laid her head on my shoulder, and held me tightly.

We stood like that for a minute. I could feel her heart beating against my chest and smell the essence of her. My head felt light. I didn't want to let go, but she pulled slowly away.

"When will I see you again?" I asked.

"Why don't you ask me for a date, smooth talker?"

"Dinner tomorrow?"

"Give me a call tomorrow afternoon."

She gave me a quick peck on the cheek and slipped behind the wheel. I watched her drive away and felt empty inside. I hadn't made love to a woman in months, and I couldn't remember ever being so damn horny.

* * *

The next morning I made several decisions. First, I needed a vehicle. I was tired of being chauffeured around town. Second, I wanted that puppy I'd seen at Dr. Stout's. Third, I was tired of not being in charge of my life. It was time for me to start performing again. And finally, I wanted to form a band with Melody as my fiddle player.

I still had money in my brokerage account because I'd been making a fair living doing studio work. I took my last taxi ride to the Jim Reed Chevrolet dealership on Broadway. I was paying the taxi driver when a salesman walked up and said, "I can put you in a new car, buddy, and you won't have to take any more taxis. How does that sound?"

I raised my eyebrows. "Well," I said, "that depends on the deal you'll give me."

"At Jim Reed's you always get a good deal. You're a fine-looking young fellow. I bet you'd like a new Corvette. I got a bright red one on the back lot. Want to see it?"

I laughed so hard, tears came to my eyes. "I was thinking more of a used pickup. What you got that fits that description?"

The man's expression changed immediately. "Well, son, I've got several pickups, but I still think you'd like that Corvette."

"Just let me see a pickup."

"Come on to the far side of the lot. My name's Charlie Drake. What's yours?"

I extended my hand and said, "Jamie Lee Coleman."

Mr. Drake showed me several trucks, but none caught my eye. We were headed back to the new car showroom when I spied a red 1965 Silverado two-door pickup. Two of the tires were flat, and the truck listed to one side. I pointed to the vehicle and asked, "How much you want for that one?"

Old Charlie was obviously distressed to even think about that particular pickup. He said, "Mr. Coleman, that doesn't look like a very good truck. It may have a lot of problems. We just took it in on a trade and haven't even had time to check it out. Probably needs a lot of work."

"How much?"

"Well, I'll have to ask the sales manager. I'm not sure we could even sell that one on time. You might have to pay cash."

"I plan to pay cash anyway. Go check for me, please. And it's got to have an automatic transmission."

An obviously disappointed Mr. Drake excused himself and disappeared into the used car office. Minutes later, he came back out with a smile on his face. "Okay," he said, "the sales manager says if you'll take it as is, he'll let it go for fifteen hundred. We'll fix the flats."

"Done. I'll write you a check."

I sat in the used car office while Mr. Drake did all the paperwork. An hour later, the truck was ready. When he handed the keys to me,

Mr. Drake said, "I can't let you drive off the lot without insurance. I would recommend State Farm. Do you know an agent?"

"No. Never had car insurance before. I never had a car or pickup before, either. How do I get car insurance?"

"My cousin, Virgil Simpson, can get it for you. Let's go back inside and I'll get him on the phone."

I spent about ten minutes on the phone with Virgil and he sent a fellow to the dealership with my insurance card and I sent a check back by his messenger. That issue taken care of, I asked Mr. Drake, "I don't have a driver's license. Reckon where I can get one?"

He laughed. "Well, son, that's a new one on me. I've never sold a car to a fellow who didn't have a driver's license. I don't reckon that's a problem unless you get stopped by a cop. There's a Department of Safety office on Murfreesboro Road out near the airport."

"Thanks, Mr. Drake. I'll drive out there and get legal."

After I took my test and passed. I received my temporary license and stuck it in my wallet. It was still early, so I headed up I-40 to Round Rock and got to the Stout farm around three. It was a chilly day, and the heater didn't work on the pickup so I shivered all the way. The sun was shining, and that did help. Perhaps I should have listened to Mr. Drake about the pickup possibly needing repairs. *Oh, well, live and learn.*

The doctor was busy tending a sick cow when I walked into his barn.

"Hi, Doc, I've come for that puppy," I said. "You've still got him, don't you?"

"I said I'd keep him for you, Jamie. He's in my office."

I found Fireman stretched sound asleep on the floor of the doctor's office. Doctor Stout had said he was a sooner, but he looked like he had a lot of Lab in him. I knelt beside him and shook him gently. He opened his eyes and gazed up at me. His tail started wagging, and he jumped up and licked my face. I could feel my heart race. This little guy was going to change my life.

"Come on, Fireman. I'm taking you home with me," I said.

Dr. Stout gave me a small amount of the dog's food, his water bowl, and his leash. Fireman sat next to me on the way back to Nashville and looked through the windshield with his tongue hanging out the corner of his mouth. By the time we passed Cookeville, he'd lost interest in scenery and had fallen asleep.

I stopped at the Kroger grocery on Harding Road in the Belle Meade Shopping Center and bought the puppy food and a chew toy. I knew puppies needed something to chomp on, and I didn't want Fireman at my boots. When we got to the apartment, I put his leash on and walked him down Twenty-First Avenue. He kept pulling me along and I had to pick up my pace to keep up with him. I felt like a new daddy out with his first kid.

Melody and I had decided we'd go to Mario's for dinner. I was delighted to be able to pick her up in my new-to-me pickup. She lived in an apartment off Murfreesboro Road. So I'd driven down Twenty-First Avenue to West End and then Broadway to Eight Avenue. When Melody opened the door, she looked fabulous. She wore black slacks and a white blouse with a black sweater thrown over her shoulders. Her hair was in a ponytail, my favorite style. She had diamond studs in her earlobes, and her lips were a burgundy color. I couldn't wait to taste them.

I'd bought new trousers and a blue blazer at Levi's men's store. I was tired of feeling scruffy all the time.

I retraced my route back to West End Avenue and parked on the street in front of Mario's. The maitre d' seated us at the same table Rhonda and I had used when we'd been there earlier. Melody and I enjoyed a leisurely dinner and returned to my apartment around nine o'clock. When I opened the door, I couldn't believe what I saw. The place was a mess. At first I thought that someone had broken in and trashed the apartment. Then I realized that Fireman had pulled the pillows off the couch, ripping them so that feathers littered the floor. Two of the lamps had been pulled from their tables, and the bed cover had been yanked off and lay on the kitchen floor. The dog was sound asleep in the middle of the living room, but when he heard Melody and me, he jumped up and ran to me.

Melody laughed so hard tears came to her eyes.

I shook my head and asked, "What have I done?"

She helped me pick up everything and restore some semblance of order to the place. I'd made a bed for the puppy in the bathroom. Melody and I took the dog for a short walk and played with him for a few minutes.

Then Melody picked Fireman up and held him in her lap as we headed for the couch. "You're going to make life interesting for Jamie, little fellow."

We sat on the couch, and I said, "I'm going to put a band together. I'd really like for you to play fiddle."

She grinned and said, "You've got to be kidding. What do you know about managing a band? And what makes you think the world needs another country band?"

"I worked in the Colt Walker Band and learned a lot. We can do this. I'm really excited about it. Don't be such a spoil sport."

"I'm just playing devil's advocate. It really is a scary business. Just a handful of artists ever make it big."

"I'm going to make it big. So big it'll blow your socks off."

"Okay. I'll play fiddle. But don't say I didn't warn you."

Fireman was sound asleep in Melody's lap. She lifted him gently, took him to the bathroom, and placed him on his make shift bed. "Sleep tight, little fellow."

We listened to a Tony Bennett cassette on the stereo, and she snuggled into my arms. I slipped my finger under her chin and lifted her face and kissed her. She opened her mouth and returned my kiss with passion, her lips pressing hard against mine. My heart pounded, and I said, "I want to make love to you. May I?"

A smile crept across her face, and she led me to the bedroom.

Chapter 19

I hadn't made love to a woman since Joy. As Melody led me to my small bedroom, I was overcome by a mixture of lust and intimidation. I turned the bed covers back, and when I turned to face Melody, she was naked. She smiled and walked into my open arms. As I wrapped my arms around her, the feel of her soft skin made me shudder. She gave me a wet open-mouth kiss. Then she started unbuttoning my shirt and pulling it out of my trousers. Within seconds she had completely undressed me, and she stepped back to admire what I hoped was a slim and muscular body. She grinned and pushed me onto the bed.

Then she mounted me and began a slow rhythmic and undulating motion that brought me to a climax in seconds. I couldn't believe I'd come so fast and felt a little embarrassed. I thought I'd mastered my premature ejaculation problem, but it was obvious that I hadn't. Pulling off me, she lay beside me and nestled her head on my shoulder.

"Now that we've got that out of the way we can spend some quality time exploring each other's bodies and minds. You okay with that?" Melody said with a grin.

I pulled her to me in a firm embrace and said, "I think that's a wonderful idea."

We held each other tightly in that manner until we both drifted off into a peaceful sleep. At some point in the night, I awoke and, pulling the sheet back, exposed Melody's pale breasts. I slowly began to kiss and suck softly on her nipples. Melody moaned, and when she opened her eyes, I kissed her on the lips. Then I explored every crease and fold of her body with my lips and tongue. By the time I slipped inside Melody, both of us were consumed by lust. We climaxed and fell into each other's arms. Soon we were both sound asleep.

I awoke around nine o'clock the next morning. I raised up on one elbow and gazed down on Melody's angelic face. Then I leaned over and whispered, "I love you."

Melody's eyes flew open, and she asked, "What did you say?"

"I love you."

"We just met and we've made love once. How could you possibly be in love with me?"

I smiled. "I'm a quick study. You're beautiful, great in bed, love my dog, are a fabulous fiddler, seem to like me, and I have the deep feeling that we'll make a great couple. You'll come around to my way of thinking eventually. Trust me."

She sat up facing me. The sheet had fallen to expose her generous breasts with their erect nipples, and she made no move to cover them. Looking me in the eye, she said, "I've never met anyone like you, Jamie. It scares me a little because I think you're probably right. I most likely will fall in love with you. What must that say about me?"

"That you're not only gorgeous but a smart woman. And like

I said, you play the violin and fiddle better than anyone I've ever heard. I'm so damn lucky I found you, it makes me a nervous wreck."

Melody wrapped the sheet around her and stepped out of bed. Heading for the bathroom, she turned back to me and said, "As soon as I get out of the shower, I'll make some scrambled eggs and coffee. You do have food in the house, don't you?"

Nodding, I said, "Yes, dear. Leave me some hot water, will you? The tank's not very big."

She came out minutes later wrapped in a bath towel, her wet hair in a hand towel. She started dressing in front of me, and I watched her the whole time. It was all I could do not to pull her back into bed. She threw me the bath towel, smiled, and said, "I left you about three seconds of hot water. You'd better hurry."

We ate breakfast with Fireman at our feet begging for bacon bits. I remembered how upset Miss Frances would get when I fed Bandit at the table. Nevertheless, I dropped a small piece of meat on the floor next to my new puppy. It was devoured in a nanosecond.

I took a sip of coffee and said, "I want you to help me put the band together. You know a lot more musicians than I do."

"I still think you're taking a big risk. But I know you well enough now to understand this is something you have to do. I'll do the best I can."

* * *

I knew exactly the kind of band I wanted. It would be different. I'd be the lead singer and guitarist. Melody would play fiddle or violin, depending on the music. We hired a fellow named Mark Doolittle for Dobro, banjo, and rhythm guitar. He was a tall skinny fellow with dark brown, thinning hair and deep set eyes that didn't seem to blink. Tommy Wallace would play drums. This old boy could reach around a basketball with one hand. His hair was a dirty blondish color that hung over his collar. Sammy Carpenter would play bass. He was a short fellow who looked overpowered standing next to his instrument. His beady eyes seemed to wander about the room and never look directly at anything. Jolly Joe Hornpepper was a round fellow who waddled when he walked and never smiled. He would be on the keyboard. No one in the group was over twenty-five.

It was an ambitious project, but I'd learned a lot from working with Colt Walker. I hired a booking company and told them we'd do any gig that paid. That meant we'd be doing small clubs and dance halls for a while. Everyone was excited. I'd done something a little unusual when I formed the band. I'd instituted a profit-sharing program. The better we did, the more money everyone would make. It was a great motivator.

The drums, keyboard, and bass took up a lot of space. I bought an enclosed trailer at a place on Murfreesboro Road next to Sears to pull behind Melody's station wagon. As soon as we started making a little money, I planned to buy a new van so we'd be more comfortable. Eventually, we'd move up to a touring bus. But we all knew that was in the future.

I laid down some stringent rules for behavior. No smoking in the car. No booze when we were working, and absolutely no coke. They could smoke pot on their own, but not while we were onstage or in a dressing room.

All of our apartments were too small for us to practice in. I talked the owner of an antique store on Eighth Avenue named John Wallace into letting us use the back of his establishment after he closed at five in the afternoon.

I'd bought a better stereo with good speakers because I wanted to play different artists and music for my guys. Our first practice session reminded me of Colt Walker's. Everyone was tense, but after an hour, things settled down.

"Don't get discouraged, guys. We'll get there eventually," I said. "I want this to be a very special band. We'll throw in a little boogie-woogie from time to time as well as some South American jazz. We might even try a little classical from time to time."

Mark Doolittle shook his head, and with a smirk, said, "Jamie, that don't make a whole lot of sense to me. How the hell am I supposed to play something classical on my damn banjo?"

"If Larry McNeely can play Beethoven's Fifth on the banjo, so can you," I said. "You'll just have to practice."

Jolly Joe piped in, "Country bands don't play classical, Jamie. Every damn fool and his brother knows that."

"I don't want us to stay a country band forever. The sooner we can cross over to mainstream popular music, the better. There's more money and better gigs. Trust me on this."

The men all shook their heads in unison and groused under their breath. Melody alone thought the idea had merit.

After that first hour, I said, "I want a repeated theme underlying the start of almost every piece we play. The closest thing I can think of is how Johnny Cash does it."

We tried a lot of ideas for the next hour and finally hit on a subtle boogie-woogie beat. It was amazing how well it worked. By the time we'd finished the first two hours of practice, everyone was excited but exhausted.

To celebrate, I took everyone to Mario's for dinner. I even let them throw down a few Italian beers. Melody started with French champagne and then switched to a California chardonnay. I sipped a Coke.

After that disastrous first night, I'd taken Fireman to an obedience class. He proved to be a smart little fellow and picked up things quickly. He went everywhere I did. While we practiced, Fireman sat patiently and watched or fell asleep.

To no one's surprise, Melody and I decided to share an apartment.

Neither of the ones we had was big enough, so we moved into a two-bedroom so that I could have an office.

I was delighted that Melody turned out to be a reader. She didn't enjoy the variety of books I did, but she consumed at least a novel a week. And she proved to be a damn good cook. In the short time we'd been together, we'd settled into a comfortable relationship. Thank goodness she loved Fireman as much as I did. When we were home together I would glance at Melody and see Fireman cuddled in her arms.

Our first gig was at a small dance hall in Clarksville, Tennessee, on the border with Kentucky where the Fort Campbell army base was located.

Not only did I want our band to sound different; I wanted us to dress in a certain way. Most country groups didn't pay much attention to that type of thing. They wore jeans and cowboy boots. Some of the old-time stars were partial to sequins and fancy jackets. I wanted something in between that looked tasteful and distinctive.

Melody was a clothes horse, so I ran all my ideas by her. We'd wear black jeans, cowboy boots, and Mexican guayabera shirts. We'd do long sleeves in the winter months and short sleeves in the summer. The one problem was that we had to have several for each band member.

At our last rehearsal before leaving for Clarksville, I said, "Melody and I've decided we're going to dress different than most bands." Then I told them what Melody and I had decided.

Mark Doolittle said, "I ain't wearing no fancy Mexican shirt. Damned things are pleated. Hell, I'd look like a damned sissy or maybe a queer."

"I'm with Mark," Tommy Wallace said. "I don't want to be taken for a fairy."

"Hell, I'm already thinking about quitting. You have too many damn rules, Jamie. We ain't used to this kind of shit," Jolly Joe said.

"It's like the drinking. Damnit, I do my best playing when I've got a little buzz. I think it's nuts, this crazy shit about us not drinking."

Mark shook his head and said, "The guys are right, Jamie. You need to back off. You're too damn strict for your own good. Hell, we're musicians, for God's sake. We ain't angels."

It was my second rebellion, and I wasn't sure how to handle it. I knew I had to be a strong boss. They were all older than me and had a lot more experience. But the die was cast so I said, "If you want to be in this band, you'll do as I say. This is not a democracy. Look, I know you guys think I'm a hard-ass, but someday you'll understand. I'm aiming for the stratosphere. You'll all be rich someday. Trust me."

Mark started to place his banjo in its case, and Tommy just stared at me. Melody broke the silence. "Come on, guys. We all need this job. None of us are exactly rolling in money."

I held my breath and waited. Finally, Mark said, "Okay. But I ain't wearing the damned thing until we go on stage."

* * *

The second Friday in April, Melody and I hooked the trailer to her station wagon and picked up each member of the band. I remember the date specifically because it was the day that Paul McCartney broke up the Beatles.

Melody had placed the guayabera shirts in plastic bags and hung them in the trailer. With all six of us crammed into the station wagon, we could barely move. I drove with Melody on the bench seat next to me, her hand resting gently on my thigh.

It was an overcast day with the temperature in the fifties. The old wagon strained up the few hills between Nashville and Clarksville. I didn't know much about the dance hall. All I had was an address. We'd decided to tailor our performance to the audience. If they wanted to dance, we'd play it straight down the middle, a typical country band. If they seemed a little adventurous, we'd try some of our other material.

Melody and I'd planned to repeat the duet that Kelly and I'd performed in Colt's band. Melody had a nice voice and probably could have made it as a singer, but her real love was the fiddle.

We arrived in Clarksville around six o'clock. The dance hall was a dump. When we walked in, Melody groaned. I looked at the guys and said, "I never promised you a rose garden."

Jolly Joe laughed and said, "Hey, man. Somebody ought to write a song called that."

The place was small and dirty. The owner was a fat guy named Walter Newberry who came waddling over to greet us, an unlit cigar hanging out of the corner of his mouth.

"Howdy, y'all tonight's band?"

I nodded. "Where's the stage and dressing rooms?"

"Stage is there," he said, pointing to a bare area in the corner. "Ain't got no dressing room."

"We need a dressing room," I said.

"I reckon you could use the bathrooms. They're right big."

It took a while to unload the trailer. I placed Tommy and his drums in the corner, and the rest of us would stand in front of him. There were two microphones, but the sound system was terrible. I decided we needed to buy our own to avoid this problem in the future.

We hadn't eaten, but I was reluctant to leave our instruments unattended so I sent Jolly Joe out for burgers. We sat in a few of the rickety chairs and ate our dinner wondering what the evening would bring.

Patrons began to filter in around eight o'clock. Within thirty minutes every table and chair was taken. The miniscule dance floor was just a bare space in front of where we'd be playing. I tried to keep a positive attitude, but I was a nervous wreck.

While we were waiting to start, I wandered over to the bar and asked the bartender, a burly guy with a shaved head, "Is this your usual crowd?"

He nodded.

"Do they like to dance or just listen to music?"

"Both."

He wasn't much help, so I moved among the patrons who seemed to be mostly blue collar workers and simply asked them. Most said they liked to drink and listen to music, but if the spirit moved them, they'd dance. This was a blue-collar crowd. I didn't see anyone who looked like a soldier. My decision was to play it straight country.

We began with a fast bluegrass piece. Mark started us off with the banjo, and Melody joined in on fiddle. Then all six of us gave it everything we had. I was pleased to notice that people were tapping their feet. When we finished that first song, we received a roaring round of applause. My heart was pounding, and everyone in the band was grinning.

After forty-five minutes of playing, I signaled a break. Without a dressing room, we just mingled with the crowd. Everyone was friendly and told us how great we were. One good old boy who'd had a few too many beers came on to Melody, and the bouncer had to intervene. It wasn't a big scene, but I was still nervous.

The cigarette smoke was so thick I couldn't breathe. I'd decided I wasn't going to sing or do our duet. We were an instrumental band that night.

We did a few dance tunes, and people jammed the dance floor.

After three forty-five minute sets, we signed off and packed up our instruments. The crowd begged us to stay, but we were exhausted. While the others were loading the trailer, I looked up the owner.

"We're heading out. I'm ready to be paid," I said.

"Y'all were great," he said, handing me a check.

"I'd prefer cash," I said.

"Don't trust me?"

I smiled. "It's not a matter of trust. I pay my guys after each gig. They want cash."

He frowned, but went behind the bar and opened the cash register. He pulled out some greenbacks and handed them to me, six one-hundred-dollar bills. I slipped them in my pocket and said, "Thanks."

"Y'all come back anytime. Our folks like you," he said.

* * *

We played so many run-down, hopeless bars and dance halls that I was about to go crazy. Then one night in Dothan, Georgia, we'd just finished our last set when a fellow wearing a big cowboy hat and alligator boots walked up to me, extended his hand, and said, "Jamie, my name's Rufus Alexander. I'm a music producer and agent. I'd like to talk to you for a few minutes."

I took his hand and said, "Pleased to meet you. What do you want to talk about?"

"Your career."

"What about my career?"

"I can help it."

I shook my head. "I'm really beat, Mr. Alexander. Can we put this off until tomorrow?"

"Okay. When you getting back to Nashville?"

"Tonight."

He handed me a card and said, "This is Wednesday. Meet me at the Holiday Inn in Nashville on Friday morning. I'll buy you breakfast. Say eight o'clock?"

I nodded. "Yeah. That's fine. I'll see you then."

On Friday morning I drove to West End Avenue and parked in the Holiday Inn lot. Mr. Alexander was waiting with a cup of coffee in his hand when I walked up to his table. I was still beat because I'd been having trouble sleeping. The guys in the band had started complaining about everything. We shook hands, and I took the chair across from him.

A waitress walked up and asked, "What you want, honey?"

I laughed, looked up at her with my bloodshot eyes, and said, "Start an IV on me and hook the coffee up."

She shook her head and poured my cup full. We ordered, and Mr. Alexander said, "I thought you guys did a good job down there in Dothan. Not too professional yet, but that'll come with time. You need some direction, son. I can help you."

"I'm not looking for an agent. I manage everything myself."

"You know what they say about a doctor who treats himself?"

"Not really."

"The doctor that treats himself has a fool for a patient."

"What does that mean exactly, and why is it relevant here?"

"A musician who manages himself has a fool for a client."

"So, what are you proposing?"

Just then the waitress brought our food to the table. We started eating and as he talked, Mr. Alexander waved his fork in the air. "Well, son. I see potential in you. I think I could help your career. Get you moving up the ladder to success in a hurry."

"Who do you currently represent?" I asked.

"Well, that's confidential."

"Do you have references? How much would you charge?"

"We make a deal, I'll give you references. I would take twenty-five percent of your gross."

I had heard that agents generally got fifteen percent of a musician's gross. Twenty-five percent sounded way too high. "I don't know, Mr. Alexander. That figure sounds a little high to me."

"You're an unknown at this point. That percentage could drop once you get more experience under your belt."

I didn't know what to do. I wished Melody had come with me.

I knew enough not to agree to anything without at least talking to Jake. "I'll have to think about this, Mr. Alexander."

He took a folded piece of paper out of his inside coat pocket and placed it on the table. "This is a letter of intention. It's not a contract. Sign this and after you think it over, if you still don't want to do it, no harm done."

I said, "Thanks for breakfast. I have your card. If I decide to sign on with you, I'll call in a couple of days."

"You're making a big mistake, son. The offer is only good for today. You walk out of here, all bets are off."

I shrugged. "I guess they're off."

"I can make it difficult for you. All I have to do is drop a few hints around town and you're finished. It's not a good idea to piss me off."

My heart was pounding and my mouth felt so dry I doubted I could swallow. I tried to stay calm, but it wasn't working very well. Was this guy bullshitting me, or was he serious? I took a deep breath and said, "I guess I'll just have to take my chances."

Then I turned and walked out of the restaurant.

By the time I got back to the apartment, my head was splitting. When I told Melody what Mr. Alexander had said, her face blanched. Then she took my hand and said, "Honey, I could be wrong, but I don't think things like that happen. You know, someone puts a hex on you."

I hoped she was right.

* * *

Six months later I had a real rebellion on my hands. One Saturday morning I opened the door of our apartment to see all four guys staring at me.

"Come in, guys. What's up?"

262

Mark was the spokesman. "We've had it, Jamie. We've played every sleazy dance hall and honky-tonk in a five-hundred-mile radius of Nashville. If you don't get us better bookings, we're quitting. All of us."

"We're not exactly a famous band. We don't have a record contract, and no one is banging on our door. But I'll talk to our booking agent and see what I can do."

"Make it happen soon, Jamie, or we're out of here. I mean it," Mark said.

The other three nodded.

Well, I have to tell you, that pissed me off and also scared the shit out of me. I couldn't do without these guys. I did need a band.

The following Monday I drove over to Music Row and talked to Pinky Albright, our booking agent. Pinky was a skinny fellow with a ring on each little finger, his trademark. His secretary ushered me into his small, crowded office where I found him chewing on an unlit cigar and reading the *Tennessean*.

"What's up, kid?" he asked.

"We're dying out there, Pinky. You've got to get us better gigs. I know we're unknown, but this shit is killing us."

The phone rang and I shook my head. When a damn phone rings, not many people can ignore it. Sometimes I had to agree with Jake. The things can be a nuisance. Pinky didn't even say "excuse me." He just picked up the receiver.

He listened for a moment and said, "Don't sweat it, man. I've got you covered. I'll call back in five or ten minutes."

Replacing the receiver, he grinned and said, "Jamie, son, ever heard that old saying about being in the right place at the right time?"

I nodded.

"That was Billy Crutchfield from Owensboro, Kentucky. He manages the Executive Inn. A lot of famous people perform there, and he's in a bind. The act he had lined up was in a bad wreck on the way down from Chicago and can't keep their date. Want a shot at it?"

I laughed. "That's like asking a starving man if he wants a T-bone steak. Hell, yes. Call him back."

The Executive Inn was a big hotel on the bank of the Ohio River in Owensboro. I'd seen ads in the *Tennessean* for the hotel and knew some good performers played there. I figured it could be the break we'd been waiting for.

Pinky got the details worked out while I stood there. It was a one-week engagement for two shows a night, one at 8:00 and a second at 11:00. The pay was excellent, and we received free rooms and meals.

I said, "Thanks, Pinky. I really appreciate this."

"Hey, man, that's my job. Good luck, son. This could be a great opportunity for you."

I felt as if I was walking on air as I rushed back to my pickup. I couldn't wait to tell Melody and the boys.

* * *

That evening I assembled the band at the antique shop on Eight Avenue promptly at seven o'clock.

"Okay, y'all. This is important as hell. For the next three nights we're going to practice and practice some more. We have to get this right."

"I have to hand it to you, Jamie. I never thought you'd be able to land us a gig like this," Mark said as he picked up his instrument.

"Oh, you of such limited faith," I said with a grin.

"I've always had faith in you, honey," Melody said.

Mark laughed. "Hell, babe, you're thinking with your ovaries again."

Melody hit him over the head with the bow of her fiddle.

"Okay, y'all. Let's get to work," I said.

For the next three hours, I pushed them hard. We had settled on a play-book by the end of the evening that I was pleased with. Every song would start out with the short, quick boogie-woogie four bars that would become our signature entrance.

* * *

We arrived at the Executive Inn around three o'clock in the afternoon of our first day's work. I checked us in and arranged to meet with the director of entertainment.

Our rooms overlooked the Ohio River. Seeing a tugboat pushing three large barges filled with coal made me think of walking the levee in New Orleans. The sun beat down on the small city from a cloudless sky. As I gazed out the window, Melody walked up behind me and placed her arms around my waist.

"I have a feeling this is going to be our big break, honey. I can feel it in my bones," she said.

"I hope so."

We unloaded the trailer and left the instruments in their cases. I'd abandoned the canvas cover for a hard case in which to store my Gibson. The Executive Inn was a classy place, so we didn't worry about someone stealing or trashing the instruments, which was a new experience for us.

Later in the afternoon, I spent some time with the director of entertainment, Justin Spears, a balding, middle-aged man.

"Could you tell me something about your clientele?" I asked. "I like to match the music to the audience. We're used to playing to a bunch of tipsy truck drivers."

Justin laughed. "There may be a few of them in the audience, but it'll be a mixed group. You know, some retirees and just plain old married folks."

The band ate dinner together in the main dining room at six

o'clock. Melody sat next to me. "Since we're working tonight, I don't want anyone drinking alcohol," I said.

"One glass of wine won't affect me," Melody said.

I shook my head.

"Hell, Jamie, I need a beer. At least one," Mark protested.

"It isn't happening, guys. This is our big chance. We're not going to blow it. I want everyone to be sharp and on their toes. I know I'm being a hard-ass, but I think it's important. We've got to be in top form. After the show tonight, you can all get knee-walking drunk for all I care. "

At five minutes to eight, we left our dressing room and assembled in the wings of the stage. Melody was adjusting her ponytail for the tenth time and biting her lower lip. The fellows seemed more relaxed. Fireman sat at my feet. He had a red bandana around his neck.

Promptly at eight, Justin walked onstage and stood facing the audience. "Ladies and gentlemen," he said, "it's my distinct pleasure to introduce Jamie Lee Coleman and his band for your entertainment this evening."

At that point, I pushed a clicker, and Fireman walked onstage and stood facing the audience. Then he lowered his front legs as if he was taking a bow. There were laughs and catcalls from the audience. Then he wandered to the side of the stage and sat facing forward.

I couldn't use my regular introduction because no one really knew me or what I'd be performing. So I walked onstage and said, "Good evening, I'm Jamie Lee Coleman, and I'd like to introduce the members of our band. You've already met our mascot, Fireman."

Melody came out first and waved to the audience, followed by Mark, Tommy, Joe, and Sammy. As each appeared I said the person's name.

I'd asked Justin not to dim the lights in the auditorium so I could see the audience. Looking out over their heads, I saw a lot of blue-rinse hair.

We'd decided to do a variety of thirties and forties tunes. Willie Nelson had been reviving some of them on his records, and with the crowd before us it seemed like a good idea. The first piece was "Stardust" followed by "Tenderly." Melody played the violin, not the fiddle.

The applause was deafening. I sang three songs in a row, and then Melody and I did a duet, "That Old Black Magic." Then I wandered down the steps and stood in front of an older couple in the first row. I thought "I Love You Truly" would be appropriate. Tears slid down the woman's wrinkled cheeks.

I climbed back onstage, and we picked up the pace with a raunchy boogie-woogie followed by a jazz piece. People were loosening up, and the applause grew louder. Mark stepped up to the microphone and started a bluegrass run, and then we all jumped in.

Perspiration beaded across everyone's forehead. The lights were hot, and we were exerting a lot of energy. I could feel sweat dribbling down my rib cage.

We'd rehearsed something that none of us was sure would work but that we thought might be fun. In the midst of the bluegrass number, I threw my Gibson to Mark, and he threw his banjo to me. I picked a few fast bars and Mark did as well. Then we switched again, and Melody and I played each other's instruments.

After an hour of playing, we were exhausted but having the time of our lives. The audience was, too. I glanced into the wings once to see Justin with a huge grin on his face.

We received three encores and finally had to stop. We needed an hour's down-time in order to do the second show.

Back in the dressing room, Melody threw her arms around my neck and kissed me hard on the lips. "Jamie, honey, we did it!" she said. "I'm so excited I could bust!"

There was a knock on the door, and when I answered it, a tall, sandy-haired man said, "I'm Maurice Ledbetter. I'd like to speak to you for a moment."

I stepped into the hall and said, "Sure. What's on your mind?"

"I'm with Ramsey Records. I'd like to offer you a contract."

Chapter 20

My heart was racing as I took the man's card. Taking a deep breath, I said, "Thank you, Mr. Ledbetter. That sounds real interesting. I'll call you as soon as we get back to Nashville."

"I think you've got a real future, Jamie. You have that special aura that makes a star."

I burst back into the dressing room with a big grin on my face. I grabbed Melody by the waist and pulled her to me. Then I kissed her. Leaning back, I said, "We're going to get a recording contract. That fellow was from Ramsey Records."

Melody started to cry. "Oh, honey, I'm so happy."

Mark came over and said, "That's great, Jamie. When?"

"After this gig, when we get back to Nashville."

The day after Mr. Ledbetter's visit, I called the City Café in Round Rock and asked Dorothy to get Jake on the phone. Minutes later, Jake said, "I'm glad to finally hear from you, Jamie. I thought maybe you'd dropped off the face of the earth."

"Sorry, Jake. We've been busier that a one-armed paper hanger in a hurricane. I need some help."

"That's a new one. I thought you were Mr. I Can Do It Myself."

"I've been offered a recording contract. I need the name of a good intellectual property attorney. Any suggestions?"

"Sam Young in Nashville. I seldom hear from you. Things must be going well."

"I promise I'll do better, Jake. Give my love to Yolanda."

I called Mr. Young and set up an appointment for the following week.

On the third night of our engagement at the Executive Inn, Justin came by our dressing room between shows with a friend. The man's name was Arthur Balance, and he owned a nightclub in Kentucky just across the river from Cincinnati, Ohio. He was a tall effeminate fellow who spoke with a lisp.

Justin introduced us, and Mr. Balance said, "Justin told me I had to catch your show. I'm glad he did. It's quite unusual. I'd like to offer you a spot at my club for a week. Are you available?"

"I've got to be back in Nashville next week for awhile. We want to cut a record, and I've got some friends I need to see. In a month we'll be available," I said.

Handing me his card, he said, "Call me and give me an exact day. I want to advertise the fact that you're coming."

I thanked him, but was puzzled. *Why would anyone advertise an unknown band?*

*   *   *

When we returned to Nashville, I went to see Mr. Young, a wiry man who looked like an aging cowboy movie star. He wore a Stetson tilted back on his head and had his boots up on his desk when I walked into his office.

He stood and offered his hand. "You Jamie Lee Coleman?" he asked.

"Yes, sir."

"Have a seat. Jake Watson said you're a special friend of his."

"He's like a father to me."

"Someone offered you a recording contract?"

I nodded. "Ramsey Records."

"Have a seat, son. Ramsey is a small outfit. They don't have any stars in their stable. Not like RCA, Mercury, or Capitol. What did they offer?"

"I didn't discuss anything with Mr. Ledbetter. I knew I wanted an attorney to make the deal."

"Smart move. The chances of a big label giving a contract to an unknown are slim. It's not a bad idea to cut a record with a small company to get your name out there. I'll negotiate a good deal for you and make sure you're able to move up to a premium label later without a penalty."

"So, what would be a good deal?" I asked.

"They're small, so you can't expect too much up front, if any at all. My take would be to ask for a good royalty. I'll try to get you at least twelve percent. You have to understand this up front. Most of the time the artists don't do very well unless they sell a ton of records. Everything is controlled by the record companies. They get paid first, and they have ways of whittling down the artist's take-home pay."

"I'm a pretty good businessman for my age, Mr. Young. I try to let no one take advantage of me if I can help it."

We shook hands and I left.

Things were looking up. Melody and I sold my pickup, her station wagon, and the trailer and bought a new blue 1970 Chevrolet van. I had the title made out in both of our names. I could feel myself becoming more and more attached to Melody. Not only was she gorgeous, but she was smart, funny, and one hell of a musician. And our sex life was fantastic. I was even thinking of marriage.

I wanted to introduce Melody to Jake and Yolanda, so the day after we bought the van, Melody, Fireman, and I drove to Round Rock.

As we headed east on I-40 I said, "I've been racking my brain trying to come up with a tag line to go after my name. Johnny Cash calls himself 'the Man in Black' and Hank Snow is 'the Singing Ranger.' What do you think?"

"How about the Sexy Yodeler?" Melody said, laughing.

"Be serious, girl. Help me here."

We batted a few ideas around, and finally Melody said, "In reality, Jamie, I think most of those tag lines come from their fans, critics, or friends. Someone call them something, and it sticks."

"Okay, you know more about this business than I do," I said. "What should we call the band?"

"The band doesn't need a name. We're the Jamie Lee Coleman Band," she said.

We arrived at Jake's house just in time for dinner. I'd called to let them know what time to expect us. As I'd hoped, Yolanda had fixed a wonderful meal of pork chops, green beans, cornbread, creamed corn, and mashed potatoes. We finished with chess pie and coffee.

At the table Jake quizzed Melody about all aspects of her life. I figured Jake could see we were in love. I'm sure he wanted to make sure she was worthy of his charge.

We adjourned to the library after dinner, and Jake and Yolanda had their usual. Melody sipped on a chardonnay, and I had a Coke. Fireman sat at my feet while we listened to "Rhapsody in Blue."

Melody, Fireman, and I went to my old room around ten o'clock.

"Do you think Jake has a problem with us sleeping together?" Melody asked.

"No. He'd be a little hypocritical if he did."

"What's that mean?"

"If you haven't picked up on it, Yolanda is more than just a housekeeper."

"They're involved?"

I nodded. "Deep, dark secret."

"I'm from Mississippi. I understand," Melody said.

Melody took the bathroom first and came back to the room wrapped in a bath towel. Her hair was brushed full and fell to her shoulders.

I took a quick shower and returned to the bedroom. She was reading when I picked up Fireman and placed him at the foot of the bed like I'd always done with Bandit. Then I slipped under the covers. She turned off the light and snuggled up against me. We kissed and fondled each other for a long time before she helped me inside her. As we climaxed, I whispered, "I love you."

She held me tightly against her and said, "And I love you with all my heart."

We lay quietly in each other's arms for a few minutes, and then I rose up on my elbows and said, "Melody my darlin' you are the love of my life, my best friend, and my lover. Will you marry me?"

Melody placed her hand behind my head and pulled me to her. I could feel the wetness of her cheeks against mine. "I think that's a wonderful idea, Jamie Lee Coleman. When?"

"As soon as we can get a license and line up a judge." Then as an afterthought, I asked, "Do you want a church wedding?"

"I don't care the first thing about a church wedding. My mother may be disappointed, but that's her problem."

I had a perplexing thought. "I guess after we're married we'll have to go visit your folks."

"There's no hurry. I've already told Mother we're too busy right now to visit. Once things settle down, then we can go see them all. My brother in Memphis and my parents in Yazoo City."

* * *

We went to the courthouse the next morning and asked for a marriage license. We discovered the requirement for a premarital blood test had been dropped and there was no waiting period. Judge Grant married us that afternoon, and Jake and Yolanda witnessed for us.

When the judge said, "You may kiss the bride," Yolanda began to bawl, tears streaming down her cheeks. Jake just had a big smile on his face. We adjourned to Jake's house where Yolanda served us ice cream and cut the cake she'd made for the occasion.

Jake raised his flute of champagne and said, "Here's to a long and prosperous life for both of you. Now I have a daughter as well as a son. I love you both so much it takes my breath."

Melody and I had decided we didn't have time for a honeymoon. There was too much to do with our new gig coming up and the possibility of cutting a record. We said good-bye to Jake and Yolanda and stopped by the City Café for a cup of coffee before the drive to Nashville.

We'd just taken our seats when Oliver Winter, a fellow I'd heard of but didn't know, walked over and asked, "Aren't you Jamie Lee Coleman?"

I stood and offered my hand. "Yes, sir," I said.

"I'm the head of the draft board, Jamie. You haven't registered."

Of course I hadn't registered. I didn't want to have anything to do with that stupid war.

"I didn't know I had to."

"Every male has to register when he turns eighteen. You could be in real trouble, son."

"If I do it now, will it be okay?"

"I'll try to smooth it over for you. But you've got to come over to the office now."

Melody's face was ashen, and she was biting her lower lip so hard I thought she might draw blood.

"Where is it?" I asked.

"I'll walk you over," Mr. Winter said.

We gulped our coffee, and I paid the bill. We followed Mr. Winter across the street to the courthouse.

I had to push the whittlers out of the way so we could climb the steps. The inside of the courthouse was dark and cool. The draft board office was in the back next to the county clerk's where we'd bought our marriage license.

The secretary had been in my high school class. Her name was Audrey Crockett, a slight girl with mousey brown hair and no chin. She smiled when she saw me.

"Hi, Jamie," she said.

Mr. Winter said, "Put Jamie on the rolls. He hasn't registered yet."

Then he turned to me and said, "There'll be another lottery soon. Be sure to give your contact information to Audrey." Then he went in his office and closed the door.

"I'm sorry about Billy," Audrey said.

"What about him?" I asked.

"You don't know? He's missing in action over there in Vietnam," she said.

Melody grabbed my arm. I'd told her about my cousin and some of our adventures.

I felt as if someone had stuck a knife in my heart. For all the distance in our relationship, I did love Billy as a comrade in arms. My God, we'd spent our childhood fighting the system. "How's Lester taking it?" I asked.

"Been drowning himself in shine. It's right sad," Audrey said.

I gave her Melody's and my address and made sure she noted that we were married. Then I said, "It's good to see you, Audrey. How's your mom?"

She smiled and said, "She's fine. I'll tell her you asked about her."

In my experience it never hurt to stay on the good side of a bureaucrat.

* * *

Melody was quiet on the drive back to Nashville. Her blue eyes were moist, and she stared through the windshield. I knew what she was thinking. I'd get drafted, sent to 'Nam, and killed. There was no way in hell that I'd let that happen. If another Pearl Harbor occurred, I'd have volunteered that fucking day. But did I give a shit if the damn country of Vietnam became Communist?

"What's running through your mind, Melody?" I asked.

"You know damn well what's running through my mind."

"Don't worry about it, sweetie. Now that we're married I'll be lower on the list. And, if push comes to shove, we're out of here. We can make our music in Canada, Australia, or any fucking place we want."

She smiled. "I'm so glad to hear you say that. I was terrified you'd want to be a fucking hero or something."

I laughed. "Do I look like a hero?"

"Come to think of it, no."

Back in Nashville, the guys in the band were delighted when Melody and I told them we were married. Jolly Joe said, "Hell, man, you had to make an honest woman out of that girl."

* * *

Mr. Young made us a good deal with Ramsey Records. The band members were excited to finally cut a vinyl. We had just enough time to produce a record before we had to be at our next gig. The words of a new song had been running through my head for a few days, so the night before we were to cut our first single I jotted down the words and chorus to "Stolen Kisses," my second composition. I hadn't received huge royalties from "Mountain Love," but it had whetted my appetite for what might happen in the future.

I had always been a fan of Marty Robbins, so I patterned the ballad after one of his. It was a sad and sentimental song with a haunting melody that told the story of a long haul truck driver who fell in love with another man's wife. The first time I sang it for Melody, she cried.

On the day of the recording session, we unloaded our instruments from the van and walked into the studio. Everyone was nervous. Mr. Ledbetter was waiting for us as we walked in.

Looking at his watch, he said, "You're cutting it a little close, Jamie."

"Sorry. We've been running late all morning," I said.

I had a strange feeling settle over me as we entered the studio. I'd been a session musician and longed for the time I'd be able to cut my own record. Now my dream was actually coming true.

We pulled our instruments out of their cases and began to tune them. Mr. Ledbetter had decided to lay the record out in several tracks. Then the sound engineer would pull it all together.

When I walked up to the microphone, my mouth felt devoid of saliva. I wasn't sure I could speak, let alone sing. Once the band started to play, I relaxed and gave it my best shot.

At the end of the four-hour session, Mr. Ledbetter was very excited. "That was awesome, Jamie. I think we may have a hit on our hands."

I smiled. "You think?"

We spent two weeks practicing for our next gig in Kentucky. Mr. Ledbetter had put a rush on the production of the single and had it to the radio stations in ten days.

I was impressed by Ramsey Records' handling of the publicity. The company's representatives descended on every major radio station in the country. None of us were prepared for the response to the single.

Soon all you could hear on country radio was our ballad. Sales skyrocketed. The royalties poured in, as did offers for gigs. My Paine Webber account was finally growing again, and I was on the phone with Mr. Hackman three or four times a day.

Had I not been well grounded from my association with Miss Frances and Jake, I might have fallen prey to the magnitude of our success. I'd watched a number of performers who let it go to their heads. A lot of them blew everything on booze, broads, and coke.

Melody, God love her, stayed grounded as well. I couldn't believe how lucky I was to have her as my wife. It was wonderful that we worked together.

* * *

By the time we arrived in Kentucky for our nightclub gig, it was almost two months since I'd made the arrangement with Mr. Balance. He'd been happy to postpone our engagement because of our sudden notoriety. Since our single hit the airwave, our whole world had changed. I couldn't believe how quickly we'd gone from obscurity to fame. I was beginning to have a little trouble keeping the guys in line, though. With the profit-sharing plan, they were making damn good money, much more than they would have in most bands. The two months off had made them a little restless and a bit lazy.

Melody and I were late getting to our dressing room the first night of our show. When we walked in, I caught Jolly Joe tipping a silver flask. He screwed the top back on and slipped it into his pocket.

"What's in the flask?" I asked.

"Sweet tea," he said with a silly grin.

I stared at him, waiting for an honest answer. When he didn't come clean, I said, "Let me have it."

"Come on, Jamie. Cut me a little slack, for Christ's sake," he said.

Glancing around the room, I looked each guy in the eye and said, "When we started this band, I told y'all the rules. You signed on to them." Then looking directly at Jolly Joe, I said, "If I *ever* catch you with that damn flask again when we're working, you're out of here. Put it on the table."

He glared at me with defiance in his eyes but did as I'd asked.

No one said a word. Melody had a stricken look on her face. Mark, to his credit, took his flask out of his pocket and placed it next to Jolly Joe's.

"Thanks," I said. "Now let's go out there and give these folks what they paid for."

We stood in the wings while Mr. Balance introduced us. He must have been a little nervous because his lisp was so bad I could barely understand him.

As always, Fireman with his bandana was at my side. I pushed the clicker, and he walked out onto the stage. He bowed among hoots and catcalls, then wandered to the side of the stage and took his post.

I went out and addressed the microphone. I stood there staring out over the heads of the audience for a few moments without saying a word. Slowly, the chatter died down, and I said, "I guess you know who I am or you wouldn't be here."

That brought a round of applause and a good bit of laughter. Then Melody, fiddle and bow in hand, walked out with a big smile on her face, and I said, "I'd like to introduce our fiddler and my wife, Melody Chapman Coleman."

Each band member was introduced as he appeared, and once assembled, we went right into "Stolen Kisses."

The response was terrific. What happened next reminded me of my first visit to the Opry with Melody. People came right up to the edge of the stage and took our picture. We were blinded by the flashes from their cameras.

Most performers prefer to have the house lights dimmed when they perform. I didn't. I wanted to see the faces of the people we entertained, their responses. Plus I planned to wander among them. It was my trademark.

We played all kinds of music that evening, everything from country to jazz and boogie-woogie. About halfway through the first show, I wandered down the steps into the audience. This was a younger crowd than we'd played to before. There were no blue-rinse hairdos. I picked a middle-aged woman with peroxide blond hair who was obviously with her husband. He was a burly guy with long gray hair hanging over his collar. I stood before her, looked into her eyes, and sang "I Love You Truly."

She turned beet red but had a smile on her face. I don't think anyone in the audience had ever heard the song. I shook her husband's hand when I finished and then walked over to another woman who looked to be in her thirties. I sang "Love Me Tender," and when I finished, she stood and threw her arms around my neck. I laughed and said, "Remember, darlin', that's my wife up there onstage."

Melody, playing her part, made a face at the woman. That brought the house down. We finished with some old standards from the forties and fifties to foot-stomping applause.

Back in the dressing room, I went over the list of engagements that our booking agent had arranged for us. It was a heavy schedule and would take us all over the country in the following weeks. We wouldn't get back to Nashville until around Christmas.

I'd leased a tour bus because it was going to be a grueling trip in a van. That way the guys could take turns driving. Melody and I had a small bedroom in the very back, and the fellows had bunk beds.

We had a twenty-inch television we could watch when we were in a city. Most of the time when we were on the road, Melody and I read, but the boys played cards.

Atlantic City, New Jersey, was our last gig before Thanksgiving. We'd left on Wednesday and were on our way to Atlanta for a show. Melody and I'd said goodnight to the fellows and gone to our bedroom. We crawled into bed and read for an hour. As I turned off the bedside lamp, Melody snuggled up to me and said, "You're going to be a daddy."

Chapter 21

Suddenly, I realized I was a few weeks shy of nineteen, married, making two hundred grand a week, and going to be a father. I snapped the light back on and stared at my wife. She had a sheepish grin on her face.

"When did this happen?" I asked.

"Six weeks ago, give or take a day or two," she said. "I hope you're happy."

"Of course I am. Are you?"

She put her arms around me and lay her head on my chest. "I've dreamed of having a child since I was a little girl playing with dolls. I'm so excited I can barely breathe."

I tilted her face toward mine and kissed her softly on the lips. I wasn't sure the timing was right, but if being pregnant made Melody happy, I was all for it. I knew some entertainers carried their young kids with them on the road. I guessed we could as well.

"Can we still make love?" I asked.

She answered me by rolling on top of me and kissing me hard, her tongue finding mine. We made gentle love for a long time and then fell into a deep sleep. I awoke around one o'clock in the morning and realized the lamp was still on. Luckily, the curtains were drawn.

The next morning I took the bathroom first. After I'd showered and shaved, I went up front and got two cups of coffee. When I got back to the bedroom, Melody had fluffed up the pillows and sat waiting for me.

"You're such a sweetie," she said. "I knew you'd bring me coffee."

I sat on the side of the bed and sipped my mug. "When should we tell the guys?" I asked.

"I don't have a problem telling them this morning," she said.

"How long will you be able to work?" I asked.

"I don't know. If you don't mind looking at a big-bellied woman, I can probably do it up to the eighth month. I'll have to ask the doctor."

I set my mug on the bedside table and leaned over and kissed her. "I think a big belly on you might be sexy."

She poked me in the ribs and pulled me to her. "I love you so much," she said.

Then we made morning love.

* * *

The Nashville elite have always had a love-hate relationship with the music industry. They appreciated what it does for the local economy but make a concerted effort to distance themselves from the rowdy image of the musicians. That's why most of the stars live in Hendersonville and along Old Hickory Lake.

Now that Melody and I were making incredible amounts of money and had a child on the way, we decided we needed a house. We wouldn't go out on the road again until spring, so we had plenty of time to find a good deal.

Returning from our tour, we'd settled in the apartment and were at the breakfast table one morning when Melody asked, "Where do you think we ought to look for a house?"

"Belle Meade," I said.

She frowned. "Most everyone lives out in Hendersonville."

"That's why I want to settle in Belle Meade. I've driven through there, and I like the way it looks. The houses are fabulous, and everything's well maintained."

"It'll be expensive," she said.

"We can afford it. While we're off the road I want to cut an album. I've been working on some new songs."

"Are we going to do Glen Campbell's show?"

"I got confirmation yesterday."

"Are we going to fly out there?" she asked.

"I've got tickets on American. We leave next Wednesday."

She reached across the table and took my hand. "Things seem to be moving so fast. It kind of scares me."

"That's the way things happen in this business. You have to be prepared to strike while the iron is hot."

"When're we going to look for a house?"

"I've contacted a real estate agent. He's going to show us some places right after lunch."

* * *

We met Sandy Benton, the real estate agent, at the corner of Belle Meade Boulevard and Harding Road at one o'clock that afternoon. He was a fellow in his mid-forties with light brown hair and steel gray eyes. He was driving a powder-blue 1970 Cadillac four-door sedan.

He jumped out of his car and ran back to introduce himself. "Y'all follow me," he said. "The first property is on this street."

The boulevard was divided by a strip of green grass and trees. We drove a mile and turned into a driveway. The house was a two-story brick with black shutters and white columns. The lawn was manicured and the trees magnificent.

Mr. Benton led us into the front hall, and we followed him from room to room. The den caught my eye because every wall was covered with walnut bookcases, and a huge brick fireplace sat at one end of the room. It reminded me of Jake's library.

The master bedroom also had a fireplace and the biggest bathroom I'd ever seen. The tub was sunk into the floor and had Jacuzzi jets, and there were two sinks. Melody's eyes were wide with excitement. I was really impressed with the place and asked Mr. Benton, "What're they asking for this?"

"Two fifty."

"Is there any room for negotiation?"

"Make an offer and I'll see what the seller says."

"What would you suggest?"

He thought for a minute and said, "I'd try two forty-five."

"Try two forty."

He nodded and said, "Will your parents be helping you with the twenty percent down payment and the mortgage?"

I shook my head. "My mother's dead and my old man's in the state pen."

Melody blanched but didn't say anything.

Mr. Benton looked a little skeptical and asked, "Mr. Coleman, how do you propose paying for this property?"

"I'll write you a check," I said, taking out my checkbook.

Benton frowned.

"Call Commerce Union Bank and give them the account number on the check," I said. "They'll verify that it's good."

"What business did you say you're in?" he asked.

"I'm in the stock market."

I don't think he believed me. I felt sure he had me pegged as a drug dealer. However, I got the distinct impression that to Mr. Benton, money was money.

He watched me closely as I wrote out the check. When I handed it to him, he asked, "How can I reach you?"

"Our phone number's on the check. We'll be home this afternoon. How soon can we move in?"

Mr. Benton obviously wasn't accustomed to cash transactions. The house was empty, so I saw no reason for it to take more than a day or two.

He cleared his throat and slipped the check into his shirt pocket. "There has to be a termite inspection and the seller must issue a title insurance policy. I could rush both, but it'll still take a week."

"You're going to make $14,400 on this sale. I think for that amount of money you can make the effort to get this done in two days, max."

He smiled and asked, "How old are you, Mr. Coleman?"

"I'll be nineteen in a few weeks."

* * *

Melody was fidgeting in her seat as we backed out of the driveway. "Jamie, honey, that's an awfully big house for two people, and so much money. You sure we can afford it?"

"We can afford it. There'll be three of us in a few months and maybe four or five not long after that," I said.

She shook her head. "I don't know, Jamie. I think you need to slow down. This whole thing is making me a nervous wreck."

"Relax, honey. I know what I'm doing. This is going to work. Trust me."

She smiled and stared out the windshield. We were on Harding Road passing the Belle Meade Shopping Center, a small strip mall on the corner of White Bridge Road.

Since we were leasing a tour bus in the spring, we didn't need the van any longer. We'd decided Melody and I needed our own vehicles. We'd discussed what cars we wanted, and Melody had chosen a station wagon because of our soon-to-be-expanded family. I figured we'd stay with Chevrolet so I drove straight to the Jim Reed dealership.

The salesman who'd sold us the van met us at the door. He was a skinny fellow named Carl Horton with the yellowed fingers of a heavy smoker.

I said, "We want to trade in the van for a couple of cars, a station wagon for Melody and a Monte Carlo for me. And I want a good deal."

He led us out to the back lot and showed us what we'd asked for. We settled on green for both vehicles. With the trade in, the price for both cars was five grand. I wrote him a check, and we waited for them to be serviced.

Melody said, "Jamie, honey, you're making my head swim. I can't believe this is happening. It just seems too fast. You're sure you know what you're doing?"

I took her hand and said, "Trust me, honey. I know what I'm doing."

While Mr. Horton was taking care of the sale, I called our State Farm agent and gave him the vehicle numbers on the two cars. About an hour later, the salesman walked into the waiting room and handed us our respective keys. Then Melody and I drove back to the apartment flush with excitement.

* * *

The phone was ringing when we walked into the living room. It was Mr. Benton. He said, "The sellers agreed to the price, and your check is good, so I'll try to get everything in order by day after tomorrow."

"Can we take possession then?"

"I'll call and meet you there with a key."

I thanked him and called our insurance agent at State Farm again so he could insure the house. Then I made sure the electricity and water were changed to our name. Things were moving a little fast for Melody. She seemed to be in a daze. I, on the other hand, felt energized.

"Let's go buy some furniture," I said.

Melody sighed and said, "Jamie, honey, we can't furnish a whole two-story house in an afternoon. To do it right, we'll need several weeks."

"No we don't. You know I like to get things done quickly."

She was standing with her hands on her hips, never a good sign with Melody.

"Damn it, Jamie. Listen to me. We are not going to furnish our new house in one afternoon. That's insane—you're insane."

"I'm not insane, just practical. What's wrong with you? Why don't you trust me?"

"Don't raise your voice to me, Jamie Lee Coleman. Don't you ever do that again. This is supposed to be a partnership. Start acting like a partner instead of a damn dictator. I'm so mad at you this moment I could spit bullets."

Melody spun around and ran from the room. I stood there like an idiot and wondered what I'd done. Then my senses came to me and I realized I'd been a total jerk. I followed Melody into the kitchen where I found her standing at the sink wiping tears from her eyes with a paper towel. I walked to her side and handed her my handkerchief.

"I'm sorry, honey. I'm an idiot. Please forgive me. We'll do it your way. I love you. I just want you to be happy."

She looked up at me with tears still sliding down her cheeks. She sniffed and smiled. She knew she'd won and was proud of herself. I let it go.

Let's just get a few things for our bedroom, the den, and the kitchen. Then we can take our time for the rest of it," Melody said with a grin.

"Well, okay. If that's what you want to do. You're the boss when it comes to the house. Hell, if I was honest with myself, you're the boss of my life, and I'm totally okay with that."

She laughed. "Is that so? I won't let you forget that one, smooth talker."

We took her car and drove to Green Hills, where there was a furniture store called Bradshaw's. Our apartment had come furnished so we didn't own a single thing, and we had to furnish part of a two-story house. I said, "Let's start with the bedroom. How's a king-sized bed sound to you?"

"I think a queen would be better. Kings take up too much room."

"Whatever you say, sweetie. May I have a recliner for the den?"

"I'm not trying to railroad you, Jamie. We need to do this together. In the first place, no one in their right mind furnishes a house this quickly. But I'm going to cut you some slack on this because I love you so much."

"Okay, darlin', but I want you to have whatever you want."

For a soon to be nineteen-year-old young man who had been raised in a tarpaper shack in sheer poverty, I was so excited I could barely contain myself. Miss Frances and Jake had taken me in and treated me well, but now I had my first chance to enjoy the fruits of my own labor. My heart raced as we entered the furniture store.

We spent two hours selecting a bed, chest, bedside tables, and lamps for our bedroom. Then Melody said, "Why don't you pick out what you want for the den? We'll need a television, too."

After arranging for the new purchases to be delivered the day we were to move in, we went to Castner-Knott department store in Green Hills to buy stuff for the kitchen. I was having fun and couldn't wait to get into our new home.

* * *

I'd arranged everything so the truck would deliver our furniture shortly after Mr. Benton handed me the keys. I'd bought two red leather chairs with ottomans similar to Jake's, and they were placed in front of the fireplace.

Melody spent the afternoon filling the bathrooms with towels and the kitchen with cooking utensils. I placed furniture and the lamps for her approval. At the end of the day we fell into each other's arms, exhausted. "That was fun, but I don't want to do this again for a while," Melody said. "We'll eventually have to furnish the rest of the house."

We didn't have any groceries, so we went out to eat at Jimmy Kelly's Steakhouse on Harding Road. We had to stand in line because the place was packed, but it only took about twenty minutes to get a table. As we walked into the dining area, I noticed Sarah Cannon seated at one of the tables with a man.

I grabbed Melody's arm, and we stopped. I said, "Mrs. Cannon, I'm Jamie Lee Coleman, and this is my wife, Melody. I met you very briefly backstage at the Opry once."

She smiled and said, "I never forget a good-looking young man, do I, Henry?"

The man answered, "No, you don't."

"We just sat down. Why don't you and your wife join us?" Mrs. Cannon said. "This is my husband, Henry."

"We'd love to, but I hate to impose," I said, taking Henry's hand.

"Nonsense. Besides, I've been hearing your name a lot in the last few weeks. I'd like to know more about you."

I pulled out a chair for Melody, and we joined the Cannons.

The four of us ordered, and I gave a very brief account of my life, leaving out Beulah Land and the fact that Pop was in the pen for murdering my mother.

Mrs. Cannon said, "I'm fascinated by how quickly some young entertainers reach the top nowadays and the amount of money they make. It's not like the old days."

"Communications are so much better now. Radio is more sophisticated, and television has made a tremendous difference," I said. "We're going on Glen Campbell's show next week, which should give us a big boost."

"Well, that's a coincidence! I'm going to be doing his show at the same time. He's such a nice young man."

"We're excited. Tell us about your career. I listened to you on a crystal radio when I was a kid."

She laughed. "Well, I'm not really from Grinder's Switch. In my early career I did the Opry and some traveling shows. I did a lot of big county fairs in the autumn. Henry flew us to a lot of those engagements. He has his own plane."

That piqued my interest so I asked, "What kind of airplane do you have, Mr. Cannon?"

"A twin-engine Beechcraft Baron," he said.

"How fast is it?"

"About two hundred miles an hour."

That started me thinking. If I learned to fly, the band could take the tour bus, and Melody and I could meet them.

"How hard is it to learn flying?" I asked.

"You just have to take lessons. Cornelia Fort Airport over in East Nashville has a flight school."

Our food arrived, and we made small talk while we ate. At the end of the meal, I thanked the Cannons for allowing us to join them. Then I picked up the bill after some good-natured arguing.

"Good luck on the Campbell show," Mrs. Cannon said as we parted.

* * *

The next morning I drove to East Nashville. I had a terrible time finding the small airport. It was right on the Cumberland River that runs through Nashville and very close to BNA, the municipal airport.

The airport was named after Cornelia Fort, an early female aviator, who was a contemporary of Amelia Earhart. She was teaching a student to fly in Hawaii the day the Japanese bombed Pearl Harbor.

A young skinny fellow with sandy hair was standing behind the counter when I walked in and he asked, "Can I help you?"

"I'd like to learn how to fly," I said.

"What's your goal, relational pilot or professional?"

"Beats me. I just want to see if I like it."

"You got time for a lesson?"

"Sure."

The man introduced himself. "I'm Webster Dunhill, one of the instructors."

I shook his hand and said, "Jamie Lee Coleman. Nice to know you."

"You the singer?"

"Yeah. You like country music?"

"I love it. And I love 'Stolen Kisses.' Every time my girlfriend hears it she cries."

"Give me a card or write your name and address on a piece of paper and I'll send you an autographed record."

"Wow! I can't wait to tell Cindy."

As we walked out to the line, he explained some things about the program. "We have two types of trainers, Cessna 152s and 172s.

The 172 is a more complicated airplane and makes it easier for you to transition, move up to larger aircraft."

"Why don't we use the 172?" I said.

He explained the preflight maneuvers a pilot must go through before even getting into the cockpit. We checked to make sure that the tie-down ropes were undone, that the wheel chocks had been removed, and that there was no water in the fuel tanks. The whole preflight took about ten minutes.

I climbed into the left-hand seat, and the instructor took the right. He handed me a laminated piece of paper and said, "Flying is all about checklists. We use them to ensure we don't forget something. There're pre-flight lists and pre-landing ones. It's a safety issue."

We went through the list and then started the engine. Webster explained the controls, and we watched the ailerons move up and down when I turned the wheel or yoke from side to side and the elevators do the same when I pushed the wheel in and pulled it back.

Taxiing out to the runway, he explained how the rudder pedals and the brakes worked. At the end of the taxiway, he had me run up the engine and check the magnetos. After making sure no one was on final approach, we pulled out onto the runway.

"We fly a left-handed pattern here, which means once we reach a thousand feet above the ground . . . we abbreviate that to AGL . . . you'll make a left turn," Webster said as he pushed forward on the throttle and we roared down the asphalt.

"Keep your hands on the yoke and follow me through on the rudders as well. At sixty-five knots we'll pull back on the yoke and lift off the runway. Our field elevation is five hundred feet so when the altimeter reads fifteen hundred feet, we'll make a left turn. Keep the nose on the horizon until we reach our altitude."

My heart was pounding, and my mouth was so dry I could barely swallow. It reminded me of my first time on stage at Play It Again

Sam's. At fifteen hundred feet he made our turn and pushed the nose of the airplane down.

"We'll stay at level flight in the pattern. Now I'm going to make another left turn and line up parallel with the runway. We'll fly past the end of the runway and then make a series of two left turns to line up for final approach to the runway. Even in the summer time we have to pull on the carburetor heat to keep the air intake from freezing and killing the engine."

My heart was in my throat as we approached the earth. Would we crash and burn? My palms were so wet I thought the wheel might slip out of my hands.

"Look ahead as we get close to the ground. The idea here is to let the airfoil stall just before we touch down. Hold the nose up and let the plane settle onto the asphalt," Webster said.

I pulled back on the wheel a little too soon, and we started back up. Webster pushed the yoke down and finished the landing. Then we took off again.

"That's called a touch-and-go," he said.

Once we were in the pattern again, Webster said, "We'll head out toward Old Hickory Lake to our practice area. Then we'll do some turns, stalls, and slow flight. I want you to get a feel for the plane." Then looking at my stricken face, he said, "Relax, Jamie. This is supposed to be fun."

After an hour, Webster said, "We don't let the first few lessons last over an hour because most people are so tense they tire easily." Then laughing, he added, "Kind of like you, Jamie."

After landing, we taxied back to the line and went through a shut-down checklist. As we climbed out of the cockpit, Webster asked, "What did you think?"

"I love it. When's my next lesson?"

Chapter 22

As I'd told Melody earlier, I'd bought tickets on American Airlines for our trip to Los Angeles. I started to get first-class tickets until the travel agent told me how much they were. We were doing well, but not that well.

We arrived at LAX right on schedule. There was a direct flight from BNA as I'd learned to call the Nashville Metropolitan Airport. I'd arranged for a Hertz van so we'd have room for our instruments. While Melody and the boys were collecting our luggage, I hopped on the Hertz bus and rode to their lot.

I got back to the baggage area just as they were dragging our stuff to the curb. We loaded everything in the back of the van, and I checked the map that the man behind the Hertz counter had given me. I'd made reservations at the Beverly Hills Hotel on Sunset Boulevard.

I handed the map to Melody and said, "Honey, you are now our navigator. Tell me what to do."

She laughed. "I'm always happy to tell you what to do, darlin'. First you've got to get on something called the San Diego Freeway and go north to Sunset Boulevard. How in the hell we're supposed to get to the damn freeway from here is anyone's guess."

As we checked out of the lot, I asked the attendant, "Can you get us from here to the freeway?"

"Sure. Turn left out of the lot and go to Sepulveda Boulevard and turn left on W. Century Boulevard. That'll take you to the freeway."

That's what I did and we entered the north entrance. Melody spotted the Sunset Boulevard exit before I did. "Get off here, Jamie. I guess we turn right."

We pulled up to the pink Beverly Hills Hotel a few minutes later. The doorman, a big fellow dressed in a uniform that made him look like a general, opened my door and asked my name. I slipped him a five-dollar bill, and he frowned. I thought it was enough, but he obviously didn't. While the bellman, a young guy who looked about eighteen, collected our baggage and instruments, Melody and I went to the reception desk to check us in.

The producer of the program had suggested the hotel; otherwise I most likely wouldn't have picked it. The lobby blew me away. Not only was the hotel pink, but most of the furniture in the lobby was pink as well.

Melody and I had a small one bedroom suite and I'd put the boys in rooms with double beds. The bellman delivered our luggage a few minutes after we walked into our suite. I tipped him and turned to see Melody looking out the window.

"Jamie, honey, come look at this pool."

It was the largest pool I'd ever seen. There were all kinds of people sitting in lounge chairs, and most of the women wore the skimpiest bikinis I'd ever seen. Melody saw my expression, and said, "Down, boy. It's okay to ogle the merchandise, but no handling."

We ate dinner in the hotel restaurant and as soon as we took our seats, I said, "Okay, guys. Tonight is special. Order anything you want. That includes beer, wine, etc."

I probably shouldn't have said that because by the time we'd finished dinner Jolly Joe wasn't feeling any pain. As we walked out of the restaurant, I pulled him to one side. "Man, I didn't mean for you to get knee-walking drunk."

"Fuck off, Jamie. We ain't in a dressing room getting ready to go onstage. Besides, you said we could drink."

"I know. Just try to keep it together until tomorrow."

He staggered off, and I knew at some point I'd have to let him go. The other guys kept their drinking under control, but not Jolly Joe.

The taping was to be in front of a live audience at CBS City the following afternoon. I asked the doorman for directions, and he said, "The studio is north of the Farmer's Market, on the corner of Fairfax Avenue and Beverly Boulevard. It's not far from here. Just follow this line I drew for you on the map."

When we pulled up to the building, we unloaded our instruments and checked in with the security people. They gave us name tags and told us where to go to the sound stage. The guard at the door told us how to find our dressing room. We'd been settled down for about fifteen minutes when the co-producer, Rick something, I can't remember his full name, knocked on the door and said, "You folks will follow Minnie Pearl. She's from Nashville. Y'all know her?"

"Yes," I said. "We know her. Great lady. Will we get to meet Glen?"

"Maybe. As you might imagine, he's tight as a tick during taping. He may look relaxed on stage, but believe me, it's just his professionalism."

We unpacked our instruments and tuned them. I was a nervous wreck. I kept pacing back and forth. Melody, God love her, sensed my mood and placed her arm around my shoulder. "It's okay, honey. We're good. Just remember that. And you're the best. Everything is going to be fine. Better than that—great."

Could anyone wonder why I loved that woman so much? I gave her a peck on the cheek and said, "I love you so much it hurts. I hope you know that."

She just smiled.

We watched Minnie Pearl do her number on a monitor in our dressing room. I continued to be amazed by her dual personality— hillbilly buffoon one minute and well-educated Bell Meade matron the next. She told one corny joke after another but the audience loved her.

We slipped out of our dressing room and stood in the wings as she finished her monologue. As she exited the stage, I grabbed her hand and said, "You're a hard act to follow, Minnie."

She laughed. "I can't wait to hear you and your band, Jamie. Go out there and knock 'em dead."

I led the way and walked out onto the stage. The lights were glaring and hot. I was glad we'd worn our short-sleeved guayabera shirts. While we were taking our places on the stage, the co-producer came over and asked, "Have you done a TV gig before?"

I shook my head.

"This is different from a live performance even though we have an audience. If you make a mistake, all we have to do is repeat the take. This is all on tape. So, relax. Y'all look like you're wound tight as a tick."

We hadn't brought Fireman with us because of the airline. And I had no idea how he'd do with all the confusion of the taping.

We started with an instrumental, leading with our boogie-woogie theme. Then we did "Stolen Kisses," our platinum single. That brought the house down. Melody and I did our duet and received a thundering applause.

At the end of our set, while we were still being taped, Glen Campbell walked over and said, "You guys were great. I can't wait to have you back. Let me borrow your banjo player so he and Larry McNeely can do a duet."

Mark had a panicked expression on his face. I pulled him aside and said, "This is why I told you to practice. You can do this. Go out there and make me proud."

Mark and Larry played one of Glen's signature songs, "The Wichita Lineman" and about half way through the instrumental, Glen walked over and sang the lyrics. It was a crowd pleaser and brought the house down. Then Glen and Larry McNeeley did a takeoff of Laurel and Hardy. I laughed so hard my sides hurt.

Back at the hotel, we were all exhausted but elated. We were so excited I doubted any of us would be able to sleep that night. Melody and I went to our suite, but the boys headed for the bar and God only knows when they finally got to bed.

* * *

We arrived back in Nashville a few days before Christmas. Melody and I loved our new home, and we were getting accustomed to the size. It didn't seem nearly as big and intimidating as it had when we'd first moved in. And Melody had taken her time to furnish the rest of the house. I thought she'd done a great job.

I was in the process of putting up our Christmas tree when the phone rang. I picked it up and said, "Coleman residence."

"Mr. Coleman, my name's Jerome Maddox. I'm with *Time* magazine. I'd like to do an interview if you have time."

"Why would you want to interview me?"

"You're a celebrity now. People want to know about you."

"All people need to know about me they can get from listening to my records and coming to my shows. My private life is no one's business but mine."

"Most celebrities feel that way, Mr. Coleman. They eventually come to the realization that they can't separate their private and professional lives."

I laughed. "Just watch me." Then I replaced the receiver.

"Who was that, Jamie?" Melody asked.

"Some guy from *Time*. Wanted an interview."

"What did you tell him?"

"Our private life is ours."

She placed her arms around my neck and said, "I'm so glad you did that. I hate all that gossip and crazy stuff they put in those magazines at the cash register in the grocery store."

It was the first time I'd declined an interview, but it wouldn't be the last.

* * *

On Christmas Eve the phone rang, and when I answered, Yolanda said, "I'm sorry, Jamie honey, but Jake passed away this morning. Dr. Kate thinks he had a stroke. At least he didn't suffer. Poor dear was at least eighty-five, though he'd never tell anyone how old he was."

I felt a pain in my chest and took a deep breath. Jake and Miss Frances had been wonderful mentors, and I'd loved them both. I knew Jake was up in years, but I wasn't prepared for his death. I'd planned to go see him right after the first of the year.

"When's the funeral?" I asked.

"He chose cremation, and he didn't want a funeral or memorial service."

"Jake always said funerals were for the living, not the dead. I would like to do something as a remembrance. What about his ashes?"

"He didn't leave any instructions."

"I have an idea. Jake loved the mountains. I'll fly over Cooper Mountain and scatter his ashes. What do you think?"

"You can fly an airplane?"

"I'm learning. My instructor will come with me."

"He left a will. The house is mine until I die, and then Round

Rock will get it for a library. He bequeathed his novels and biographies, stereo equipment, records, and cassettes to you. You're welcome to come get them whenever you want. The law books go to Vanderbilt."

What a treasure trove! I felt speechless and my eyes moistened. I said, "Thank you, Yolanda. I know you'll miss Jake. If there's anything Melody and I can do for you, please let us know."

"I will, dear. Just come to see me soon."

* * *

After the first of the year, Webster and I flew a Cessna 172 to the small Livingston airport. We had a hard time finding it. We had a sectional map, but the airfield just didn't seem to be where the map said it was. After circling over the town for a few minutes, we spotted the airfield. The reason we'd had trouble was that it was located on the top of a hill. As I set up my final approach to the runway, I realized I was looking at a cliff beneath the tarmac. If I came in too low, we'd crash. My palms were sweaty as I pulled out the carburetor heat and lowered the flaps.

After we touched down, I taxied us up to the FBO and shut down the engine. Webster jumped out and threw some chocks under the nose wheel and a line boy came out and asked, "Y'all need some avgas?"

Webster said, "Yeah. Top us off."

I went into the office and asked the guy behind the desk, "I need a rental car. Do you have one?"

He smiled and said, "I reckon not, mister. Don't get much transients coming through here. Most of our folks are locals."

"Any suggestions?" I asked.

The fellow tilted his head back and his eyes turned to one side. "How much you willing to pay? How long you need it?"

"I just need to drive up to Round Rock for a few minutes. I'll give you a hundred dollars. How's that sound?"

"Like a winner." Then handing me a set of keys said, "Dodge pickup in the lot. Don't look like much but she runs damn good for a '68 model."

I took a hundred dollar bill out of my wallet and handed it to the guy. Then Webster and I walked out to the lot and climbed into the pickup. Webster had never been to that part of Tennessee, and he couldn't believe the road from Livingston to Round Rock. It was one hairpin curve after another. At least it was a nice day. There were a few cumulonimbus clouds hanging over the mountains to the east and the temperature hovered in the high thirties.

Yolanda looked sad when she answered the door, but she smiled when she saw me. I'd called and told her we were coming, and she had Jake's urn ready for us. She invited us in for coffee, so we could discuss the books and stereo equipment.

After introducing her to Webster, I said, "I'm devastated to lose Jake. I know you must be, too. I was coming to visit next week. I wish I'd come last week."

"We never know when someone's going to die, honey. There's no way you could have known that. Don't fret over it."

"I'll rent a U-Haul truck and come for everything right after my birthday."

"Just come when it's convenient, honey. I'll keep everything just as it is."

We finished our coffee, and I gave Yolanda a hug. "I'm serious, Yolanda. If you need anything, you let me know. You've been like a mother to me. I love you."

Her lips rose slowly into a smile and she said, "And I love you, honey. All I ask is that you come to see me every once in awhile. I know how busy you are now that you're famous."

"Melody and I will both come. I promise."

Webster and I drove back to Livingston with Jake's urn on the seat between us. I was overcome with grief. I simply couldn't believe my dear friend was dead. Now I'd lost my last mentor from my childhood.

I'd needed some cross-country flight training anyway, so it worked out well for us to make the trip to East Tennessee. Webster and I took off and set course for Cooper Mountain. As we passed over Round Rock and Beulah Land, I was struck by how small and insignificant they both appeared from the air. I could see trails of black smoke rising from the tin chimneys atop the tarpaper shacks of my kin. Then I thought how far I'd come in my nineteen years.

Over the mountain, I opened the small window beside me, and Webster handed me the urn. I turned it upside down and watched the ashes of my dear friend float toward earth like snowflakes. I bit my lower lip and whispered, "Good-bye, Jake. I'll miss you, old buddy. Thank you for all your kindness." The tears that flooded my eyes blurred the instruments on the panel and I turned to Webster and said, "Take the yoke. I can't see a damned thing."

I banked the plane and turned back toward Nashville. I thought it was ironic that one life had ended and another was just beginning. Soon I would have an heir—a son or daughter. And I knew I'd be a better father because of all I'd learned from Jake. I had started my life in that terrible place known as Beulah Land, but I now had a great future. I felt a lump in my throat at the thought of my two marvelous mentors, Miss Frances and Jake Watson.

In a hoarse whisper, I said, "Jamie Lee Coleman, you're one lucky fellow."

* * *

When I got to the house, I couldn't find Melody. We usually left notes for each other on the refrigerator door, so I went into the kitchen to look for one. There it was, scribbled on a small piece of paper and held in place by a magnet. *I'm at the Vanderbilt ER.*

"Oh, shit," I whispered under my breath and ran out to my car. I flew down Harding Road to Blakemore and over to Twenty-first Avenue. I turned into the Vanderbilt parking lot, where the emergency room was situated under the hospital.

I ran to the information desk and asked, "Where's Melody Coleman?"

"Are you Mr. Coleman?"

"Yes. I'm looking for my wife. Where is she?"

"In an exam room. Follow me."

The woman took me to a room down the hall where I found Melody lying on a wheeled stretcher. She wore a white hospital gown. Rushing to her side, I asked, "What's wrong?"

Tears flooded her eyes and she couldn't speak. Just then a young resident doctor walked in and said, "I've called Dr. Montgomery. He's on his way."

I took Melody's hand in mine and brought it to my lips. I just held it tightly while she tried to compose herself. Finally, she whispered, "I lost the baby."

A black cloud settled over me, and my knees felt weak. *How do you lose a baby?* I wondered. *What does that mean?* I was obviously in denial. Hell, I knew what it meant. Our baby was dead. Jesus, how did that happen?

I turned to the doctor. He said, "Your wife has had a miscarriage. Her private doctor's on the way."

Then he left Melody and me alone. Tears slid down her smooth cheeks, and I tried to blank the scene from my mind.

Twenty minutes later Melody's OB, Dr. Montgomery, walked in. He took Melody's other hand and said, "We need to do a D and C. That stands for a dilation and curettage of your uterus to remove any remaining tissue. We'll put you to sleep, and you can go home in the morning."

"How dangerous is this procedure?" I asked.

"The main risk is anesthesia, but it's minimal. Melody's going to be fine. Please don't worry."

I kissed her on the lips and a nurse rolled her out. I went to the surgery waiting room and got a cup of bitter, terrible coffee out of the vending machine. Then I spent the longest two hours of my life while they operated on Melody.

Dr. Montgomery, a slight fellow with gray hair and the fingers of a pianist, finally walked in and said, "She's doing fine. But there's a bit of bad news. Melody won't be able to have children in the future."

"I don't understand," I said.

"Melody had a severe case of endometriosis. That's caused by the lining of the uterus or womb migrating into the abdominal cavity. I'm surprised she got pregnant in the first place. I had to do a hyster-ectomy, remove the uterus. Melody and I discussed this possibility before the D and C. She didn't want to worry you. I'm very sorry. I'll tell her when she's fully awake."

I watched him leave the room and wondered how Melody would take the news. From what she'd told me when she first got pregnant, I didn't think she'd handle it very well. I felt a sadness settle over me as I thought of what the doctor had said. I'd been looking forward to having a child.

Minutes later a black nurse walked in and asked, "Are you Mr. Coleman?"

"Yes."

"Your wife is resting quietly in the recovery room. As soon as she's fully awake, she'll be moved to a room. You can go see her then."

About an hour later, they took her to the maternity floor. I found her room and went to her side. Her eyes were red and watery. When she gazed into mine, she started to cry. I kissed her on the lips and said, "I talked to the doctor. I'm sorry."

She just shook her head and looked away. I was devastated to see how she was taking the news.

I sat in a straight-back chair beside her bed and stared at the wall. Melody went to sleep and mumbled incoherently. I felt sure she was dreaming. I knew they couldn't be good or happy ones.

* * *

The guys in the band sent a huge bouquet of flowers to the house. They'd wanted to visit Melody, but I told them to hold off. I wasn't sure how things would be when I brought her home. The first week was the toughest. Melody was very quiet and slept a good part of every day.

After her post-operative visit to the doctor, her mood lightened. When we were finally able to discuss the situation, Melody said, "I'm sorry, honey. I know you wanted a baby as much as I did."

I'd been thinking a lot about everything for days. I knew what a child meant to Melody, so I said, "We could always adopt one. There're lots of deserving kids out there."

She took my hand and said, "I'll think about it. I just wanted your child so badly. I wanted it to have both our genes. With our lifestyle, I'm not sure having a child is a good idea anyway."

I suspected that statement had more to do with Melody trying to come to grips with her loss than anything else. "Let's wait and see," I said. "There's no hurry."

* * *

We all went to Round Rock to pick up Jake's books. I drove the U-Haul truck with Melody sitting beside me, and Mark brought the guys in Melody's station wagon. I'd bought almost a hundred boxes from the moving company, and they were stacked in the back of the truck.

Yolanda opened the door and when she saw all of us standing

there, she said, "Well, I reckon it's a good thing I cooked a ham. Y'all hungry?"

I hugged her and said, "This crew is always hungry. Thanks, Yolanda."

"Well, come in. You know where the dining room is. Make yourselves at home."

"Yolanda, these are the members of our band. I've been telling them what a great cook you are."

I introduced everyone and we sat down. Melody was at my side. Yolanda had cooked a small honey ham, and the table was laden with creamed corn, mashed potatoes, gravy, and biscuits. Needless to say, our crew made short order of everything.

Afterward, Melody taped all the boxes together, and the guys and I filled them with books. There must have been a thousand. They'd certainly fill all the bookcases in our den. I might even have a few left over. I'd turned one of the two extra bedrooms in our house into an office. I figured I could always have the walls covered with shelves.

We packed the stereo equipment, records, and cassettes in those plastic peanuts that everyone hates. By the time we finished, the truck was full. As I carried boxes out and up the ramp, it reminded me of the times I'd helped Pop load an eighteen-wheeler at the shirt factory loading dock. Thinking of those days made my stomach churn.

I walked back into the library and stared at the empty book cases. The place looked so vacant, so devoid of substance, that it made me think of an empty skull.

I found Yolanda in the kitchen. "We're loaded and ready to roll. Thanks for lunch. The guys will be talking about it for weeks."

She walked toward me, drying her hands on a dish towel. "You and Melody come to see me, Jamie. You promise me this minute."

"I promise. And if you need anything—anything at all—you call."

"You know I will. Now, drive safe."

It was pitch black by the time we drove up Belle Meade Boulevard. I parked the truck in the driveway and asked the guys to come back the following morning so we could unload. I figured it would take the better part of the day.

Melody fixed us some scrambled eggs and bacon for dinner, and we went to bed early. We were both exhausted. We read for a while, and then I turned off the bedside light. Melody rolled over to my side of the bed and kissed me on the lips. "Dr. Montgomery said we shouldn't have sex for about four weeks. You okay with that?"

"Just having you next to me is fine. I know how much you love me, and you know how much I love you. We don't have to prove it to each other by making love. Cuddling with you is all I need."

"You're such a sweetie. No wonder I love you so much," Melody said.

The guys showed up at nine o'clock the next morning, and we unloaded boxes and placed books in shelves for most of the day. Melody made sandwiches for lunch, and we took an hour break. I set up the stereo equipment and stacked records and cassettes in special racks I'd bought at Castner-Knott.

* * *

I'd written five new songs, and in February we cut an album at Ramsey Records. I'd had a few calls from the major studios, but I'd been happy with how Mr. Ledbetter had managed our single.

We continued to vary our music and style. The album had five instrumentals as well as my vocals. Melody and I did a duet that I wrote just for the occasion. We'd been able to weave that boogie-woogie undercurrent into the start of every piece we played. It was rapidly becoming a trademark.

Mr. Ledbetter walked into the studio just as we were finishing the recording session. He waved me over and said, "I'd like to talk to you for a minute, Jamie. Let's go into my office."

I followed him into his cluttered office, wondering what he wanted. He sat in the chair behind his desk, and I took the one opposite him.

"As you've probably heard, Mr. Ramsey had a heart attack yesterday and died. He was eighty-one. His family has no interest in the company and wants to sell it. I thought you might want to buy the assets. I'd be willing to stay on and run the day-to-day operation."

I was flabbergasted. In my wildest dreams I'd never thought of owning a record company. The idea was intriguing. Depending on the price, it could be a great investment.

"Any idea what they want?" I asked.

"I think they'll be reasonable. It's a small private company without any major artist under contract. Frankly, you're our biggest star."

"You'll stay on?"

"Yes."

"Okay. See what you can work out. I'd like for you to be the CEO and I'll stay in the background. The first thing we'll do is start looking for talent, people who're good but haven't been discovered yet."

"Sounds like a good way to go," he said.

We closed the deal the following week. I changed the name to Star Search Records to emphasize our basic business plan. Every disc we cut after that was on our own label. It allowed me to have complete control of my career. I'd always acted as our agent, and I would later purchase a booking company.

Nashville is a lot like L.A. when it comes to talented people. Almost every waiter who works in a restaurant is a musician and/or a singer. Some are exceptional and struggle for years before they make it to the top. Very few are overnight sensations. And, of course, some talented people never make it—never get past the bar or dance hall circuit. I've never really figured out why that is. I think some of them are truly talented but simply don't have the ability to promote themselves.

I called Mr. Ledbetter the week after the deal closed and said, "Why don't you start going to some of the bars around town that have live music? Maybe you'll see someone who is really good. It wouldn't be a bad idea to check out Austin, Texas. I've heard they have a lot of live music venues."

"Good idea. I've decided to make the rounds to all the major country stations in the country. You okay with footing the bill for that?"

"Of course. We need to move quickly."

*　*　*

We were to start our tour in April. Around the middle of March, Webster, my flight instructor, started talking about letting me solo. I wasn't sure I was ready. In fact, the thought of being alone in the air made me a nervous wreck.

On a Wednesday afternoon, Webster and I were doing touch-and-goes when he said, "Pull onto the taxiway and let me out."

My mouth went dry, and I could feel perspiration seep from my palms. I did as I was told, and he jumped to the ground and slammed the door.

"Good luck," he said.

I taxied to the end of the runway and started my takeoff run. At sixty-five knots I pulled back on the yoke, lifting the nose toward the sky. As I felt the wheels leave the asphalt, my heart was in my throat.

I glanced at the altimeter, and it read eight hundred feet AGL. I shifted my eyes back to the windshield and saw that it was filled with a Boeing 737. At the same instant, I heard a voice say, "American Airline flight 362 on downwind for Cornelia Fort Airport."

That little airport had a runway long enough for a light twin, not a jet. The fixed base operator used a radio frequency called a Unicom. All airplane radios have that standard frequency, and when there isn't a tower, pilots use it to state their intentions as they approach an airfield.

My rational mind told me the captain of the jet was playing a joke on the guys behind the desk in the airport office, but my emotional mind told me I was about to have a midair collision. I was on the verge of making a radical maneuver to avoid the jet when my rational mind took charge.

I made my usual left-hand turn at one thousand feet AGL and entered my downwind leg of the pattern. I pulled the throttle and set the flaps at fifteen degrees as I set up for my final approach. On the glide slope for touchdown I pulled on the carburetor heat, adjusted my angle of descent, and added another fifteen degrees of flaps.

The main landing gear touched the asphalt, and I held the nose wheel off the ground until it settled on its own. Then I taxied back to where Webster waited for me. He had a big grin on his face as he climbed back into the passenger seat.

"Great job," he said.

I eventually went on to obtain multiengine and instrument ratings. I'd loved flying from that first lesson. It was almost as exciting as playing to a live audience. When I'm in the air, my mind is so focused that I can't think of anything else. It's a perfect escape. Over the years I've owned a number of airplanes, and at this writing I have over six thousand hours in the air.

My first twin was a Beechcraft Baron like Henry Cannon's. Then I moved up to a Piper Navajo. Melody and I would fly to our engagements while the band took our tour bus. That gave me more time to take care of my various business interests.

Part Three

Chapter 23

By 1988 I was a well-known entertainer who had crossed over and was no longer thought of as a country singer. Melody and I'd unlisted our telephone number from the very beginning, and both of us used the Star Search Records address on our drivers' licenses. No one knew where we lived or how to get in touch with us at home. And we made an effort not to know our neighbors on Belle Meade Boulevard.

Our record company was doing great. Not only was it producing my albums, but we had a wonderful line-up of young stars. Mr. Ledbetter turned out to be a tremendous asset, and I'd increased his salary each year.

We'd done a few television specials in the mid- to late seventies and played the Strip in Las Vegas numerous times. Reporters continued to pester me for interviews even though I always refused.

I'd turned down *Time, Newsweek, People, Parade, The New York Times*, and countless others.

If your picture isn't spread all over magazines and grocery store tabloids, it's possible to mingle in public without people pestering you. Melody and I frequented restaurants in Nashville and other cities in complete privacy.

There was one woman reporter I really liked who worked for *Star Power* magazine in Los Angeles.

We were doing a series of concerts on the West Coast in 1978. We'd started in San Diego and were to play Los Angeles, Bakersfield, and San Francisco. All the original members of the band were still with me with the exception of Jolly Joe. He could never keep his drinking under control, so I had to let him go. I'd replaced him with a young guy named Jack Tudor, a fabulous keyboard master.

In Bakersfield, we'd just finished our show and were relaxing in our dressing room when there was a knock on the door. Melody answered it, and a woman said, "Mrs. Coleman, my name is Scarlett Gibson. May I speak to your husband for a moment?"

Melody glanced at me, and I nodded. I felt sure she was a reporter, but I always made an effort to be civil. I had enough jealous musicians to deal with. I didn't need enemies.

"Come in," I said. "What can I do for you?"

She was an attractive woman who looked to be in her early thirties. She had light brown hair cropped short and wore no makeup. She was dressed in a tailored pants suit and stood on high-heeled pumps. Her smile was infectious.

"I know you don't do interviews, but I wondered if you might make an exception in my case," she said.

"What makes you think I'd do that?"

"For one thing, I'd be careful to keep your private life out of my article. I'd limit my questions to your professional efforts. I'm interested in your music, how you write your songs, that sort of thing."

"You're the first reporter who's ever said they'd keep my private life out of their write-up. But if I let you do a piece on me, then I'd open myself up for an onslaught of questions by other reporters. I hope you understand."

She sighed and shook her head. "I really don't understand why you're so secretive. People want to know about you."

"I know it's late, but have you had dinner?" I asked her.

"No."

"Join Melody and me. We seldom eat until after our show," I said.

She agreed, and the three of us found a nice Italian restaurant that stayed open until midnight. We took a booth in the back and ordered. While we waited for our food, I asked Scarlett, "Do you keep up with new artists?"

"That's part of my job."

"I guess you know we own Star Search Records."

She nodded.

"I'm always looking for new musicians. Do you know a hot talent who hasn't been noticed yet?"

"I'll trade you that information for an interview," she said with a smile.

"You're a smooth one," I said.

Melody had been listening to this exchange with some interest. She was never jealous of the attention I received from women because she knew I was madly in love with her. The groupies could flirt with me and even get possessive, but Melody kept her cool. She had always supported me in my attempts to keep our private lives to ourselves.

Knowing this, I was a little surprised when Melody said, "Maybe you ought to let Scarlett ask you some questions about your record company."

I shook my head. "I'm sorry, Scarlett. Think about what I asked you. You could really help a struggling young musician."

"How can I contact you, Mr. Secret?"

"Call the record company. We're in the Nashville yellow pages."

* * *

Melody continued to play violin with the symphony when we were in Nashville, and I went to all her performances. She'd been discussing my participation as a soloist with the conductor, Kenneth Schermerhorn. Tall and slim, the Maestro was a flamboyant and ruggedly handsome man with a mane of silver hair. Dressed in white tie and tails, he'd step onto the stage from the wings and walk confidently to the podium, face the audience, bow, and then lead the orchestra with incredible energy and artistic flair.

Maestro Schermerhorn and I agreed on Beethoven's Symphony No. 9 in D minor, the third movement. I later learned it was one of the Maestro's favorites.

We'd been out of the city doing a show and didn't get back in time to do a rehearsal with the symphony. That meant I'd have to go on cold. The maestro was extremely upset, but there was nothing I could do about it. We'd been in Oklahoma City when a tornado had touched down and decimated the general aviation airport. Numerous planes had been destroyed. Luckily, our bird was in a hangar, but we couldn't take off until the one runway had been cleared. That set us back a whole day.

The evening we were to perform, Melody and I went to our other favorite restaurant, Julian's on West End Avenue. Peter, the maitre d', seated us at a table on the second floor in the back of the dining room. We normally didn't eat before a show, but on this particular night I wanted something in my stomach.

We ordered a light meal. As always, Peter stopped by our table to discuss the stock market. He'd just bought some Harley-Davidson stock and wanted to know what I thought.

After dinner, we parked in the legislative garage and walked across Sixth Avenue to the Tennessee Performing Arts Center. Melody led me backstage to a dressing room. I'd actually bought a tuxedo for the occasion and felt a little uncomfortable. My old Gibson had been enshrined in our library, and I'd acquired a beautiful new Martin with an incredibly mellow tone.

During the first piece of the evening, Melody and I stood in the wings and watched the conductor. They were playing Igor Stravinsky's *The Firebird,* and the Maestro's silver hair was flying about his head as he flung his baton to set the time of the music.

At the intermission, as one of the musicians walked past us, I heard him say, "I can't believe some country singer's going to do a guitar solo with us."

I could feel my face flush, and Melody put her arm around my waist. "Don't let it bother you, honey," she said. "Once you start playing, their doubts will vanish."

The Ninth Symphony was in the second half of the program. Maestro Schermerhorn strode out to the podium, and I followed him. There was a single chair in front of the violin section. Melody played in the second row.

I took my seat, and when my time came to play, I gave it everything I had. The acoustics in the auditorium were excellent. That was good because I never used amplification on my guitar. At the end of the performance, the musicians and I received a standing ovation. We were called back for two encores. I had arranged with Maestro Schermerhorn to do short pieces I'd learned from listening to Segovia records.

As we mingled backstage, the man who had made the disparaging remark came over and shook my hand. "That was a remarkable performance, Mr. Coleman. I'm duly impressed."

* * *

The following Monday, I received a call from Dr. Kate. Yolanda had died early that morning of an apparent heart attack. I felt a sadness settle over me like a black cloud. She was the last of my caretakers. I'd planned to visit her that week. I'd learned a valuable lesson that day. When you love someone, you should never put off visiting him or her. We'd kept in constant contact since Jake's death, and I'd thought she was in good health.

The funeral was to be on Wednesday at the black Baptist church. Melody and I drove to Round Rock that morning and arrived around noon for the two o'clock service. We went to the City Café for lunch. Melody ordered the daily special, meatloaf and mashed potatoes, and I had a hamburger.

While we were eating, a fellow who I didn't know came to our table and introduced himself. "Mr. Coleman, my name's Jack Raymond. I sell real estate and wondered if you might be interested in a farm since you're from around these parts."

"Have a seat," I said. "Tell me what's available."

"I've got two parcels. One is a hundred acres and the other, one fifty. They're adjacent to each other, so you could get a total of two fifty."

"If I were to buy them, could we keep my name out of the transaction?"

"Sure, if you used a corporate name."

I'd been thinking of buying some land in Parsons County. I liked living in Nashville, but at heart, I'd always been a country boy. While I had unpleasant memories of Round Rock—Beulah Land—I also had pleasant ones. I'd loved living on Miss Frances's farm.

"I'd be interested in putting together about a thousand acres over a period of time. I don't want my name used because that would just drive up the price," I said to Mr. Raymond.

"You're right about that," Mr. Raymond said. "I think I can piece together a parcel you'd like. Are there any specific needs?"

"Yes. I want to build a house into a mountain, and I need a flat area to place a runway for my plane. I'm thinking of getting a new jet, so I'll need at least seven thousand feet of flat pasture. Can you handle that?"

"That's a tall order for Parsons County, but I think I can," he said, handing me his card. We shook hands and he left.

Melody said, "I didn't know that you were getting a new jet or that you wanted to build a house up here."

"I'm still thinking about it."

"It would be nice if you shared these things with me," she said.

"Wouldn't you like to live on a farm?" I asked.

"Not particularly. I like living in Nashville. I'm not a country girl."

I felt badly that I hadn't shared my vision for the future with my wife. I depended upon her good sense for most of my decisions. I said, "I'm sorry, Melody. I should have said something to you. I apologize."

She smiled. "Thank you. Do we really need a new jet?"

After I started making real money, I sold the Baron and purchased the Navajo. Next was a Navajo conversion called a Panther. They built them at the Cornelia Fort Airport in East Nashville where I'd learned to fly. The plane had bigger engines, and I considered it safer than the standard models. While it was fast and comfortable, I wanted something faster and larger, so I'd bought a Cessna Citation jet. It could be flown single pilot, but I always had a copilot with me. I knew it was safer for Melody.

We'd been getting some offers to play Europe, and I didn't like flying commercial airlines. The new plane under consideration, a Gulfstream IV, was manufactured in Savannah, Georgia. At that time it was a thirty- to fifty-million-dollar machine. But it could be outfitted like our tour bus with a bedroom for Melody and me.

My copilot and mechanic was a fellow named Ernie Sloan from

Round Rock. Ernie's grandfather, Abel Sloan, had owned Round Rock's only hardware store until he died and Ernie's brother took it over. Ernie was a slight guy with a small pot belly hanging over the belt of his jeans. He'd lost most of his hair, and what was left just sat like puffs of cotton over his big ears. We'd met at the municipal airport in Nashville a few years before. Ernie already had an airline transport pilot and an airframe and power plant licenses. I'd obtained my ATP in 1975.

I took Melody's hand in mine and squeezed it. "If we're going to play Europe we'll need a larger plane, one that has at least a five-thousand-mile range."

"Okay. I'll have to think about living up here, though. I'm not sure about that."

"We'll continue to live in Nashville. I just want this place for weekends and as a retreat," I said.

We finished our meal and arrived at the black Baptist church at one forty-five. While the civil rights movement had basically done away with segregation, African Americans in Tennessee, by and large, continued to prefer their own churches, particularly in small towns like Round Rock.

Miss Frances had dragged me to the First Baptist Church on Main Street when I'd lived with her, but Brother Abernathy had never been able to baptize me. The evangelical fundamentalist approach to religion simply put me off. The only time I entered a church was for a wedding or funeral.

I remembered the black choir from Miss Frances's funeral. They had incredible voices, and the spirituals they sang made chills run up my spine. I was looking forward to hearing them again.

Brother Longworth was still the minister. I'd met him on one of my trips back to Round Rock. He was a big man with a booming voice that swept across the small church like a tidal wave.

Yolanda's open casket sat in front of the preacher's podium. Open casket funerals are still popular in the South. I consider them bar-baric. A long line of mourners filed past it as a woman played hymns on the organ. I couldn't bear to see Yolanda's body and stayed in the back pew where Melody and I'd chosen to sit. Ours were the only white faces in the crowd.

When the service started, the preacher led the congregation in a prayer and then gave a stirring eulogy. The choir sang several spiri-tuals, and they had the same effect on me as they had before. Melo-dy's eyes were moist when I glanced at her.

The church had its own cemetery next to the building so we attended the graveside service as well. Several of Yolanda's rela-tives came up to Melody and me and thanked us for coming to the funeral.

All the people I cared about in Round Rock were now dead. I still had kin in Beulah Land, but I'd cut off all contact with them years before.

* * *

I'd always found it interesting that Nashville was called Music City when it had only a handful of live venues for musicians to display their talent. The Opry was by invitation only. There were a few bars on Lower Broad where you could have a beer and hear some unknown band or singer.

There were two exceptions. The Station Inn opened in 1974 and showcased bluegrass musicians and bands. I'd caught John Hart-ford, the song writer and banjo player, there a couple of times when Melody and I went looking for talent for our record company.

The Bluebird Café in Green Hills did a commendable job in book-ing young talent. It had opened sometime in the early 1980s. To play the Bluebird was a stepping-stone, sometimes leading to a recording contract. Mr. Ledbetter and I'd signed a few good acts there.

Melody and I went there often when we were in town and mingled with the patrons without being recognized. Not being in the tabloids constantly made it easy for us to wander around incognito. That, of course, was why I didn't give interviews. I usually dressed in jeans and wore a baseball cap. Melody just sort of blended in.

We were there one evening when a young woman carrying an old Gibson guitar stepped onto the stage. She looked to be about nineteen or twenty years old. She had a mane of luxurious blonde hair and sparkling blue eyes. They reminded me of Melody's. She walked confidently to a ladder-back chair and sat down. Her guitar was to be her only accompaniment for she had no band to back her up. She looked out over the crowd, smiled a fourteen-carat gold smile, and said, "Hi, y'all. My name is Sarah, Sarah Updike. I so hope you'll like my music."

Then she began to pick a haunting melody on that old Gibson that made chills run up my spine. When she started to sing, Melody grabbed my wrist and squeezed so hard I thought her fingernails would bring blood. Sarah had the most lyrical voice I'd ever heard. I could feel moisture in my eyes. When she finished that first song, there was a hushed silence hanging over the audience. She had a look of concern on her face until the crowd burst into foot-stomping applause. It was a rousing reception that brought back that fourteen-carat smile. She played for another thirty minutes and then stood, bowed at the waist, and left the stage.

I called our waiter to our table and handed him a card. "Would you please give this to Sarah?"

A few minutes later Sarah approached our table and sat across from me. She had a bewildered expression on her face. "Mr. Coleman, I've always been a great fan of your music. I'm so honored to meet you," she said.

"You have an incredible voice, Sarah. Melody and I love your music. By the way, this is my wife, Melody. Would you like to have something to drink?"

She shook her head. "Thank you so much. That means a lot to me for you to say that, Mr. Coleman."

"Call me Jamie. Everyone does. Melody and I own Star Search Records. Do you have a recording contract?"

"No, sir. My agent hasn't been able to get me one. I thought he'd never get me into the Bluebird."

"What's his name?"

"Rufus Alexander."

Jesus, I thought, *what a tragedy.* That jerk had ruined the careers of more young artists than any other agent or producer in the business. He preyed on naive upstarts who rolled into Nashville looking for their first big break. They were vulnerable and easy marks. He'd sign them to slave contracts and promise them the moon. Then he'd milk them dry. Take most of what they earned. A real scumbag in my opinion.

"Sarah, I hate to tell you this, but Rufus is not an honest man and he's a terrible agent."

"I know that now, Jamie. I'm sick about it, but I don't know what to do."

"Let me help you. Contracts can be broken. It just takes a sharp lawyer and a little cash to make it happen. Give me your phone number and I'll have my attorney contact you. Once that's accomplished, I want to give you a contract with Star Search Records. With the right management, you can be a star. Not just a star, but a huge star."

Tears were streaming down her smooth cheeks and her lips trembled. She reached across the table and grabbed my forearm. I thought she'd bring blood, too.

"How can I ever thank you? I've been so discouraged this last year. If I hadn't gotten this gig at the Bluebird, I was going home."

Melody reached across the table and dabbed Sarah's eyes dry with her handkerchief. "Jamie's right, Sarah. You've got a great future. We'll help you. Where is home?"

Sniffing loudly, Sarah said, "Carthage, Tennessee. You know, on the Cumberland River where the big bluff is."

Melody and I both knew where Carthage was. We'd driven through there numerous times over the years. It was where Senator Albert Gore Sr. and his son, the vice president, were from. Cordell Hull was from Carthage as well. He'd been a U.S. senator and later Secretary of State under Franklin Roosevelt. He was also instrumental in establishing the United Nations. So, Carthage had produced some pretty famous native sons. And I predicted that Sarah Updike would soon be a famous native daughter.

I paid the bill, and as we stood to leave, Melody put her arms around Sarah and gave her a hug. I shook hands with Sarah, and we left. The next morning I placed a call to my attorney, Jack Robbins.

The other city known for its music was Austin, Texas. It was called the Live Music Capital of the World. Right after I'd bought Ramsey Records, I'd sent Mr. Ledbetter to scout the Austin music scene for young talent. There were bars and auditoriums scattered around the city where countless musicians played every night, and *Austin City Limits* was filmed at the University of Texas and shown through the auspices of KLRU, the public television station. Big-name acts performed there on a regular basis. Willie Nelson lived in Austin instead of Nashville.

I was making huge amounts of money from touring and the record company. And I received royalties from the songs I'd written. Some other performers had recorded my songs, and every time one was played on the radio or television, I got paid.

In addition to the cash flow, my stock market accounts were growing at an astounding rate. There'd been a slowdown in the early 1970s, but things picked up until the October crash in 1987. I managed to survive those problems because Mr. Hickman and I were very careful about how we picked my stocks.

Melody and I supported the symphony, ballet, and fledging opera in Nashville. And we gave large sums to United Way and the Salvation Army. I also sent money to the Southern Poverty Law Center in Montgomery, Alabama.

While most of the records we produced were by country stars, we also did some classical recordings. Mr. Arbuckle and I produced an album dedicated to Segovia. It wasn't a big seller, but we didn't expect it to be. It was a project of love.

Chapter 24

In the summer of 1993, we played Madison Square Garden in Manhattan. I'd enlarged the band considerably by then because we were more mainstream than country. All the original musicians were still with me except for Jolly Joe. I'd added a tenor saxophone, trumpet, and clarinet. Our shows still featured country and bluegrass, but we threw in a lot of jazz and Latin music. It was the versatility that made us popular.

Anytime we played the Big Apple, Melody and I stayed at the Carlyle Hotel on Seventy-sixth and Madison Avenue because the hotel allowed dogs. I'd always try to catch Bobby Short in the Café Carlyle when we were in town because I was a great fan of his music.

The evening of our performance, Melody and I hopped a cab to the MSG Theater on Seventh Avenue where we were to entertain a huge crowd. We were all excited because so many famous people had played the Garden. I knew Elvis and my idol, Frank Sinatra, had been there as well as countless others.

I paid the taxi driver, and Melody and I went to the stage door. The security guard let us in and directed us to our dressing room. When I opened the door, I saw everyone waiting on us except for Roger Apple, our tenor sax man. "Where's Roger?" I asked.

Mark shook his head and shrugged his shoulders.

"Well, we can go on without him if we have to," I said. "Surely he'd let us know if something was wrong."

There was a commotion in the hallway outside the dressing room, and when I opened the door, I saw Roger wrestling with the security man. His hair was disheveled and his face flushed. I stepped out into the hallway and asked no one in particular, "What's going on?"

By now the security man had Roger in a head-lock. He looked at me and said, "This fellow's high as a kite on something, Mr. Coleman. He's caused a ruckus since he walked in the door."

"Please let him go. I'll get to the bottom of this."

Once free, Roger shook his head and stared at me, his eyes glazed, his pupils dilated. I shook my head and said to the security man, "Please call the EMS and ask them to take Roger to a hospital. He's obviously in bad shape. I suspect it's cocaine."

Then turning back to Roger, I said, "When you're sober, contact Lucy Davenport and pick up your last check."

I went back into the dressing room and shut the door. I glanced at Melody and said, "We need to find a new sax man. Please put out some feelers when we get home."

The rest of the band members had a stricken expression on their faces. I looked at them and said, "You all know the rules. Roger's getting off easy."

Fireman had passed on in 1980, and we'd picked up another rescued dog from Dr. Stout soon after. We'd named this one Roscoe. He was part golden retriever and had a sweet disposition. Because we had our own airplane, we took him with us everywhere we went.

We'd trained Roscoe to do all the tricks Fireman had known, and he started our show the same way. I wasn't too sure how it would go over in a place like New York City, but the crowd went wild when he walked out on the stage and took his bow.

I'd heard for years that New Yorkers were difficult people to get along with, but that wasn't my experience. My theory has always been, treat people well, and they'll reciprocate.

The band and I played together for an hour, and then they took a break. I sat on the stage alone for thirty minutes with Roscoe at my side and played the guitar and sang. Then the band came back, and we did another hour.

The audience was great. We were called back for three encores and finally had to beg off. In the dressing room, I was placing my Martin in its case when there was a knock on the door. I opened it to find Scarlett Gibson standing there. She smiled and said, "You guys were great tonight. Have you got a minute, Jamie?"

"For you, darlin', I've always got a minute. Come in, girl."

All the band members knew Scarlet and liked her. Melody gave her a hug. I asked her, "What's up? This a social visit?"

"I've quit asking for interviews, Mr. Secret. I've got a new singer I want you to check out. Her name's Molly Mac. You'll want to give her a recording contract."

"She live in Nashville?"

"Asheville, North Carolina. Has a small bluegrass band. Plays small gigs but has great potential."

"Thanks, Scarlett. You're the best. Want to have dinner with us?"

She shook her head. "Can't. But thanks anyway."

Needless to say, we were exhausted by the time we got back to the hotel. Melody and I took Roscoe for a quick walk before going into the lobby. I'd arranged with the maitre d' of the dining room to have our dinner sent to our suite because I knew we'd get back after they'd closed.

We ate, took quick showers, and went to bed. Neither of us bothered to read. I slept lightly and heard Melody up once or twice during the night. We were leaving for Savannah and New Orleans the next morning.

* * *

We'd landed at Teterboro Airport in Jersey City, New Jersey, across from lower Manhattan. As soon as Melody got her face on, I called Ernie Sloan on his mobile and said, "Morning, Ernie. You all set?"

"Fuel truck is topping us off now. You on your way?"

"Yeah. We'll be there in about thirty minutes. Stock the bar with some Cokes and stuff."

Melody, Roscoe, and I took a limousine through the Holland Tunnel to New Jersey and arrived at the airport around eleven o'clock. Ernie had the plane waiting on the tarmac. The Citation had been a wonderful plane for us, but I was set on a G-IV.

Ernie had filed an IFR flight plan for Savannah before Melody and I arrived, and as soon as I climbed into the left seat, he started the port engine. By the time I was buckled in, the starboard had been lit. I keyed the microphone on my headset and said, "Ground Control, this is five, five Poppa Mike requesting permission to taxi to the active runway."

Teterboro was an incredibly busy airport serving general aviation and required all the same procedures that a commercial one did.

There were three planes in front of us, and we'd have to wait until they took off before we could take our turn.

"Five, five Poppa Mike. Contact the tower on one nineteen-point-five."

"Roger, one nineteen-point-five."

I contacted the tower, and they had us hold on the taxiway while the other planes departed. When our turn came, the tower operator said, "Five, five, Poppa Mike taxi to the runway and hold."

"Roger, five, five Poppa Mike."

We sat there for a few moments, and then the tower said, "Five, five Poppa Mike, cleared for takeoff. Contact Departure Control on one two six-point-seven."

I keyed the microphone and said, "Roger, one two six-point-seven."

I taxied out onto the runway and pushed the throttles forward with Ernie's hand following through with mine. At rotation speed, I pulled back on the yoke and lifted the jet off the asphalt.

Once clear of the airport we signed off with Departure Control and on with the first in-flight service center. Then we climbed to an altitude of forty thousand feet for our cruise south to Savannah.

One of the things I loved most about flying was the precision of IFR. It continued to fascinate me that we could descend on a glide slope through heavy clouds with no outside visual clues and find the end of the runway every time.

Our N number, that's the number painted on the tail of the airplane, like an automobile license plate, was five, five Poppa Mike. We had to use that in all of our radio communications. I'd just been passed to the next ground station when the radio operator asked, "That you, Jamie or Ernie?"

They aren't supposed to do that, but most would say something friendly when we were passed from one station to another.

"It's Jamie," I said. "You fellows behaving yourselves?"

"Oh, yeah," he said with a laugh.

When we got close to Savannah, we went through the reverse of what we'd done at Teterboro, contacting Approach Control and then the tower. After we landed, I taxied to the Signature FOB and shut down the engines.

As usual I'd rented a Hertz car for our trip to the Gulfstream factory. I had a hand-held GPS that I carried for such occasions. I typed in the address on Gulfstream Road and hit navigate.

A few minutes later, we parked at a visitor's spot in their lot. I'd arranged for a salesman to meet us for a tour of the factory and to place an order. At the reception desk, I asked, "Could you locate Bob Lowery for me?"

Bob was a tall, lanky fellow in his late forties. He walked with a confident stride and shook all our hands when he entered the room. "Welcome to Gulfstream, Mr. Coleman. You're interested in a new G-IV?"

"Yes. We need the range and size of the four. We have a Citation now."

"Well, follow me and we'll look around the factory a bit and then get down to specifics."

After a quick tour of the factory, Bob took us to his office in the administration area of the building. His desk was cluttered with blue-prints and various papers. I considered that a good sign.

"So, what configuration do you have in mind?" Bob asked.

"We want to set it up similar to our tour bus. I understand there'll be room for a small galley and a bedroom in the aft part of the fuselage."

"That's correct. Typical configuration forward. How many band members will accompany you?"

"There are three long time members of our band. They will always travel with us. Three additional members sometimes come with us but usually fly commercial. They'll do that when we go to Europe. We always rent a set of drums in whatever city we play in because they take up so much room."

"There'll be plenty of room." Then turning to Melody, he asked, "Will you be picking the interior, Mrs. Coleman?"

She laughed. "You bet. These guys have the aesthetic taste of an orangutan."

Ernie and I excused ourselves so we could get a cup of coffee in the lobby while Melody spent time with the company interior decorator. After coffee, Ernie and I talked to Bob Lowery about avionics. Those are the instruments on the panel the pilot uses to fly the airplane. Altimeter, air speed indicator, autopilot, GPS, engine instruments, etc. We could have bought a used G-IV, but it would have had to be gutted to meet our needs.

At the end of our sessions, Bob said, "It's been a pleasure working with you. It's always a pleasure to work with someone who knows exactly what he wants."

"When do you think we can take possession?" I asked.

"About a year. I think it would be a good idea for you and Mr. Sloan to start working on our simulator in a few months. The G-IV could be ready sooner than I think."

"Sounds good."

We shook hands, and the three of us walked back to the parking lot and got into the rental car.

Melody had an excited expression as she said, "This is so exciting. I wasn't all that set on another plane until we saw the Gulfstream. By now I should know just to trust your instincts, Jamie."

"I've been telling you that for years."

After a quick lunch, we were back in the Citation and headed for New Orleans.

* * *

I'd kept up with my New Orleans family over the years and tried to visit as often as possible. Casey continued to work as a waitress despite the fact I'd set up a Paine Webber account in her name with five million dollars in it.

Axelrod, then in his eighties, still played the bars on Bourbon Street. I'd offered to buy him his own place, but he'd refused, saying, "If I owned the place, I couldn't complain about the boss. Hell, Jamie, that's half the fun."

Sam was no spring chicken himself, but he continued to manage the bar. Melody and I checked into a suite at the Royal Sonesta Hotel on Bourbon Street. Ernie took a room down the hall. The suite was spectacular, two stories with a wrought-iron spiral staircase between floors.

I'd invited Sam, Axelrod, and Casey to dinner at Begue's Restaurant in the hotel at eight. We were seated right on schedule, and everyone but me had a round of highballs. Melody ordered the wine, and we enjoyed a good French meal, finishing off with a salad, coffee, and dessert.

Casey took a sip from her china cup and said, "I always feel strange having people wait on me. I can't get the waitress out of my blood."

"Why do you still work?" I asked her. "You don't have to."

"I know. And I really appreciate what you've done for me, honey. It's just that I feel guilty if I'm not working. Besides, it keeps me out of trouble."

I still had feelings for Casey. Not sexual ones; I got all of that I could handle with Melody. The feelings went back to our first encounter and the fact she'd initiated me into the act of lovemaking. Then she'd brought me back from the brink when I broke my neck and lost Joy. There would always be a place in my heart for Casey. Melody knew about my previous relationship and wasn't jealous. That was one of the greatest things about being married to Melody. She was a very secure person.

"You're going to do a short gig at the bar, aren't you?" Sam asked.

"Play It Again Sam is where I got my start. As long as you want me, I'll do a gig for you."

"There're not many big stars who'd play a bar for a friend," Axelrod said.

"You would," I said.

"I ain't no big star," Axelrod said.

"You are in my book," I said.

"That's what I like about you, honey. You're still the same old Jamie I knew when you were a green sixteen-year-old," Casey said.

"You told me you were eighteen," Sam said with a smile. "Hell, I suspected you were lying, but you were such an incredible musician, I let it pass."

Melody followed the conversation with tolerance. She'd heard it all before. Finally, she asked, "What time do you want Jamie at the bar, Sam?"

"Eight o'clock would be great."

"Whatever happened to Triple J?" I asked.

Axelrod shook his head. "Fat bastard kicked the bucket two years ago. Just ate himself to death. Good riddance as far as I'm concerned."

I had no love for Triple J, but he'd given me my first job. That counted for something in my book.

* * *

Melody and I arrived at Sam's about ten minutes till eight. The place was packed. He never said anything when I was going to drop in and didn't advertise the fact. It was a surprise he liked to spring on his patrons.

At eight on the dot, Sam walked up on the stage and addressed the audience. He gazed out over their heads and said, "Ladies and gentlemen, may I have your attention? Our jazz trio couldn't make their appearance tonight, so I've arranged a substitution for your entertainment. Please welcome Jamie Lee Coleman."

A stunned silence swept over the room. I stepped onstage, sat in my old chair, and stared at the audience. Then I played my old stand-by, the Count Basie boogie-woogie piece I'd learned at age sixteen.

I ran through a series of songs I'd made famous and once or twice caught myself glancing at the bar, looking for Joy. I knew that made no sense, but she'd been a special person in my life, my first love. I don't think you ever forget that individual as long as you live.

It had been a long time since I'd played in an intimate situation. Just before I quit, I stepped off the stage and approached an older couple at a table in the middle of the room.

I sang "I Love You Truly" to the woman, and tears slid down her wrinkled cheeks. That song really gets to the geriatric crowd. Then I wandered over to Melody and Sam's table and sang to my wife "Love Me Tender." Elvis's old song had always been a favorite of hers. When I finished, she stood and planted a wet kiss on my lips.

Turning to the crowd, I said, "It's okay, folks. This is Melody, my wife."

That produced a round of applause. I went back onto the stage and played for another thirty minutes. I loved entertaining people, and the smaller venues were my favorite because I could see the responses on their faces. After I walked off the stage, Sam tried to pay me, but I said, "You can't afford me, Sam."

When we got back to the hotel, Melody and I took a bath together in the big Jacuzzi tub and then made love on the bathmat. We just couldn't make it to the bed.

* * *

I was lucky as hell to have acquired a set of fabulous in-laws. Melody's parents were both retired schoolteachers. We tried to visit as often as possible, which usually worked out to about once every three or four months. We'd fly into Jackson because the Yazoo City airport didn't have a long enough runway for the Citation. Her father would pick us up in his ancient Suburban and tell us jokes all the way home.

They lived in an old part of the small city in a two-story frame house. Mr. Chapman kept it and the yard in immaculate condition. He was a tall, slender man with white hair and a sparkle in his eyes.

He had Melody's disposition, which made him easy to get along with. I figured he was about seventy-five.

Melody got her looks from her mother. Mrs. Chapman had been a finalist in one of the Miss America pageants. When she told me how many of those queens had come from Mississippi, I couldn't believe it. I think she was seventy, though she kept her hair as blonde as it'd been in her youth, and her blue eyes were radiant and her pale skin devoid of wrinkles. She looked about fifty at the most.

When Melody and I'd first married, Mrs. Chapman had inquired about my family. I was up front with her and didn't spare any details of my childhood. She was understanding and non-judgmental. Her name was Naomi, and she'd been a librarian when she taught. She was an avid book lover, so we'd formed an immediate bond.

On our last visit, Naomi and Melody cornered me in the kitchen and said they wanted to talk to me. Naomi said, "Melody and I have been thinking about your relationship with your father. Or your lack of a relationship. We know it's a painful subject, but we think you should seek closure with him. It's not healthy to carry hate in your heart."

Had I not loved these two women, I would have walked out of the room and never spoken with them again. But I did love and respect them. How could they expect me to make up with Pop? The bastard had killed my mother right before my eyes.

I just stared at Mrs. Chapman because, in truth, I was speechless. Melody put her arm around my waist and pulled me to her. "I think Mother's right, Jamie. I think you should go see him."

I laughed. "You do remember he's in the penitentiary."

"They have visiting hours," Naomi said. "And Melody tells me it's right there in Nashville."

I went over to the refrigerator and took out a bottle of Coke, twisted off the top, and took a swig. All kinds of crazy thoughts were running through my head. What if I got in the visiting area and attacked the old bastard, tried to kill him again?

Naomi and Melody stood next to the sink and waited for me to say something. Finally, I said, "I don't know what purpose that would serve. But if Melody wants me to see the old . . . " I didn't finish the sentence because Naomi hated profanity.

* * *

I kept putting off the inevitable, thinking Melody would forget about the whole affair. But she had a memory like an elephant.

In late summer of that year, I called the prison and asked when visiting hours were. Then I made arrangements with the warden to see Pop.

The day I was to visit, I had a burning in my stomach that just wouldn't go away. Melody gave me a Zantac, but it didn't help. My old anxiety response kicked in, and my hands were so wet, I could barely hold onto the steering wheel.

Like most people, I had no sympathy for jailbirds. Most of them deserved to be incarcerated. I never understood why Johnny Cash identified with those people. As far as I knew, he'd only spent one night in jail.

I waited in line like the other visitors for about ten minutes before the gate opened and we all filed in. I wore jeans and a baseball cap so no one recognized me, which was a blessing. We were herded up a flight of stairs to a big room with two long tables, one on each side of a thick glass partition. Telephones allowed visitors to talk to inmates.

When he entered the room, I recognized him immediately. I couldn't even remember how many years it'd been since I'd seen him. He looked haggard, old, and pitiful. His teeth, never good, were now stained black. I later learned he smoked a pipe anytime he wasn't working at some task for the state.

He knew I was coming, but I don't think he thought I'd really show up. When he recognized me, a slow smile spread across his wrinkled face. He was wearing an orange jumpsuit and some type of old tennis shoes. He sat down and picked up the receiver. I did the same.

"How're you doing, son?" he asked.

Having him call me son sent a chill up my back. My mouth was so dry, I could barely swallow. I didn't know how to answer him. I wondered why in the world I'd come. I almost stood and walked out, but I didn't. I just stared at him.

Then he said, "Shine always got me in trouble, Jamie. I ain't had none in all these years, and I've had a heap of time to think about my sins. I reckon the Lord ain't too happy with me. I'm real sorry I kilt your mom. I just needed to say that."

I don't know what I'd expected him to say. Certainly not a confession or that he was sorry. He looked so pitiful, I almost felt sorry for *him*.

Looking into his bloodshot eyes, I shook my head and said, "I've hated you for the better part of my life. I don't know if I can stop now or ever."

"I know, son. I ain't been a good daddy to you. All I can say is I'm a better person when I ain't drinking shine."

I nodded. I did have some memories of him when he'd been sober. They weren't great memories, but at least he hadn't been beating the shit out of me. I wondered if I could really forgive the old bastard.

"I hope you'll came back to see me, Jamie. I get right lonesome. Lester don't come no more now that Billy's dead."

There'd been a positive identification of Billy's body, and he'd been flown back to Round Rock in a black body bag.

Standing, I said, "I don't know if I'll be back or not, Pop. I'll think about it." Then I replaced the receiver and left.

Had I been a drinking man, I'd have headed for a bar.

Chapter 25

In the summer of 1994, I traded the Citation in on the G-IV. Ernie and I took delivery of the new plane and had to go through some more intense training. It was a much more complicated ship than the small Citation. A good bit of our instruction was in a flight simulator. If nothing else, it saved on the consumption of Jet A fuel. And we could both make a mistake, crash the plane, and still walk away. Simulators are awesome.

Melody and Roscoe stayed home in Nashville. She referred to herself during these aviation exercises as a "flying widow." Naomi had come to keep her company for the two weeks I'd be gone.

Working through Mr. Raymond in Round Rock, I'd acquired a little over a thousand acres in Parsons County. I'd finally convinced Melody that living in the country part time would be good for us. We traveled so much I thought the tranquility would ease our sometimes jagged nerves. Melody had been working with an architect in

Nashville to develop a set of construction plans. We knew exactly what we wanted and had decided on its location at the farm.

The runway and hangar were to be built first so we could fly up from the John Tune Airport when we wanted to check on the construction. We'd hired a general contractor from Cookeville. I'd had my attorney draw up the contract with a time constraint. If the house wasn't finished on schedule, he'd lose money.

Ashland Oil had a refinery in Ashland City, Kentucky, just over the state line, and I arranged to purchase my Jet A fuel directly from them. We set up our private aviation activities like a real general aviation airport. The runway was built by a company specializing in that type of construction. Huge fuel tanks were sunk in the ground. The hangar was made of steel beams bolted together with corrugated sides and roof. Big bi-fold doors kept the elements out. I even installed a set of approach lights and an ILS glide slope so we could make instrument landings.

The property was fenced with four strands of barbwire. A brick entrance was constructed with an ornamental gate containing the initials J. L. C. It worked on a keypad and remote controls.

We purchased a herd of black Angus, and they roamed freely around the property though we had a large barn for them. Dr. Stout had been instrumental in locating the animals and was responsible for their health and well-being.

Once she got into the planning, Melody was excited about all the activity. She and Naomi had spent hours working on the design of the house and its furnishings. Because of all the excitement of building the house, Melody had decided that she would like to live on the farm fulltime. I'd contacted Sandy Benton and asked him to place the Belle Meade house on the market. We'd paid two-forty for the place in 1970 and had it on the market for a million-three in 1994.

We flew up to the farm at least three times a week. Some of the band members were from the country, and a few of them purchased land in Parsons County. Ernie Sloan had a small acreage that had been in his family for years. He was in the process of building a new house as well.

I had no desire for a swimming pool, but Melody insisted we have one. It was to be heated so she could use it year-round. I'd grown up swimming at a deep hole in Widow's Creek over in Moodyville. I can assure you that it was not heated.

Melody had hired a full time maid in Nashville to help her with housework and look after the place when we were on tour. The woman had no desire to leave the city. I asked around Round Rock for a housekeeper and got good references for a woman named Magnolia Summerfield.

She came to the construction site for an interview on a Friday afternoon in a beat-up Honda Civic. As she stepped out of the small car, I noticed that she was a tall woman in her mid-fifties with silver hair that almost touched the ground. I'd met Crystal Gayle a few times, and she was the only other individual I'd ever seen with such a hairstyle.

Roscoe and I walked over to the car, and I said, "You must be Magnolia."

She took my hand and replied, "That's me."

"Come on over to our construction trailer and we can talk. I want you to meet my wife, Melody."

Roscoe, Magnolia, and I trudged across the construction site to our trailer. It was a stripped down thirty-foot house trailer. Inside, Melody was taking a percolator off the gas range.

"Honey, this is Magnolia Summerfield," I said.

"Y'all sit at the table. Everyone want coffee?"

"I do. How about you, Magnolia?"

"I reckon. You got any real cream, honey? I ain't fond of that artificial crap."

I chuckled under my breath. Magnolia was definitely not bashful. Melody filled three mugs and took a seat beside me.

"We're looking for someone to help Melody with the housework. If I'm here by myself, I'd want you to fix my meals. We'd want you to live on the premises. There'll be a small apartment just off the kitchen. Do you have a problem with that?" I asked.

Magnolia shook her head. "No. I ain't got no problem with that. What y'all like to eat?"

"Parsons County fare is fine," I said, though Melody did not like the amount of grease that floated on most country plates. But then, Magnolia would only cook when Melody was away.

"What y'all paying?" Magnolia asked.

"How does fifteen hundred a month sound?"

"Like a fist full of money. That's right generous of you, Mr. Coleman."

"Please call me Jamie. Everyone who works for me calls me Jamie."

"You offering me the job?"

"Yes. Will you take it?"

"I reckon."

* * *

We were to move into the house in the summer of 1996. In the fall of 1995 we did a tour of England. The main reason I'd bought the Gulfstream was so we could fly ourselves to Europe. Ernie and I worked on the IRF flight plan for several days so we'd have it set in our minds before we actually filed it. The route would take us in a big arc from Nashville up over New England, then Nova Scotia, the tip of Greenland, over Ireland, and then to London. I won't bore you with the details, but Ernie and I were a little stressed at first. Once we got into it, we had a blast. Even though the operators spoke beautiful English, I'd had a little trouble understanding Approach Control and the Tower operator at the London City Airport because of their accents, but we managed to do everything correctly. We landed and taxied to their corporate jet center. We were able to go through Customs there and change dollars to pounds.

Our travel agent had booked us in the Lanesborough Hotel in the Hyde Park section of London. She'd failed to tell me how expensive it was. When I saw the rate for two nights, I took a deep breath. Our Royal Suite had three bedrooms, a drawing room, a private dining room, a living area, and a kitchen.

Melody wandered through the big suite with a look of wonder on her face. "How much is this costing us, Jamie?"

"Don't worry about it, sweetie. The promoters are picking up the tab."

"Glad to hear that. I think I'll pamper myself and soak in that big bathtub. Want to join me?"

"You know I can't turn down an invitation like that," I said with a grin.

I simply marveled at how lucky I'd been to find and marry Melody. I loved her so much it hurt. She was my lover, confidant, and best friend. I simply had no idea how I would ever manage without her. I just hoped I'd never have to.

We were set to play the London Palladium two days hence. We'd arrived early because I wanted plenty of time to adjust to the change of time zone. Melody and I had never been overseas before, but I'd heard horror stories about jet lag and wanted to make sure we had time to adapt. We were excited to see the sights and couldn't wait to take a tour.

The following day we took a taxi to Piccadilly Circus. I paid the driver in pounds, which presented a challenge for an old country boy from Parsons County. I'd wanted to take one of those red double-deck buses, but Melody thought we'd get lost. Shaftesbury

Memorial Fountain sat in the middle of the area, and the steps were crowded with people sitting and observing the crowd. The guide book said the fountain had been built in 1893.

We wandered around for several minutes just listening to the people talk. Melody and I were fascinated by their accents. Some were so thick that neither of us could understand a word. Around noon, we went into a pub and ordered lunch. Later, we went on a tour of the Tower of London. I had no idea the place was so big. From my reading, I thought it was just one big tower. I remembered it was a place where they kept people as prisoners and that Anne Boleyn, Henry VIII's second wife, had spent some time there before he had her head chopped off. I never did think that was very nice of the old monarch. I mean, after all, she was his wife.

It took several hours to tour the Tower of London, and we still didn't see everything. I was really fascinated with the suits of armor. At six two, I thought those men from the Middle Ages seemed rather small in stature. But then, I'd read that somewhere.

The evening of our concert, Melody and I arrived at the Palladium in a limousine supplied by the promoters. The boys followed in a large van. I knew I'd never hear the last of that one. Our show was scheduled for nine o'clock and the crowd was to be warmed up at eight by a new act I'd signed to Star Search Records. It was a duo called Johnny and Jack, and they reminded me a lot of Brooks and Dunn.

Our band sat in our dressing room and watched the two singers on a closed circuit television monitor. Seeing the response of the audience, I knew I'd made the correct decision to book the act.

Promptly at nine o'clock, Roscoe walked onstage and took his bow. I don't believe that English audience knew exactly what to think, but by the time he'd wandered over to the side of the stage and taken his place, the audience erupted in applause.

I walked out next as always, introduced Melody and then the

boys. We played for an hour, and I stayed on stage alone for thirty minutes with just my guitar and a straight-back chair. Then the band came back, and we played for another hour. The crowd was terrific. They loved our music, and we loved their response. We finally had to shut it down after four encores.

Back at the hotel, Melody and I said goodnight as the fellows went to the bar. We were exhausted and all either of us could think of was sleep.

Our second gig was in Manchester. We were booked into a large suite in the Lowry Hotel. It was a five-star property, but extremely reasonable compared to the Lanesborough. Our performance was in the Manchester Evening News Arena. It was huge, seating almost twenty thousand people.

Basically, we performed the same music and songs that we'd done at the Palladium. The only difference was when Roscoe walked onstage, the audience hooted and hollered at the top of their lungs. I figured the crowd was more working class than the folks in London.

We'd filled every seat and received a similar reception to the one we'd enjoyed in London. After three encores, we had to beg off.

All in all Melody and I loved England, and she insisted we book another tour the following year. It was an easy sell. While we were in Manchester, much to my surprise, we ran into Scarlett Gibson.

We had just returned to the hotel after our show when I spotted her across the lobby and motioned for her to join us.

"What are you doing here?" I asked.

"I *am* a reporter. I'm here covering the London music scene. It was a double pleasure to see that you had a show here."

"This is our first trip overseas. It's been very exciting for us. I'm glad to see you, girl. Want to join us in the bar?"

"I thought you didn't drink."

"I don't, but Melody will have a glass of wine. I'll sip a Coke."

The bar was empty when we walked in except for two men seated on stools talking to the bartender. They looked like they might be salesmen.

Spotting us, the bartender said, "Have a seat anywhere. The waitress will be with you in a minute."

We picked a booth in the back and I slid in beside Melody; Scarlett sat opposite us. The waitress materialized moments later. She was an attractive young blonde in a very short outfit that barely covered her ass. She had a pretty smile but had the bad teeth the British are famous for.

"Ladies?"

Melody said, "I'd like a glass of Merlot. French preferably."

My, my, I thought. *My little wife is getting more sophisticated by the day.*

Scarlett smiled and said, "I'll have the same."

I piped in, "You can bring me a Coke."

Turning to Scarlett I asked, "Have you run into any good, new talent since you've been here?"

"Actually I have. There's a young fellow by the name of Sylvester Hornblower who has a beautiful voice. He sings country, but a lot of his songs are old English ballads. I didn't think too much of his band, but he'd probably sound good on a record cut in Nashville with some good musicians."

"Could you give me some contact information?"

"Sure," Scarlett said, picking up a paper napkin. She took a pen out of her purse and scribbled his name and phone number on it. Handing it to me, she said, "You know, Jamie, I've been supplying you with new talent for some time now and I get nothing in return. Do you think that's fair?"

I could feel my face flush. No, I didn't think it was fair, but what could I do? I'd created this persona of extreme privacy, and if I let Scarlett pierce it, I'd open myself up to an onslaught of reporters.

I shook my head and said, "No. It isn't fair and I'm sorry. What if I gave you a commission for every good lead you give me? Would that help?"

She sighed heavily and said, "You can't buy your way out of this one, Jamie. I don't want your money. I want to know how you feel about your success—I want to know how you write your songs. I want to know *you*."

I reached across the table and took her hand in mine. "Scarlett, honey, if I ever give an interview, you will be that person. That's all I can say." Then glancing at my watch, I said, "Melody and I need to hit the sack. Please keep in touch, Scarlett. And thanks for Sylvester's number."

* * *

When the house was finally finished, we hired a local company to move all our belongings from the Belle Meade house to the farm. The Nashville house had sold the month before, and we'd gotten what we'd asked. Mr. Benton was walking on air.

At our new home, it took several days to get all the pictures hung and the books placed on the library shelves. Naomi and John Chapman had come up to help us. Without them and Magnolia, I don't think Melody and I could have done it on our own.

I'd been back to visit Pop several times and was making some progress in my feelings about him. I knew I'd never like him, but I did feel sorry for him. I sent him a little allowance every month so he could buy pipe tobacco, cigarettes, and things in the commissary. He'd been asking me to check on Lester.

Junior, who'd been sent to the state penitentiary for manslaughter, had been killed by a fellow inmate with a shank sometime in the 1970s. That meant Lester was my only uncle. I'd never had any problem with Lester, and I'd always liked Aunt Lulu. And I wondered why I hadn't looked them up, particularly since they'd lost Billy.

A week after moving into the new house, I got in my Chevy crew-cab pickup and drove to Beulah Land. There was still no electricity or indoor plumbing. I parked on the highway beside the old hand pump and wondered if the well still held water. And, if so, was the water still laced with sulfur?

Looking up the hill, I noticed the vacant spot where our shack had once stood. Dr. Kate had told me it burned to the ground soon after Pop went to prison. Lester's place seemed the same. I guessed Aunt Lulu was the breadwinner now because I understood Lester seldom left the shack. I think he stayed drunk most days. It was a Saturday, so I figured they'd be there.

There always seemed to be snotty-nosed kids running around Beulah Land. That day was no exception. One scantily clad, bare-foot young girl followed me up the hill.

"Who're you, mister?" she asked.

"Lester's kin," I said.

She accepted that explanation and fell into stride with me. At Lester's door, she said, "Old Lester don't come out much. I reckon he stays shined up most days."

The child couldn't have been more than ten years old, and she knew about moonshine. Then I remembered I was ten myself when I first met Miss Frances. What did that say about the girl's world? I'd almost forgotten what stark poverty those people lived in. If it hadn't been for Miss Frances and Jake, where would I be? The thought made me shudder.

I knocked on the plywood door, and moments later Aunt Lulu opened it. She stared at me for a second and asked, "That you, Jamie?"

"Yes, ma'am. How are you?"

"Right well for an old woman. Come in and say hello to your uncle."

The interior of the shack was just as I'd remembered. *Dark, musty,* and *hot* were words that came to mind. As my eyes adjusted, I saw the outline of Lester asleep on the worn couch. He gurgled as he snored. Lulu was barefoot and wore a large sack-like dress that hid her fat rolls. Her hair, uncombed, greasy, and stringy, stuck out in every direction.

She padded over to the couch and shook her husband's shoulder. He turned over, farted, but didn't respond. She shook him again, and he said, "Stop that, woman. Leave me alone."

"Jamie came to see you, Lester. Wake up and say hello to the boy."

He sat up and tried to adjust his bleary eyes. They were blood-shot, and he had difficulty focusing. He stared at me for several seconds, his mind trying to place my face. Nothing seemed to register. Then he flopped down and drifted off to sleep.

Lulu, not to be ignored, shook him again. "Wake up, Lester," she said.

This time he sat up and swung his feet to the floor. Still looking at me with confusion, he asked, "Who're you?"

"It's Jamie, Uncle Lester. I've come to see you."

He tried to stand but fell back to the couch. He shook his head and said, "That really you, Jamie? You ain't shittin' me?"

"It's really me, Lester. I wanted to tell you and Aunt Lulu how sorry I am about Billy."

"A damn shame, that's what it is. Government sending our boys off to them foreign countries to get kilt for nothing. I say fuck the bastards."

Lulu was nodding, but she didn't say anything. I couldn't argue with Lester. I'd never understood the Vietnam War.

It was so hot in the shack I could feel perspiration trickle down my rib cage. It felt stuffy as well, and Lester's breath, laced with shine, was making me nauseous. I needed to get out of there.

I felt sorry for Lester and Aunt Lulu; there's no denying it. I had so much, and they so little. I made a quick decision that day. I said, "Good-bye, Lester." Then turning to Lulu, I said, "Step outside with me."

She followed me outdoors, and I squinted against the afternoon sun. She stood close to me, her body odor penetrating my being like a knife. I said, "I've done real well, Aunt Lulu. I want to help you and Lester."

Confusion flooded her face. "I don't understand, honey. Help us what?"

"I'm going to buy y'all a house in town and move you out of Beulah Land. Then I want someone to help Lester get off the shine and deal with his loss. I hate seeing him drink himself to death."

Her eyes moistened, and tears slid down her fat cheeks. Then her lips began to tremble. She grabbed me with both arms and pulled me to her. I thought for a moment she would crush my rib cage. I tried to free myself but to no avail. She had me in a death grip.

Finally, she released me and said, "I heard you'd done real well, Jamie. I'm right proud for you. I know Lester is, too."

"There's a Mr. Raymond in Round Rock who does real estate. I'm going to have him find you a house. Then I'll talk to Dr. Kate and ask her to find a place you can send Lester to dry him out. That okay with you?"

"Yes, son, that sounds just fine. God bless you."

She looked as if she might hug me again, so I said, "I've got to go now. Mr. Raymond will come see you soon. Bye, Aunt Lulu. Come see me when you can."

"I will, Jamie. I heard that house of yours is one of them mansions."

As I walked down the hill, the little girl slipped in beside me. I asked her, "What's your name, honey?"

"Lily"

"Your last name?"

"Crockett."

"What grade are you in?"

"Fourth."

"You like to read?"

"I can read."

"But do you like it?"

She had a puzzled look on her face as if to say, *What's there to like about reading?*

I knelt in front of her and said, "Take me to you mother."

Lily ran up the hill to a shack above Lester's, and I followed. She flung the door open and yelled, "Momma, come here!"

Minutes later a woman who looked fifty but was probably in her early thirties came to the door. She had mousey brown hair, wore a baggy housedress, and was barefoot.

"Are you Lily's mother?" I asked.

"Who wants to know?"

"Could we talk alone for a moment?"

She frowned. I could see fear in her dull brown eyes.

"Don't be afraid, Mrs. Crockett. My name is Jamie Lee Coleman. I'm Lester's nephew. I've just moved back to Parsons County."

"You the singer fellow built that big house?"

"Yes, ma'am. Could we talk?"

"I reckon. You stay out here, Lily."

She stepped back inside and waved me in. "I ain't got nothing to give you," she said. "I ain't been to the store in a few days."

I pulled out a rickety chair and sat at her table. She did the same. It was as dark, stuffy, and hot in her shack as it had been in Lester's. I couldn't imagine living like that and then remembered, I once had. Mrs. Crockett continued to have a confused look on her face.

"What does your husband do?" I asked her.

"He works at the shirt factory," she said. "It ain't steady, though."

"I'm going to need some help on my place. You reckon he'd be interested in seeing me about that?"

A smile formed on her haggard face, revealing a set of teeth that reminded me of my mom's. Nodding, she said, "Yes, sir, I reckon he would."

"I have one other request," I said.

She stared at me.

"I'd like to have Lily come visit me and my wife. I want to show her my library and my books."

I might as well have said, I want to send your daughter to the moon. Mrs. Crockett looked at me as if she had a bad taste in her mouth.

"How you reckon she'd get over there?"

"Your husband could bring her when he comes to work and then take her home when he's finished. My wife and I travel a lot, so we won't be there all the time."

"I'll have to ask Walt what he thinks," she said.

"Have him come see me. The gate code is 1952," I said. Then wondering if she knew what I meant, I said, "We have a gate to keep the cows in. There's a keypad like on a telephone. He'll have to push those numbers for the gate to open."

She nodded, and I said, "Have him come this afternoon if he can."

Chapter 26

Like all of us, Walter Crockett was a product of his genes and environment. He was thirty-five and looked fifty-five with a receding hairline and furrowed cheeks. His teeth were tobacco-yellowed and sparse with several molars missing.

He displayed good manners by taking off his baseball cap when he entered the house. I'd asked Melody to join me for the interview. I always depended on her good judgment. We sat in the great room to talk.

I explained what I had in mind for the job. It would consist of keeping the grounds, mowing the lawn, cleaning the pool, and taking care of the cattle. And I explained that I didn't tolerate alcohol.

He seemed to understand what his duties would be and said, "I'd like the job, Mr. Coleman."

"Call me Jamie. Everyone who works for me does. When can you start?"

"Tomorrow, if that's okay. They don't need me at the shirt factory again until next month so it won't cause them no problem."

"Good. Did your wife tell you about my interest in Lily?"

He nodded.

"That okay with you?"

"I reckon. She's a smart girl."

I'd shared with Melody my desire to influence Lily's life. I had been overcome with sadness the day I'd visited Lester and Lulu. Seeing that child trapped in hopeless poverty had pulled at my heart strings. She seemed bright and quizzical. I wanted to mentor Lily, open new worlds for her just as Miss Frances had for me.

As in all my endeavors, Melody supported me one hundred percent. The next day when father and daughter arrived, Melody hugged the child and took her to Cookeville where she bought her new clothes, just as Miss Frances had done for me.

Due to our hectic schedule, Melody and I had decided after she lost the baby that we wouldn't adopt a child. We figured it would be too difficult to raise one correctly. But we had no such misgivings about taking Lily into our lives. After all, she had a mother and father to look after her when we weren't around.

That afternoon when Melody and Lily returned, I showed Lily my library and said, "I'm going to read you a story. Would you like that?"

She looked at me with a noncommittal expression.

"What kind of story?" she asked.

"It's a story about a young girl who lived in the mountains of Switzerland. It's called *Heidi*."

Melody had made us hot chocolate, and we sat in the big red leather chairs facing each other. I began to read the story, and Lily's eyes brightened. I couldn't take on the voice of the characters like Miss Frances did, so I read the sentences straight. After two chapters, I gave the book to Lily so she could continue. She took it home that evening, and when she returned the following day, she'd finished it. Next, I gave her *Tom Sawyer*. She sat in the library all day reading.

I had no idea where my relationship would go with Lily. She was responding to me as I had to Miss Frances. Perhaps she would be able to pull herself out of her morass as I had out of mine.

* * *

A month after we'd moved into our new home, Melody and I were reading in bed one evening. I turned off my bedside lamp and she did the same. When I pulled her to me, I noticed a lump about the size of a Robin's egg on her rib cage next to her left breast.

Turning the light back on, I said, "Honey, pull up your night-gown and let me check something."

"I'm not in the mood, sweetie," she said with a smile.

"You're always in the mood. I felt a lump on your rib cage," I said.

She rolled her eyes to the ceiling and did as I'd asked. I saw the small mass and touched it. "Does it hurt when I push on it?"

"No. I didn't know it was there."

"Please go see Dr. Kate in the morning," I said.

"I've got too much to do tomorrow. I'll go next week."

I shook my head. "Tomorrow. *Please.*"

* * *

When Melody returned from Dr. Kate's office, she had a worried look on her face.

"What did Kate say?" I asked.

"She found several more small lumps on my body that I'd never noticed. She said they were swollen lymph nodes, and since I didn't have an infection, at least one of them needed a biopsy."

"When's she going to do it?"

"She referred me to a specialist in Nashville."

I could feel my pulse quicken. To me, biopsy meant something bad. I didn't want to even go there. "When's the appointment?" I asked.

"Next week . . . Tuesday at two o'clock."

"What's the doctor's name?"

"Dr. Smithson. He's a general surgeon."

I picked up the phone and dialed information. I got the doctor's number and called his office. When the receptionist answered, I said, "My name is Jamie Lee Coleman. My wife, Melody, has an appointment with your doctor next Tuesday. I'd like him to see her today."

"He's got a full schedule this afternoon. I just can't get her in."

"Darlin', can't just isn't in my vocabulary. I have to get her in this afternoon or I'll go stark raving mad. I'll be a damn mental case. You don't want to be responsible for that now do you?"

She laughed. "I recognize that darlin' inflection, Mr. Coleman. You are the singer, right?"

"Got me."

"Okay. Be here at five o'clock. I'll get him to see her as his last patient. And remember, buster, you owe me one."

* * *

Dr. Smithson turned out to be the chief of surgery at Vanderbilt University Hospital. The doctor was in his mid-fifties with brown hair graying at the temples. His dark eyes looked as if they could see right through you. He was tall and athletic, his stride confident. He interviewed us in his office and then asked a nurse to escort Melody to an examination room. I sat in the waiting room and stared at the walls.

Several minutes later, his nurse took me back to his office. Melody was already there. The doctor came in and said, "I need to do a fine-needle biopsy of the largest node. Otherwise, I can't make a diagnosis. This can be done under local anesthesia. It's up to you whether we do it this afternoon or not. Frankly, I believe the sooner the better."

"What are we dealing with?" I asked.

"I'm thinking some type of lymphoma."

Melody asked, "What's that?"

The doctor had a soft, reassuring voice and radiated a sense of warmth and caring. I could see compassion in his eyes when he said, "It's a type of cancer that affects the lymphatic system. There're different types depending on the cells involved."

I was stunned. Melody had always been healthy and strong as a horse. How could she have cancer? And what was the lymphatic system?

"The lymph nodes are part of the body's defense against infection. They're connected by small vessels similar to veins and carry a clear liquid known as lymph. Besides the nodes, there are other organs such as the spleen, tonsils, and adenoids that contain lymphoid tissue. I know that's a lot to digest, but I've made it as simple as I could," he said.

I let out a deep sigh and, looking at Melody, said, "I think you should do it this afternoon."

She nodded. "I agree."

Dr. Smithson said, "I'll give you a little sedation and do the biopsy in about thirty minutes. I've got to do evening rounds in the hospital, and when I get back, I'll do the biopsy."

"When will we have an answer?" I asked.

"About this time tomorrow," the doctor said.

* * *

After the biopsy, Melody and I went directly to the Vanderbilt Plaza

Hotel on West End Avenue across from the Vanderbilt campus. I saw no point in flying back to the farm. Melody was pensive as I checked us in. "I'll need to go down the street to the pharmacy," she said. "We don't even have a toothbrush with us."

"I'll do it. You're still groggy from the sedation," I said.

She didn't argue, and when we got to the room, she pulled the bedspread back and lay down. I sat next to her, picked up her hand, and said, "We'll get through this together."

"I'd be lying, Jamie, if I said I wasn't a little scared," she said. "But I'll deal with it."

"You're a strong woman. I know you will. What do you want besides toothbrushes and paste?"

She told me and I purchased all the toiletries we'd need for a one-night stand. We had dinner that evening at Julian's and went to bed early. We didn't have any books with us, so we went directly to sleep or, more correctly, tried to sleep. At one o'clock in the morning I knew Melody was still awake.

"You okay, darlin'?" I asked.

"Yes. I should have asked the doctor for a sleeping pill."

"I could call his answering service," I said. "The farmers' market pharmacy stays open all night."

"No, please don't bother the doctor. We'll be okay without one night of sleep."

* * *

Dr. Smithson wore a grave expression when he ushered us into his office the next afternoon. "The diagnosis is an unspecified peripheral T-cell lymphoma. It's a rare form of non-Hodgkin's lymphoma, very fast growing and generally widespread. Even with treatment the prognosis isn't good."

"But I feel fine," Melody said.

"That's the nature of the disease."

"What's the treatment?" I asked.

"Chemotherapy."

"Where's the best place for it?" I asked.

"The two largest cancer centers are Sloan Kettering in New York City and M. D. Anderson in Houston. They're both outstanding. We have excellent oncologists here as well."

"Please don't take offense, Doctor, but I'd prefer to go where they have the most experience," I said.

"That's not a problem. I have friends at both institutions. I can arrange for an appointment."

*　*　*

We chose M. D. Anderson because it was in Houston and easier for us to fly to. Dr. Smithson was able to get us an appointment with one of his friends the following day. So we flew back to the farm to collect our clothes. Melody and Magnolia worked out what would need to be done in our absence, and I told Walt that Lily could take home any book she wanted from the library.

Ernie had the G-IV in front of the hangar the following morning and had filed an IFR flight plan by the time I climbed into the left seat. We arrived in Houston an hour and a half later and landed at the David Wayne Hooks Municipal Airport. I taxied up the Tomball Jet Center and shut down both engines. Ernie was going to fly the plane back to the farm as soon as it was fueled. Melody was dealing with everything remarkably well. I, on the other hand, was a basket case. The only reason I'd insisted on acting as pilot in command had been to keep my mind off the damn lymphoma.

I'd rented a Hertz car for our trip to the hotel and later the hospital. I'd made reservations for us at the Four Seasons Hotel. Melody sat in one of the lobby chairs while I filled out the paper-work for the car and paid for the Jet A fuel.

Ernie was fidgeting, walking up and down in front of the desk. He turned to me and asked, "Why can't I stay with you folks? There's nothing I need to be doing back in Round Rock."

"I appreciate that, Ernie. I really do. Melody and I need to do this by ourselves. When we need the plane, I'll call your cell."

"If you need anything, man, please call. I'll be here in a flash."

"I know you will and that's very reassuring. Now, get the bird home."

I watched Ernie take off and then walked over to where Melody sat, staring at the wall in front of her. I extended my hand and said, "Let's go to the hotel, honey. You can rest a little before we go to the hospital."

She nodded and followed me out to the car. I punched the address on Lamar Street for the hotel and followed the directions. I had arranged for a suite, and we arrived about two hours before we were due at M. D. Anderson. We knew we were going to be there for a few weeks so we'd brought a lot of luggage. While I checked us in, Melody supervised the loading of our things on the bellhop's cart. The Presidential Suite was magnificent. Nothing like the Lanesborough Hotel in London, but still spectacular.

Melody and I took a light lunch in our rooms, and she lay on the big four-poster bed for about an hour, though I don't think she was able to sleep. I read a book that I'd brought with me.

We left the hotel about thirty minutes before our appointment, arrived at the hospital, and found the oncology clinic. The doctors at Anderson were professional and efficient. The lead oncologist was a young doctor by the name of Walter Abramson. A nurse ushered us into one of his examination rooms about twenty minutes after we arrived.

Melody sat on the examination table and twisted her wristwatch band around and around. She had a stoic expression on her face, but I knew she was scared. Hell, I was terrified.

Dr. Abramson walked in with a chart in his hand. He was about my height with sandy hair. He had a well-trimmed goatee and a pleasant smile.

"Mrs. Coleman, I'm Dr. Abramson. I'm sorry that you have this problem. I'm going to do the best I can to get you well." Then turning to me, he asked, "You're Mr. Coleman?"

"Yes. We know this is bad, doctor. We want you to level with us."

"Of course. The next few weeks are not going to be easy. Chemotherapy is always difficult. After all, we are going to give you terrible poisons in hopes that they will kill the cancer cells. Unfortunately, they will make you very ill. We do have a new drug that is wonderful for nausea."

"How long will this take?" I asked.

"It depends upon the response we get. Anywhere from three to six weeks."

"So we'll stay here?"

"Yes. I'll oversee all treatments. Most will be by intravenous injection, but some will be given orally. Now, if you don't mind, Mr. Coleman, the nurse and I will examine your wife. Please step outside."

* * *

The six weeks we stayed in Houston were a nightmare. Melody, God love her, did better than me. I had to take a sleeping pill every night. For about five days after each treatment, she experienced muscle aching and nausea. I'd bought her a wig because she'd lost all of her beautiful blonde hair. She wore it during the day. Seeing her bald head at night made me so sad I wanted to scream. I'd told her she looked sexy that way, but I knew she hadn't bought it.

The steroids were awful. They made her face puffy, and she gained about fifteen or twenty pounds. She looked in the mirror at the hotel one day and said, "Jamie, honey, I look like a fat pig."

I pulled her to me and kissed her hard on the lips. "You look beautiful to me, darlin'. Please don't say things like that."

She lay her head back and looked me in the eye. "Oh, Jamie, I'm terrified. This is the worst thing I've ever had to deal with. I'm not sure I can do it."

"If anyone can do it, you can," I said. "You're a strong woman."

* * *

We arrived back at the farm in September. I'd canceled our fall tour and all my other business activities to spend every waking hour with Melody. We walked around the property every day, taking pleasure in little things like watching squirrels scamper up and down our trees. The weather was cold and damp at times, but that didn't seem to bother Melody. She'd just bundle up and wrap a scarf around her long, beautiful neck. A small creek ran behind the barn, and we'd watch minnows dart back and forth in the clear water, much as Bandit and I had done at the Washington farm. Roscoe accompanied us on all our walks and stayed unusually close to Melody.

We'd just come back from the creek one day when Melody said, "Jamie, honey, you know I love spending this time with you. It's really wonderful. I'm just worried that you're not paying attention to business. You know, all those things you usually do."

"My only business these days is you, Melody."

"But I'm fine. I feel good. I've got a lot of energy. I was thinking about picking up my fiddle and playing a little music. You're making me feel guilty—taking all your time."

"Do you want to do a duet? Do you feel up to that?"

"I'd love to. Let's go to the library."

So that's what we did. Melody took her violin out of its case, and I grabbed my guitar out of my study. We started out with a few of our old familiar songs that we'd played over the years.

Melody frowned once when she missed a note, but otherwise her performance was remarkable. It felt wonderful to be making music together. We played for about an hour, and then I could tell Melody was beginning to tire.

I said, "Wow! You haven't lost your touch, Melody. I need to rest awhile. My fingers are aching."

She laughed. "You're just looking out for me. There's nothing wrong with your fingers."

* * *

Things didn't really start to deteriorate until around Thanksgiving. The symptoms were subtle at first, a general fatigue that followed even moderate exertion. By the time Christmas rolled around, Melody was bedridden. Her eyes were sunken and dull, her pale skin pasty white. I made myself sit with her even though I wanted to cry each time I looked at her.

Naomi and John had come to be with their daughter in her last hours and were a great source of strength for Melody and me. Magnolia kept the house immaculate and cooked all our meals. When I wasn't with my wife, I moped around the premises looking for things to keep my mind occupied.

The day after Christmas, Melody asked her mother to find me. I was in the barn stacking hay for the cows. When I got to our bedroom, Melody patted the mattress and said, "Come sit with me, Jamie."

I thought she looked beautiful. She'd put on some lipstick and combed her new growth of thin, sparse hair back from her forehead. I sat next to her and said, "You look lovely today."

"You always were a smooth talker," she said. "And, at times, a terrible liar."

"You know I love you more than anything in the world," I said.

"Yes. But I'm worried about you, Jamie. You're not dealing very well with this situation. We've had a wonderful life together. We've worked side by side, had an incredible physical and spiritual . . ."

Tears flooded her eyes when she couldn't finish her sentence. I couldn't believe how brave she was. I took her hand and raised it to my lips. Then I leaned over and kissed her. It took every ounce of self-control I had to keep from screaming at the top of my lungs.

She inhaled deeply and said, "I wish we'd had children. They could look after you when you're old."

I didn't say anything. I just held her hand.

"I want you to promise me something, Jamie," she said with a sober expression.

"Anything."

"When I'm gone, I want you to go on with your life. You have so much to offer the world. And you need to be here for Lily. She loves you so much, and she's blossomed from your mentoring. Don't you dare mope around this house feeling sorry for yourself."

Tears slid down my cheeks as I tried to answer her. I bit my lip and waited for a few seconds before I tried to speak. Finally, I said, "You know I would promise you anything. To be honest, I'm not sure I can do what you ask. I will be lost without you in my life. I'm not sure I can survive."

"If you want me to die in peace, please promise me."

I'd always been honest with Melody. I had never lied to her. But that day I did. I squeezed her hand and said, "I promise you I will go on with my life."

She smiled and fell asleep. I looked at her angelic face and shook my head. *I'm sorry I lied to you, girl. I really am.*

* * *

Melody died in her sleep sometime that evening. Naomi found her the next morning. I'd been staying in the second guest room. When she told me, I felt as if someone had stuck a knife in my heart. I felt hot all over, and a terrible melancholy settled over me like a black shroud. I wondered if I could even get dressed, let alone face the day.

When I finally made it out of bed, I stood in a hot shower for a long, long time letting the water cascade over my tense neck. I took deep breaths trying to calm my jagged nerves. I took so many that I became light-headed and almost passed out. I cut myself three times shaving and broke my comb trying to arrange my hair. I was a mess.

There's always a lot to do when someone dies. It's one of the things that helps people deal with their sorrow. After I left the bathroom, I dressed and called the funeral home in Livingston. Melody, her parents, and I had discussed the arrangements that were to be made.

Melody wanted to be buried in Mississippi in a plot that her parents had reserved for their family. I'd been told there was a space for me should I want it. I hadn't known quite how to respond. Finally, I'd said, "At least we'll be together."

The funeral home hearse drove Melody to Yazoo City the following day. The service was to be the day after. The Chapmans were Methodists. Melody had told me once that it was easy to be a Methodist because they didn't have real strong feelings about much of anything.

Ernie and I flew the Chapmans to Mississippi the day the hearse left Livingston. The Yazoo City County Airport had a five thousand foot runway so we were able to land there. I'd arranged for a Hertz car so I could drive John and Naomi to their home.

Naomi insisted that Ernie and I stay at their house. They had a garage apartment with a private entrance. We hadn't brought much with us. I simply had an overnight bag filled with a clean shirt and my toilet articles. I didn't plan on staying very long. We all went out to dinner that evening so Naomi wouldn't have to cook.

I got up the day of the funeral in a daze. My head hurt so bad and my neck was so stiff I didn't think I could drive to the church. In fact, I found Ernie in the kitchen and said, "Man, you'll have to drive us to the church. I'm a fucking mess this morning."

"No sweat. You look like hell, Jamie. You've got to get hold of yourself."

"Yeah. Easier said than done, buddy."

The Methodist Church was in a quiet part of town and was a red brick structure with a large cross on top of a white steeple. When Ernie and I drove up, the parking lot was already full, and there didn't appear to be any parking places on the street. Ernie drove two blocks before he found a spot. The Chapmans, Melody included, were very popular in their home town.

The boys in the band had wanted to come, but I'd asked them not to. Rhonda stood on the porch of the church waiting for me as Ernie and I walked up.

"I'm so sorry, honey," she said, pulling me to her. "I know you loved her so much."

"I'll always love her, Rhonda. Just because she's dead doesn't mean I don't love her anymore."

Tears flooded her eyes, and she said, "I know that, Jamie. I wasn't denying the fact that you'll always love her. I'll always love her, too. God, I'm going to miss her so much."

John and Naomi had wanted me to sit in the front pew with them but I declined. The one thing I had insisted upon was no open casket. I couldn't tolerate the idea of people gawking at my dead wife. Ernie, Rhonda, and I sat on the back pew by ourselves.

The preacher motioned for us to stand and said, "Let us pray. Dear Lord, please take Melody into Your Heavenly Kingdome. She has been a good Christian all her life. She taught Sunday school when she was just a teenager, and she touched many, many hearts with her music. She will be greatly missed by her family and friends.

We can all take comfort in the knowledge she is in Your good hands. In the hands of Jesus, our Lord and Savior. We ask this in Your name. Amen. Amen."

Melody's brother stood and walked to the podium. He looked out over the mourners and said, "My sister was a beautiful soul. She never met a stranger, and she was the go to person in our family. She was always there for us. In fact, she was always there for anyone who needed help in any way. The essence of the good Samaritan."

He continued for the next fifteen minutes, but I tuned him out. I knew everything he was saying. My thoughts drifted back to that day in Nashville when I'd opened the door of Rhonda's apartment and first laid eyes on Melody Chapman. I remembered her angelic face, her beautiful blonde hair, her pale complexion, her ruby red lips, and her figure to die for. I'm quite sure I didn't go to sleep, but at the end of the service I couldn't have told anyone what had transpired after her brother took the podium.

Ernie and I followed the hearse to the local cemetery where the Chapmans had bought their plots. It belonged to the county, and I was pleased to see that it was well maintained. The funeral home had placed a tarp over the fresh pile of earth next to the open grave. Six feet of earth soon to be pushed on top of my darlin's coffin. Jesus, that thought made me retch. I wasn't sure I could go through with the whole barbaric ritual. But I did. Just before they lowered the casket, I touched the fingers of my right hand to my lips and gave the love of my life one last kiss. My eyes were so blurred with tears that, thank God, I couldn't see the dirt being shoveled into the grave.

I wandered back to our rental car in a daze. Ernie walked along beside me, holding the elbow of my right arm in a firm grasp. Had he not done that, I'm sure I'd have fallen. I'd told Naomi that I would come by the house after the graveside service, but I just couldn't. Once in the car, I turned to Ernie and said, "Let's go home, Ernie. I can't take any more of this."

Ernie and I flew back to the farm that afternoon. I let him take the left seat, and I half heartedly acted as co-pilot. There was a storm brewing on our weather scope just south of Round Rock and we thought we might have to divert to Nashville. By the time we arrived, however, the area had cleared, but the ceiling was low. About four hundred feet. We'd called the house and asked Magnolia what it looked like outside. We used our ILS glide slope to make our landing and broke out of the clouds lined up perfectly for the runway.

I couldn't sleep in our bed that first night knowing Melody had died there. In fact, the next day I had it removed from the house and replaced with another.

During the entire episode of Melody's illness, I hadn't picked up my guitar except for the short duel Melody and I'd done that day in the library. During those first weeks after her death, I wasn't sure I ever would. I had placed her violin in the library on a top shelf. Every time I looked at it, my stomach churned. Finally, I called Rhonda.

She picked up on the second ring. "Hello."

"Rhonda, it's Jamie."

"Hi, honey. I'm so sorry about Melody. I know you miss her. Is there anything I can do to help you?"

"Would you take her violin? I just can't look at it. I think she'd want you to have it."

I could hear her catch her breath and choke up. "Yes. I'd love to have it. I'll take really good care of it. Please don't worry. Oh, Jamie, this makes me so sad."

"I know. I'll have one of the boys drive down to Nashville and give it to you."

Chapter 27

I'd canceled all our engagements until further notice. I continued to pay the guys in the band and told them if they wanted to quit, I'd understand. They all stood by me. Mr. Ledbetter took care of the record company, and Mr. Hickman managed my brokerage accounts. For the first week after Melody's death I sat in the library and stared at the walls. At night I wandered aimlessly around the house flipping lights on and off in a daze. Then one night I found myself in the kitchen pantry. Why? I had no idea. I stood there, my eyes drifting from soup cans to jelly jars to bottles of olives. Then I saw the Merlot that Melody kept for special occasions. I lifted it off the shelf and went back into the kitchen. Fumbling through Melody's domain I found the cork screw and eased the cork out of the bottle, I had no idea where she kept the wine glasses so I filled a tumbler and tipped my head back. Two more and I was so groggy that I wandered back to my bedroom and fell into bed.

Magnolia cooked for me, but I seldom ate, and thirty pounds melted away. I depleted the Merlot supply two days after I'd found the first bottle. The closest liquor store was in Cookeville, so the next day I waited until Magnolia went to Round Rock for groceries, then climbed behind the wheel of my pickup.

I don't even remember driving through Livingston. Once in Cookeville, I wandered up one street after another looking for a liquor store. When I found one, I parked the truck and sat there for a few minutes trying to clear my muddled brain. I'm sure my eyes were blood shot. My head pounded and a dull headache pressed both temples.

The front door had a sign that said pull but I pushed instead. Confused, I waited for a patron to come out and then I wandered in. I was still functioning well enough to realize what I was doing but I didn't give a shit. I pulled two large bottles of vodka off a shelf and carried them to the counter. I dropped one and it exploded on the tile floor splashing the clear liquid on my jeans.

"Shit. Add it to the fucking bill and get me another one."

"You okay?"

"I'm fine. Mind your own damned business."

"You driving?"

"You want to sell this fucking vodka or not?"

"Take it easy, fellow. You look awfully familiar. I know you?"

By then I'd turned my back and walked to the vodka shelf. I grabbed a second bottle and slammed it on the counter.

"What I owe you? Three?"

"Cash or credit?"

Fumbling in my jeans' pocket I grabbed a wad of twenties and handed him a fist full. He counted out what I owed and gave the rest back. I grabbed the sack and when I turned I lost my balance and damned near fell on my ass. Black spots floated in front of my eyes and the horizon tilted. I grabbed the counter and waited until the spell passed, then with as much dignity as I could muster, walked out of the fucking store.

I damned near made it back to the farm when I misjudged that sharp curve about a mile from my front gate. The pickup sailed off the black top and rolled three times before it collided with a big maple. I was upside down, no seat belt, head bleeding like a slaughtered pig, and blood filling my eyes. I pulled my handkerchief from the back pocket of my jeans and held it to my head. The door was open, so I rolled out onto the ground and lay there for several minutes.

When I walked into the house I yelled for Magnolia. She came scrambling out of the kitchen and when she saw my bloodied head screamed, "Jamie. What happened?"

"Turned the fucking pickup over. Take me to Dr. Kate, please."

When we walked into the Round Rock Medical Clinic, Jazz took one look at me and ushered us back to an exam room. Moments later, Dr. Kate entered the room,

"What happened, Jamie? Let me take a look."

She pealed the handkerchief away and examined the wound. It hurt like hell because the handkerchief had stuck to the cut edges of the skin.

"How'd you do this? It's going to require stitches."

"He rolled his pickup," Magnolia said.

"Lie down on the exam table, Jamie. I've got to deaden this first."

She injected the wound and then cleaned it. It only took ten stitches so I figured I'd gotten off easy. After she'd bandaged it, she asked, "Have you been drinking?"

I ignored her.

"Jamie?"

I simply got off the table and walked out of the room. Looking back over my shoulder, I said, "Magnolia will pay you."

When Magnolia slipped behind the steering wheel of her Honda, she said, "That weren't no way to treat Dr. Kate, Jamie, and you know it. You ought to be ashamed of yourself."

I looked out the window. "Can we just go home. When we get to the truck, stop. I've got to get something out of it."

When she saw the pickup, Magnolia slowed down and pulled onto the shoulder. I climbed out of the Civic and stumbled down the hill to the totalled truck. The bottles, for some reason I'll never understand, survived the crash. They were still in the brown paper sack, so I stuck it under my arm and climbed back up the hill. As I slipped into the passenger seat, Magnolia asked, "What's in the sack, Jamie?"

I didn't answer. She shifted the little car into drive and spun the wheels on the gravel of the shoulder. Back at the house I went into the kitchen and found a bottle of orange juice. I still remembered how to make a Screwdriver. The first one went down in one gulp. The rest I sipped. In thirty minutes they'd numbed my soul enough that I could sit motionless for hours on end without a coherent thought. After all, that was my aim.

Magnolia called Dr. Kate one day and asked her to make a house call. I didn't know anything about it until the doctor rang the doorbell. Magnolia escorted Kate into the library. She took one look at me and said, "Jamie, you've got to eat and you've got to stop this drinking. You can't go on like this. At least let me give you an antidepressant."

I shook my head. "I don't want any pills. Just leave me alone."

She sat in the chair next to mine and said, "Please let me help you."

Shaking my head, I said, "I'm sorry, Kate. Please leave."

"Melody wouldn't like this, Jamie. You know she wouldn't."

"Don't mention Melody. Leave me alone."

I stared right through Kate.

"This isn't good. You've got to deal with this in a rational way.

You need help. I'm worried you'll do something harmful to yourself."

"I haven't the energy to kill myself if that's what you're thinking. Please leave me alone. Go away."

She stood, looked at me for a moment, shook her head, and left the room.

* * *

Roscoe didn't come when I called him one morning, and I found him beside his water bowl. He'd died in his sleep, like Melody. He was an old dog and I'd expected it, but losing him was yet another blow to my fragile existence. I collapsed next to his limp body and felt my shoulders shake. I cried so hard I couldn't catch my breath. I sat there for the better part of an hour. Then I called Ernie, and he buried Roscoe for me in the back pasture. I didn't want another dog. I couldn't imagine loving and losing anything ever again.

It was Lily, like Casey before her, who brought me back to the living. It was the last weekend in February. There was a three-inch snow on the ground, and I had a roaring fire going in the library. I sat staring at the flames, lost to the world. I sensed a presence and turned to see Lily standing next to me, an angelic expression on her face.

"Mister Jamie, you know Miss Melody is with the Lord," she said. "She's with Jesus."

I simply stared at the child. Brother Abernathy's preaching and Miss Frances's prodding had never convinced me that there was a God. I'd never believed in heaven or hell. As far as I was concerned, when you died, everything just went black. But the thought that Melody might live on in some other form grabbed me that day. What if those people were right? What if there was a God after all? What if I was wrong?

Whether or not I was truly convinced or just wanted to believe in something again, I'll never know for sure. But for a time at least, I bought into the whole idea. I simply accepted the fact that Melody was in a better place. I didn't start praying or going to church, but I decided religion did help some people deal with their problems. That it helped them accept death as an extension of life.

There'd been a transformation in Lily. She was eleven years old and blossoming. She'd become an avid reader, and her grades had improved. I knew I'd have to get her out of Beulah Land for her to thrive.

One afternoon after Lily had told me Melody was with Jesus, I walked down to the barn so I could talk to Walt. He was stacking bales of hay in one corner of the loft.

"You got a minute, Walt?" I asked.

He dropped a bale, wiped his forehead with his handkerchief, and said, "Sure. Let me climb down the ladder."

When he stepped onto the barn floor, he said, "What's up, Jamie?"

"As you know, I've become very fond of Lily. She's a bright girl, and she seems to be doing well in school. I know the conditions you and your family live in. I once lived in Beulah Land myself. It's not a good environment for a blossoming young girl like Lily."

"I know that, Jamie. Me and my wife been thinking about moving into town now that I've got this here job."

"I've got a better idea. I'd like to build you a house here on the farm."

"That's mighty nice of you, Jamie. We can afford to pay you rent."

"No. The house will be yours rent free. In fact, I plan to place the house and the one-acre it sits on in your name."

Walt's eyes moistened and he sniffed loudly. "Jamie, you're the finest man I've ever known. Thank you so much."

* * *

I'd stopped the vodka cold turkey the day Lillie told me Melody was with Jesus. The withdrawal wasn't as bad as I'd feared. There were night sweats, insomnia, periodic shakes, and terrible headaches, but I made it through them and I'd slowly come out of my depression, taking each day at a time. In the spring, I'd wander down to the creek and watch the crawfish and minnows like I'd done with Bandit and later Melody and Roscoe. Often on weekends, Lily would accompany me.

On a Saturday morning in May, Lily found me in the library. I'd begun to read again, and on occasion, I'd even pick up my guitar. She walked over to my chair and said, "It's a pretty day, Mr. Jamie. Reckon we could wander down by the creek? I'd like to tell you about a book I'm reading."

"You don't have to call me Mr. Jamie, Lily. Please call me Jamie like everyone else."

"I didn't reckon that would be my place. You know, seeing you're my elder and all."

I laughed. "You don't have to make me feel that old. I don't think of myself as an elder individual."

"Well, okay. I'll call you Jamie like everyone else. So, Jamie, want to walk down to the creek?"

"I'd love to."

It was a lovely day. The air was crisp and there wasn't a cloud in the sky. A gentle breeze blew the new leaves on the maple trees, and when I took a deep breath, I could smell honeysuckle. Turning to Lily, I said, "I'm glad you got me out of the house. You're right, this is a pretty day. Now, tell me what you're reading."

"*Cold Mountain*," she said. "Are you familiar with it?"

"I've heard of it, but haven't read it. What do you think?"

"It's about the Civil War. Our Civil War. I don't like the thought of war, Jamie. Why do people fight wars anyway?"

"That's a complicated subject. I guess there are times when war is necessary. Our Civil War was fought to preserve the integrity of the Union and to free the slaves. And the Second World War was fought to save Europe. And, of course, the Japanese had attacked us at Pearl Harbor. In my opinion, the Korean War and the Vietnam War were ill-conceived and served no purpose."

"I hope we don't have any more wars. Justified or not," she said with a determination unusual for such a young girl.

We sat by the creek and watched the minnows scurry around. Beams of sunlight shone like spotlights through the canopy of maple trees. It was such a peaceful place that I lay back in the soft grass and closed my eyes. Thoughts of Bandit, Melody, Fireman, and Roscoe drifted aimlessly through my mind.

I felt a tickle under my nose and opened my eyes to see Lily tickling me with a leaf. She grinned and said, "Wake up, Jamie. We need to go back to the house."

* * *

The Crockett family moved into their new home in July. It was a simple three-bedroom house set on a one-acre lot next to the hangar. It had its own entrance off the county blacktop as well as access to the farm. I'd hired a decorator out of Cookeville to furnish and decorate it for them. They'd never had running water or indoor plumbing, and I think it took them a while to get used to both. Lily adapted easily and told me one day, "It's nice having hot water and a bathtub, Jamie. I sure appreciate what you've done for us."

"And I appreciate what you've done for me, Lily," I said.

And I meant every word. Had it not been for Lily, I'm not at all sure I would have survived after Melody's death.

* * *

I pulled the band back together in the fall of 1997 and booked a tour to start in Atlanta and extend into the Northeast coast. I'd called Rhonda, and when she answered, I said, "Rhonda, honey, it's Jamie."

"You don't have to tell me who you are. My God, Jamie, I know your voice the second I hear it. How are you?"

"Recovering. In fact, I'm activating the band. Would you consider playing fiddle with us?"

There was a long silence, and then she said, "You're sure you want a fiddle? You don't really need one at this point. It might make you think of Melody."

"It will make me think of Melody, but if you're the fiddler, I can live with it. The only thing I ask is that you don't use Melody's violin. You okay with that?"

"Of course. I'd be honored to play with your band. When do you want me?"

"We'll be practicing here at the farm. I'd like for you to come to the house and stay in one of the guest rooms. Can you be here next week?"

"Yes. All I'm doing is studio work. I'll be there Monday."

We practiced at the recording studio I'd built in one end of the hangar, and it took a while for us to get back in shape. Rhonda was a good musician, but she couldn't play as well as Melody. During the last days of my recovery, I'd written a few songs that I tried out on the guys. Some they liked, and some they didn't. We decided to do only the ones everyone liked.

The tour was to start in October, and I was walking the fence line at the farm one day when I received a call from Dr. Stout on my cell phone.

"Jamie, I've got two golden retriever puppies over here who're looking for a home," he said. "Think you could take them off my hands?"

"I don't know, Doc. How old are they?"

"Eight weeks. Both are males and purebreds."

I picked them up that afternoon. Needless to say, they were cute as they could be, and I fell in love with them immediately. I had no idea what I'd name them and decided to wait a few days to see what their personalities suggested.

Magnolia wasn't too happy that I'd brought two puppies home, but they soon won her over. I bought them chew toys so they'd leave our furniture alone, and I started training them. They were smart little fellows and caught on quickly. I still hadn't been able to come up with names when Lily solved the problem.

"I think you should call this one Mutt and this one Jeff," she said.

"Sounds like a plan to me," I said.

* * *

I'd kept up with Amy over the years. She was married to a doctor and lived in Columbus, Ohio. She had two girls who were in school at Ohio State. She'd call from time to time when she was visiting her parents in Cookeville, and we'd get together.

Just before the tour was to start, I received a call from her saying she was in Cookeville and wanted to drive up to the farm. She arrived around one o'clock that afternoon.

Amy was in her mother's car, a 1996 Chevrolet sedan. I always had to stop and think how old we were. I was forty-five so I had to assume she was as well. She'd aged well. Her hair was still the same bright red it'd always been and her pale skin was devoid of the freckles I'd remembered. It occurred to me that Amy might have had a little help with her youthful looks, but I certainly didn't care one way or the other.

"You're looking good, girl," I said, walking up to the car. "Give me a hug."

She put her arms around my neck and kissed me on the cheek.

"I'm so sorry about Melody," she said.

"It was terrible, but I'm dealing with it. Come in the house and tell me about you," I said.

Magnolia made us coffee, and we sat in the living room. Amy seemed preoccupied. Finally, I said, "What's going on?"

"Is it that obvious?"

"Yes. I've known you almost my whole life."

She shrugged. "Harry left me."

"I'm sorry. Another woman?"

"A man, if you can believe that. Harry was gay and never admitted it to himself until he fell in love with his accountant. I was devastated, but couldn't be mad at him."

"It's hard for straight people to understand homosexuality. I'm convinced they're born that way. I've never thought it was a matter of choice," I said.

"Me either," she said. "The girls have been terrific and very understanding. But now in mid-life I'm alone, and it scares the hell out of me, Jamie."

I walked over to her chair and sat on the arm. I pulled her to me and said, "You're a beautiful, sexy woman with a lot to offer. You'll find someone soon. I know you will."

She smiled for the first time and asked, "You interested?"

I kissed her forehead. "I'm just now walking among the living, Amy. You'll have found someone by the time I'm available."

She grabbed my hand and squeezed it so hard I yelled. She smiled and said, "Sorry. I need you now! I don't want to wait. I need you *now!*"

"Don't do this, honey. I would love to have you for my own, but it's just not possible. If you want to wait me out, that's your prerogative. All I'm saying is that it'll be a long time, and you deserve someone now. Not five years from now."

She dabbed at her eyes, and said, "Okay, Jamie. I do love you. I guess you know that. I've loved you since that first day we played Miss Frances's piano. I guess I'll always love you."

I didn't know what to say. I did love Amy on some level. Not like I'd loved Joy or Melody, but on some level I did love Amy. I smiled and said, "I love you, too, honey. It's just not the right time."

As she drove down the long driveway to the county blacktop, I hoped that she'd find a good man. Whoever he was, I doubt he'd know how lucky he was to have her.

* * *

It felt strange being on tour without Melody. The Golden Retrievers were too young and not well trained enough to open the show, but they went with us everywhere. I was already in love with the little guys. I'd bought them matching bandanas, and they wore them every day.

We'd just finished the show in Atlanta and I was unwinding in my dressing room when there was a knock on the door.

"Come in," I said.

I couldn't believe my eyes. Colt and Kelly Walker entered the room with big smiles on their faces. I hadn't seen them since I'd left their band. I knew they were still in business because I'd occasionally hear about them. And every once in awhile, they'd get a single on the charts.

"Look who the cat dragged in," I said. "How the hell are you folks?"

Kelly came over and planted a deep, erotic kiss on my lips. They tasted of bourbon. Colt shook my hand.

"We weren't sure you'd remember us now that you're a famous star," Colt said. "But we all knew you'd eventually be one."

"How could you even say something like that?" I asked. Y'all gave me my first break."

"Even if you were just sixteen," Kelly said.

"I never told you that," I said.

"Casey told me before we went on tour. She made me promise to look after you," Colt said.

"She was my guardian angel in more than one way," I said. "What are you folks up to?"

"We're still working honky-tonks and dance halls," Colt said. "Haven't come up in the world like some people I know."

"You playing around here?" I asked.

"Yeah, at a good-sized dance hall up Highway 400 in Alpharetta, Georgia," Kelly said. "It's about thirty miles north of downtown Atlanta."

"We're not due in Atlantic City until Saturday. Want an itinerant guitar picker to jam with you tonight?" I asked with a grin.

"You shitting me?" Colt asked.

"Might be fun. Just don't tell anyone about it. I'll just step out on the stage with y'all like old times. Where y'all staying?"

"Alpharetta Marriott on Windward," Kelly said.

"I'll get Ernie and me rooms there for tomorrow night."

*　*　*

Ernie and I checked into the Marriott, and then we met up with Colt and Kelly for dinner in the hotel restaurant. Kelly looked great in a tight skirt and cowboy boots. Her hair was in a ponytail tied with a red ribbon. I had to admit, she looked damn good.

"I still can't believe you're doing this, Jamie," Colt said.

"You taught me the ropes. I wouldn't be where I am today without you," I said.

"Well, that's stretching it a bit. But I'm really excited about tonight."

"How long you reckon it'll take the folks to recognize you, Jamie? Kelly asked.

"Beats me. Who cares, really? All we want to do is entertain the folks," I said.

Ernie sat back and enjoyed our banter. He'd heard me talk about the Walkers a lot. Particularly Kelly. We all tried not to eat too much. Never a good idea to go onstage with a bloated stomach. After dinner, we all drove to the dance hall and arrived at a little before eight o'clock. Colt hadn't said a word to the guys in his band.

The club manager's name was Claude Blank, and he looked hard at me when we walked backstage and entered the dressing room. The fellows in the band recognized me immediately and thought it'd be a blast to have me play with them. Ernie kept Mutt and Jeff in the dressing room with him after we went on. He watched everything on a closed circuit TV monitor.

It was a big dance hall, and the place was jammed. Colt and his band had done really well on the dance hall circuit and were in great demand. He'd been self-effacing when he'd said they were *just* doing dance halls.

We all walked out on the stage at once. I wore jeans and a regular cowboy shirt like the other fellows. Kelly had on a tight shirt with the two top buttons undone. She was bulging so much I wondered if she'd had a little help from a plastic surgeon.

Colt started off with a fast bluegrass number, and Kelly joined in on her fiddle. I played rhythm guitar along with his regular guy. No one in the audience paid much attention to me because I was just one of the fellows onstage.

On the second number, I stepped up to the microphone and picked the melody. Halfway through I stepped back and Kelly moved forward to do a fiddle solo. The crowd was appreciative and clapped with enthusiasm.

Then I winked at Kelly and asked, "You still remember 'Mountain Love?'"

She answered by doing a quick run on her fiddle. Then we sang the duet as if we'd never parted. The response from the audience was terrific. Then I sang "Stolen Kisses," and there was little question in anyone's mind who the extra guy was on the stage.

Almost immediately the whole atmosphere changed. People stopped dancing and crowded up to the edge of the stage. We played nonstop for two hours. Colt and his band were great. They knew every song I'd ever written.

The audience refused to let us leave the stage. I was having a blast. I'd always loved to entertain people, and I loved to perform with friends. After five encores, we begged off. Back in the dressing room everyone dropped exhausted into their chairs. Mutt and Jeff came over and licked me in the face, and I rubbed their ears.

Colt was beside himself with glee. He kept saying, "Those folks ain't never going to forget this night. Hell, I ain't either. No, sir, I ain't never going to forget this night."

Kelly was quiet. She just sort of stared at me every once in a while.

* * *

We got back to the hotel, and Colt insisted we all congregate in his and Kelly's suite. They hadn't changed any of their vices. Colt was throwing back beers and Kelly was sipping Black Jack. The fellows either drank beer or smoked weed. The sweet odor penetrated everything.

No one was feeling any pain by the time I got up to leave. I shook hands all around and hugged Kelly. She gave me a peck on the cheek. Colt thanked me again, and I left.

I'd been in my suite for about five minutes when I heard a knock at the door. I opened it to see Kelly standing there, fully clothed, with a drink in her hand. I didn't invite her in. She just stepped through the threshold and went directly to the couch and sat down.

"I've got a question for you, Jamie," she said. "Come and sit with me."

I didn't know what to do. I was tired and wanted to go to sleep. Ernie and I were to leave in the G-IV around ten the next morning. And I knew Kelly was drunk.

She kept patting the cushion beside her, so I walked over and joined her. "What's the question?" I asked.

"That night I came to your room naked as a jaybird, why didn't you fuck me?"

"You remember that night?"

"Parts of it," she said with a grin.

"You were drunk and Colt's wife. That's why I didn't fuck you. What do you remember?"

"I remember crawling on top of you and then waking up outside my room wrapped in a damn blanket. And I knew I hadn't been fucked."

"I'm amazed that you can remember anything that happened that night," I said.

"Did you like the way I looked naked?"

"I'd be lying if I said I didn't."

"Want to see me naked again?"

I hadn't had sex in almost a year and was just beginning to think about it once again. Kelly was a sexy woman, and she obviously wanted me. Damn if I wasn't tempted.

"You're drunk, Kelly, and you're still Colt's wife. It wouldn't be a good idea."

"Colt fucks around," she said.

"That doesn't mean you have to," I said.

She pursed her lips and then took a sip of her drink. Smiling, she asked, "Do you know how this makes me feel?"

"I'm not following you."

"Forget it," she said as she staggered to her feet.

She fell to the floor and lay there like a beached whale. I picked her up and, hugged her, and she lay her head on my shoulder. We stood that way for several moments. I could feel her heart beating in time with mine.

"Come on, Kelly," I said. "I'll walk you back to your suite."

Chapter 28

In the spring of 2003, Lily graduated from high school. I'd set up a trust fund for her after Melody's death. Lily had blossomed into an articulate and beautiful young woman. She'd been accepted to Harvard and planned to major in English literature. I expected her to obtain a PhD and become a college professor. Miss Frances would have been proud.

For a graduation present I gave Lily a new Ford Taurus. It was red with black leather seats. As she walked off the stage clutching her diploma, I stood at the back of the auditorium and waited for the ceremony to end. She had been the valedictorian of her class and the speech she gave sent chills up my spine. I was so proud of her I couldn't hold back the tears. And I was proud of what I'd been able to do for her and her family.

As everyone filed out of the auditorium, I motioned for her to join me. She walked over and gave me a big hug. Then she said,

"Thank you, Jamie. None of this would have been possible without you. And Melody."

Then I handed her the keys.

She looked at me quizzically, and asked, "What are these?"

"Car keys. Let's go out to the parking lot and see if you can find a car that they fit."

A smile formed on her lips and she ran toward the door, her black robe flowing behind her. In the school parking lot, she darted from car to car looking for a paper temporary license tag. When she saw the Taurus, her eyes lit up like neon signs. She inserted the key into the driver's side door and opened it. Then she sat behind the steering wheel and started the engine.

After blowing the horn about ten times, she motioned for me to get into the car. As I slid into the passenger seat, she said, "Thank you so much, Jamie. I'd hoped you'd give me a watch for graduation. I never dreamed you'd do this. How can I ever thank you for coming into my life?"

"Hey," I said. "I should be thanking you. You've enriched my life so much it's immeasurable. And you brought me back from the brink when Melody died. You saved my life, girl. I'll always be indebted to you."

"I guess you need a ride home," she said.

"Yes. I drove the Taurus here. I was hoping I'd be the first one to ride in it with you driving."

* * *

My life had settled down considerably. I still missed Melody, but I'd accepted the fact that I might someday marry again, though there were no prospects on the horizon. I'd heard that Kelly and Colt had gotten a divorce sometime in 1999. Our paths hadn't crossed since the night I played the dance hall with them. Amy had married a high school math teacher and lived in Cookeville once again. I saw them occasionally.

Overseeing the record company and my various businesses and touring kept me extremely busy. And, I continued to enjoy an incredible career.

In July I was invited to Dr. Kate's eighty-third birthday party. The G-IV was in Savannah undergoing its annual inspection so we were using our old tour bus. We'd done a TV special at the new Opry House in Nashville and were on our way to Charlotte, North Carolina, for a show.

We left I-40 at Cookeville and drove up the new four-lane to Livingston and then on to Round Rock. The party was in full swing when we arrived.

Dr. Kate's hair was silver, and she wore it cropped short. Jazz still acted as the clinic's receptionist. Kate's assistant, Dr. Wally Johnson, had joined Kate in 1978 and had taken a lot of the load off her shoulders.

One of the guests was a cousin of mine, Shenandoah Coleman. She'd written a book in the 1950s about a politician in Memphis and had been a reporter for NPR. We'd met a few times over the years. I think perhaps we were the only two of the Coleman clan who had ever made it out of Beulah Land.

The whole crowd sang "Happy Birthday" to Dr. Kate, and then she made a wish and blew out her candles. "All I can say is, I'm glad Jazz used one candle for each decade and not the full eighty-three," she'd said.

After she'd opened her presents, I wandered over and said, "I'd like to see you in private for a moment."

"Come back to my office," she said.

I followed her down a long hallway to her cluttered office. She sat in her chair and motioned for me to take the one opposite.

"What's up, Jamie?"

"I've been stumbling lately. If I was a drinking man, I'd think I was drunk."

She frowned. "How long has this been going on?"

"About a month and it's getting a little worse. I kind of drag my right foot a little."

"What's your schedule look like?"

"We've got a show in Charlotte, then we're off for a few months."

"I want you to see a neurologist in Nashville next week."

"What's going on?"

"You'll need some tests. I'm not qualified to deal with this. I don't want to make any predictions."

* * *

The Charlotte show went well. Had I realized at the time that it would be my last, perhaps I would have played a solo for longer than my usual thirty minutes. Since we were on the tour bus, I had to sleep in the bed that Melody and I had used during the days before we obtained our airplanes. The band and I got back to the farm a couple of days after the show. The problem with my foot was driving me nuts. If it didn't get better soon, I'd never be able to manage the rudders on the G-IV. I was already having difficulty with the accelerator and brake on my truck.

I'd arranged for an appointment with the neurologist at Vanderbilt before I left Dr. Kate's office the day of her birthday party. Ernie and I drove the pickup to Nashville and used the valet parking service. I had planned to go by myself, but Ernie insisted on driving me. Now that Melody was gone, I considered him my best friend. We had no secrets between us.

I checked into the clinic office in the new Bill Wilkerson Hearing and Balance Center where the doctor's office was located. It housed the ENT, internal medicine, and neurology departments. The nurse called my name about twenty minutes later and took me to an examination room. Ernie stayed in the waiting room.

Dr. Lewis, the neurologist, was in his early thirties so I figured he'd just gotten out of his residency. He had a good bedside manner for a specialist and put me at ease immediately.

He examined me and said, "We need to do some tests. The EMG will be done here in this clinic. That's a procedure that tests the integrity of your muscles. Then I want an MRI of the brain. I guess you know what that is."

I nodded. "Any thoughts at this point?"

"Too early to say. You have some obvious weakness in your right leg, and your reflex is diminished."

"Can we do those today?" I asked.

"We just had a cancellation. I think we can work you in if the Medical Imaging Department can."

"Can I get the results today?"

"No. That's pushing it a bit. I can see you early in the morning. Tell the receptionist to make you an eight o'clock appointment."

When I walked back into the waiting room, Ernie flagged me down. "What did he say?"

"I have to do a couple of test this afternoon. He'll see me in the morning."

"He have a guess?"

"Didn't want to commit."

The EMG reminded me of an EKG I'd once had at Dr. Kate's office. That took about forty-five minutes. Then I went to the imaging department for the MRI. I'm glad I've never suffered from claustrophobia. My shoulders barely fit in the narrow machine. As the technician was adjusting my head, I asked, "How do people with claustrophobia manage this?"

She smiled. "I tell them to think of the MRI machine as their coffin."

I guess she thought that was funny, but I didn't. I couldn't believe how noisy that damn machine was. They did give me some ear plugs, or I'm sure I'd have developed hearing loss. I was happy to finally be able to sit up. My back was killing me.

We left the clinic and drove over to the Vanderbilt Plaza Hotel and checked in. Then we ate at the Ruth Chris's restaurant in the basement. This time I'd thought ahead and brought a book. I had a restless night and didn't sleep worth a damn. It reminded me of the sleepless night Melody and I'd spent the day of her first examination. All through the night I'd dream and then wake up. The recurring dream had to do with Pop. He kept hitting me in my eye and slapping my head. I wanted to kill him.

At breakfast, I only had a cup of coffee. My usual scrambled eggs, bacon, and grits just didn't appeal to me. Ernie glanced across the table and said, "You've got to eat, man. This ain't good."

"I can't eat until I know what's going on."

We checked out of the hotel and drove back to Vanderbilt University Medical Center. We used the valet parking system again and went up to the neurology clinic. I checked in and the nurse called me back immediately. Ernie had a worried expression as he picked up a *Popular Mechanics* magazine to read while I saw the doctor.

Dr. Lewis's nurse took me to an examination room where I read a month-old issue of *Time* until the doctor came in. He sat in his chair and said, "The news isn't good, Mr. Coleman. I'm sorry, but I believe you have amyotrophic lateral sclerosis, commonly known as Lou Gehrig's disease."

To say I was stunned would be a gross understatement. I stared at the doctor in a state of disbelief and confusion. I knew what ALS was, what it did to your body. When I was in Charity Hospital in New Orleans, the man in the bed next to me had ALS.

"You're positive?"

"Yes. Are you familiar with ALS?"

I nodded. "I had a broken neck when I was about sixteen. The neurosurgeon took great care of me and I had a full recovery. I know ALS will eventually paralyze me. I'll be nothing but a vegetable on life support."

"You have the peripheral form. Over a period of time the paralysis will progress up your legs to your chest and arms. You are correct. You'll eventually be a quadriplegic and at some point on a respirator."

I stood and took the doctor's hand. "Thank you for your time, Doctor. I appreciate your frankness."

I settled up with the front desk because I hadn't paid them my co-pay as required by my insurance. Ernie could tell the news wasn't good by the expression on my face, but he didn't say anything. We got back to the garage and waited for the pickup. I kept taking deep breaths, trying to control my anxiety. Finally, I had to hold my breath because I realized I was hyperventilating and actually getting dizzy.

*　*　*

Ernie and I didn't talk for a long time on the way back to the farm. We'd been together for many years, and he could read me like a book.

As we passed Lebanon, he finally asked, "How bad is it, Jamie?"

"Nothing serious, just a temporary weakness in my right leg."

He didn't say anything for a few miles. "Don't shit me, man."

"Would I do that?"

"Hell, yes. Tell me the truth."

I shook my head and refused to answer him. I alone had to deal with the situation. I didn't want anyone's advice or sympathy. I already knew how I was going to handle the problem. Straight forward.

"The G-IV will be ready tomorrow. Get someone to go with you to pick it up. I'll need it in a couple of days," I said.

Ernie glared at me. "Damnit, Jamie. Tell me what the doctor said. I may have to beat the shit out of you if you don't."

I laughed. "When was the last time you beat the shit out of anyone, Ernie? Hell, you're a damn creampuff."

He continued to glare at me periodically until we got back to the farm around three that afternoon. As soon as Ernie parked the pickup, I went to my study. I had a lot of work to do. I hadn't updated my will since Melody's death so I called my attorney and asked him to come the following day. Then I jotted down all the changes I wanted made in the document.

Jack Robbins, my Nashville attorney, arrived around ten o'clock the next morning, and I met him at the front door. We shook hands and he said, "You were insistent that I come this morning. Something going on I need to know about?"

"You know me, Jack. Once I get a thought in my head I can't sit on it."

We went to my study and settled in. Magnolia brought us coffee, and after filling our cups she left. I took a sip off mine and said, "I've jotted down all the changes I want."

I handed him my notes and he quickly scanned them. "When do you want the final document?" he asked.

"Tomorrow. FedEx it to me. I want it here by ten o'clock."

"Jesus, Jamie. I'm not a fucking robot. I need at least two days."

"Nope. Tomorrow. I've made you a rich man over the years, Jack. This is how you can pay me back."

He shook his head. "Yeah. You have done well by me, Jamie. I'll have it here by ten in the morning. You're sure nothing is going on I need to know about?"

"I'm just an impatient man."

We shook hands and Jack left.

I had one other detail to take care of. I'd treated my dear friend Dr. Kate terribly, and I felt humiliated and very ashamed. I climbed into my new Ford 150 King Ranch pickup and drove to Round Rock. I parked in front of the Round Rock Medical Clinic and climbed the stairs. Patients who couldn't find a seat in the crowed waiting room sat on the steps and stood on the sidewalk waiting their turn to see Dr. Kate or Dr. Wally. I simply climbed the steps past them and walked up to the window that Jazz guarded with her life. When I rang the bell, she slid the frosted window back.

"What you want, Jamie Lee Coleman? We're a might busy today."

"I need to talk to Dr. Kate for a few minutes. It won't take any time at all."

"You see all these people waiting to see her. You something special?"

"Jazz, you know me better than that. Please, just put me back in a room and let me talk to her. It won't take but a minute. *Please!*

Jazz sighed heavily. "If I didn't love you so much, I'd tell you to go jump off a bridge. Hold on. I'll see what I can do."

She got up and walked back into the catacombs of the clinic. Moments later she returned and said, "She'll see you for just a few minutes. You're really pushing this, Jamie. That's not like you."

"I know and I'm sorry."

"Come on. Follow me.

She led me down a long hall to an exam room that I'd been ushered into more than once in my youth. Moments later, the good doctor entered with a haggard expression. "You okay, Jamie? Jazz says you're agitated."

"I just need to talk to you for a few minutes. Nothing serious."

She looked at me with an expression of doubt. "What's up, Jamie. You don't usually bust in here without notice and demand to see me."

I felt like a ten-year-old waiting for a penicillin shot. "I need to apologize. I feel terrible for the way I treated you when I was morning Melody. I'm so sorry. Could you ever forgive me?'

She looked at me with a withering glance. I could see suspicion in those royal blue eyes.

"Jamie, honey, I delivered you in that terrible shack in Beulah Land some fifty-three years ago. I took care of you when you were a snotty-nosed kid and gave you numerous penicillin shots despite your inflammatory cursing. Don't bullshit me. What's going on? What did the neurologist say?"

"That's it's nothing serious. Just a temporary weakness of the muscles in my right leg."

"As the referring doctor, you know he will send me a full report."

"That's what it'll say. Anyway, I just wanted to come by and tell you how sorry I am that I treated you so badly. I'm right ashamed of myself. You will forgive me, won't you?"

"There's nothing to forgive, Jamie. I believe I've earned the truth. Please level with me."

I grabbed her and gave her a bear hug. I couldn't help myself. Tears flooded my eyes and I kissed her on the cheek. She had been one of the most enduring friends I ever had. And she'd outlived Miss Frances, Jake, and Yolanda. She was the one last person from my childhood who I could always count on. I would miss her with all my heart.

As I walked out of the room, I looked over my shoulder and saw tears streaming down her wrinkled cheeks. I knew at that moment she'd figured out my plan. I actually felt sorry for her.

When I got back to the farm, I went into my study and called Scarlett Gibson's home in Santa Monica. The answering machine picked up, and I left a message. I hoped she wasn't out of town. I had a job for her.

She called me back but I couldn't take the call because I was on the john. I called her again, and did something I'm not proud of.

I lied to her. I led her to believe she was coming to see me for that long-denied interview. She jumped at the chance, of course, and said she'd be there the following afternoon. That time frame would work well and allow me to get my affairs in order.

My attorney delivered the will the next morning as requested, and I checked it over. Everything I'd requested was in there. I heard the G-IV do a flyover and walked out on the terrace to watch Ernie land the plane, then watched him taxi to the hangar and wished I'd been at the controls. I was overcome with sadness as I realized I would never fly that graceful bird again. It made me think of just taking her up for a few-touch-and-goes. But I had to put that desire behind me like all the others.

Scarlett arrived with her dog that afternoon, and we had supper together. She wanted to start the interview after supper, but I begged off. I excused myself and went to my study where I sit now finishing this autobiography. I started it following Melody's death. It kept my mind busy and helped me deal with my loss.

On my desk before me lies a Glock 9mm semiautomatic pistol. It's one of many guns I've owned over the years. I'm a gun nut, what can I say? I've never believed in killing innocent animals and I've never understood the mind-set of hunters. No, my fascination with guns is more cerebral. I respect the sheer beauty of their mechanical mechanisms. The way all the parts fit together and work in unison. Not unlike the members of a band. So, over the years I've honed my skills at target practice. It's been a hobby I've thoroughly enjoyed for a long time.

I've had an incredible life filled with equal measures of success and failure, happiness and sadness. But most people's lives are that way. I have no intention of living out the remainder of my days as a quadriplegic. Been there, done that when I had my broken neck.

The thought of never again picking up my guitar was the defining moment for me. Knowing I'd never sing or face an audience simply reinforced my decision. Some people might think of me as a coward for taking my own life instead of facing my destiny. Others would say I shouldn't interfere with God's plan. I've sort of drifted away from the idea of God so that didn't influence me. No, to be honest, I want to stay in control of my life while I still can. If I wait too long, I'll be at the mercy of others.

Glancing at the clock, I see that it's almost two in the morning, August 3, 2003. I've asked Scarlett to seek a publisher for my life story. That was the real reason I'd asked her to come to Round Rock. I know she'll do the best she can. I'm going to place this manuscript in the wall safe, and then I'm out of here.

Try to remember me as a man who had a talent he couldn't explain and tried to live his life with honor and dignity. If there is a God, surely He or She is compassionate and forgiving. Considering what lies ahead of me, perhaps God will cut me a little slack for what I'm about to do.

Jamie Lee Coleman
Round Rock, Tennessee

Reading Group Questions

1. In contrast to the first two titles in the Round Rock series, *Little Joe* and *The Trial of Dr. Kate*, the author writes *The Life and Times of Jamie Lee Coleman* from the first person, on the premise that we're reading a book written by the title character himself. How does this technique create a different reading experience from the previous two books in the series?

2. What might Jamie Lee's childhood have been like had he remained in Beulah Land? In your opinion, would his innate musical talents have found some other means of expressing themselves, or would they never have emerged? In general, how important do you think mentor figures are in helping us develop?

3. Throughout the book, Jamie Lee Coleman becomes involved with several different women, among them, Amy, Joy, Casey, Kelly, and Melody. How do you feel about each of these relationships? In what ways is Jamie Lee a good romantic partner? In what ways might he be a problematic one?

4. *The Life and Times of Jamie Lee Coleman* makes use of characters repeated from the prior books in the series—Frances Washington, Dr. Kate, Jake Watson, Joe Stout, etc. (Jamie Lee Coleman himself makes his first appearance as a baby in *The Trial of Dr. Kate*.) How does the author's use of this technique help to build a sense of history around the setting and the characters? Do the characters seem to evolve between the different books?

5. For the first time in the Round Rock series, characters travel for extended periods to parts of the country far from Round Rock: New Orleans, Nashville, New York City. How effective do you find the author's portrayal of each of these other locales? What crucial differences are there between the social world of Round Rock, Tennessee, and the social world of the French Quarter in New Orleans as shown in the novel?

6. Late in the book, Jamie Lee Coleman has a meeting with his father in prison. When his father asks Jamie if he'll come back to see him, Jamie first says not to count on a visit, and later says he'll think about it. Do you think that Jamie ultimately made the right decision in trying to reconnect with his father? If you were in Jamie's position, would you have forgiven your father?

7. Throughout Jamie Lee Coleman's life, when faced with terrible setbacks, Jamie sometimes responds by sliding into extreme depressions combined with alcohol abuse. Alcoholism has been a theme in the author's work, from the more serious treatment in *The Trial of Dr. Kate* to the more humorous portrayal in the novella *My Life Among the Fairies of Walnut Ridge*. How does Jamie's use of alcohol compare to these other books? How might Jamie's desire to maintain absolute control over his life and career relate to his tendency toward depression?

8. Do you think Jamie's attempts to "give back" to Round Rock and to rescue Lily Crockett from a childhood in Beulah Land are ultimately successful? Do you think Beulah Land will be in any way changed by Jamie Lee's efforts? As a mentor figure, in what ways is Jamie Lee like Frances Washington or Jake Watson, and in what ways is he different from his mentors?

9. What do you think about Jamie's final decision to end his life in response to his diagnosis? Do his reasons make sense? Do you agree or disagree with his decision? How might other characters in the Round Rock universe react to learn about his suicide?

Author Q&A

1. Your style of writing changed dramatically with this book, compared to the first two books in the Round Rock series. What gave you the idea to tell this story from the first-person point of view of Jamie Lee Coleman, through his autobiography?

For a story like this I believe the first person narrative is essential. By using the first person narrative, the story unfolds as Jamie Lee Coleman tells it. I believe this makes the story seem more real.

2. With scenes ranging from small French Quarter clubs to the Grand Ole Opry itself, this book paints a truly detailed picture of the country music scene in the 1960s and beyond. What kinds of research did you do in order to write this book?

I've lived in Nashville but not New Orleans. I practiced ear surgery in Nashville, Tennessee for thirty years, and I had several country singers as patients. Minnie Pearl was a personal friend.

3. What made you interested in writing about this kind of music from this time period? Are there any artists—either those who make cameos in the book or those who don't—that you particularly enjoy?

Johnny Cash was always a favorite.

4. The story of Jamie Lee Coleman is a true rags to riches story, with Jamie going from a childhood in extreme poverty to many decades of fame, financial stability, and success in the world of country music. What is it that appeals to you about writing this kind of story?

I've always been drawn to rags to riches stories.

5. Each of the Round Rock books so far has dealt directly with themes of racial prejudice within the South. In this book, the most compelling such story has to do with Jake Watson and his "housekeeper," Yolanda. Was this a common arrangement at the time, and did people tend to respond to it in the same way the characters in this book respond to Jake and Yolanda?

The South has always been known for its hypocrisy. Say one thing and do another.

6. After Shenandoah in *The Trial of Dr. Kate,* this is the second time you've written the story of a Coleman who breaks free of Beulah Land. What was different about the experience of writing about Jamie Lee Coleman compared to writing about Shenandoah Coleman?

Shenandoah had to make her way on her own, while Jamie had Miss Frances as a mentor. Mentors are very important. I'm not sure Jamie would have survived his father's beatings without one.

7. Could you talk about the ending of the book, and why you chose to have Jamie Lee Coleman take his life in response to his diagnosis? Is the ALS material in the book based on experiences from you or for anyone you may have known?

I had two dear friends die from ALS. Jamie's is a personal decision that depends upon one's moral and religious base. Some people would say he was justified and others would say he wasn't.

8. Finally: it was interesting to encounter Joe Stout again in this book as an adult, and fascinating to get brief glimpses of his later life through Jamie Lee Coleman's eyes. Do you plan to work with this character more in the future?

The fourth book in the Round Rock Series, *The Veterinarian Joe Stout*, due out in 2015, is about Joe Stout (Little Joe) as an adult living in Utopia, Texas.

More Books By Michael E. Glasscock III

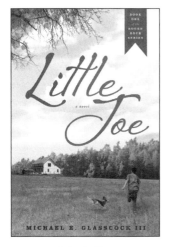

Little Joe

When Little Joe Stout survives the car accident that took his parents' lives, he is sent to live with his maternal grandparents in the small town of Round Rock, Tennessee. Orphaned and missing his Texas home, Little Joe is reluctant to adapt. But his grandparents, especially his grandmother, are up to the challenge of raising him despite their own struggles. Set against the drama of World War II and the first sparks of the civil rights movement, Little Joe's new home is a microcosm of America in the 1940s as local events mirror the radio broadcasts that bring the news of the day into his grandmother's kitchen. *Little Joe* begins the four-part Round Rock series.

ISBN 978-1-60832-566-5
Greenleaf Book Group Press

The Trial of Dr. Kate

In the summer of 1952, Lillian Johnson was found dead in her home—an overdose of barbiturate had triggered a heart attack, but the scene was not quite right. It looked as though someone other than Lillian herself had injected the fatal dose. Dr. Kate Marlow, Lillian's physician and best friend, now sits in the Round Rock city jail. The only country doctor for miles, Kate cannot remember her whereabouts at the time of Lillian's death. *The Trial of Dr. Kate* is the second novel in the four-part Round Rock series.

ISBN 978-1-62634-013-8
Greenleaf Book Group Press

For more information about any of these books, go to www.michaelglasscockiii.com.

More Books By Michael E. Glasscock III

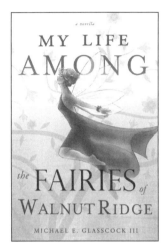

My Life Among the Fairies of Walnut Ridge

When Preacher Jack tells you that he's fallen in love with a tiny Celtic fairy who's lived in Walnut Ridge for more than two hundred years, he knows you won't believe his story. But when he meets the fairy Maybelle by the creek in his back yard, his life begins to turn around—and upside down—in this fast-paced story filled with fairy dances, flying trucks, small-town drug hustlers, and strange, new-blooming romance. And when Jack and Maybelle come face to face with an all-too-modern political evil, it's up to the two of them to work to take their town—and their country—back. *My Life Among the Fairies of Walnut Ridge* is a fantastical, Southern-tinged detour into a world of strange magic that exists just beyond our sight—a world maybe closer to our own than we believe.

eBook ISBN 978-1-938416-72-9
River Grove Books

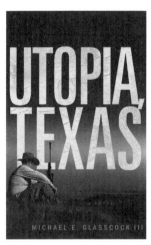

Utopia, Texas

In the quiet town of Utopia, Texas, life is simple. Local game warden Monty Kilpatrick does his duty catching poachers, smokes too many cigarettes, and tries to keep his marriage afloat. But just across the border in Mexico, drug cartel kingpin Juan Diaz is running his empire with an iron fist. Utopia is along the cartel's main trafficking routes, and when Monty arrests Diaz's brother during what he thought was a routine traffic stop, the men's paths cross. In a flash, the formerly peaceful Utopia becomes a war zone. In order to save his town, his wife, and his pride, Monty must be ready to lose everything he holds true.

ISBN 978-1-60832-416-3
Greenleaf Book Group Press

**For more information about any of these books, go to
www.michaelglasscockiii.com.**